Highland Grace
The Macleans

The Second Book in The Medieval Highlanders Series

K.E. SAXON

Copyright © 2008 K.E. Saxon

All rights reserved. No part of this book may be used or reproduced by any means, graphic, electronic, or mechanical including photocopying, recording, taping, or by any information storage retrieval system without the written permission of the author K.E. Saxon, the copyright owner and publisher of this book, except in the case of brief quotations embodied in critical articles or reviews.

This is a work of fiction. Names, characters, places, brands, media, and incidents either are the product of the author's imagination or are used fictitiously. Any resemblance to actual events, locales, organizations, or persons, living or dead, is entirely coincidental and beyond the intent of the publisher. The author acknowledges the trademarked status and trademark owners of various products referenced in its work of fiction, which have been used without permission. The publication/use of these trademarks is not authorized, associated with, or sponsored by the trademark owners.

Cover Design created by Angela Waters Graphic Art & Design

* * * *

ISBN: 1499701772
ISBN-13: 978-1499701777

CONTEMPORARY BOOKS BY K.E. SAXON

Sensual Contemporary Romance
Love Is The Drug
A Stranger's Kiss (novella)
A Heart Is A Home: Christmas in Texas (novella)

Sensual Romantic Comedy/Fantasy Romance
Diamonds and Toads: A Modern Fairy Tale

ACKNOWLEDGEMENTS

I am eternally grateful to a wonderful new Welsh writer friend, Elin Gregory, who kindly and generously supplied the phonetic pronunciations of two of the Welsh terms in my glossary. This, after many long, hair-pulling months of trying to find them on my own. Thank you again, Elin!

K.E. Saxon

AUTHOR'S NOTE

The twelfth and thirteenth century Scottish Highlands is a fascinating time in history. Although much is known, there is still much that remains in shadow and supposition. The old laws of succession, and the old Celtic systems were mixing with the new feudal systems brought in by the Norman-influenced kings of Scots (the first key figure in this being David I, who became king of Scots in 1124).

Although, by the time of William the Lion (William I), who ruled Scotland from 1165 to 1214, the feudal systems were more firmly established in the southern region of Scotland, the king had managed to exert his influence and sway in the wilder northern and western regions as well. Mostly through alliances with foreigners to whom he chartered land, or to natives who sought a royal charter for their land in order to secure it for their own offspring.

My vision, therefore, was of a kind of "melting pot." The old ways, not completely abandoned, yet the new coming to be embraced.

Although I did many, many (many) months of research into this time in the Scottish Highlands history, I still found it necessary to take some creative license on certain aspects in order to fulfill my vision for the romance, and allow for less confusion to the romance reader. I won't list the licenses I took, but hope that the history purists will close an eye to these instances and simply enjoy the tale.

K.E. Saxon

* * *

GLOSSARY

Alban Eiler \ all-ben A-ler \: The feast of the vernal equinox. Lit.: Light of the earth.

crwth \ krooth \: an ancient Celtic musical instrument with the strings stretched over a rectangular frame, played with a bow.

Cymru \ kumree \: Welsh for 'Wales'.

Hogmanay \ hog-m*uh*-**ney** \: The eve of New Year's Day.

kraken \ **krah**-k*uh*n \: According to Viking legend, a sea monster large enough to swallow a whole boat.

Matins \ 'mætinz \: Morning prayers at sunrise.

Pencerdd \ Penkerth \: the chief poet in a welsh court.

penteulu \ pentaylee \: head of Prince Llywelyn ap Iorwerth's *uchelwyr teulu*, his noble warriors.

Sext \ sekst \: The fourth of the seven canonical hours, or the service for it, originally fixed for the sixth hour of the day taken as noon.

Terce \ turs \: The third of the seven canonical hours of the divine office, originally fixed at the third hour of the day, about 9 a.m.

uisge beatha \ ishka beyha \: Lit: 'Water of Life', a.k.a. whiskey.

Uphalieday \ Up-helly-a \: January 6, the Feast of the Epiphany, a.k.a. 'Twelfth Night'.

* * *

PROLOGUE
Perth, The Highlands, Scotland 1204

"Relax and let me love you."

"Aye," she murmured between the hot, wet kisses she blazed across his neck and chest.

Through the slits of his half-opened eyes, he watched her. Watched as her gloriously blushed breasts bounced in time to his rhythm, as her nipples grew ever more tightly wound.

He bent forward and greedily sucked one of them into his mouth. She climaxed instantly, the undulating walls of her taut canal squeezing and caressing him as they milked him into a long release as well. At its peak, he arched his back and choked out, "Oh, God!" as the head of his erupting sex rammed against her womb, flooding it with his hot seed.

* * *

Bao woke with a start and sat up, rubbing the base of his palms against his eyes. He wiped the sticky discharge off of his belly and thigh with the wool blanket before tossing it aside, feeling like a callow youth, surging with carnal urges so intense that he spewed seed as he slept. But the dream had been vivid, his mind's perfect reflection of his and the flaxen-haired goddess's only time together. Even now, over two moons later, he could almost taste her on his tongue.

After rising, he walked to the wash basin and poured water from the earthen pitcher into its base. He pulled the top portion of his long, straight black hair back and tied it with a leather thong and scrubbed his stubbled face with the cold water. After drying it with a cloth, he took up the silver platter he used as a mirror and began his morning shave.

He lit a candle and looked at his reflection. The image he saw was haggard and sad. His eyes were red from lack of sleep the past few nights; the green flecks in his umber eyes, a direct contrast. They were puffy as well, causing them to have a more pronounced slant. He ran the sharpened knife against the edge of his jaw, nicking the place next to the dent in his chin. "Ouch! Dammit."

Stop thinking about her! Her family profited from your mother's enslavement!

A knock sounded on the door and Bao called out, "Enter!" relieved at the interruption.

"A missive just arrived for you, sire, from the King" his servant said and handed the scroll to him.

"My thanks," Bao said absently, unfurling the parchment as the man departed. Another assignment, no doubt.

As his eyes scanned the words, his heart began to

speed. 'Twas a demand that he escort one of the ladies of the court as far as his brother's holding so that her husband could meet her there and escort her the rest of the way home, along with a proposal that he remain there with his family through the coming holy days, if he so desired.

He'd sworn a vow to himself not to return to that holding—at least not until his brother found a suitable husband for their sister. But, as a soldier and liege to William, King of Scots, he had little choice in the matter.

His fate set, he gathered his belongings, arranged his affairs and set his course for the Maclean holding. *Only long enough to transfer the lady into her husband's hands*, he told himself, *and tell his brother what he'd learned about Jesslyn's kin as well.* He'd stay clear of the flaxen-haired widow. Well clear.

* * *

CHAPTER 1
The Maclean Holding, The Highlands, Scotland 1204

Jesslyn MacCreary sat with her hands tightly clasped and pressed firmly into her lap as she received the interrogation by her good friend and protector, Laird Daniel MacLaurin, chieftain to both the MacLaurin and Maclean clans.

"Who did this to you? I demand to know!" he shouted and then continued without waiting for an answer, "'Twas my cousin, Callum MacGregor, was it not? It had to be." He turned and stormed across the room a few paces, running his hand through his already tousled auburn hair, before turning back to Jesslyn.

"Nay, 'twas not Callum," she replied in low tones.

"Thank Christ for that, since he's been wed to the daughter of Laird Gordon these past moons. Who then? One of my Maclean warriors? The man will wed you and make this babe lawful, I swear it."

"It makes no difference who the father is. And I'm

perfectly capable of raising this bairn on my own, you needn't worry," she replied with more confidence than she actually felt.

"Aye, it matters. It matters a great deal. The clan elders may insist on banishing you, tho' my grandmother and I will not let that come to pass." Daniel walked over to the stool across from her and sat down. Leaning forward, he placed his hands over her clenched fists and said, "Now, tell me who did this to you, Jesslyn. No more delaying."

Realizing he'd not relent until she'd given him the information he was seeking and seeing the worry in his familiar green eyes, she finally said, "'Twas one of the traveling minstrels—a one-time encounter. And there's no need for you to worry; I'm resigned to my situation—in fact, I revel in it." She rose and stepped toward the hearth. Keeping her back turned to Daniel, she clasped her hands at her waist and twisted her fingers together. *Not a complete falsehood*, she told her chiding conscience. Her gaze dropped to the rapid pulse of her guilty heart beating in her wrist. *Aye, but not the complete truth, either*, it answered back.

She felt the weight of his gaze on her as he said, "Nay, I've known you for too many years not to see through your charade. 'Twas *not* a traveling player, Jesslyn. But I shall plague you no further about his identity, at least for the moment."

She turned back to him with a nod of relief.

"I'm not surprised to hear that you're glad at the prospect of a babe; after all, you've craved more bairns for a long time now. In fact, 'twas one of the reasons you agreed to wed me."

"Aye, well, you're well-wed to Maryn now."

"The threat of a clan war and much needed profits from shipping saw to that."

Jesslyn nodded. "Not *such* a hardship, I trow," she teased, though her heart wasn't truly in it.

Daniel smiled and that calmed her. "Nay, not at all, as Maryn is my one and true mate," he said.

Taking a deep breath, Jesslyn closed her eyes and forced herself to tell Daniel the plan she'd been formulating since suspecting her condition several sennights past. "I think it best that Alleck and I leave here and go back to the MacLaurin holding. I can easily say that I've been widowed once again," she said hopefully. Peeking back over her shoulder, she continued, "You know that they'll believe me—my good character is well known to them." Embarrassed by the subject, she dipped her head and regarded her nerveless hands once more, saying softly, "They'd never think to suspect that the bairn was conceived outside of wedlock. And you did bring me here with the clear purpose of finding a husband for me."

"Aye, but how do you suppose you'll support your bairns if you return there? On your ale-making?"

Irritated at the derogatory tone in his voice, she turned fully to face him again. Placing her hands on her hips, she said, "Aye, why not? 'Tis a good profession."

"Aye, if 'twere your only choice. But 'tis not. What of my vow to your husband as he lay dying on the field of battle? That I'd take care of the two of you, that I'd see that Alleck was trained to be a warrior when the

Highland Grace

time came?" Daniel shook his head. "Nay, Maryn and I think it best that you and Alleck move up to the keep and reside with us under our full protection, at least until the babe is born. And my grandmother is in full agreement."

Jesslyn turned back to gaze at the crackling flames in the hearth as she considered the arrangement. 'Twas so like Maryn, with her generous nature, to want to protect them from censure. Jesslyn was still amazed that she and Daniel's wife had become such good friends, especially considering their troubled beginning. But having the support of Lady Maclean as well, the grandmother of the babe's father, left Jesslyn with an even heavier feeling of guilt for denying that lady her great-grandchild. Could she live under the same roof as the older woman and continue to withhold that knowledge? She didn't know if she could. But she owed it to her late husband's memory to do as he wished and keep their son under Daniel's guardianship, which, ultimately, forced her decision. "Aye, that seems a good solution." Turning back to Daniel, she continued, "And this, you believe, will bolster your defense against my banishment?"

"Aye, it will. In fact, your possessions should be transferred up there forthwith. I shall send several servants down here to retrieve them as soon as you have them packed and ready. Since your condition is not yet known to anyone other than the four of us, we have some time to get you settled before I take the information to the clan elders."

"I just wish that I'd had a bit more time before my

situation was discovered," Jesslyn said.

"You may wish it, but 'tis glad I am that I found out now rather than later. At least I have some time to deal with the clan before your condition is apparent. Just think how much worse 'twould have been had one of the other clan members realized the truth behind your squeamish behavior of late before Maryn did," Daniel replied. "Will you at least tell me when you expect this babe to arrive? And please do not lie to me again. 'Twill do no good, as I shall figure it out on my own in a few sennights' time anyway, if only by the signs you give."

Seeing the truth in that, Jesslyn gave him the answer he sought. "I expect the babe around the time of *Bealltainn.*"

Daniel nodded and by the look of surety in his eye, he was no doubt still believing 'twas Callum's bairn she carried. Thankfully, he made no further queries, simply rose and walked toward the door. After opening it, he turned back to her, his lips pressed into a thin line as he gave her a penetrating look before saying, "You'll have an hour's time to get everything packed and ready to be moved up to the keep. I shall go to Niall's house to retrieve Alleck and then I shall tell him that we wanted the two of you to live there with us. That should suffice until you are able to explain your condition to him."

Jesslyn started at the sound of the door slamming shut. He was still angry, it seemed. Sighing, she walked toward her bedchamber, her mind swirling with disjointed thoughts. Thoughts of packing her things and moving to the keep. Thoughts of the reception she'd receive and the questions she was sure to have to answer, shrouded in half-truths. Thoughts of her babe. Thoughts of its father.

She absently felt for the foreign coin that resided around her neck on a leather thong. 'Twas the one Bao's mother had given him as a bairn, he'd told her. Jesslyn had kept it hidden under her clothing and cradled between her breasts next to her heart ever since she'd found it under her pillow the morning he departed for Perth late last summer. A parting memento from her unborn babe's father—tho' he'd certainly not known of her condition at the time, as he'd left within mere sennights of their interlude.

Her eyes blurred with unshed tears. She gritted her teeth and swallowed past the lump in her throat, refusing to give in to the weakness. But one fell. And then another. And in a moment's time she was across the chamber and lying face down on her bed, quietly sobbing. A phalanx of emotions crowded her being. Humiliation, dread, joy, sadness, relief, anger, remorse, longing; all of them melded together to form a tight ache in her chest.

Unable to control her emotions, she indulged them, hoping that in doing so, it would lessen the need for such outbursts in the future. The thought of breaking down in front of Lady Maclean mortified her. And she certainly couldn't allow her son to see her in this condition. That image alone was enough to dry her tears.

She sat up.

After a moment, she walked to the washstand and poured water into the basin before dousing her swollen eyes and heated cheeks with the cool liquid. She grabbed a dry cloth from the stack that lay next to the bowl and pressed it to her face, turning as she did so to plan her packing procedure. 'Twas time to gather up their belongings, she could defer it no longer.

It didn't take her long to finish the task, as they'd brought few things with them when they'd traveled here from their home on the MacLaurin holding almost seven moons prior.

Jesslyn opened the door to the cottage and then turned. With her hand on the handle, she took one last look at the place she and her son had called home for these past moons, images flitting through her mind. Of Daniel questioning her behavior when she'd kissed him in the tower chamber, causing his new bride to leave him; of Callum playing knucklebones with Alleck; of Maryn generously offering Jesslyn her friendship and support; of Bao.... She smiled then, tho' 'twas bittersweet. Aye, Bao. Daniel's half-brother did so delight that day in her berry tarts.

With a jagged sigh, she turned and walked out, leaving her past behind as she forced her feet to carry her toward her future.

* * *

CHAPTER 2

"Remember you when your friend, Coby, back on the MacLaurin holding, told you his mama was making a babe in her belly and, once it was finished, he was going to be a brother?" Jesslyn said to her son as she sat on the edge of the bed next to his reclining form. She lifted her hand and gently stroked the pale blond hair off of his forehead.

Alleck's brows furrowed. "Aye, and then his blabbin' wee sister was borned."

Jesslyn smiled. "I thought you liked Christy. She certainly seemed to like you."

Alleck shrugged and rubbed his chin on his shoulder. "She's all right. But she don't know how to keep a secret. And she can't play knucklebones good, either."

"Well, you weren't very good at the game when you were a bairn of three summers, either. I'm sure she's much better at it, now that she's older." She tapped her son's nose. "And telling me that you were trying to lower yourself into the well was *not* blabbing," she chastened. "She was worried that you'd get hurt." Jesslyn leveled a stern look on her son then. "Which, you most definitely could have done, laddie."

Alleck's lower lip extended, but he didn't argue, clearly not wanting to get another lecture from her.

Realizing the subject of her discussion had gone off course, Jesslyn said, "A while back, you told me that you wished you could have a brother." She drew in a deep breath and slowly released it before continuing, "You may get your wish, for I'm making a babe in my belly now."

Alleck sat up so quickly he nearly toppled her off her perch. "Truly?" he said excitedly, bouncing up and down. He stilled and cocked his head to the side. "But I thought you could only make a babe if you was wed—that's what you told me."

"Aye, and that is mostly true. But, sometimes, just sometimes, a lady will make a babe when she is *not* wed," Jesslyn replied. Due to the babe's bastardy, it would need a strong foundation of love and support and she thought to begin building it now. "'Tis not very usual, and that's why we must feel doubly blessed."

"I can't wait to tell Niall I'm going to have a brother!"

Jesslyn cringed inwardly. Taking both her son's hands in her own, she said, "Nay, Alleck, you mustn't tell Niall about the babe yet. 'Tis going to be a secret that only you, Daniel, Maryn, Grandmother Maclean, and I know. At least for a while. And I cannot promise you that you'll get a brother—the babe may be a lass, we will not know for sure until the birth."

Alleck's shoulders slumped. "Aye, Mama."

"That's a good lad. Lie back down now and I shall tell you a tale of a mighty warrior who was given a kingdom after he slew the horrible dragon that had been rampaging the countryside."

Alleck hurriedly lay back down.

Jesslyn began her tale in low, reverent tones. *"Many years ago, not far from this very keep, there once lived a great and powerful warrior...."*

* * *

"I believe Callum to be the father, tho' Jesslyn has stubbornly refused to verify my suspicion," Daniel said to both his grandmother and his wife late that evening. They'd agreed to meet in the solar after Jesslyn and Alleck had gone to their chambers for the night. "I cannot blame her for not wanting to name him, since, if it were revealed, it might cause Callum problems with his new bride, not to mention his in-laws."

"Aye, I suppose I can see the wisdom in keeping our kinship to the babe a secret," Lady Maclean said to Daniel. "But only for a while. Callum deserves to know of his bairn, and if we wait, say, a year after the babe's birth, that should be enough time to lessen the blow to his relationship with his wife and her family.

"And if the babe is not Callum's?" Maryn asked.

Daniel scrubbed his fingers over his stubbled chin and said, "I've thought about this for hours now, and can think of no other with whom she'd have had the opportunity to conceive a babe." He shook his head and shrugged. "Nay, it *must* be my cousin who did the deed." Struck by a new thought, he narrowed his eyes at his very pregnant, bronze-haired wife. "Do *you* suspect someone else?"

"Well, there did seem to be some sort of connection between her and Bao, if you remember."

"Bao! They'd only met two days before we left to negotiate a settlement between the MacGregors and the Gordons, and then he left a fortnight after we returned. Are you suggesting that Jesslyn would have had carnal knowledge of a man she barely knew?" Daniel vehemently shook his head. "Nay, the father is *not* Bao."

"I must agree with Daniel, Maryn. If only because of the lack of opportunity." Lady Maclean sighed. "Callum is the father, I doubt it not."

"I admit, the possibility does seem awfully remote," Maryn said, "but I keep remembering how avidly they gazed upon each other as Jesslyn handed those tarts up to Bao, just before he rode out of the courtyard that day. There was something between them."

"Aye, there may have been an attraction brewing, but that still doesn't lead me to believe Jesslyn would have lain with the man after barely meeting him."

Maryn sighed. "Aye, I suppose you're right. Tho' I cannot help wishing that it *were* Bao; 'twould make things so much easier. After all, *he* is free to wed."

"Except, he's now miles away in Perth," Daniel reminded her.

Lady Maclean straightened on her stool and placed her hands over her knees. "So, 'tis settled then? We agree that Callum fathered the bairn and that we must speak to Jesslyn about revealing such on the babe's first birthday?"

"Aye," Daniel and Maryn said at the same time.

"We must tell Branwenn before you speak to the elders. 'Twould not do for her to find out afterward," Maryn said to her husband. "Her feelings would surely be crushed—you know how sensitive the lass is."

"Aye. I should have spoken to her before supper this eve, but there simply wasn't enough time to do so. I know she was highly curious as to the reason we asked Jesslyn and Alleck to move to the keep, but,"— Daniel turned his gaze to his grandmother— "your training has gone well, because she kept her own counsel and did not question the decision publicly."

Lady Maclean nodded. "She's a good lass. And 'twas not my training, but her brother, Bao's. She's amazingly well-mannered, considering the upbringing she's had."

"I've been surprised, as well," Maryn said. "Bao had to have been gone quite a bit on the king's campaigns. Yet, Branwenn and he are so close. I hope 'twill not be too many more moons before he visits."

Daniel turned the focus back onto their original topic. "I must begin my search for a suitable husband for Jesslyn forthwith." He looked at his wife and said, "I expect your full support this time."

"Aye, you shall have it. But I insist on helping you to find the man. Steward Ranald and Derek, your lieutenant, must not be considered again, agreed?"

Daniel nodded. "We'll begin the search on the

morrow. Noticing that his very pregnant wife had begun to knead her lower back, Daniel assisted her to her feet, saying, "For now, let us retire to our bedchambers and get some rest." He turned then to his grandmother and helped her to rise as well. "We must also speak to the clan elders on the morrow. I've arranged for them to gather in the great hall at noon."

"With our support behind her, Jesslyn will not be banished," Maryn said.

He placed his arm around his wife's back to give her support as they moved toward the door. "Nay, she'll not. But the sooner she's wed, the better."

"Aye," Lady Maclean agreed.

* * *

The meeting with the clan elders went much as Daniel had expected, he told Jesslyn afterward. At first, they'd insisted that she be sent back to the MacLaurins, which, of course, would have suited Jesslyn, but Daniel and his grandmother managed to dissuade them of that notion. And, as Daniel had suspected it would, the fact that she and her son would be residing at the keep under his and Lady Maclean's protection had aided the elders in changing their opinion.

* * *

The next sennight was filled with activity as Jesslyn was admonished to begin sewing swaddling clothes for her babe. She now sat with Maryn, Branwenn, and Lady Maclean in the solar working on the second of her feeble attempts and listening as the ladies made plans for the *Hogmanay* feast in a bit over a moon's time.

"Callum and his new wife will be attending, so we

must make sure to have his chamber furnished with more hooks for his wife to hang her clothing upon while she is here," Lady Maclean said.

"'Twill be good to see Callum again. I do hope he's happy in his union, he deserves to be," Jesslyn said.

"Daniel assures me that Callum was pleased enough with the match, even tho' 'twas contrived to keep peace between the clans. He said the lass is quite pretty—and Callum does love a pretty face," Maryn replied. "I remember how unsure I felt when I arrived at the MacLaurin holding and knew no one, so I shall give the lady a special welcome. Some cut flowers and herbs placed in their chamber will do nicely, I think."

"She will appreciate the gesture, I'm sure," Jesslyn said.

"My father will also be attending. I'm looking so forward to seeing him again," Maryn said, her smile broadening.

"And I as well. We'll serve swan again, I think," Lady Maclean replied. She looked up from her sewing and asked Maryn, "It *is* Laird Donald's favorite, is it not?"

Maryn nodded, her smile shifting, becoming wry. "Aye, tho' I've yet to see him turn away anything he's been offered. Ouch!" Her hand flew to her stomach. "The babe's a bit restless, it seems."

Lady Maclean studied her. "'Twill not be many more sennights until your babe makes his appearance. Mayhap, even while our guests are here."

"Aye, 'tis what Daniel keeps saying, tho' I hope 'tis *after* the festival. For everyone's sake."

Jesslyn smiled. There was much to celebrate, it seemed.

"I only wish Bao would be here," Branwenn lamented.

Jesslyn's shoulders stiffened at the sound of her babe's father's name, but she quickly let go of the tension. 'Twould not do for anyone to suspect her secret. And, thank heaven, she'd managed to defer Daniel's decision to find her a suitable husband until after the new year. That would, at least, give her some time to accustom herself to the prospect once again.

"Aye, that would truly make my old heart sing if all my grandsons would be at my side for the holiday," Lady Maclean replied.

"Daniel sent a missive to him, but, curiously, we have yet to receive a reply," Maryn said worriedly.

Jesslyn's heart tripped and her head shot up. "I…I doubt he'd travel all the way back here so soon, anyway," she said a bit breathlessly to Maryn, then turned her gaze on Branwenn. There was a much-too-wise look in Branwenn's big violet-colored eyes before the lass looked away, which unsettled Jesslyn further. Branwenn had been acting very peculiarly toward her since being informed of Jesslyn's pregnancy. She watched her constantly. Surely, Bao hadn't told his sister about their tryst? Nay, he was much too protective of the lass's innocence to have done such a thing. A blush formed on Branwenn's cheeks and Jesslyn became even more alarmed that she somehow knew the truth. If Daniel ever found out, he'd bring Bao back and force him to wed her. And she could think of no greater torture than to be wed to a man that would resent her for all his days for taking away his much-desired freedom.

"Branwenn, you look flushed. Are you feeling well?" Lady Maclean asked.

"I do feel a bit tired, Grandmother Maclean. May I go to my bedchamber and lie down for a while?"

"Aye, lass, I think it a good idea. We can't have you catching a fever."

Branwenn rose and placed the garment she was working on in the basket next to Lady Maclean's stool.

"I'll send Daniel up to see you. He may have some herbs that will help you to feel better," Maryn said.

"Nay, that will not be necessary," Branwenn said in a hurry. "I'm sure I shall feel much revived after a nap."

Maryn nodded and turned her attention back to the seam she was working on.

After Branwenn departed, Jesslyn and the other two ladies continued their sewing in silence for a time, each in their own quiet contemplation. They'd been thus for a bit over a quarter-hour when Maryn turned to Jesslyn and asked, "Have you felt the babe move yet?"

Jesslyn placed her hand over her slightly rounded tummy and replied, "Nay, not yet. Surely, 'twill not be many more days hence."

Lady Maclean nodded. "You said you believe the babe will arrive at *Bealltainn*? By my calculations, the babe should quicken in about three sennights' time."

"I pray you are right," Jesslyn replied.

* * *

That night, Jesslyn lay in her bed, her mind churning. Ever since she'd learned that Daniel had invited Bao here for *Hogmanay*, she'd been filled with apprehension. Mayhap she shouldn't wait until the new year to find a husband. At least the man she chose would go into the union willingly. And he'd be well aware of her childing state as well, and have agreed to wed her anyway. Surely, that match would be, if not joyous, quite comfortable. She could live with that.

Jesslyn pressed her fingers over her eyelids in an attempt to stave off the tears she felt pooling in them. "Ow!" She'd forgotten about her newly pricked fingers. She was *no* seamstress. Sighing, she settled that same hand behind her head and stared up into the darkness. But what if Bao actually *wanted* this babe? That question had been plaguing her since she'd first discovered her condition and decided to keep the babe's paternity a secret. Could she truly refuse the chance to give this bairn a life with its natural father? And what of Bao? If the roles were reversed— impossible, but still—would he keep the knowledge of the babe's blood tie to her a secret? She shook her head. Nay, he would not. For, tho' everyone believed that she and Bao barely knew each other, that was not the case. They had met in secret a couple of times prior to their tryst. Had actually formed a bond, a friendship, she believed. And she did know him. He was both loving and responsible. Nay, he would never keep such a thing from her. She sighed in resignation. And neither, it seemed, could she any longer.

* * *

CHAPTER 3
The Highlands, Scotland 1204

Jesslyn was in the tower larder counting the number of bags of grain they had in preparation for the *Hogmanay* feast when the news of Bao's arrival was given to her by a kitchen maid who'd been sent in to retrieve her.

"Tell Laird MacLaurin I shall be in the great hall in just a moment," she said to the lass.

The servant nodded. "Aye, m'lady," she replied before turning and scurrying away.

Jesslyn hurriedly took off the soiled tunic she'd put on over her silver-blue woolen gown and tried desperately to realign her veil and filet, stuffing her bedraggled, thick flaxen braid back under the covering.

She had yet to make her confessions to the others, as she'd sworn to herself she'd do this day. Nay, she'd intended on giving them her admission when they broke their fast together later in the morn. She'd thought it a good idea to include her son in the discussion as well; allow him to have his say amongst the others, as this new babe in her womb affected his life as well. She knew without being told that he'd be over the moon with gladness that Bao was the babe's father, however.

But now, it seemed, she'd hesitated too long. For 'twas vital that she speak with Bao first and find out his true thoughts on his pending fatherhood before she convey the babe's father's identity to Bao's family members.

As she hustled toward the keep, she agonized over the coming reunion. Had he thought of her at all these past moons, as she had so often thought of him? Would he be pleased to see her, or think her a nuisance?

Oh, God! She pressed her hand over her pounding heart. What if Daniel had already told Bao that she was with child before she'd had a moment to speak with him in privy? Jesslyn doubled her speed, hoping to get to the great hall before Daniel had had a chance to explain her condition to Bao. She would discreetly tell Daniel that she did not want him to speak of her childing state now. That she would prefer that he spoke of it later, after the family members had had some time to enjoy each other's company.

The family, as well as a very beautiful raven-haired woman of evident wealth, were already assembled by the time Jesslyn arrived, but it quickly became clear that Bao had not been told of her condition as yet, for which Jesslyn gave a mental sigh of relief.

Highland Grace

She stood in the entryway a moment, the others not having noticed her arrival as of yet, and stared at Bao. Her breath caught in her lungs. He had grown more masculine in the passing moons, it seemed to her. More vividly beautiful. His black hair, that fell in a straight line down his neck and ended at his broad shoulders, shone with blue highlights that could be seen even from across the room. And that massive *uisge beatha*-hued frame. The well-thewed chest, the mighty arms, the trim waist. Fortunately for her thrumming nerve-endings, the green woolen tunic he wore hid the long, sinewy legs and thighs she knew he possessed, else she would surely melt into a puddle of desire where she stood.

"I'd wondered why I'd not received a reply to my missive. You must have only just departed Perth when I sent it," she heard Maryn say to him.

He smiled. "Aye, tho' knowing now that you'd threatened to bring the family to me would have brought me here to you in any case."

"And why is that? I believe I would enjoy visiting that town. After all, 'tis near the abbey at Scone, where our king was crowned. There must be quite a bit to keep one entertained there," Maryn replied.

"Aye, there is!" Branwenn piped in. "We simply must make a journey there." She turned to Daniel and said, "Can we? Please?"

For a split second, a look of alarm crossed Bao's countenance before he blinked it away, and Jesslyn knew why: 'twas to do with the other trade in which he was secretly involved.

"Have you forgotten my wife's delicate condition?" Daniel asked her. "I don't think a journey will be likely to happen for quite some time to come."

The woman saw her first and settled her hand on Bao's shoulder, leaning with intimacy and familiarity into him as she whispered something to him and tilted her head in Jesslyn's direction. The same carnal smile he'd bestowed on Jesslyn so often, darkened his features as he gazed at his companion. Jealousy, molten and quick, pounded through her veins. 'Twas clear that the lady was much more than a responsibility to him. *Was she one of the ladies who paid him for his services?*

He swung his gaze to Jesslyn. His eyes flashed with what she believed to be lust, but instantly disintegrated into a look of bored disinterest. It cleaved her chest like a sword. He gave her a nod. "Jesslyn." Mayhap the friendship they'd managed to salvage last summer was an illusion on her part. Which told her that he would not be happy about the babe, and would be better off not knowing he'd fathered it.

"G'morn," Jesslyn replied shakily, with a quick dip of courtesy.

"Come inside." Daniel broke from the circle they'd formed by the hearth and walked over to her, placing her hand in the crook of his arm as he began escorting her toward the others.

"I beg you, don't say anything about my condition just yet, will you?" she said *sotto voce* as she walked beside him.

Daniel narrowed a gaze at her, but nodded his agreement.

* * *

Bao stepped to the other side of Lady MacGhille, in hopes that Daniel would step into the void with Jesslyn, so that Bao could keep his distance from her. Unfortunately, Daniel chose to neatly tuck Jesslyn between them. Almost instantly, the scent of lavender assailed his senses, and brought forth a visceral memory of the glide of her silken skin against his abdomen, the cushion of her full breasts against his chest. *Blood of Christ!* He had to get a grip on this hunger for her. They'd parted friends the last they met, but his discovery of her brother's perfidy—and her family's own profit from that perfidy in specific regard to Bao's mother—had killed those warm feelings he'd held for her for good. Now all he needed was for his body's desire for her to die a quick death as well. He was here for only as long as it took to transfer Lady MacGhille to her husband, and then he would be off again. No *Hogmanay* festival, no rekindling of the flame between himself and the widow.

Derek, Daniel's lieutenant, came through the entry at that moment. "Lady MacGhille's husband has arrived. He gives his thanks and his regret, but is pressed to take his wife immediately to their holding, as the King has requested his swift return to court on urgent business. I am to escort the lady to her palfrey."

Daniel stepped toward him. "I shall come with you and greet Laird MacGhille."

Bao stepped forward. "I'll come as well."

The two men left with Lady MacGhille on Daniel's arm.

* * *

A half-hour later, all were gathered once more in the great hall.

"The meal should be ready to be served in a few more moments," Bao's grandmother said to him. "I've requested a bit heartier of a fare than we usually have at this time of day, since you've been traveling for so many days and are in need of meat."

Bao grinned down into her unusual eyes, one blue, one green, and put his arm around her waist, giving it a squeeze. Was she thinner than she'd been a few moons past? She somehow seemed more fragile to him than she'd been before. And her hair seemed even more gray than it had been then, as well. But her cheeks were rosy, and that boded well for her health, surely. "My thanks to you for that, Grandmother. Oat cakes and ale have been our main sustenance for most of our journey. I believe I could eat an entire sheep, were it placed before me now—hooves and all!"

"Bao, if you ate the hooves, I'd swallow a toad!" Branwenn said.

"Alive or dead?" Bao replied, a sinister gleam in his eye.

Daniel and Maryn laughed.

"Boiled or raw," Branwenn rejoined, the devil in her eye.

Maryn laughed so hard she snorted, which caused his brother to howl even louder.

Jesslyn's hand flew to her mouth, hiding a smile that sent warm sunbeams through Bao's center, which he viciously squelched.

"Now, now, my wee bairns, no one is eating hooves *or* toads, so cease this silliness and find your seat at the table," his grandmother said as she pressed her hands into the curve of both their backs and urged them forward. "Daniel, will you escort your wife and Jesslyn to the table?"

Bao reached around his grandmother and tugged on his sister's straight black locks that had grown past her shoulders in his absence.

"Ow! Stop that you buffoon!" she yelled and slapped at his hand.

His grandmother halted and grabbed a fistful of each of their outer clothing, forcing them to stop their forward motion as well. "Branwenn, that was extremely unladylike. Beg forgiveness from your brother for raising your voice."

"But Grandmother Maclean, he started it! He pulled my hair!"

"You are my ward and I've promised to train you to be a lady. A lady may not have control over another's actions, but she most assuredly has control over her response. You have just shamed me with your behavior."

Branwenn's eyes got misty as bright flags of fury—and no doubt mortification, Bao was sure—slashed across her cheeks, but she blinked away the tears and turned to him. "I'm sorry I yelled at you, Bao," she said in a strained voice.

Bao felt horrible. He'd just been so happy to see her and had fallen easily back into his life-long habit of teasing and tormenting her. But, his grandmother was right. He'd asked her to train his sister so that she could make a good match for husband, and he must learn to treat her differently, at least in front of others. "'Twas I who was wrong to treat you as a bairn, when 'tis so obvious that you are a young lady now. I beg your forgiveness."

Branwenn nodded.

Bao looked into the sad, purple pools of his sister's eyes and resolved to spend some time with her alone as soon as they could arrange it. He needed to soothe his niggling worry and conscience that his sister was not settling in here.

His grandmother lifted her hand to his sister's fiery cheek and pressed a kiss to the other one. "That was as gracious an apology as I've ever heard. You're a beautiful young lady, I simply want your behavior to match your appearance."

"Aye, Grandmother," she said and leaned into her embrace.

"Shall we join the others at the table then?" Bao asked. Maryn, Daniel, and Jesslyn had discreetly left the three to their discussion and had already settled at their places.

"Aye, let us dine," his grandmother said. "Otherwise, we *all* may become so hungry we'd eat hooves."

Bao and Branwenn grinned at her jest. This time, Bao moved between the two ladies and led them toward the others. He gently held his sister's delicate-boned, tiny hand in his beefy, calloused one and the warm glow that filled his heart expanded further.

Highland Grace

After seating his grandmother, he settled his sister onto her stool and bent low, whispering in her ear, "Will you take a walk with me after we break our fast?"

Branwenn nodded. "Aye."

He took the place his grandmother indicated, the same place he'd had when he'd been here last summer. Next to Jesslyn. *All right. After the meal, after the walk with Branwenn, I'm gone from here.* Before he could stop himself, he stole a glance at her. *Why did she have to wear the same damned gown she'd worn the day he'd plundered her?*

As if his sister had read his mind, she leaned around him and said to Jesslyn, "The silvery-blue of your gown makes your eyes even bluer. You look lovely."

Jesslyn's gaze lifted from her seemingly intent study of the trencher. "My thanks. Malcolm, my late brother bought the material for me with his earnings in the holy lands and sent it to me. He wrote that he'd purchased the cloth with that precise thought in mind."

Every muscle in Bao's body went rigid and he was sure the hate he felt showed in his gaze when he moved it over the garment.

"Then your brother was a very wise man," Branwenn said.

His sister's voice brought reason back and he turned his attention to the trencher. Leaning forward, he inhaled deeply. "The rabbit stew smells good, Grandmother." With effort, he brought forth some semblance of manners for the others' benefit, and glanced at Jesslyn again, saying, "The meat is in quite large portions; shall I cut it a bit more for you?" tho' he couldn't keep the ribbon of steel from underlaying the polite words.

Confused by Bao's cold, distant behavior, Jesslyn replied, "Aye, that would be quite helpful. My thanks." *Why?* It seemed to be more than just disinterest. There was brooding displeasure there as well. And that venomous look he'd just given her. What was that about?

* * *

"Mama! Mama! Is Bao really home?!" A loud boom sounded following the query, and 'twas clear to Bao that Jesslyn's son had thrown the door to the keep so wide it banged against the wall. He stood and turned. No matter his feelings for the mother, the lad had found a permanent place in his heart. When Alleck finally entered the great hall, Bao stepped off of the dais and strode toward him. "Good morn, Alleck. I wondered where you were."

Just as he'd done so often before, Alleck flew at him, wrapping his arms around Bao's lower legs and holding tight. "Bao!" He looked up into his face and said, "You said you wouldn't come back here for *Hogmanay*, but I'm glad you did anyway."

Deciding not to disabuse the lad of the false notion, he said only, "I'm glad I came back as well. Have you been at Niall's then?"

Alleck nodded his head with vigor. "We're buildin' a big"—he thrust his arms out wide—"fortr'ss around this ol' cart outside the blacksmith's."

"'Tis a sound undertaking, I trow. Will you show it to me when you've finished building it?"

"Aye."

"Come, have a seat at the table and we'll break our fast together." Turning, Bao placed his hand on the lad's back and pressed him forward.

A stool was placed to the right of Jesslyn. "You'll sit next to me, Alleck. We're having rabbit stew—are you hungry?"

"Aye! How come we get to eat stew so early, Mama?" He squirmed and fidgeted on his seat.

"Because Bao's been traveling for days now and needed something a bit heavier than bread and cheese for his meal."

"How is the fortress building coming along, Alleck?" Daniel inquired.

Alleck chewed faster and swallowed his bite of stew with a loud gulp. Bao grinned. Clearly Jesslyn had tutored the lad not to speak with his mouth full. "Good. But we hafta find somethin' we can use to make our mang'nel."

Lady Maclean's gaze sharpened in alarm. Looking from Alleck to Daniel and then back to Alleck, she said, "Mangonel! I hardly think you lads need weapons. You might hurt yourselves, or someone else."

"I agree," Jesslyn said. "I thought you two were building a privy place for you and your other friends—that hardly requires a missile-lobbing engine."

Alleck's brows slammed together. "But how are we s'pose to keep the lasses out of our fortr'ss if we can't blast stuff at 'em?" He crossed his arms over his chest and pursed his lips in a defiant pout.

"You'll simply have to think of another plan, laddie," Jesslyn said. "And straighten up. No more of your peevish behavior or I shall send you to your bedchamber."

Alleck huffed a loud sigh and Bao hid an even broader grin behind his fist. "Aye, Mama," the lad replied sullenly. After another moment, he dug back into his meal, the episode seemingly forgotten.

* * *

Maryn leaned into Daniel's side, needing the added support now that the babe had grown so big in her belly, and said softly, "Have you noticed the way Bao and Jesslyn keep looking at each other when the other doesn't see? There is definitely an attraction between them."

Daniel looked over at the two and watched them a moment. "Aye. 'Tis almost palpable, is it not? Although, my brother does seem to be fighting against it awfully hard." He narrowed his eyes, his mind filled with new possibilities. "'Twould certainly make things easier if Bao would wed Jesslyn. The babe would then be a legitimate Maclean."

"That's a fine idea!" she said. "But do you think he'd wed? He's been so set on keeping his life free of further involvements."

Daniel shrugged. "He asked to speak with me in privy later this afternoon. I shall broach the subject then and try to overcome his objections."

"Will you tell him of her babe?"

Daniel nodded. "Aye. And I shall tell him who I believe the father of the babe to be." He looked directly at her then and continued, "He's family; he should be told for that reason alone. But, because of our blood tie, 'twill also allow him to see the importance of keeping the babe within the family as well."

* * *

"Would you like more water?" Bao asked Jesslyn, still all politeness but no warmth.

"Aye. My thanks," she replied.

Alleck leaned forward and looked past Jesslyn at Bao. "Mama's got a babe in her belly, jus' like Maryn."

Jesslyn sucked in a sharp breath and squeezed her eyes shut. *Oh, God! He'll know. He'll know and he'll hate me.*

The tense silence that followed pressed down on her like a slab of granite.

"Al—" Daniel began.

"I'm gonna have a wee brother soon."

Jesslyn expelled the breath she'd been holding. When she finally managed to force her eyes open, they were instantly captured by the shocked and horror-filled eyes of her babe's father.

* * *

"Is that so?" Bao said, dread, fascination, and disgust warring inside him. "And when will your brother arrive, Alleck?"

"Mama says the babe should be ready by *Bealltainn*."

Bao's stomach did a flip.

"But you mustn't tell anyone about it, yet."

Out of the corner of his eye, Bao saw Alleck nod his head in emphasis. "Mama says so."

Bao turned his gaze on the lad and took in a deep breath. "Mayhap, if 'tis a secret, you weren't supposed to tell me either." Was that his voice? It sounded higher than normal.

The lad's eyes widened and he swung his gaze to his mother. "Is it all right that I told Bao, Mama? You didn't tell me I couldn't tell him 'bout the babe. And Branwenn knows."

Jesslyn turned her gaze to the lad. "Aye, 'tis all right. We were going to tell him about the babe after the meal."

Branwenn leaned into Bao's side and whispered in his ear, "She will not tell anyone who the father is."

Bao nodded once, but said naught. He knew who the father was. Him.

His grandmother motioned to one of the servants and requested another stool be placed next to her. "Alleck, come sit by me. I'm quite curious about this fortress you and your friend are building."

While Alleck made his way around the table and settled himself on the stool, Jesslyn said in a quick whisper, "I need to speak with you as soon as possible after the meal. Alone. Can we meet in the wood, at the place we first met?"

He frowned as he studied her a moment before slowly nodding. "Aye. I asked Branwenn to take a walk with me, but I shall delay that until later in the day," he whispered in reply. His jaw tensed. "And wear a different gown."

Her brows slammed together in both perplexity and annoyance, but she nodded. "Aye, all right."

The remainder of the meal was spent catching up on events and planning for the coming celebration in a few sennights' time. Both Bao and Jesslyn were relieved when the meal finally ended.

"Alleck, I'll walk back with you to Niall's house. I'd like to speak with his mother a moment," Jesslyn said as the others went their separate ways.

Bao watched her leave. When she took her son by the hand as they strolled from the great hall, he fought hard against the feelings of wonder and tenderness that threatened to overtake his other, more logical feelings of disgust and betrayal. But even with that, there was only one thing for him to do. And he would do it. No one would ever say that Bao did not know and do the right thing, no matter how vile the thing he did might be to him.

He felt Branwenn's gaze on him as she walked toward him. "I suppose our walk together must wait until another time?" she said in a low voice once she'd reached his side.

Bao looked down into his sister's all-too-aware eyes and narrowed his own. "You know!" he accused. "How?"

Color shot up her neck and washed over her face. She turned her gaze away from him. Then she coughed and cleared her throat several times, an old ruse, he knew, to stall for time. "Sorry," she said hoarsely, "I swallowed wrong."

"Braaanweennn," he drawled in the same tone he'd used on her as a bairn when he knew she was lying to him about some mischief she'd gotten herself into.

Her shoulders drooped. Wringing her hands, she walked away from him and stood facing the hearth. "I was there that day. At the waterfall," she said in a barely audible voice. "I saw *everything*."

Bao strode over to her and grabbed her by her upper arms, turning her to face him. His voice shook when he said, "You *watched* us? I can't even begin to find the words to say how wrong that was." He shook her ever so slightly as his grip on her arms increased. "This is exactly why I insisted that you stay on here to receive training from my grandmother. No decently raised young lass would *ever* do that!"

Her eyes filled as her throat worked. Finally she said in an anguished whisper, "I'm sorry!" before her face crumpled and the floodgates opened in earnest.

With a jerk, Bao released his grip on her arms and turned away. Needing to gain control of his anger before he hurt his sister's feelings further with more harsh words, he strode across the room, cupping his hands behind his head. He stopped and stared at naught, his mind focused on the events of that fateful day. "You followed me?" he finally asked.

When she didn't answer, he turned and looked at her. Her face was a mask of misery, soaked with her salty tears. She was such a tiny thing; she always had been. Since the moment of her birth on the four-wheeled cart his father had stolen from some pilgrims he'd murdered on one of his many freebooting rampages. Branwenn's mother had been stolen in a raid by Bao's father as well—and then the man had been violently angry when he'd discovered she was carrying her husband's babe in her belly. But, somehow, the woman had survived his father's beatings and kept her babe inside of her. But when she'd delivered Branwenn into this world, she'd taken her last breath. Jamison Maclean had been intent on dumping the babe on the side of the road, but Bao had convinced him to allow him to keep her—for a price. That had been the night he'd agreed to work the venereal trade for his father. And it hadn't been many hours past that time that he had been initiated into the darkest side of human bondage.

With a mental shake, Bao shrugged away those dismal memories and focused once more on his sister. He'd kept her innocent. Innocent of that side of his life, and certainly physically innocent. He'd wanted a better life for her, and he'd made sure she'd had a clean and stable home, as well as plenty of food and clothing. But, being raised as she was near the court, and having a brother who was gone much of the time on the king's campaigns, had allowed her to develop her already independent nature to a level that had been troublesome, to say the least, much of the time he'd raised her. And was this latest mischief so unforgivable? Nay, 'twas not. Especially since he must admit his own culpability in her behavior.

He walked over to her and took her in his arms, holding her and stroking her silky hair. "Do you know what your first word was? 'Twas my name. Well, not *exactly* my name, but quite close," he said, reminiscing in the age-old way he'd used all her life to comfort her.

She nodded beneath his palm. "I called you 'Gow'. I remember," she said wistfully.

Bao smiled and kissed her forehead. "Nay, you can't possibly remember. You were too young."

"Well, it seems like a memory since you've told me of it so oft," she replied.

Bao hugged her more tightly and let out a loud sigh. "I'm sorry," he finally said. "I shouldn't have spoken so harshly to you. I was just shocked, but I'm calmer now."

She relaxed further into his embrace. "I know I shouldn't have stayed and watched, but I was just so curious. Why is it so awful for a lass to know how 'tis done before she is expected to *do* it the night she's wed?" She pulled back and looked up at him, ire at the injustice of society's rules written on her countenance. "Lads are *encouraged* to learn how 'tis done, 'tis so unfair!"

Bao's lips came together in a grim line as he pressed his finger and thumb against his eyelids. After a moment, he shook his head. "I know not." He looked into his sister's upturned face once more and continued, "'Tis just the way things are—and always have been, as far as I know." He shrugged. "Well-bred, unwed lasses must remain virtuous and ignorant of those things." Placing his hands on her shoulders, he said gravely, "I'm sure it has quite a bit to do with keeping the lass from finding herself in the same condition Jesslyn is in right now."

She bowed her head and nodded. "Aye, I suppose you are right." She stepped away and sat on one of the stools next to the hearth. "What are you going to do? Will you wed her?"

"Aye."

Branwenn squealed with glee. Bounding to her feet

once more, she flew to him and threw her arms around him again. "I cannot believe it! You swore you'd never wed!" she said, her cheek pressed tightly against his chest.

Bao chuckled and scrubbed his knuckles across the crown of her head, knocking her filet even further askew. "Fate, it seems, has made that vow one I will have to break."

She slapped at his hand and leapt out of his reach. "Then you'll be staying on here?" she asked as she righted her hair ornament.

"Aye, so it seems. But first, I must obtain the mother's agreement."

"She'll say aye—she obviously likes you—otherwise, she wouldn't have"—she fluttered her hand a few times—"you know, with you."

Aye, he knew. 'Twas that thing, however, that he *would* forget. "I suppose I should be off now to speak with her." He turned and strode toward the doorway, but swung back to Branwenn before he departed. "I truly am sorry for treating you like a bairn in front of the others earlier. 'Twill not happen again. And I still want to spend some time with you later—I want to hear how you have truly been getting on here."

She nodded. "I'd like that as well. Mayhap, after supper this eve?"

"Aye, after supper," he replied. "I missed you."

Her eyes misted again and she blinked. "I missed

you too. Now, go find the mother of your babe and set a date to wed."

* * *

CHAPTER 4

Jesslyn pulled the fur-lined mantle tighter around her arms and shoulders as she paced in front of the opening to the shallow cave where she and Bao had first met—the setting of their last private talk, as well, before he'd left last summer. The vines, that had once been so full of leaves, serving to cloak the entry, were now dry brown stems—a somewhat sinister version of their former selves, or so it seemed to her. Thankfully, the snow flurries had stopped some time earlier, but there was still a thin layer of frost on the ground, and it weighted down the pine and juniper branches as well.

Where was Bao? She'd been waiting here for what seemed an half-hour. Mayhap, he'd changed his mind. After all, his reaction to the news of the babe had been distress and alarm. Exactly what she'd expected after the cool reception she'd received from him. Mayhap, he was afraid she would confirm that he'd fathered the babe and he would feel honor-bound to wed her.

But he had naught to fear, for she had no intention of wedding him under these circumstances. Nay, he'd made it more than plain last summer that he desired an unfettered life. And with his distant manner today, this course seemed even more imperative. Besides, she had little doubt that he'd resent her for forcing him into an unwanted union, and a life filled with anger and bitterness was not the life she would have for her babe, her lad, or herself.

Deciding it would be foolish for her to wait for him any longer, she turned to leave. She hadn't walked more than two paces when the sound of a horse whinnying brought her up short. Her gaze riveted on Bao as he walked with masculine grace over the snow and ice-covered forest floor toward her, leading his stallion by the reins.

"I hope you haven't been here long," he said, his tone rigid, when he was close enough for her to hear him. "It took more time than I'd expected to delay the walk I'd planned with my sister." His breath formed puffs of gray misty fog as he spoke, his movements stiff as he tethered his horse to the trunk of a nearby pine. When he'd completed the task, he turned toward her and his eyes swept her violently trembling form. "'Tis bitter cold out here, I'd best make a fire before you become ill." All his words were right, but his voice remained steely.

"My thanks. I should have made one myself, but I wasn't aware of the cold until just now." She heard her own overly cheerful tone and berated herself. *Why do you care if he likes or hates you? You'll not be seeing much of him after today*.

An awkward silence ensued as she watched him build a fire near the opening to the cave before pulling back the bare stems of the vines and bringing the two stools made from portions of pine trunks forward.

Hating the silence, she asked, "I've often wondered: How did you manage to make those stools and the table while you dwelled in the forest? Did you actually travel with such cumbrous tools?"

Bao looked toward her. "Nay, we brought only a few satchels filled with the minimum for our needs—and my weapons, of course." He shrugged and shook his head. "The stools and table were here when I found the cave. I know not from where they came."

"Hmm," she replied with a nod.

"Come, sit by the fire." Bao unclasped the circular gold pin at his shoulder. "Take my mantel," he said, shrugging one shoulder out of the heavy brown covering.

"Nay, the fire will be sufficient to warm me." She settled on a stool and leaned forward with her palms raised toward the heat of the flames.

He refastened the pin and crossed his arms over his chest, his look once more brooding and tense. It made Jesslyn glad that she could hide most of her visage within her own mantel's fur-lined hood.

"We'll wed, of course," he stated.

Jesslyn's heart slammed against her ribcage. She shook her head. "Nay, we will *not*."

"We will."

She swallowed hard. "'Tis not yours."

His eyes widened. "'Tis not *mine?*"

"Nay, 'tis not," she said with more force. "I knew you'd think it was the moment you heard of my condition," she rushed to say, "and that is why I wanted to meet with you forthwith...to explain."

"Whose else could it be?" he asked harshly, tugging her hood down off of her head. With narrowed eyes, he studied her, then shook his head. "You lie."

Jesslyn rose and strode away from him, her hands clasped over her belly. "Nay, I do not. I told you after we..."—she shrugged—"that I'd just past my monthly courses."

"If I didn't father this babe, who did?" There was a note of angry disbelief in his tone.

"It matters not, the deed is done and the man is miles away and wed to another."

"Wed to another?" There was a long pause and then his eyes narrowed once more. "Are you saying 'tis Callum's bairn you carry?" After only a slight pause, he said, "Nay, I think not. 'Twas clear when I had you, you hadn't been with anyone since your husband."

Oh, lord. Of course, *he* would be able to *tell* whether she'd lain with anyone recently. A man with his sordid experience. "I only lay with the father once."

"Aye, *that*, at least, is true." In the next instant, he was behind her, swinging her around to face him, tipping her chin up, forcing her to meet his eye. In spite of everything, her body betrayed her, sending a tremor of awareness across her nerve endings and making her womb pulse. She darted her tongue over dry lips.

She saw his reaction as well. His eyes widened then

settled, their coal-black centers a near eclipse of their surrounding umber. She heard his harsh intake of breath, saw his nostrils flare and before she knew what was happening, he enveloped her in his strong embrace and devoured her mouth. No gentle kiss, this, but open-mouthed, tongue-thrusting, teeth-grinding near-brutal domination and pleasuring.

And her body responded. Hot, hard need burned her insides. *This.* This was what she'd once dreamed of having with him. After their time together. Before he'd dashed all her hopes of a marriage between them and returned to his life of soldiering and pleasuring of ladies in the King's court.

Which he would return to again, quickly and with relief, once she'd convinced him about the babe. She twisted her head to the side and broke the kiss. "Nay! We mustn't."

As if scorched, he let go of her and took a step back. She stumbled, but managed to right herself without falling. His breath harsh and loud, he pressed his arm to his mouth. After a split moment, he said, "Aye, that much is true." Then with a glare that pierced through her, made it impossible to breathe, he added, "But wed, we will."

She felt her alarm like a swift silver-cold tide rush up her spine and into her brain. Crossing her arms, she said, "You want no part of marriage! Why do you demand it now, when I've told you the babe I carry is not yours?"

Arms akimbo, he stood with legs spread, like an ancient statue of some conquering god of war.

"Because you lie. It *is* my babe you carry in your belly."

"I do not! The father is someone else entirely. Why will you not believe me?"

"Because, though you may own other loathsome faults, this I know: You would never lay with a married man, Jesslyn."

Loathsome faults? Which are? She didn't have the courage to ask. And besides it only proved her belief that they should *never* wed. But he was right about her and married men. Another tack then. "All right! I'll tell you the truth."

He crossed his arms over his chest as if in judgment. "Finally."

"I've told no one who fathered this babe because I wanted to speak to the man first, which I have recently done." Feeling chilled once again, she moved over to stand by the fire and lifted her hood back over her head. "The babe's father is Steward Ranald."

"Steward Ranald! Daniel's fleshy, foolish steward?" He snorted and strode to the other side of the fire so that, once again, they faced each other. "He's old enough to be your father!"

"He's agreed to wed me," she said, keeping her eyes on the fire. "So you see, there's truly no reason for you to sacrifice your freedom for me." And tho' she hadn't in truth spoken with the steward yet, the man had been so avid for her that she was sure that she could convince him to wed her—and lie about his fathering her bairn. And it wouldn't be *such* a bad match. Oh, he was a bit too zealous in his attentions to her. But surely, over time, his enthusiasm would wane, would it not? And a mature man would be good to have as husband because he wouldn't require the same amount of attention—would he? Nay, surely not. And, really, his portliness was not *so* unattractive, now was it? Nay, 'twas not.

"So the steward is now miles away and wed to another," Bao said, his voice jeering. "Was it his twin who showed me into the great hall earlier, then?"

Jesslyn nibbled on her bottom lip. *Damn!* She'd forgotten she'd said that. "Nay. I confess, I lied about that. Pray pardon me." With more strength, she added, "The steward *is* the babe's father, however, and he is quite free to wed me."

"I see," he said. "Hmm. So...you and he...lay together only once? Or was that a lie too?"

Jesslyn began to feel as if she were walking into a trap, but had no idea how to get herself out of the mess. She fidgeted with the pin that held her mantle together. "Nay, 'twas no lie."

Bao crossed his arms over his chest. "Under what circumstances? I'm curious how he won your favor, as I would never have had the pleasure had you not believed me, in the beginning, to be your husband back from the dead."

She lifted her head and narrowed her eyes at him. "Of what matter is it? We did the deed and he fathered my bairn—'tis all that you need to know."

"Beg pardon. I'm just having a hard time seeing the two of you together, 'tis all." After a brief, but tension-filled moment, he rose from the stool. "Well, I suppose there's naught else to be said, then." He turned his attention to the fire, kicking snow onto the flames. "You should leave here first and I'll follow a bit later after I've put this out and taken the stools back inside the cave."

"Aye, that would be best." Relieved, and aye, a bit saddened that she'd so easily convinced him that she wouldn't wed him, she turned and moved quickly toward the break in the trees that led into the glen.

* * *

"I spoke with Jesslyn after the meal this morn. She told me Steward Ranald fathered her bairn," Bao said to his brother later that day. It'd taken a while after his meeting with Jesslyn to map out a course of action.

"So now she's saying the father is my *steward?* Ha! I trow that's even more fantastic than her tale that a traveling minstrel fathered the bairn!" Daniel replied before turning his focus back on his sword.

The two were seated near the hearth in the great hall, each using the time to clean their weapons while they had their discussion.

Bao cocked his head and regarded his brother. "She told you that the bairn's father was a *traveling minstrel?*" He shook his head and rearranged the oiled cloth against the steel blade. "Why does she bother lying? 'Tis clear she's quite bad at it."

"I know not," Daniel replied.

"I intend to wed her," Bao stated.

Daniel grinned. "Good. I'm glad I will not have to compel you to do so, as I'd thought I would."

Bao looked at his brother's profile. 'Twas clear he knew naught of his and Jesslyn's tryst, so.... "You were going to try to compel me into wedding her? Why?"

He met Bao's eye. "I think it quite obvious. The bairn must be Callum's. Callum's mother is a Maclean. You're a Maclean. Wedding Jesslyn will keep the bairn in the family."

"The bairn's not Callum's, it's mine."

His brother nearly dropped his sword. Eyes wide with shock, he said, "Did you just say *you* are the babe's father?"

The tension in Bao's neck tripled. "Aye."

"How? How is that possible? And don't even think to give me a lesson in anatomy—you know what I mean."

"Last summer, before I came forward to reveal my identity to you, I met Jesslyn in the wood a few times."

"A few—"

Bao held up his hand. "Nay, we only lay together once, but we did meet in the wood a couple of times prior to that."

"I think you should start at the beginning," his brother said, his eyes drilling into Bao's. "How did you first meet?"

"She came to the forest the first time a few sennights before I met with you. She was looking for a waterfall that her husband had beckoned her toward in a dream. She said the dream had seemed so real to her that she wanted to find out if the place existed in truth."

Daniel's brows slammed together in confusion and surprise. "And *is* there such a fall?"

Bao sighed. "Aye, there is." He placed his sword

on the floor and got up. He took several steps away from Daniel before turning to face him once more. "I'd dreamt of the waterfall as well, not long after Branwenn and I had arrived on this holding—and Jesslyn was part of my dream."

"You dreamed of Jesslyn before ever meeting her?" Daniel's eyes grew wider still. "This whole tale is becoming more fantastic by the moment."

"Aye. Believe me, I know how strange it sounds, but 'tis true. I, too, was driven to find this mystical place after seeing it in my dream, and I found it only days afterward."

"But how did you meet Jesslyn in truth? We trekked the wood thoroughly in search of you—Alleck's 'magic giant'—but found no trace. Did she somehow stumble upon your cave?"

"Nay, I saw Jesslyn coming through the trees one day and, tho' 'twas against my better judgment, I made my presence known to her." After a brief pause, he explained further, "My seeing her first in a dream was the reason I felt so impelled to speak with her, give her my story."

"Let us leave the subject of the dreams for another time. For now, I want more details of Jesslyn's part in keeping my brother and sister's existence a secret from me for *several sennights.*"

It galled him to take her part in this matter, but he'd given her his vow to do so, and he'd not break it. "She didn't know of our kinship, nor did she know of Branwenn until we brought her here. But, she knew I was waiting in the wood, waiting for the right time to speak with you. And that I intended no harm."

His brother jumped up and began to pace. "I can't believe her perfidy! We've been friends since we were bairns, how could she—"

"Calm yourself, Daniel." Bao strode over and clamped his hand on his shoulder. "I made Jesslyn promise to give me a bit more time. I convinced her that you weren't ready to hear what I had to say yet and I vowed that I would make it right, should you learn of her secrecy and be angered by it."

Daniel looked at him and a gleam came into his eye. "I've a hankering to finish our wrestling match, what say you?"

Bao grinned in spite of his dark mood. "I look forward to it. But don't think you'll get off so easily this time. I've been training rather vigorously the past moons and I'm in much better condition to best you."

"We shall see," Daniel replied smugly. "So...at what point did you lay with Jesslyn?" he said, turning the subject back to their original discussion. "Was it after you'd moved into the keep with us?"

"Nay, 'twas before that time." Bao sighed and scrubbed his fingers across his brow. "The day after we first met each other, I showed her the way to the waterfall, and that was the last I saw of her until the day before I came to the keep to meet with you. I'd decided to take a last swim at the fall, but Jesslyn was already there." An image of her standing, bared before him, arms outstretched, her luminous hair and smooth white skin glimmering as the blinding sun made prisms of the water droplets running down those lush breasts and thighs, raced through his mind and dazzled him once more. Until the sobering words of Alan, Constable of Scotland—his first glimpse of her true nature—crowded it out and enveloped his heart in a sheath of ice once more. *"Jesslyn MacCreary, the slave-trader's sister abides at the Maclean holding under your half-brother's protection, does she not?"* Bao swung around, stalked back to his place by the hearth and sat down. He snatched up his sword and resumed cleaning the blade with much more vigor than before. "Suffice it to say,"—he heard the ill-temper in his voice and softened it—"we did all that was necessary to conceive a bairn." He'd deal with Jesslyn's inhumane, selfish greed on his own terms, *after* they were wed, and with no input from his half-brother. This he'd decided after seeing her again, after learning she carried his babe and would gladly let another man raise it.

Daniel shook his head in wonder. "I confess, I'm having a hard time believing this." He placed his hands behind his back and began to pace, looking at the floor as he moved.

"I assure you, 'tis true," Bao said.

"But 'tis just so unlike her. She's always been quite adamant about being wed before she'd lay with a man." Daniel stopped and faced Bao once more. "Even Graeme, her husband, whom she loved deeply, was obliged to wait until they'd wed. Which was why, I'm sure, he'd insisted on wedding her so quickly once she'd accepted his troth." Daniel's all-too shrewd eyes drilled into Bao. "Yet, according to you, Jesslyn had only met you twice before she allowed such intimacy. Something in this tale is just not fitting together."

Bao refused to give any further specifics. The intimate details of that day were between him and Jesslyn. "As I said, 'tis the truth. And the only thing that matters is that I convince her to wed me."

"Oh, she'll wed you. I shall see to it," Daniel replied.

Bao balanced the flat of his sword on his thighs and leaned forward, resting his elbows on his knees. "I've already asked her, and she refused me. Twice."

Daniel walked back to his stool and sat down. "Ah, but now you have my backing as well. And Maryn and our grandmother's, too." He laughed then, a diabolical gleam in his eye. "And Alleck will not let her rest until you two are wed, once the idea is given to him."

Bao sat back and crossed his arms over his chest, a smile of satisfaction lighting his countenance. He'd wed her and put her in a hell of imprisonment, just as his mother had been.

* * *

CHAPTER 5

Three days later, Jesslyn was busily stirring her pottage on the cookfire when a knock came to her door. "Enter," she called out and turned back to her task.

"G'day, Jesslyn," Maryn said, "I've been inveigled by Bao to come speak to you about relenting and giving him your troth."

Jesslyn rolled her eyes. "Ayyy. Will no one let it rest?" She rose to her feet and placed the spoon on the table next to her. "Why will you not just let me wed the steward, as I've said I would?"

Maryn walked over to a stool and settled on it, saying, "Because, the babe's not the *steward's*. 'Tis Bao's. And he deserves to raise the bairn as his own."

Jesslyn twisted her fingers together and twirled around, beginning to pace. "He's much changed since last we met." She turned a steady gaze on her friend. "Much changed."

Highland Grace

Maryn's look was disbelieving. "In what way? He's still the bold warrior, still the gentle, loving brother that we all met this summer past."

Jesslyn rushed over and sat on the seat in front of Maryn, taking hold of her friend's hands. "Do you not see? With me, he is not that man. I truly believe he wants to do the right thing, to wed me, be responsible for us, and yet, he resents the doing of it. I see it in his eyes, hear it in his voice each time we speak."

"All men *think* they do not want marriage—and just look how contented they become after the deed is done."

She sat back. "Not this time, not Bao."

"Alleck wants a father."

"The stew—"

"Will be a horrid father to the lad. He's too old—I still cannot *believe* my husband ever thought the man was a decent match for you—he's pompous, and he's not the patience required to raise a lad as active as is your son, Alleck."

She spoke the truth, and Jesslyn knew it, but still she struggled with her dread. "What if he begins to miss his life in Perth?" *The life that no-one else knew of but her.* "He may grow to hate me."

Maryn put her hand on Jesslyn's knee. "He'd *never* do that. You are the mother of his bairn, for one thing. But for another,"—an impish grin lit her countenance—"I do believe he *likes* you well. And you *like* him. Why else would the two of you have found yourselves in this situation?" She sat back. "That alone bodes well for a well-made match. Believe me, I've personal, expert knowledge of such."

The smell of burning pottage wafted over to Jesslyn and she hurried over to stir it once more, but her mind spun with all her friend had said. Maryn was right. And, besides, could she really allow another man to raise Bao's bairn, when its father had proved his desire to do the deed? And, of course, there was Alleck. He'd not stopped hounding her to wed the man since first learning of the possibility days ago. After the fourth rotation around the pot with the spoon, Jesslyn finally turned to Maryn and said, "All right. I'll wed him."

* * *

They were bound in wedlock by sundown. The celebration of the wedding was deferred until the next day, so the two were left with the evening and night to spend alone together.

And now they stood in the cottage that Jesslyn and Alleck had lived in prior to moving to the keep. It had been decided that the newlyweds should have a bit more privacy this first night, so the cottage had been prepared—supplied with the essentials for their comfort.

Jesslyn was as jumpy as a rabbit. She couldn't believe she was a wife once more. And to this carnally charged, darkly brooding warrior-god. He stood with his feet planted wide and his arms crossed over his chest, just staring at her. Didn't he know he was making her even more nervous with that intent gaze?

"Bring me the gown you wore the morn I arrived back here."

"Why?"

Highland Grace

"You shall see soon enough."

Alarm bells went off in her head, but she saw no way around giving in to his strange mood. "Al-all right." She scurried into her bedchamber and took it from its hook on the wall, then hurried it to him. She gasped when he ripped it from her fingers, ripped it from neck to skirt hem. "What are you doing! Stop!" She tried to take it from him, but he swung it out of her reach then proceeded to make long shreds in the material with the blade of his dirk. "You'll have no more need of this."

Her heart pounded so hard, it made a weighted ball in her throat that she could barely speak around. "Why did you do that? I told you that was a precious gift from my late brother." Her palms began to sweat.

"'Tis not for you to know your master's inclinations. 'Tis only for you to obey and serve his needs."

Her breath caught. "M-my *master's* inclinations?"

"Aye. Your lord and master. And from this moment forward there will be some changes in your attire and your demeanor."

A high-pitched ringing swirled in her head, in her ears. "What is this about? Why are you behaving this way—we are friends, at least, are we not?"

"Ha! Nay. To look upon you makes me want to heave my meal. I hate the sight of you."

She swayed on her feet. "Then why did you wed me? I would have wed the steward, or some other suitable match, and your precious freedom would never have been violated."

"Ah, but do you not see? Then I would not have the

pleasure of seeing you grovel, the way my mother groveled at my father's feet. And that is the only thing that the likes of you deserve."

She stared at him. *Who is this? This is not Bao.* Not the warm, strong, gentle Bao she'd grown a hair's breadth from falling in love with last summer. Nay, this man was hard, cold, cruel.

He settled with disgusting ease on one of her stools and said, "And then of course, there is the matter of my babe. I'll not have another taking the name 'father' for a bairn of my loins. I do not take my duties lightly."

"I'll petition for an annulment."

"On what grounds? Tho' our clans are related, you admitted I fathered the babe, and I admitted that 'tis true. You were a widow and I was blissfully unshackled. The church will not allow it. Nay, you are mine to do with as I will."

Another set of alarm bells sounded. "A-as you will?"

He smirked. "Worry not, I'll not ride between your thighs again. I prefer a woman with more…experience—and I find I have no stomach for fucking slaves."

Slave! "Wh—?" Surely, 'twas meant to shock, not meant as truth!

"Go to bed, Jesslyn. We've a long life ahead of us. And do not think to speak a word of this conversation to my family, for if you do, I'll sweep you off to Perth so quickly—without Alleck, I might add—that your brain will scramble. Nay, to all we shall appear the happy, loving couple."

* * *

Highland Grace

Over the next sennight, Jesslyn's misgivings grew. Bao had insisted that Alleck remain at the keep, and she'd complied, as she had no belief that she could keep up the pretense of happiness in her home as well as in her dealings with Bao's family. Added to which, she held hope that she could assuage his anger if they were left to deal with each other in privy. So she had questioned Bao, pleaded with him to give her some reason for his loathing of her, but he'd thus far remained mute. What could have happened between the day of his departure from here when he'd smiled with genuine friendship and gratitude after receiving her gift of berry tarts and the day he'd returned? If only she could speak to Daniel about it, she was sure he could learn the cause, but she had little doubt that Bao would do as he'd threatened and separate her from her home—her son—if she did so, with few or no pangs of conscience.

She wandered through the wood in search of any last chance of mushrooms for their supper and was just coming through the trees when she glanced in the direction of the burn. She smiled and blushed when she saw a young couple lying half-clothed on the banks, kissing. Longing pricked her heart and she began to turn away when the man lifted his head and grinned down at his young amour. Her heart tripped then twisted. *Twas Bao!*

What to do? He'd told her he'd find his pleasure with another, and truth to tell, that suited her. It did! For his cruel and angry manner had suffocated any last feelings of desire she'd been harboring for him since their conversation in the wood. But she'd wither of mortification if any learned of his disinterest. She worried her lip with her teeth. Nay. Nay. 'Twould not happen. Bao was just as adamant that they give his family the belief that all was well and good with their marriage. He'd be discreet.

Pushing down the jealousy that threatened to rise within her, she turned and ran back to their cottage.

* * *

Bao watched Jesslyn's flight, his jaw clenched, his eyes narrowed, and when she was out of sight, rolled from the lass beneath him and said, "Cover yourself, your work is done. The coin I promised is in the pouch on my belt." He leveled his gaze on the mussed creature. "You did well, and there's another coin in it for you if you keep this bargain to yourself." After the lass retrieved her pay, he stood and helped her to rise with a grasp of her hand. "I shall give you notice if I need your services again. G'day, Brigid."

* * *

Later that afternoon, Bao strode in with a rather rough looking peddler. "Go fetch our guest some fresh water."

Jesslyn gave a brief nod and grabbed up the bucket and ladle. She wasn't gone more than ten minutes, but when she returned, the peddler was settled on his cart and *all her sundries and belongings were piled upon it!*

"Bao!" She dropped the bucket and the ladle went flying. "What are you doing! These are—These are mine!" The dress made from the material her husband bought for her on his fatal last journey poked out in bunches from the lid of her chest. She bunted Bao aside and started hauling the chest out of the cart. But he gripped her wrist and forced her to release her hold. "It displeases me to see you in such rags. I've purchased others for you. Come inside and I'll show you." He turned to the peddler. "Enjoy whatever coin you can gain from these items, good man."

Her eye fell on a small wooden box, the one that held all her son's secret boyhood treasures. *"Wait!* That's Alleck's—he'll be much grieved at it's loss!"

Bao lifted the box from the cart and tucked it under his arm. He hauled her into the cottage then and slammed the door. "Do not ever gainsay my decisions. You will do as I will." His smile was dark, brutal, when he said, "I saw you in the wood earlier. Do you miss the fucking, dove?"

Fire licked her neck, her cheeks and she shook her head.

His eyes narrowed. "Go into your bedchamber and change into the gown I left lying on the bed."

Seeing no way around his bitterness and wanting only a bit of peace, she did as he demanded. Her eyes scanned her chamber, emptied of her precious possessions, and they welled, but she swallowed the tears down. *Nay. Do not think of things you cannot control.* She walked over and stood at the edge of the bed. Her breath caught when she saw the fineness of the ruby-colored material, but when she lifted it, she gasped. 'Twas as sheer as a spider's web and just as daunting. What game was he playing? She could not be seen in public wearing this. She'd be banished.

This had gone far enough. She whirled around with the gown fisted in her hand and stormed into the front chamber. "I'll not wear this to supper with your family, 'tis unseemly!"

He laughed for the first time since they'd wed. A real, honest, joyful laugh that reached his eyes and reminded her of his old self. "Nay, you shall not!" He sobered and the anger came into his eyes again. "But you *shall* wear it for your master."

Oh, God. She took the gown back into her bedchamber and felt proud of herself when she closed the door a bit louder than she normally did. Just wanting to get through whatever bitter, resentful game he'd planned for her, she quickly doffed her gray gown and cotton chemise and replaced them with the gossamer pale-rose colored chemise and ruby gown. She kept her muddy boots on and walked back into the front chamber. "What would you like from me now, m'lord?" She had yet to call him 'master' as he'd demanded repeatedly she do in privy. 'Twas a small rebellion, and one that he clearly believed not worth the trouble of punishing her for, so she'd continued it with a secret pleasure.

"Come here, slave. Show me what hangs so coarsely around that white neck of yours."

The coin! The coin *her* Bao, the real Bao, had given her last summer. Why had she not remembered to take it off! With a sinking feeling in the pit of her stomach, she stumbled forward and drew the leather thong from around her neck. "I believe this is yours," she said with a note of sadness, holding it out to him.

Highland Grace

He fingered the gold piece as if it were the made of the finest silk. "My mother's last treasure," he said, his voice, far away. But when his gaze lifted, it snapped and spit daggers at her again. "If I'd only known to whom I'd bestowed this gift, I'd never have done it. 'Twas a mockery of my mother's memory."

"Please, Bao. Tell me what it is you think I've done—what have I done to deserve so much censure from you? What?"

"Ask your brother."

That gave her pause. "He's dead. I told you."

"Then I suppose 'twill be for you to puzzle out, will it not?" A gleam lit his eye. "Come closer."

Her pulse raced. "Why?"

"Come closer."

She took a step toward him. They were a mere few inches from each other now and she could feel the waves of heat flowing from him and moving over her skin. He trailed his finger along the neckline of her chemise and she jumped. In spite of her belief that she held no warm feelings for this twisted version of Bao, her skin tingled and burned where he touched her. And when the digit did a slow glide over the mound of her breast, circled its peak, her center melted, her breath caught.

He bent and slid his tongue over her lower lip. "Remember me tonight while I'm between my lover's thighs," he murmured and then he left. Left her standing, stupefied and unsatisfied, in the center of the front chamber of her cottage.

After a moment, she stomped her feet, yelling,

"Ahhh! I hate you!" then flew into her chamber and threw herself across her bed. Stuffing her pillow into her mouth, she screamed for all she was worth.

* * *

Bao heard the angry outburst and grinned in spite of his pique. 'Twas good to finally get a rise out of her after all these days. But for now, a long, icy dip at the waterfall should cool his raging lust for her. Certainly fucking other women wasn't the answer. His body hadn't cooperated in that endeavor since his first and only taste of her. His one and only attempt to service a client back in Perth after returning had ended in disgrace for him and recriminations from the lady.

And what he was going to do to kill the vestiges of tenderness he still felt for Jesslyn, he had no clue. His anger was working against him. Where he'd thought to humiliate, he'd only succeeded in raising his own need. And Jesslyn's calm compliance had been like steel talons shredding his insides. 'Twas too much as his mother had been with his father—and that made Bao's stomach churn. He wanted her to know what it was to be under another's control—to have pride, but to be punished for asserting it. He wanted her to feel remorse for what her greed had wrought. He never wanted to break her spirit completely.

Besides, this anger, this bitterness, couldn't go on much longer. Even with the role she'd played in his mother's downfall, he couldn't live with her day after day and continue the acrimony. For one thing, she carried his child, and that child deserved a—if not loving home—a home with no rancor. And so did

Alleck. Alleck had asked repeatedly for them to come back to the keep. He wanted them close by. And Bao was having a harder and harder time coming up with excuses why that could not be.

But something in him couldn't let go of the need to punish her. Not yet. So, with a sigh of resignation he headed toward the waterfall.

* * *

A bit over a sennight later, Daniel detained Bao in the great hall after the rest of the family retired for the evening. "What the hell is going on between you and Jesslyn?"

Bao crossed his arms over his chest and scowled. "Why is this your business?"

"She's the widow of my best friend, and I swore to protect her."

"She's *my wife*, not *his* widow."

"Aye, and I haven't seen one smile reach her eyes in the days since you made her such." His gaze narrowed on Bao. "And now that I think on it, I've not seen such from you, either."

Bao shrugged.

"Branwenn believes you're much changed from the man she's known all her life. She sees more anger in you, a sharpness of tongue that wasn't there before and worries that you are flaying Jesslyn with it."

"What's between Jesslyn and me will remain *between Jesslyn and me.*"

"Not if I banish you from the keep."

"She'll go with me."

"Nay, she'll not. Both she and Alleck are my

responsibility and I'll not stand silent while they are hurt."

Bao growled and leapt on Daniel. They both fell to the floor and Bao held Daniel down with his arm over Daniel's throat. "Do not threaten me, *brother*, else you'll feel the full measure of my wrath."

Daniel kneed him in the groin and Bao rolled off of him. "You fight like a lass," Bao wheezed.

"Either tell me what's going on or leave—and one more attack like that and I'll call the guards. You'll be out without horse or weapon."

Bao rolled to his side and lay there unmoving for a minute or two more, waiting for the stars to clear and the searing pain to recede.

He heard the sound of his brother's footsteps as he walked over to the buttery, heard the familiar sound of liquid pouring into metal cups, and finally Daniel's footsteps coming toward him once more. Bao felt him standing over him and cracked an eye open. "All right. I'll tell you."

* * *

"After the Constable's words to me," Bao said a few minutes later, "I found and spoke with several knights—all of them squires at the time—who'd made the journey with Malcolm to fight the infidels in the holy land. They confirmed that he'd left his post and become a slave trader. Evidently, 'twas a much more profitable venture." Bao's hands fisted at his sides. "My suspicion—my curiosity—was heightened, and I couldn't rest until I knew whether 'twas him that sold my mother to our father."

"And was it?"

"Aye. Malcolm MacGorie used thieves to fill his slave cages. This was unusual, as most slaves are spoils of war. All knew it, and all knew how he obtained his prizes, but still it was allowed. My mother's capture had been a boon to Malcolm, for she'd been a relative to royalty and worth a much higher price on the slave block."

Daniel nodded, rubbing his finger across his lower lip as he gazed at the fire crackling in the hearth. "That would have been early on, mayhap as early as 1177 or 78, which is five or six years prior to Jesslyn's birth—tell me why you blame *her* for this."

"Because she profited from my mother's and others' misfortune!"

"But, if she did not know, how is she culpable?"

"Ahh, but she did."

"Why has she never said such to me? She's only spoken of him as her brave brother, a knight fighting for God in the holy land against the infidels."

"I know not. But 'tis truth. I've got a missive from the brother which proves it."

"Show it to me."

Bao reached into the pouch on his belt.

"You carry it with you?"

"Aye, I'm never without it. I look at it whenever I feel myself mellowing in my anger toward her." He handed the small scroll to his brother. As Daniel untied the ribbon, Bao said, "The knight who gave this to me lost both legs in battle, so was never able to deliver it. When he learned that I knew the family and was asking questions about the brother, he contacted me and gave me this. Malcolm had paid a scribe to write it out for him."

He watched his brother's eyes scan the page. "Hmm. Well you are right, Malcolm makes it plain that he's obtaining his coin from selling slaves. But…nay, this is not to Jesslyn."

"Aye, it is. See? It says, 'To my dear sister' and then it speaks of her husband Graeme."

"Aye, but 'tis dated in the year prior to Jesslyn's marriage to Graham. This missive is to his other sister—Janet."

Bao's heart plummeted into his stomach and his jaw dropped open. "Jesslyn's *sister* was wed to Graeme first?"

"Aye, but that's a tale I'll leave for Jesslyn to tell—if she chooses. For now, just know this: you've built a grudge for the wrong sister. And I know Jesslyn, if she'd had any knowledge of her brother's activities, she would not have lied about it—to me at least."

"Aye, but would she still have accepted the gifts with as much zeal as her sister who did know?"

"She'll do what she must for the welfare of her family, but only for pleasure? Nay. Nay, she would not." Daniel handed the scroll back to him.

"I'll leave you now," Bao said. "You've given me much to think on."

* * *

The front chamber of the cottage was quiet and dark but for the orange and yellow glow of embers coming from the hearth. Bao closed the door with little sound and, on silent tread, made his way toward Jesslyn's bedchamber, his purpose: to gain her forgiveness and to regain her trust. But he must somehow do so without telling her of her brother's perfidy. To hurt her again, after all that he'd already done these past days, was more than cruel, more than he was willing to do.

The moonlight streaming in through the opened shutter slats played over her flaxen hair like silver starshine. She lay on her back with one arm arced over her head and the other resting across her abdomen. The blanket had slipped down, revealing her full, naked breasts and Bao's pulse raced. His mouth watered. His manhood came to attention. His fists clenched. His throat worked.

He took the last step to the bed and succumbed to his desire.

* * *

Jesslyn dreamed that a hot, humid mouth clamped her nipple and that the much-remembered strum of a broad finger set fire to her center. "Mmm." She widened her thighs and the finger entered her and began to stroke.

"You're so narrow, love. So wet."

Jesslyn jerked awake. "Get off of me!" But suddenly recalling his threat, she said, "Or is this now part of the bargain as well? My body in exchange for not leaving my son?"

"Jesslyn...oh, God, Jesslyn. I'm sorry. I was wrong. I'll do whatever penance you require. I admit, this might not have been the best way to go about it, but I want us to be wed in truth, and I wanted to show you just how much I wanted us to be such."

She rolled on her side, turning her back to him. "And what, pray, were you wrong about, Bao?"

"You. I will not tell you the whole of it for I'm done with hurting you. Just know that I've discovered my error and am set to do whatever it takes to win your friendship, be wed to you in truth."

"We *are* wed in truth, and as you told me the day of our wedding, there's naught to be done about it, but if you mean what you say, then I see no other course but to try to get along. I want my son back with me."

"We shall move into our quarters in the keep on the morrow."

"I'll not bed you."

She heard him sigh and then he said, "I understand. You need more time."

Aye, and more proof that he'd not turn into the angry devil again, defile their vows by continuing to sleep with others.

* * *

CHAPTER 6

The next day Jesslyn decided to test Bao's commitment to his promise of the night before. While Bao still slept in Alleck's chamber, Jesslyn stealthily made her way to his sword and lifted it. She emitted a soft grunt. It weighed more than she'd expected, but was not so heavy that she couldn't carry it. With slow, steady steps, she walked out of the chamber and toward the door to the cottage. As she quietly opened it, she only allowed herself one quick look back before departing.

She'd already set up most of the scene earlier. She'd strategically placed several mauled-looking pieces of chopped firewood next to the chopping block and hidden the ax. Now, she would wait. She sat down on the block of wood and looked in the direction from which Bao would arrive. She'd asked her son's friend Niall to relay a message to Bao that she requested his presence by the wood stack. There was no way he was going to pass this trial. No way on this earth. And then she'd know for all time that she could never trust him again.

Jesslyn didn't have to wait more than a quarter hour for Bao. She was first made aware of his immanent arrival by the sound of his whistling. Leaping to her feet, she grabbed the weapon and placed a piece of wood on the block. She lifted the sword high above her head with both hands around the hilt and waited for him to turn the corner before she let the blade drop.

"What the hell are you doing!" He sprinted over to her and yanked the sword from her grasp. He examined it, running his fingers along the flat edge of the blade, looking for nicks, she presumed.

"I'm chopping a few more pieces of wood for my cookfire," she said innocently. "I hope you don't mind, but I couldn't find the ax anywhere and I needed more to heat the fire. I'm making berry tarts—your favorite!—and peat ruins their taste."

His gaze settled on her middle. "You shouldn't be chopping wood," he said, a note of concern in his voice. "'Tis too much exertion for your delicate condition."

"Oh, I'm quite used to such work, I assure you. 'Tis really not difficult at all, at least not with the right tool."

* * *

Bao gave his sword another quick examination. Seeing no damage had been done to the blade, he looked again at the chopped wood on the ground and a suspicion began to form. Was this a bit of retribution on Jesslyn's part? Since the blade was still in the condition he'd last left it in, he assumed she only meant to pique his anger. But she would be disappointed. For whatever she demanded of him to get back in her good graces, he would do. Handing her the sword, he said, "If you'll show me that you can do this without straining yourself or the babe, I shall not say another word against it." He cringed inside at the thought of her damaging his weapon, but she was a much more precious prize to him than his sword would ever be.

Clearly confounded, she slowly grasped the hilt in her hands and studied his face. A mischievous light came into her cerulean blue gaze that told Bao that she was not finished testing him. She turned and lifted the weapon over her head once again and when she brought it down, she brought it down hard against the wood, making a terrible splintering sound as the blade entered the piece.

Bao gritted his teeth, but managed to keep from groaning aloud.

She strained to pull it out, but could not.

With a long stride, Bao stepped up to the chopping block and, taking hold of the hilt, released his sword from its prison. With eyes focused away from the blade's edge, he handed the sword back to Jesslyn, saying, "'Twas not quite hard enough, sweet. You'll need to put more force behind it next time."

* * *

A tremor ran down Jesslyn's spine at the warm timbre of Bao's voice when he used that endearment for her. She couldn't bring herself to truly ruin Bao's weapon. Not only because of its value,—its worth was enough to keep them in luxury for a year—but because it held meaning for Bao in other ways as well. She took a close look at the blade's edge, running her fingers along it the way she'd seen Bao do moments before. Luckily, she'd put no chips in it. But it did need a good polishing now, she could tell. Biting her lip, she handed the weapon back to him. "I've changed my mind. I find I'm too weary to do such work. I shall do as you said and refrain from such activity until after my babe is born."

Bao nodded. "Good. And I hope that means you will not do any other work that requires heavy lifting until *our* babe has arrived."

Jesslyn nodded and the ice around her heart melted a little more. This was the Bao she'd known last summer. But for how long? She still had no idea what she'd done to set him against her—or, more precisely, what he'd *believed* she'd done—and that alone sparked fear in her heart that he'd change again without notice into the beast she'd wed over a fortnight past. And what of his woodland lover? At one and the same time, she wanted not to care and cared much more than she should.

"Let us go back to the cottage and break our fast. The babe is surely hungry by now," he said. Jesslyn stiffened but allowed Bao to settle her hand in the crook of his arm as they walked the distance to her home.

* * *

Not long afterward, Bao sat at the table as Jesslyn quietly prepared their meal. He reveled in her lithe grace as she walked over to the hearth, lifted the lid on the pottage and took a whiff. Then, setting the lid to the side, she turned and took a rounded loaf of day-old bread from the basket and sliced it in half before she cut the center from it and made trenchers for their meal. Did she have any idea how beautiful she was? He watched her as she scooped the pottage into the trenchers and placed them on the table.

She was still rising from her bent position when she gasped. Her hands flew to her abdomen and Bao's heart took a dive into his stomach before it lodged like a shot from a manganel in his throat. He bolted to her side and grasped her upper arms. "What? What ails you?" He stepped in closer, placing a hand over the one she held to her stomach. She tensed at his touch, which put an answering vise grip on his heart, but allowed the contact. "Is it the babe?" he asked.

"I believe the babe just quickened." She held her gaze on her belly. "'Twas a light tapping feeling. I was beginning to worry that I wouldn't recognize it, but"—she smiled and her voice held wonder—"I did!"

"Of what are you speaking, Jesslyn? How could you not recognize something you've already gone through before?"

She went still. A look of dread washed over her face followed instantly by a mask of serenity and she took several paces away from him. He narrowed his eyes and said, "Is there something you are not telling me?"

The silence that followed held weight, but finally, with a sigh, she walked to the table, took her place and said, "Sit. I shall explain while we eat our meal."

Bao sat down and took several bites of the pottage

and watched her do the same before saying, "I'm glad to know the babe is hale, but why did you worry that you wouldn't know when the babe quickened?"

She lifted her eyes from her trencher. "I've never had a babe before."

Bao sat forward. "Wha—?"

"Alleck is the offspring of my sister and Graeme, my husband."

"Your *sister*? Alleck is your *sister's* bairn? Does Alleck know this?"

Jesslyn pushed her trencher out of the way. Leaning forward, she rested her crossed arms on the table and studied the remnants of the pottage as she replied, "Aye, I told him a bit o'er a year ago."

Bao was stunned. "How came it that you and Graeme wed?"

"My sister was living at the MacBean holding. Graeme had been gone warring for almost the entire time Janet carried his babe. She became ill and needed to remain abed the last four moons of the pregnancy and sent me a missive requesting that I move from the MacLaurin holding, where we were raised, to the MacBean holding and take care of her while she regained her strength. I, of course, agreed." Jesslyn's mouth turned down at the corners. "Unfortunately, she died delivering Alleck."

"Aye, I assumed that to be the case. Where were your parents—your mother?"

Her eyes closed tight and her brow furrowed. He was beginning to think she would not answer when she said, "My father was one of the men who died that bloody day of the massacre at the MacLaurin holding. He was Laird MacLaurin's lieutenant."

Bao leapt from his seat and leaned toward her. "Christ's bones! Are you saying *my father* was responsible for your father's death?"

Her eyes still tightly shut, she nodded.

And he'd thought her brother's perfidy unforgivable. The fact that she'd known this and held no rancor for Bao because of it tore at his already stinging conscience like the cut of a thousand blades. He turned and stormed across the room. Bao's mind reeled with the recollection of all Daniel had told him of that fatal, fateful day. Laird MacLaurin had sent most of his men to find the culprits who had set fires and killed livestock along three different MacLaurin borders. Thinking 'twas some mischief his rival, the MacPherson, was up to, Daniel's grandfather had kept only a few men back to guard the keep. But, in fact, it had been a well-organized trap their father and his band of corrupt soldiers had set. The real attack came once the keep was left undefended. In an act of bloody vengeance, Jamison Maclean had abused and executed the wife who'd left him and the father-in-law who'd sheltered her. Daniel, only thirteen moons at the time, had been fishing at the loch and had only survived because Jamison had not known of his existence.

Standing with his back to her and his head bowed, he asked grimly, "Was he one of those massacred, or did he die defending the keep?"

"He was one of the first killed defending the keep when the marauders rushed through the opened portcullis into the courtyard."

He swung around to face her once more. "What of your mother—what of you and your sister? Where were all of you that day?"

"There was a cattle fair in the next town. My mother had taken my sister and me in hopes that she might find a merchant selling fine cloth for new gowns she wanted to make for us."

"My God. When I think of what would have happened to you had you remained...."

"Nay, don't think on it. We survived, as did Daniel, and we flourished," Jesslyn replied.

Bao nodded and walked back to his stool. Sitting down, he asked, "And your mother? She's alive, then?"

Jesslyn's lips pressed into a straight line and she shook her head. "Nay, nay. She became ill from a lung fever one very cold winter. In truth, 'twas the year before Alleck was born. She never recovered."

"I see. So you were all alone at the MacLaurin holding for quite a time it seems."

Her smile was sad. "Aye, but I managed. I make very good ale—did Daniel tell you?"

Bao cocked his head to the side and gave her a lopsided grin as he looked at her in a new light. "Nay," he said, shaking his head. "Nay, he did not."

Jesslyn placed her hand over her belly and her eyes glowed.

"The babe?"

"Aye."

It took every bit of will he had not to take her in his arms and kiss that warm smile, but somehow he managed it. He took a gulp of his ale. As he settled the cup at the side of his trencher, he said, "Mayhap you should continue telling me how you and Graeme came to wed each other."

Jesslyn rose from her stool and began clearing off the table, clearly unsettled by the subject she was to relate. "I'd never met Graeme," she said finally. "My sister was betrothed to him by contract and she was escorted to the MacBean holding for the wedding. I was not allowed to attend, as I was but ten summers at the time and deemed too young to travel that far a distance. They were wed for five years before she got with child." Jesslyn tipped her head back and lifted her gaze to some unknown place above, a wistful smile on her lips. She shook her head, saying, "She was so happy."

"And then what happened?" Bao prompted when Jesslyn hadn't resumed her tale after a moment.

Jesslyn turned her head, a look of surprise on her countenance, as if she'd forgotten his presence. "Before she died, she made me promise that I would take care of her bairn, that I wouldn't leave it to be taken care of by one of the women at the keep. I swore my allegiance to her and waited for Graeme to return. When he came back, he was told of the death by Lady MacBean, and that I was there to take care of the babe. He ran to find me." Taking a deep breath and letting it out on a sigh, she turned and faced Bao. Crossing her arms over her chest, she began to rub them as she said, "I was at the well with some of the other lasses of the village. He drew me away from them and asked me to wed him. I did, and we raised Alleck as if he were mine."

"Yet you didn't wed him solely to keep your promise to your sister," Bao stated.

"Aye, you are right. There was an immediate attraction between us."

Bao studied her, saw the residue of grief in her eyes. "You still love him. And I believe that even now, after almost three years have passed, you still mourn for him."

Jesslyn dipped her head. "Aye, I suppose I shall always love him."

Bao's heart twisted. "I won't ask for your love, for I know I'm not worthy of it. But is there *naught* I can do to win your forgiveness, your friendship?"

She looked at him for a long moment before she finally answered, "I think not. But, only time will tell. For as you said, we have a long life ahead of us."

* * *

A sennight later, Bao took a step into their chamber in the keep just after the nooning meal and stopped short. Jesslyn stood with her arms crossed next to the clothing chest he'd placed there earlier. "I see you've found my gift."

She bent down and retrieved the coin that lay on top of the shimmery blue gown he'd added to the largesse and marched it over to him. "I shall, of course, accept the return of my possessions and the new gown as well, as you destroyed one of my own, but I have no need, nor desire, for this."

It took a moment for Bao to respond as his eyes

fastened on the gold circle swinging in slow sweeps from the worn leather thong to which it was attached. Finally, with a sinking heart, he stepped forward and took it. "I understand. I…" He swallowed and cleared his throat. "I have a bit of business to attend to with my brother. G'day to you." He hauled around and bolted out of the room.

He plopped himself against the stone wall outside the chamber and banged his head against it in frustration, then lifted his fingers to the sharp sting and massaged it. *What the hell was he going to do?* Everything—everything was fighting against him. His own vile behavior, his father's even worse destruction. Her love for her dead husband. Added to which was her belief of his adulterous interlude that he had no means of proving 'twas not true. Aye, he could bring the lass before her, have the lass explain their arrangement—but would Jesslyn believe? After their earlier conversation and her continued cool reserve, he had no hope she would. What a fool he'd been to take the 'lesson' that far. But he'd thought that at least the return of her belongings would soften her resentment toward him. Mayhap not to the ultimate point he sought, but at least a move in that direction. Instead, she was colder than she had been before. As if the gift served more as a reminder of his deeds than as a reminder of his better, nobler self.

She wasn't happy. She never raised her voice to him, was biddable enough, and certainly maintained the appearance that all was well between them when they were with his family, but her only smiles were for others, never for him. He was out of ideas. He wasn't a man to give up a fight, but every warrior knew when to stay in the battle and when to retreat. And it was clearly time to retreat.

* * *

CHAPTER 7

Jesslyn was back at her cottage an hour later, having fled there after her encounter with Bao in order to keep from being trapped into sewing with the ladies in the solar. Firstly, because she didn't think she could keep the calm and contented manner she presented to them from slipping, and secondly, because she needed some busy work to keep her mind off of the heavy ache in her heart.

She had just started crushing the malt for the ale she planned to brew when a knock came on the door.

"Enter!"

She was more than surprised when Daniel sauntered in. "I thought you two had moved back to the keep for good."

"We have, but your grandmother said 'twas fine for me to use the cottage to make my ale."

"Ah." He took a seat next to the fire where she had the iron caldron of water hanging, heating water. He studied his fingernails, which put her immediately on guard. There was something much too relaxed in his behavior, yet she could see the tension in his jaw and around his eyes. "I suppose you are aware that your husband is in the courtyard about to take his leave back to Perth. Shouldn't you at least say farewell to him?"

Alarm tensed her muscles. "Why is he leaving? What about his babe?"

"He's leaving because you will not forgive him for how he reacted to the letter, how he blamed you falsely."

"Of what letter do you speak?"

"He told you not?"

"Nay! What letter?"

"Bao discovered that your brother was a slave trader in the Holy Lands. He—"

"Wh—!"

"—was the man who sold Bao's mother to our father, Jamison Maclean."

"Oh God. Nay. This cannot be." Jesslyn sank onto the stool and leaned heavily against the table.

"'Tis true. And what is more, he acquired a letter from your brother that was never delivered to your sister in which it is made plain that she was well aware of how he made the coin he sent to fill your family coffers all those years."

Light-headed, she rested her forehead in her hand. "And he thought 'twas me to whom my brother wrote."

"Aye."

"He wouldn't tell me. He said 'twould only hurt me and he couldn't bear to hurt me more than he already had with his false beliefs." Her eyes shot to Daniel's. "We cannot let him leave. Take me to him!"

* * *

Branwenn met Jesslyn as she rushed through the entrance to the courtyard. "Whatever he's done, forgive him! See this! He's given me his mother's coin to keep safe for his bairn. I think he plans not to return. Go speak to him, I beg you!"

Jesslyn nodded and hurried over to where Bao stood speaking to his grandmother. "My pardon, Lady Maclean, but I must have a moment in privy with my husband."

Lady Maclean gave her a look that said she understood more than she'd let them believe and stepped away.

"You were going to leave without telling me?"

"Nay, I sent Daniel to give you the tidings."

"What about Alleck? Does he know?"

Bao's lips thinned and he shook his head. "I—I needed to leave in haste, and that farewell may have made it impossible. I intended to send him a letter along with the first of the purchases and coin I will be proffering for your support." He finally met her gaze. "I take care of my own, so have no worry. You shall want for naught. I'll see to it."

"I want the father of my babe here with us."

"You know what I am, what I've done. The babe will not suffer with my absence."

"A bairn needs it's father."

"Even if that father was unforgivably cruel to its mother?"

Jesslyn placed her hand on his arm. "I know about the letter. How can I not now feel understanding for your actions?" *Even your finding comfort with another woman.* How could he possibly feel truly wed to her when he saw her as his enemy?

He growled. "I told Daniel not to give you those tidings!" His jaw clenched as he shot a venomous look in his brother's direction. "I shall enjoy trouncing him in a match the next we meet."

"Do not leave. There is hope for this union, I trow."

"Hope? Even tho' you still pine for another? Detest my touch?"

She smiled, stood on her tiptoes, and gave him a soft kiss on his cheek. "I pine more for a strong, *living,* husband. And I do not detest your touch."

He looked at her a long moment. Finally, he grinned, and with a wave of his arm, he called the stableman over. After taking his satchel from the horse, he told the man to take his steed back to its stall.

* * *

After supper later that night, Bao watched Jesslyn nervously twisting her fingers as she stood staring into the hearthfire.

His hopes for the evening plummeted. He walked to the bed and sat down. Clearly, she was not yet ready to give him her body. But at least the icy reserve she'd held in his presence prior to this afternoon had thawed. If he was mindful and cunning, he might be able to build a bridge between them through seduction. He looked at her again. Eventually.

He unlaced and took off first one boot and then the

other before dropping each to the floor. It didn't escape his notice that she started at the sound. Aye, slow and steady would be his strategy.

He bent down and lined his boots up like soldiers next to the bed and then lay down, propping his head on his hands and crossing one leg over the other. "Do you mind bringing that stool to the side of the bed?"

She started again but nodded and walked toward the stool.

She stumbled on her way and Bao bolted upright. He settled back when she didn't fall and continued to regard her.

Her hands trembled as she picked up the wooden seat and brought it to the bedside. "Where would you like me to place it?" she murmured.

"You can put it down right where you are." He saw the dew on her brow and asked, "Are you warm? Mayhap the fire's too high." He swung his leg over the side of the bed in a motion to rise, but she stopped him with a shake of her head. "Nay, I'm fine," she told him.

"Will you sit down upon this, Jesslyn?" he said, indicating the seat.

"I-I'd prefer to stand, if you don't mind."

"Oh, I do mind. Please?"

"A...All right," she replied. She sat down facing him.

"Turn around, sweet, that's not how I want you," he said.

Her eyes dipped then widened momentarily on his erection. He knew it pushed against the cloth of his tunic, but he was helpless to control his body's reaction to her.

"Jesslyn, please turn around," he stated again. "I've no presumption that we shall couple this eve."

Her gaze jumped to his and her cheeks flushed crimson, but she did as he requested.

He sat up and placed his knees on either side of her before reaching for the brush and placing it next to him on the bed.

When he tilted her head back, she jolted. *Aye, nervous as a rabbit.* First, he pulled the filet and the veil from their positions, and then he leaned down and took in a deep breath of lavender scented air.

As he gently unwound the golden tresses that she'd had arranged under her veil, Bao was reminded once more of their time at the fall, of his first reaction to the texture and sheen of her magnificent golden locks, glorying in the fact that they were still as soft and bright as he'd remembered. And the scent of it! God, he could drown in her scent. Remembering that he'd become intoxicated on this very fragrance while he moved inside of her made him grind his teeth in agony. But release would not come this night. Nor, mayhap, many nights ahead. For now, he must simply enjoy the pleasure of touching her where e're she allowed it. He lifted the brush and gently pulled it through the long mane he had clasped in his hand. "'Tis a bit tangled," he said, "let me know if I tug too hard."

She sighed. He felt her relax, her breathing slow, saw her eyes drift shut. "Aye, I will," she finally replied. "How did you learn to brush a woman's hair so well?" she said, her voice dreamy, but with a tinge of surprise.

Highland Grace

Bao chuckled. "Remember you, I have a sister?"

He saw her mouth turn up in a smile and his heart answered.

"But her hair is so short, 'tis not the same thing at all," she said.

"Ah, but until just before I made myself known to Daniel last summer, she'd had hair longer than yours. It was down past her knees and in a constant tangle, it seemed. No doubt because she has always been so active, and so opposed to covering her head!"

Bao tipped Jesslyn's head forward a bit and lifted the hair he held in his hand, then brought the brush up from the back of her neck and down through the long strands.

"You may do this every eve, if you wish," she said.

"You would like that, then?" Bao asked.

"Aye, very much."

"Then, aye, I wish." *Good.* And with any luck at all, that would be her reaction to every liberty she allowed him.

* * *

"You are not truly going to do my sewing for me today?" Jesslyn asked the next morning.

Bao grinned at her and gave her a light peck on the nose. "Aye, I am." He turned and looked around the chamber. "Now, where is your kit?"

She swallowed a sigh of pure lust and blinked away what she knew must be stardust twinkling in her eyes and walked over to her chest. She took out the small basket and held it out to him.

He took it and saluted her, then walked toward the

door, saying, "This should be fodder for Daniel's black sense of humor for many annals!"

After he exited the chamber, she giggled and whirled around to gaze out the window. She'd had one of the best night's sleep she'd had in many moons last eve, after her husband's sensual hair brushing, followed by the heavy weight of his arm over her, the warm heat of his body at her back while she slept. 'Twas heaven.

And this morn, after she'd mentioned how little she liked sewing, how she'd prick her fingers and bleed all over the linen, Bao had actually offered to do it for her!

If he continued in this manner, she had little doubt that her niggling doubts about his character would flee to the four corners of the earth. And then they could take this marriage up in truth.

Lord knew, her body was more than ready for that to happen. She'd nearly climbed on top of him last eve when she saw his reaction to her.

Nearly.

* * *

"I've spoken to the clan elders and they've agreed to consider my suggestion that you be named chieftain of clan Maclean in my stead," Daniel told Bao several days later as they sat by the hearth in the great hall having a tankard of some of Jesslyn's ale.

Bao gave his brother a sharp look. "I have no desire for that title, so you may as well go back to them and withdraw the proposition."

"Ah, but you see, neither do I," Daniel replied. "I only accepted the lairdship as a two-year contract while they searched for a replacement for Callum."

Bao cocked his head in confusion. "Callum was laird here?"

"Aye, but he was much too immature for such responsibility at the time and the elders lost confidence in him."

"What happened?" Bao asked.

Daniel sighed. "He was lax in his government of the keep and the people who support it. The elders were becoming more and more dismayed with him as time went by, but the final blow came when Maryn stole the Maclean horses out of the keep."

"Which she did because the horse marshal wasn't taking care of the poor beasts," Bao said. "Aye, I remember hearing the tale last summer after the man attempted to kill Maryn."

"Thank God we were able to find her in time," Daniel said grimly.

Bao nodded. After a moment, he asked, "So how did they come to ask you to be chieftain?"

Daniel shrugged. "I was the most likely choice." He gave his brother an uncompromising look. "At the time."

"But, if you don't desire the title, as you just told me, why did you agree to accept it—even for a short time?"

Daniel's right brow lifted and lowered. "Firstly, because I—and my clan—were guaranteed a significant percentage of the Maclean shipping interests." A sheepish grin spread over his countenance as he continued, "But, most *enticingly*, because Maryn was offered as part of the package. She was an irresistible lure, which I found I couldn't possibly refuse."

"Maryn was part of the contract?"

"Aye," Daniel replied, "You see, Callum wanted to wed Maryn but her father had refused to consider it. Our cousin used the horse theft as an excuse to blackmail Laird Donald into agreeing to the match. He threatened a clan war otherwise."

"I'm confused. I thought you said he was ousted after the horse theft."

Daniel shook his head. "Nay, not directly after. It wasn't until he began the blackmail scheme and got both clans in a froth that the elders began to seriously discuss replacing him," Daniel said. "And Laird Donald, being the great mediator, ultimately came up with the plan to offer the lairdship for a short time, along with his daughter, for a lifetime—as a blood tie between the two clans. A combination I found extremely appealing."

Bao looked at him shrewdly. "And now, you believe you've found the perfect replacement. Are you that anxious to return to the MacLaurin holding, then?"

Daniel's gaze turned wistful as he looked into the distance. "Aye, I am. I miss my people, my land, my fortress. I built it up from the rubble our father left behind into a stronghold that, I hope, is impossible to breach." He turned and faced Bao. "I want to go home."

"How can I refuse you, then? I will need to buy out my contract with the king and find lodgers for my cottage in Perth, but if the elders agree to it, I shall become the new laird and chieftain to the Macleans."

* * *

Highland Grace

A sennight later, Jesslyn sat with the rest of the family in the great hall enjoying a traveling band of players. Holly decorated the hall, and mistletoe hung above every doorway. The Yule log lay next to the hearth, waiting to be placed on the fire later. For this day they celebrated the Yule, and the air was filled with all kinds of scents. There were scents of sweet confections, scents of meat roasting on the spit, woodsy scents from the pine log, mistletoe and holly. Jesslyn could even smell the snow. It combined with the sweet lad-smell of her son's hair and she pressed her nose to his warm flaxen pate to breathe in more of it.

"Will th' minstrels get to eat some of the Yule feast, Mama?" Alleck asked her in a loud whisper, his eyes never leaving the dancer's feet.

"Aye, I'm sure they will," she replied. She pulled him higher up onto her lap using the arm she had curled over his stomach. He'd been fidgeting so much that he'd nearly slid off of his perch.

"Here, let me take him," Bao said. And in a trice, Alleck was straddled over Bao's knee.

Jesslyn caught Bao's eye and smiled her thanks.

He smiled back, holding her gaze captive a moment before turning back to watch the minstrels' performance.

She was profoundly aware of him physically; she found she always was whenever he was near. And his gentle manner was wearing down her resolve to wait a bit longer, mind his character a bit more, before committing her body and heart to him.

But the fact that he'd sewn swaddling clothes for

their babe in her stead every day had tipped the scales in his favor. Especially with his brother's good-natured tormenting added in.

And surprisingly, he was good with a needle, certainly better than she was herself. In fact, Maryn and Lady Maclean were so impressed with his handiwork that they'd asked him if he'd make a few shirts for the babe as well. Jesslyn swallowed a giggle, but it turned into a snort, which she quickly shaped into a sound of clearing her throat. She coughed into her hand for good measure.

Bao turned around and grabbed a chalice of water from the table and handed it to her. "Are you chilled? I'll get your cloak from our chamber, if you'd like."

Shaking her head, she replied, "Nay, I'm quite warm." After swallowing down several mouthfuls, she said, "My throat was a bit dry. The water has helped. My thanks."

Taking the cup from her hands, Bao placed it back on the table behind him before settling his eyes on her countenance once more. "You look a bit flushed. Are you sure you're feeling well enough to join the feast?"

She tensed. Was this the third or *fourth* time he'd asked that same question? This excessive solicitude was scraping against her nerves. "I'm well! I promise you!" *Lord!*

"Aye," he replied, and she pressed her lips together to keep the smile from forming, for she could see that he literally bit his tongue to keep from arguing with her.

Except it irritated her too. He hadn't shown an ounce of peeve since he'd come to her bed all those nights ago and begged her forgiveness. She crossed her arms over her chest and stewed. The man must be a saint. She'd been goading him for days now and he'd still not lost his temper with her. She supposed she was simply going to have to admit that he'd passed this trial as well.

And he *was* slowly driving her mad with his oh-so-innocent requests that still managed to make her burn for him. Like the last one. As he'd removed her shoes, he'd asked her to remove her hose as well. And then he'd not only massaged her feet, he'd bathed them! In the most luxuriously warm, scented water she'd ever been fortunate enough to enjoy. And it had made her wish he'd asked for *all* her clothing, so that he could minister to her entire body with as much utter care as he gave her feet. Her mouth grew dry at the thought. She turned and grasped the chalice of water once more, bringing it to her parched lips.

As she drank, her husband, whom she'd felt watching her as she picked up the chalice, leaned down and whispered in her ear, "I'll be back in a moment. I'm going to take Alleck to sit with Daniel and Branwenn for a while."

She nodded. "He'll like that." She watched Bao move through the throng, carrying Alleck on his shoulders, which greatly amused her son. Alleck had wrapped his arms around Bao's forehead and Bao held her son's upper arms to keep him steady. And those massive hands of Bao's, which had been playing such havoc with her senses, now seemed quite safe as they cradled her son.

* * *

"I need to take Jesslyn up to our chamber," Bao said to Daniel after handing Alleck over to Branwenn. "She's not well, I fear." He cocked his head in his wife's direction. "See you how flushed her face has become?"

Daniel nodded, a frown furrowing his brow. "Aye. And her eyes are a bit glassy, as well. Think you she has a fever?"

"Aye, but she's been so contrary lately that I didn't want to upset her further by feeling her forehead."

"Take her up to your chamber and I'll meet you there in half an hour with my healer's box," Daniel said. He put his hand on Bao's shoulder. "Calm yourself. She may simply be feeling the effects of her condition. And the closeness of the hall now that 'tis filled with this crush of people doesn't help, I'm sure. Maryn went up to our chamber not an hour past with that same complaint."

Bao nodded briefly and turned, striding back to Jesslyn's side. "You need to lie down," he said, and before she could protest, he lifted her into his arms and carried her toward the doorway of the great hall.

* * *

Having grown dizzy in Bao's absence, she made no complaint, simply rested her head on his shoulder and closed her eyes. She was just so weary, and her head ached a bit as well.

With long strides, her husband cut across the antechamber outside the great hall and took the stairs two at a time to their third-level bedchamber. He flung the door open and then kicked it closed behind him, not stopping his forward motion until he was at the bedside. His voice was gentle when he said, "Will you be able to get out of this gown on your own?"

Jesslyn's stomach roiled. All she wanted to do was be very, very still so she didn't lose her meal. "Nay," she whispered.

"Do you think you can stand a moment while I do it then?"

She swallowed hard against the bile that threatened to rise from her stomach and gave her head a slight shake. "Mmm-mmm." She was afraid to open her mouth, lest she should spew.

"All right. I'll just lay you down on the bed and see if I can loosen the laces of this tight gown enough to pull it off of you."

Jesslyn nodded, rubbing her cheek against his muscled chest. She hadn't opened her eyes since he'd lifted her into his arms downstairs. It helped to keep the room from spinning.

After placing her on the bed, his quick and nimble fingers loosed the laces on the side of her gown and stripped them from their holes. The fabric gaped open enough to work it off of her with minimum effort on her part.

"I'm hot."

* * *

Bao felt her forehead. 'Twas warm, but not hot, as he'd feared. Mayhap she'd just become overheated downstairs, as Daniel had suggested. He prayed so. He walked over to the table that held a pitcher and basin for cleansing. After pouring water into the bowl, he tossed one of the cloths that lay folded next to the pitcher into the cool liquid and brought the basin over to the bedside. He wrung out the cloth and used it to cool her, blowing on each section of skin after he'd dampened it with the cloth. He couldn't help noticing the changes in her, now that he was able to see her shape more clearly. The thin material of her chemise clung to her body like a second skin. He could see the aureoles of her breasts, darker now than they had been, through the material. And her bosom was even more full, more rounded, now that she carried a babe. God, how he craved to lose himself in them, in her, once more. He doused the cloth again and wrung it out before skimming it over her arms, down to her hands. His eyes dropped to her belly. 'Twas rounded now, her childing state obvious. Through the clinging fabric, he could see the outline of her thighs, and at its apex, the mons of her sex. His goddess. His fertile goddess. His fertile, flushed, goddess. He prayed she hadn't caught a fever.

* * *

"That feels good," Jesslyn said blissfully. She opened her eyes and, for the first time, realized the depth of worry Bao was feeling for her when she saw the white line of tension around his mouth. She lifted her hand to his jaw to draw his eyes to her face. "I'm feeling much better now." She dropped her hand to her stomach and continued, "And, thankfully, my stomach no longer churns. I suppose I'm just a bit more sensitive to the heat these days."

"I hope you're right," Bao replied. "But, just to be certain, Daniel will be here in a few moments to check on you."

Jesslyn tried to sit up, but found she was still too dizzy. "Hand me my gown! Make haste!"

"Nay. You need your rest."

"Are you daft? I'm not going to lie here half-dressed with Daniel in the chamber! Now, *hand me my gown!*"

"I shall cover you with a blanket. Will that suffice?"

Realizing she'd lost the battle since she didn't have enough strength to put the gown back on by herself, Jesslyn sighed in frustration and nodded her head.

"That's a good lass," Bao said. Picking up the basin, he took it back over to the table.

While Bao's back was turned, Jesslyn made a face at him. *"That's a good lass,"* she mimicked under her breath.

* * *

The Yule celebration came and went without Jesslyn ever leaving her chamber. Under orders from Daniel, and subsequently Bao, she was confined to her bed for two days. Daniel had forced her to drink an awful-tasting herbal concoction the past morn after Bao had brought her up from the great hall. But it had mostly been a precautionary measure, since she hadn't been running a fever. And now, she was restless and bored. The celebration ended an hour or two past and she was a bit annoyed that not even her son had come to see her.

She nearly jumped out of her skin when the door flew open. "Oh, 'tis you," she said petulantly, crossing her arms over her chest.

Her husband grinned and put his hand over his heart. "Ah, my beautiful, sweet-tempered bride, I'm glad to see you, too."

"My! How merry we are this eve. I suppose you've been nipping into the *uisge beatha*?" Jesslyn didn't know why she felt so compelled to spew venom at her almost-husband, but something about his ability to withstand her worst moods without losing his temper—especially after she'd been subjected to the darker side of his character for two sennights—just set her blood to boiling.

"Nay, my sweet, not *uisge beatha*, but your delectable berry tarts."

She uncrossed her arms. "Oh," she said less forcefully. Picking at a loose thread on the blanket that covered her legs, she said, "I suppose the whole family was downstairs earlier, enjoying the minstrels and the feast." She gave a wistful sigh. Her eyes filled with tears. "I'll bet no one even considered bringing some up to me!" she wailed.

Bao rushed over to the bed and sat down next to her, pulling her into his arms. "Shhshh. Of course we wanted to bring some of the fare up to you, but we worried we'd wake you. You've been sleeping so much these past two days, Daniel and I thought it best to let you rest."

She sniffled. Then sniffled again. Her voice thick, she said, "I'm lon"—*hic!*—"nely...y...y!" Pushing out of Bao's embrace, she railed, "*And 'tis all your fault!*"

Bao's eyes grew stormy and a tick started in his

cheek. "*My* fault? Why, pray, is it *my* fault?"

"Because you forced me to stay up here the past two days, even after you knew I hadn't caught a fever!"

* * *

Bao took a deep breath. And then another. And then one more. His grandmother had explained to him that Jesslyn's moodiness was due to her condition and that the best thing to do was to appease her. "Forgive me, sweet. I see now that I am fully to blame, as you said."

She stopped crying for a moment and gazed at him through the tears that still puddled in her eyes, a look of shock on her face. "Nay, 'tis me! I'm to blame, 'tis my fault!"

Bao watched in alarm as her face scrunched up and the tears poured forth once more. But, if he'd learned naught else about women in all his years on this earth, he knew this: Never agree with any negative statement a woman makes about herself. Never. Ever. "Nay, 'twas my fault. I was wrong to leave you up here all by yourself for so many hours."

Bao rose and dampened a cloth to cool Jesslyn's fiery cheeks and rinse off her tears. He settled back on the edge of the bed and leaned forward, softly stroking the cool material over her face and eyes.

"My thanks," she murmured.

She'd stopped crying, thank the heavens.

"Will you hold me, Bao? Just for a while?"

"Aye." Bao looked around, trying to figure out how he could hold her without lying down. Definitely not a good idea. There wasn't a suitable chair in the chamber, and the stools weren't large enough. Aye, a chair would be a much better option, if only there was one. He determined in that moment to have one brought up on the morrow. His gaze lighted once again on Jesslyn. He bit back a sigh. The bed it would have to be, then. "I'll need you to move forward a minute, so I can climb in behind you."

"All right," Jesslyn replied, and did as he instructed.

Bao took off his boots and settled in behind Jesslyn, placing his legs on either side of her hips. He put his arms around her and pulled her back to lean against his chest, resting his arms under her bosom, just above her swollen belly. "Would you like me to brush your hair later—or bathe your feet again, mayhap?" Bao said after a time.

"Aye, both would be nice. Do you mind?"

"Nay, I don't mind. I enjoy the effort. Quite a lot, actually," he replied. Unable to resist the temptation any longer, he brought his hand down over her tummy and softly caressed it. "How fares our babe?"

Jesslyn smiled and looked down. "Well. In fact, the babe's been quite active this day." She put her hand on top of his and shifted it. "There! Do you feel it? Tap...tap."

Bao grinned and nodded. "Aye, she's a restless wee thing, is she not?"

"Aye," Jesslyn replied. "You think the babe's a lass?" she asked, surprise tingeing her voice.

Bao shrugged. "I know not, it just seems my likely fate. But a son would be welcome as well." He kissed the top of her head and said, "I ordered a meal be sent up here in about an hour; I'm sure 'twill include quite a bit of what was offered at table earlier."

Her smile broadened. "Good, I'm famished." She tilted her head back and to the side, looking up at him, "I am so sorry for how I behaved earlier. I honestly don't understand what's wrong with me. I'm usually much more reserved."

Bao lifted his hand to her cheek and held her chin in the palm of his hand. "'Tis the babe. I understand. And, I beg you, don't fret over it a moment longer."

Her eyes darkened and then she surprised the hell out of him when she looped her arm around the back of his head and brought him down to meet her open mouth. She kissed him ravenously, tugging on his bottom lip with her teeth and then soothing it with her tongue. God, how he wanted to take this to its natural conclusion. But 'twas too soon, and she needed her rest.

By an act of pure will, he managed to draw his lips from hers. Breathing hard, he pressed his cheek to her forehead. "That was incredible," he said gruffly. "But mayhap I should brush your hair now."

She nodded and he turned her back around. After he grabbed the brush off of the table next to the bed, he said, "Move forward a bit so I have room to work."

She nodded again and did as he requested.

Bao leaned forward and kissed the back of her head, running his hand down her arm. "You are so..."—he breathed her in—"lovely." Setting the brush to the side a moment he wrapped his arms around her and pulled her back to rest against his chest once more, pressing his cheek to her crown. "I will never hurt you again, Jesslyn."

"I'm beginning to believe that." She sighed. "Just a bit more time...all right?"

Bao nodded, rubbing his cheek against the soft hair on top of her head. "Aye, whatever you need."

* * *

CHAPTER 8

Callum and his bride, Lara, arrived the day before the *Hogmanay* feast. Jesslyn was the only one in the great hall at the time of their arrival, having awakened later than usual. She had just finished breaking her fast when the guests were announced. Rising to her feet she stepped off the dais and moved to the center of the room facing the entrance as she watched her auburn-haired ex-betrothed escort his bride into the hall.

"'Tis good to see you again, Jesslyn," Callum said, a twinkle in his emerald-green eyes. Taking both her hands in his, he gave her a quick peck on the cheek.

Smiling with pleasure, Jesslyn replied, "Aye, 'tis good seeing you as well." She stood back a bit and looked from one end of his shoulders to the other. "Lord, but you're broader now than you were the last we saw each other. Why, your shoulders are the size of Daniel's now, I trow!—have the MacGregors been working you hard, then?"

Callum's grin turned sheepish. He shrugged. "I enjoy the exercise."

"Ahhh," she replied with a nod and a wink, "that's good." Turning then to his bride, she said, "And you are Lara. You're as beautiful as Daniel and Bao told us you were." The lady was of medium height and several years older than Jesslyn, mayhap twenty-five summers. But her skin was clear and white, with just the right amount of color to her cheeks. She'd forgone wearing a veil, simply placing a gold filet over the crown of her chestnut-colored curls. A vanity of hers, it seemed. Her eyes were almond-shaped and a darker hue of blue than Jesslyn's, her features delicate. Tho' she was older than her husband by several years, her beauty matched his own fine looks quite well. They made a pretty pair, Jesslyn decided.

"My thanks, you are kind to say so," Lara replied stiltedly, removing her mantle and handing it to a servant.

Jesslyn's gaze dipped momentarily to Lara's quite-rounded stomach and her eyes widened in shock. She quickly composed her features before lifting her gaze once more to the lady's countenance. She shouldn't be further along than Jesslyn was herself, Callum having only met and wed her around the same time as Jesslyn and Bao had had their tryst, yet she looked to be a good seven moons into her childing state.

* * *

Lara smirked at the flaxen-haired beauty Callum had been waxing lyrical about for many days now.

Evidently, she had no knowledge of who Lara was to her.

And as far as the babe in her belly, well, 'twas no secret that Callum hadn't fathered it. Not any longer. And 'twas no secret that she'd been forced to wed him because of it. Of course, Callum hadn't been told of the babe prior to their wedding; after all, their union had been arranged merely as a means of negotiating peace between her clan, the Gordons, and his clan, the MacGregors. Her father, Laird Gordon, had thought it a nice trick to hand over his strumpet of a daughter and her bastard babe to the clan that had been a thorn in his side since they'd been allotted the holding by the king. The holding, that according to their royal survey said they owned the rights to a particular tract of land, and according to the MacGregor's older royal survey said the MacGregor's owned rights to it.

Lara smirked even more when she saw Jesslyn's cheeks flame with embarrassment before she asked, "Would you care for something to drink? Eat?"

Callum, clearly oblivious to the exchange between her and Jesslyn, looked around the hall, saying, "Nay, we broke our fast earlier. Is Daniel still on the training field?"

Jesslyn nodded. "Aye, he and Bao both are."

Grinning, Callum said, "Bao? He's here as well, then?"

Lara's eyebrow rose in interest. Bao? Bao Xiong? The most popular and exclusive male whore at court? The one who'd given her her first set of orgasms? The man whom she'd paid to do so again every year since?

How amusing. This visit, which she'd believed would be dull, might just turn out to be quite interesting after all. This past summer, when she'd discovered that he was a member of the Maclean clan and an integral part of the peace negotiations between the Gordons and the MacGregors, her interest had been piqued. She'd tried her best to gain a moment in privy with him before her wedding, but he and that brother of his had never left Callum's side. But this time, she'd surely have more opportunity. And she intended to take full advantage of it. She'd not told Callum of his cousin's secret occupation, of course. She'd found in her life that juicy tidbits should be hoarded, not recklessly shared. They often turned into easy means of obtaining her own ends.

An old woman, whom she assumed to be Callum's grandmother came into the hall just then with an impishly lovely dark-haired lass trailing a bit behind. Her face beaming with pleasure, the old woman cried, "Callum, my dear!" With arms outstretched, she propelled herself into his embrace.

Callum hugged her and gave her a kiss on the cheek before pulling back and giving her a long perusal. "How fare you? Are you well? I trow, you've more gray than black to your hair, even since the summer," he teased.

"My hair is precisely the same color as the last time you saw me," the old woman said, tweaking his nose. But then, with a grin, she said, "Aye, I'm well. Tho' better still, now that you've arrived." She turned her gaze to Lara. "So this is your bride, then." Once again,

Highland Grace

Lara saw instant shock quickly hidden behind a mask of civility. "What a pretty lass you are! Come, give me a kiss on the cheek."

"Good morn, Grandmother Maclean," she said. She moved forward and did as the old woman asked, nearly gagging when she caught the pungent scent of oil of juniper on the woman's skin.

Then Callum took Lara by the elbow and said, "And this fine lass is my cousin Branwenn. She's sister to Daniel and Bao."

Lara's eyebrow quirked. "Good morn," she said. *This must be the lass for whom that blasted stepbrother of mine pines! Would he not drool to know I've found her at last!*

The lass dipped her head in a brief courtesy. "Good morn," she replied. She turned to Callum then, the wide grin on her countenance making the dimples in her cheeks more pronounced, and thrust out her hand, palm-side down. "You may kiss it, if you wish. I promise not to wipe it off this time."

* * *

Callum saw Jesslyn's hand fly to her mouth as she silently laughed into it and his jaw tensed.

Forcing a good-natured chuckle, he took Branwenn's outstretched hand, raised it to his lips and placed a courtly kiss on the appendage. Lifting his eyes to her face, he said, hoping to goad her, "Was it better this time, or shall I try another?"

She jerked her hand from his grasp. "Nay, no need. You've improved greatly."

Callum nodded, trying hard to hide his irritation. Her sharp tongue hadn't dulled over the past moons, as he'd hoped when he'd seen her ladylike manner as she'd entered with his Grandmother. For some unknown reason, she pricked his pride in a way that no one else had ever done. Callum turned back to his grandmother and said, "Will Maryn be joining us soon?"

"Nay, lad, she will not. She's been abed the past two days. Her feet and ankles have become so swollen that Daniel thought it best for her to keep them raised and not exert herself other than walking around her chamber. She's due any day now, you know."

"Aye, I remember. And knowing Maryn, she's as chafed as an old bear. Will we be allowed to visit her in her chamber? I'd like to introduce her to Lara."

His grandmother nodded. "Aye. Maryn would never forgive us if we kept you from it."

"Do you mind if we do so now? Then, if it please you, I'd like to leave my fair Lara with you and go out on the training field to meet with Daniel and Bao."

His grandmother took Lara's hand. "Aye, that's a sound plan."

Callum bowed to his three hosts and took his wife's hand, leading her from the hall.

* * *

After the two were well away, Lady Maclean said, "The size of the lass's belly doesn't fit the length of time she's known my grandson. Something is amiss, and I intend to find it out."

"Aye, I thought the same thing," Jesslyn said. "And she's a bit churlish as well."

"But very beautiful," Branwenn said softly. "Did you see the gemstones lining the neckline and sleeves of her saffron gown? They looked to be sapphires and rubies."

"Aye, and 'twas woven of the finest silk. She's evidently used to a much more luxurious lifestyle than ours," Lady Maclean said.

"Or, mayhap, she simply wanted to look her best upon meeting you for the first time, Grandmother," Jesslyn said, feeling a bit guilty for speaking poorly of Callum's new wife. Deciding it best to give the lady the benefit of the doubt for the time being, she continued, "Mayhap what I perceived as bitterness of nature was only nervousness."

"Nay, there is arrogance there, and treachery as well," Lady Maclean said. "I don't believe that Callum was made aware of her condition prior to the union, else the rest of us would have known before now as well."

"'Tis curious that Callum didn't send us a missive telling us of his wife's childing state," Branwenn said. "And did you notice that neither one of them brought up the subject?"

Jesslyn nodded. "Aye, which is why I thought it best not to mention my own condition. And I was proved right when, even after Grandmother Maclean spoke of the pending birth of Daniel and Maryn's babe, they still said naught."

"Aye, but your condition is not as obvious yet. It could easily be taken as the result of too many berry tarts," Branwenn said.

"My thanks," Jesslyn replied sarcastically.

"Not at all," Branwenn rejoined.

Lady Maclean clearly too caught up in her worry over Callum, ignored the interaction, saying once again, "*Something* is amiss."

* * *

"I never thought I'd say this but, cousin, I'm glad now that Laird Donald foiled my scheme to wed Maryn. She's much too difficult for my disposition," Callum jested later as he stood next to Daniel and Bao in the courtyard outside the lower bailey where the training field lay.

Daniel grinned. "Aye, she's beautiful, but she's deadly," he said.

"Aye, *hugely* so."

Daniel narrowed his eyes at his cousin. "Pardon?"

"But in a good way," Callum added, raising his hands to shield his face.

Daniel nodded. "Exactly. And you deceive yourself if you think your own wife will not be just as hard to deal with in her last days before the babe arrives."

"That's what servants are for," Callum said, his tongue firmly tucked in his cheek.

"Aye, that ought to go over well with your wife," Daniel replied.

Bao laughed at the exchange between the two. Daniel had told him there had been tension between them when they first met last spring, but whatever had caused it had evidently passed. Now they seemed content to bait each other with their sharp wit.

Callum sobered and said, "In truth, Maryn was very sweet to Lara, which pleased me greatly. I worried how my wife would be received by the ladies of the household once they realized how far into her childing state she is."

"You should have given us some warning, cousin." Daniel chided. "'Twas a bit much to ask that we not have any negative reaction to the shock of seeing her thus."

"Aye, you're right. But Lara was insistent that I not explain things in a missive. She'd promised her father that the details would never be written out nor given to anyone outside the family."

"When were you told of her condition?" Bao asked.

"The morn after we consummated our union."

"Convenient," Daniel said.

Callum shook his head. "Nay, do not think ill of her. She did as she was told to do by her father. And she had no idea that I would have stayed with her, regardless of the timing of the confession, to keep the peace between the clans."

"Know you who fathered the babe?" Bao asked.

Callum sighed and combed his fingers through his hair. "Nay, she will not tell me." Looking from one to the other of them, he said, "But I care not. I claim the babe as my own, and he'll be raised a MacGregor."

Daniel exchanged a quick look with Bao. "Jesslyn's with child also. She's a bit over four moons along."

Callum's brows slammed together. He shook his head, clearly shocked. "Who on earth fathered the babe?"

"I did."

Callum gave Bao an intent look. "Is that why you two wed then? Because of the babe?"

"Nay, I can admit that now. But the babe did help me to gain my purpose more quickly."

"Come, I've a thirst for some ale," Daniel said. "Let us continue this discussion in the great hall."

Bao and Callum nodded and the three left the courtyard behind. With long strides they moved in the direction of the keep.

"I still cannot believe it. You and Jesslyn," Callum said in wonder, shaking his head.

"Believe it," Bao said.

* * *

"Ahh, 'tis glad I am I found you."

Jesslyn's hand stilled on the handle to her bedchamber door and she turned toward the voice. "G'day to you Lara. Are you in need of something? I could find a servant for you."

"Nay, 'tis you with whom I crave a word."

"All right. Would you like to come inside?"

"Nay, here will do. You have no notion of who I am, do you?"

For reasons Jesslyn had no understanding of, her heart started to pound. "Aye. You are Callum's new wife."

"There is that, aye. But you and I, we have a much older relationship. Can you not guess?"

Thoroughly confused and growing more wary by the moment, as Lara's smile held venom and smug conceit, she said, "Nay. Who are you?"

"Why, I'm your dear departed husband's favorite lover—you do remember Graeme kept a lover, do you not? I suppose you just weren't enough for him."

Jesslyn felt dizzy. She swayed and placed her palm on the door for balance. "That was only the one time."

"Is that what he told you?" Lara's head went back when she laughed. "Nay, 'twas *many* more times than just the one. Our dalliance started while he was still wed to Janet, in fact, and carried on into your own marriage for quite a time."

Jesslyn felt faint. *Graeme had continued the affair, even after assuring her he'd broken ties with the woman?*

Lara studied her nails. "He was quite smitten with me, you know. He would have wed me instead of you, I'm sure, if I had been there when he arrived back home to find his wife dead."

"I-I have to go." Jesslyn scrambled blindly for the door handle and fled inside, leaning heavily upon it for a moment before staggering over to the bed and flinging herself face down on the fur covering.

He'd deceived her. Betrayed her and deceived her. What a fool she'd been all these moons, pining away for her perfect, lost love. Had it all been a lie? Even up to the end? A whimper escaped and she closed her throat to hold back another one. No. She'd not believe it. Graeme had loved her, been devoted to her. They'd shared a life together, built a family.

Laura, her words and her smug grin flashed through her mind, followed swiftly by the image of Bao and the lass in the wood, and all her doubts came tumbling back into place.

She covered her face with her hands. What was wrong with her? Why did men think 'twas all right to forget their vows when wed to her? She was weak, she didn't stand up for herself, that was why.

She sat up. *If Bao ever does it to me again, I'll leave him.* She'd tried her best to forget the last incident, since their union had not truly started at that point, but now that it had—well, except for the bedding—she'd not stand by like some pitiful fool while her husband collected lovers.

* * *

Bao was feeling a bit woozy after partaking in two hours of drinking, so he used the curving stone wall for support as he ascended the stairs to his bedchamber. Daniel was decidedly a bad influence on him. He'd drunk more since he'd come back to the holding than he had in the entire year prior to that. Granted, he'd only had two flagons of ale, which was his normal consumption. 'Twas that *uisge beatha* that Daniel later brought out that had got his head to spinning. At least he'd only had the one portion this time.

* * *

Lara, having grown bored with her own company these two hours since her successful encounter with Jesslyn, slowly descended the stairs in quest of a bit of entertainment. Mayhap, if she were lucky, she'd meet up with Bao, and she could pursue her desire to revisit the passion she'd shared with him.

Because of her need to watch her step, Lara accidentally bumped into someone as she went around the curve. Barely lifting her gaze to the man, she said, "Beg pardon, sir." Then as recognition dawned, she smiled and said, "Good day to you, Bao."

'Twas clear by his struggle to focus upon her that he

was a bit into his cups, which Lara decided might work in her favor, since he might be resistant to performing a service while visiting his family.

"'Tis good seeing you again, Lara," he replied at last.

She did a slow scan of him with her eyes. The man was still as carnally captivating as he was on their last encounter a year ago. And he was enormous *everywhere*. A thrill shot through her. But, she wondered, would he service a pregnant woman? After the rigid performance of her wedding night, Lara had not allowed her husband to touch her again, even tho' he was not badly proportioned. She supposed she was simply too angered by the fact that she had been forced to wed him to ever enjoy coupling with him. And her stepbrother's awkward rutting between her thighs had been more an act of violence on both their parts than about pleasure—unfortunately for her, this last time had produced a bairn as well. "'Tis good to see you, too," she purred. *Would* Bao give her the sensual pleasure she craved? She was more than willing to find out. She swayed. "Oh, my!" She swept the back of her hand up to her forehead and fell forward with as much grace as she could manage.

His arms lunged out and caught her in a light embrace. "Where is your bedchamber?" he asked, his gaze sharp with concern. "I shall carry you there, if you wish."

She nodded and bit back a smug smile. "'Tis just above, on the next level. The third door down."

After lifting her into his arms, he quickly climbed the remaining stairs and strode through the door she'd indicated. As he placed her on the bed, he said, "I'll summon a maid for you."

She grasped his hand when he began to turn away. "Nay, stay a moment. I'm feeling less faint now and wish to become better acquainted with you."

She could tell he wanted to say her nay, but evidently deciding 'twould be rude to do so, pulled up a stool next to the bed and sat down. "What would you like to know?" he asked.

"How much you would charge a woman round with child?"

* * *

It took Bao a moment to realize her meaning. Sobering even further, he sat forward and narrowed his eyes at her. "Pardon?" he said.

"How much would you charge to fuck me now that I've a child in my belly."

Bao's ears started ringing. "I'm out of commission."

She gave him a knowing smile as she scooted off the bed and walked over to her clothes chest. She bent and retrieved something then turned and, when she did, Bao gasped.

"Ah, so you *do* remember me. Come now, once more for old time's sake?"

Bao stood up. "You!" She was wearing the mask one of his clients always wore, for discretion. Warm damp soaked the shirt under his tunic, quickly becoming clammy. "How?"

Her laughter trilled, scraping over Bao's nerve endings, as she sauntered back over to the bed and sat down. "The first time 'twas my sister's doing—Edina?

Edina Stewart? Her husb—"

"I know who she is, to whom she is wed." He crossed his arms. Edina had been the lady he'd been with last. The one whom he'd not been able to complete the deed with who'd been so angered that she'd thrown him out.

"Well, she is the one who purchased you for me that first time five years ago. 'Twas after my lover married and refused to continue our affair. Edina had heard that you could give satisfaction to even the most notoriously unresponsive of the ladies at the royal court and, until that first time with you, I had had that same problem, even with my lover."

"I'll not do it."

"But I've an entire casket of jewels from which you may choose! Do you not want to add to your coffers?"

"Nay," he said, his voice harsh now, "I've plenty already. And I'll never fuck the wife of my cousin."

"How about just the thing you do with your mouth, then?" She lifted her skirts and spread her legs wide and all Bao wanted to do was bolt. He got to his feet and threw her skirts back over her legs. "Nay."

Did she know of her stepbrother's vile plot to take Branwenn from him and make her his slave mistress? "My sister knows naught of this, so do not tell her."

She inched the skirts back up a bit, showing off her bare legs and Bao gritted his teeth. "That little innocent? Nay, I'll not say a word."

"And your stepbrother? Where is he?"

"Giric? Oh, he's still in Perth I assume, why?"

"'Tis a privy matter between him and me." Mayhap

she didn't know that side of things. Praise be. "I think it time for you to get a bit of rest." He turned and stormed toward the door. He was halfway through it before he swung back around, saying, "Don't try this ploy on me again. I'm wed. Happily so." And then he left, shutting the door with a loud *snick*.

* * *

Bao leaned against the wall outside his cousin's bedchamber door with his eyes squeezed tightly shut. Breathing hard, his brow damp with sweat, he relived the past moments, horror, shame and dread commingling in his chest to form a painful vise. He pushed himself away from the wall. Taking the stairs two at a time down to the lower level, he continued on, not stopping until he'd made it through the arched entrance of the lower bailey. He needed the demands of physical exertion to tamp down his demons.

* * *

CHAPTER 9

Laird Donald arrived the next morn, and on his heels, Lady MacGregor, Callum's mother and Lady Maclean's daughter.

The preparations for the *Hogmanay* feast were at their peak. Maryn, who was still obliged to stay abed, was supervising the activities from her bedchamber, with the help of Branwenn, who was the youngest and most agile of the ladies and, therefore, able to make numerous trips up and down the stairs to receive Maryn's instructions.

Lady Maclean and her daughter were busy overseeing the household staff as the entire keep was cleaned. The floors were cleared of their rush mats, swept, and replaced with new ones, the hearths were cleared of ashes, silver was polished, tapestries were shaken of their dust and rehung on the walls. Casks of ale were being brought from the tower cellar and the kitchens were filled with cook staff bustling about preparing the many courses for the feast.

Jesslyn and Lara were called upon to have branches of the rowan tree placed above doorways for luck and to see that the wine, made from its fermented berries, was ready for the celebration. They also made certain that mistletoe, to prevent illness; holly, to keep out mischievous faeries; and hazel, for protection, were all placed in each chamber.

The scent of juniper enveloped the hall. It was being burned throughout the keep as the cleaning and preparations were made, to clear out any evil spirits that may have moved in during the past year. The doors and windows would be flung wide to air the chambers out before the feasting began.

The men had been sent out to the upper bailey to build the pyre for the bonfire later that night.

"Do you mind if I step out for a while?" Lara asked Jesslyn. "I feel a bit ill from the biting smell in here."

Jesslyn, who'd been swallowing her dislike and anger for the sake of keeping the peace, lifted her eyes from her task and, noticing Lara's pallid complexion, replied, "Nay, do as you must. We've almost finished with the preparations anyway."

* * *

Lara walked out of the keep toward the upper bailey. Ever since Bao had left her chamber the day before, she'd been dwelling on the conversation they'd had, and his parting words to her. He'd said he was happily wed and it hadn't taken her long to find out to whom. The fates were surely smiling on her. How wonderful to rub salt in Jesslyn's wound, to say that she'd had *both* husbands rutting for her! Especially after Graeme had crushed her pride, first by wedding Jesslyn and then by sending her a letter attempting to curtail their affair.

Lara laughed. Of course, once she'd arrived back there, he'd soon forgotten his decision. 'Twas near a year later that he'd broken their arrangement in truth—all for that *lady* Jesslyn.

She nibbled her nail. She just had to have Bao again. Not only for the pleasure he offered, but because her chaste little nemesis had him. And this time, she'd make sure that Jesslyn was full aware of her new husband's adultery. That should put a damper on their passion for some time to come. Jesslyn had ruined Lara's relationship with Graeme, 'twas the least she deserved to have Lara ruin her relationship with Bao.

Aye, she'd do or say whatever she must to attain that goal. The promise of jewels had not moved him, but Lara had no doubt her next ploy would.

She strolled up and stood next to her quarry. As she watched Callum and Daniel lift another log onto the pyre, she said, "My husband certainly does his best to prove his strength matches the two of yours."

He gave her a pointed look. "His strength *does* match ours. And his warrioring skills are some of the best I've seen. You'd do well to be thankful for the good fortune you had in wedding such a man." He left her side and took Callum's place, indicating to his cousin with a jerk of his head that she was near.

Her husband grinned and jogged over to her. As he halted in front of her, he said, "How are the preparations coming for the *Hogmanay* feast this afternoon?"

"Quite well. I was feeling a bit ill from the smell of the burning juniper, so I came out for a bit of fresh air."

He put his hand on her arm and it was all she could do not to cringe. "Mayhap you should rest awhile." He looked around and then took hold of her hand. "Let us walk to the well. I shall lift you up onto the edge," he said, leading her away from the pyre.

* * *

Bao gave a mental sigh of relief when he saw his cousin stroll away with his mischief-making wife. He could see that Callum was trying very hard to make the best of his unenviable situation. He treated the lady with a gentleness and consideration that was clearly not returned.

Daniel followed the line of Bao's vision. "He seems to care for her," he said.

Bao nodded grimly. "Aye."

Taking his gaze from the couple, Daniel turned it on Bao. Narrowing his eyes, he stated, "You like her not."

Shrugging, Bao turned and picked up the end of another log. "'Tis more that I do not trust her. She is like the restless ladies of the court."

"Because she wears fine clothes and jewels?

Bao shrugged again. He would like naught more than to confess all to his brother, but he could see no good coming from it, only more heartache for Callum, more problems for him and Jesslyn, and more danger for Branwenn.

"I hardly think that a good reason to judge her so

harshly."

"I suppose you are right," Bao replied. "Are you going to pick up the other end of this log before the sun sets? I grow tired of holding it."

Daniel laughed good-naturedly and lifted his end of the wood. "Let's finish this and go to the loch to retrieve my father-in-law and Alleck. I doubt not that they've caught a few trout by now, tho' this was their first attempt at ice fishing."

Bao nodded. With so many people visiting the keep, surely Callum's wife wouldn't solicit his services again. But she'd be leaving in a few days in any event, so he'd simply make sure he stayed clear of her until then.

* * *

"The woman hasn't stopped complaining since she arrived, Mama," Maggie, Lady MacGregor, said. "The furniture isn't nice enough, the food doesn't taste good, the wine is off, the staff are prone to idleness. I'm at the end of my patience."

Lady Maclean looked up from her task and gazed at her still-youthful looking, though middle-aged daughter. She'd gotten her black hair from her mother, but had inherited her green eyes from her father. Evidently, she had inherited his impatience towards indulgence as well. "Have you spoken to Callum? What says he?"

"He says that she's captious because of her condition. He refuses to speak to her about her behavior—in fact, he seems set on pampering the lass." She fluttered her hands in the air in agitation. "He buys for her whatever she asks," Lady MacGregor replied irritably.

"Does he love her then?"

Lady MacGregor shook her head. "Nay...nay, I do not believe that he does." She made a quick count of the number of candlesticks placed on each trestle table and nodded her approval to the servant who waited close by before continuing, "But, he cares for the babe. And he wants its mother to be happy."

"How has Chalmers reacted to her spoiled behavior?"

"My husband said naught for a long time, hoping Callum would deal with his wife. But, finally, a few days prior to their departure to journey here, he had a discussion with her." Grinning, Lady MacGregor said, "In the same way he'd deal with a spoiled bairn, he sent her to the priest for lessons in humility. The priest made her put on old, scratchy clothes and dust and polish the pews!"

Nodding, Lady Maclean said, "Mayhap that's the reason she hasn't given us as much trouble."

"Aye, that seems likely."

* * *

"'Tis a shame your uncle could not attend the feast," Lara heard Jesslyn say to Callum. They were seated at the table on the dais enjoying the last course of their meal.

"Aye, but I'm glad he at least allowed my mother to attend. The MacGregors celebrate *Hogmanay* in much the same fashion, and he, as chieftain of the clan, was obliged to o'ersee the thing. Actually, my mother had thought it best if she stay, since it is her first *Hogmanay* as the laird's wife, but my uncle insisted that she visit her mother instead. After all, she's not been back here since she left almost a year ago."

"Aye," Lara interjected, "your uncle is *such* a dear soul." She hoped he choked on a bone in their absence. Every time she remembered the torment he and that evil wee goblin of a priest put her through, she had to fight back a shudder of hatred.

Her husband took her hand and raised it to his lips, kissing her fingers. "You're kind to say so, my dear."

Lara gave him a wooden smile. He was a fool. Could he not see what an ass he was making of himself? 'Twould be best for all involved if they simply tolerated each other. His constant show of concern, which she was beginning to understand was genuine, was more than she could bear. She only hoped that he would cease his attentions to her once the babe was born. "When will we go out to view the bonfire?"

"The players are to entertain us first," he replied.

Lara nodded. After taking a sip of wine from the silver cup, she leaned forward a bit, pretending to inspect the area where the players were to perform. In fact, she was avidly watching Bao from the corner of her eye. She'd been unable to get him alone these past hours as he seemed to be in constant company of another. But the bonfire would serve her purpose, and she had the perfect plan.

* * *

A drop of wine nearly ran down Jesslyn's chin before she stopped it with a sweep of her tongue. She felt her husband's gaze on her just before he dipped his head and whispered into her ear, "You look lovely this eve. The color of your gown matches the ruby of your lips."

Her breath hitched. "My lips are not so deeply tinged," she countered.

"Aye, they are. Deep and red and full. Like the tender petals of a rose. Beautiful."

Jesslyn trembled. The feel of Bao's mouth so close to the shell of her ear made her long to feel their caress on other, more sensitive, portions of her body. "My thanks."

She'd made her decision. This night, after the celebration, she would give herself to him. He'd proven himself to her over and over again these past sennights with his kindness, his devotion to her, to Alleck, to the babe in her belly. And what was more, he'd barely even glanced in Lara's direction. In fact, it seemed to her that Lara vexed Bao, for each time he heard her speak, Jesslyn saw his jaw tighten, tho' he was careful in all other respects to keep an amiable façade.

Aye, she was through with her reticence, her fear. She turned her gaze on him. "Will you meet me later? I'd like to speak with you alone."

A spark of intrigue lit his eye. "Aye. When?"

"We'll wait until after the bonfire is lit. I don't want to seem rude and leave too early."

He nodded and his thumb stroked her cheek. "How do you feel? Are you too warm?"

Jesslyn smiled. "Nay, I'm fit. My thanks for your concern." She turned her mouth into his palm and bestowed a kiss upon it.

* * *

Highland Grace

Bao's manhood shot to full attention. He longed to rock against the ruby-red lips he'd been speaking of in truth as her hot sheath squeezed him in its grip. Bao swallowed a groan of pure agony and slowly took his hand from her grasp. Turning on his stool, he stared blankly at the players, who'd begun their entertainment while he and his bride spoke.

He was close to his limit for biding her surrender to him. He'd wanted to wait for her, and he had. He hadn't found relief since that morn in Perth when he'd awakened from the nearly tangible dream of their only time together.

So, he hoped fervently that with a bit of luck and a lot of skill, this might just be the night that saw the end of his celibacy for good.

* * *

Lara waited until she saw Jesslyn walk with Lady Maclean around to the other side of the bonfire before she excused herself from her husband, saying that she was weary and would retire to their chamber. After receiving a nod from him and a quick peck on the cheek, she walked in the direction of the keep. She saw Bao standing with Laird Donald near the entryway. Perfect. "Good eve, Bao. Good eve, Laird Donald," she said as she approached. Turning her gaze to the dark-haired object of her forbidden desires, she said, "Jesslyn asked me to tell you that she'd like to meet you in the top chamber of the store tower."

Bao smiled and nodded. The store tower. This night might prove to be more interesting than he'd originally hoped. He turned to Laird Donald and said, "It seems

I've been summoned."

Laird Donald laughed. "Aye, lad, that you have. And you mustn't keep your lady waiting."

* * *

Lara nodded a brief farewell to the two men and walked past them to enter the keep. But she didn't go up to her chamber. Instead, she made her way across the great hall and through the door in the back wall that led toward the kitchens. She'd get to the store tower via the herb garden.

* * *

Using the flint and striker he found just inside the door at ground level, Bao lit one of the candles that intermittently hung from sconces along the wall of the stairs. After climbing the stone steps and entering the room above, he made a quick scan of the chamber. Jesslyn hadn't arrived yet, it seemed. But she'd evidently planned this interlude quite well; there were blankets and pillows on the floor, and a flagon of wine was resting on a crate with a silver chalice sitting next to it.

Moving around the chamber, he lit the candles in the two sconces on the wall and then placed the taper he held in his hand onto the bronze candlestick positioned next to the chalice on the crate.

He turned toward the door when he heard the soft pad of footsteps coming from the stairs. When he saw who it was that entered, his heart dipped into his stomach and catapulted back to throb in dread against his breast bone. "What the hell are you doing here?" he said. 'Twas Callum's mischief-making wife that stood before him in a state of dishabille.

She leaned against the door frame, her arms crossed beneath her breasts, pushing them up so that they spilled from the loosened bodice of her chemise. She'd removed her gown sometime prior to entering, for it was not in sight. Tho' her belly was round with child, she was still quite slim and, he already knew from past experience, she knew how to make herself alluring to men.

"Giving you another chance to change your mind, of course," she replied, straightening and moving further into the chamber.

She shrugged and her chemise dropped off of her shoulders, leaving her breasts bare, her nipples pebbling as they came in contact with the chill air of the room. "After all, what's so terrible about a friendly fuck between cousins-in-law? Especially now that there's no danger of getting me with child." She giggled. "Nay, that deed has already been done by Giric!—Damn!" Her hand flew to her mouth. "That was supposed to be a secret."

"Are you drunk?"

"Mayhap a wee bit, but isn't this the night for such behavior?"

"Get the hell out before my wife finds you here."

She laughed throatily. "You foolish man, have you still no apprehension? Your wife remains below enjoying the bonfire—'twas I who created this lover's bower." She walked toward him, her arms outstretched and her chemise slipping to the floor. "Show me heaven, do to me all the things you've done before."

"Nay," Bao said, striding around her toward the open door.

"Not even for the entire casket of jewels?" She pointed to the corner where the container lay. "You can look inside if you like."

Bao halted in the doorway, his back to her, grasping the doorframe in both his hands. "Go to your husband for your pleasures. I've no desire to bed you, for any amount of riches."

Her purring voice turned spiteful. "But would you, in exchange for your sister's freedom? Or do you want my stepbrother to know where your precious Branwenn dwells? 'Tis not in a nunnery as you've convinced him, is it, *dear* Bao?"

He fisted his hands at his sides to keep from strangling her then and there and whirled to face her. "You'll not say a word to your brother about my sister's whereabouts. Not a word."

Clearly unabashed by her own nakedness, she tossed her head as she stormed toward the table with her arms akimbo. Cocking her hip to the side and keeping one hand at her waist, she lazily ran her finger around the silver rim of the chalice as she asked, "Aye. Not a word—*if* you give me this one little boon."

"Nay, I'll not. For, you could easily break your word afterward." Bao scanned her too-knowing visage. "Just how much do you know of why your stepbrother wants my sister?"

She shrugged. "He says he owns her by right and that you are keeping him from what is his."

"He doesn't own her. I've paid him many times over

the price he paid my father for her years ago."

She cocked a brow at him. "He has a deed of ownership."

Bao ground his teeth before he answered. "Aye, I've paid his debts, paid him his annual fees for her continued freedom for nigh on fifteen annals trying to get my hands on it—and keep his hands off her." A flash-memory of Giric looming over his bed when Bao was a young squire sent an all-too familiar tremor of dread and revolt through his system and he clenched his fists to fight it off.

Lara laughed. "Aye, Giric does like to toy with people."

"He does more than toy with his mistresses. Two have gone missing under very mysterious circumstances, to which the King turns a blind eye, as the women were of low birth."

Her mouth turned down into a frown, but she shrugged as if forcing a look of disinterest. "He has a bit of a cruel streak. Many men do."

"'Tis more than cruelty, 'tis violent, mayhap even murderous." *And, at the minimum, perverse.* "I shall *never* put my sister in his clutches."

Her laughter trilled, echoing off the stone walls. "Then, 'tis clear what you must do, is it not?" She threw her head back and gave a much more deep-throated laugh. "And this time, Bao Xiong Maclean, *you* shall pay *me* for the privilege."

"Not without surety that my sister will remain unharmed and free of him until I can get her well-wed."

Her gaze turned calculating. She sighed. "I was

hoping I could keep this little bit of revenge on him in my possession, as he deserves to suffer for what he's done to me, but…but what if I gave you the deed of ownership? I stole it from him several moons ago, after I discovered my childing state. Once it's in your hands, 'twould matter less if my stepbrother found out where your sister dwells, would it not?" She shrugged and turned, walking toward the bedding she'd arranged on the floor. "Anyway, I have naught against the lass—and I know first hand Giric's proclivities. I'll not give her away—not if you service me well."

"Where is the deed now? I won't agree to a thing until I see it with my own eyes."

"I'll not say where, but I can promise you that you shall see it, own it, this very night, if you agree to my terms."

"I want to see it first."

"Nay, not until *after*."

"I must know it's the deed that my father used to barter Branwenn."

"Oh, it is. Why don't I tell you a bit about it? Will that do as proof?" She looked up at the ceiling beams and said, "'Twas dated the twelfth day of January, in the year of our Lord, eleven-ninty. It states that for a price of three silver pennies, one 2-year-old war horse of healthy stock, and a chain mail, the babe, Branwenn, would be given in slavery to Giric MacBean."

'Twas just as his father had told him. It took Bao less than a second to decide. "I'll meet you in the stables in an hour. Bring it with you." Bao left then, flying down the stairs and out into the courtyard. The woman was a menace. But, if he could do as she wanted, by the end of it, he'd finally have his sister's freedom. He'd also have betrayed the one woman he wanted desperately to love him.

He needed a drink. With purposeful strides, he moved toward the keep. Some of Daniel's *uisge beatha* would do. It might numb the edges enough so that when he tried to do the deed, he would succeed this time. And he *must* succeed.

* * *

Laird Donald strolled up to stand beside Lady Maclean. The bonfire was at full blaze now, the heat from it reaching several feet from its edges, warming those who stood in its sphere. The upper bailey had been cleared of all carts and other articles made of wood or cloth that might accidently ignite from a stray spark. "This be as fine a display as I've seen in years."

Lady Maclean nodded. "Aye, my grandsons did a fine job on this."

"Where's my son-in-law? I'd like to congratulate him on his success."

"He's with Maryn. She's awfully close to having her babe, and Daniel doesn't want to leave her side for very long. He shall be down here again soon, I'm sure."

"Branwenn seems to be settling in nicely. I saw her dancing with some of the other young lads and lasses a few moments past."

"Aye, she's coming along just fine. Tho' she's still set against wedding."

Laird Donald looked at her in surprise. "You've given her a choice?"

Lady Maclean's lips thinned and she shook her head. "Nay, I've not. But, because of her unusual upbringing, I'm giving her a bit more time to become accustomed to her fate. I've not argued the point with her as of yet."

"Do you have anyone in mind for her?"

"Several, actually. They're all from good families and not so old that they'd not tolerate her active nature."

"That's good. The lass has spirit, and 'twouldn't do for her to be wed to a man that couldn't appreciate it."

* * *

Jesslyn wandered over to stand with Callum as he watched the clan youth enjoying another dance. She followed Callum's gaze and saw Branwenn. "She's got such impish beauty, does she not?" Jesslyn said.

"Aye, as long as she doesn't speak," Callum replied. "And she's much too wild. Grandmother should put a stop to this display forthwith."

Jesslyn took hold of Callum's sleeve when he started to turn in the direction of Lady Maclean. "You've certainly become stern since last we met. Leave the lass be; she's only enjoying the festivities a bit."

"You think me too stern? When both you and my wife are proof of what can happen to a lass if she doesn't guard her virtue as she should?" Callum pulled from Jesslyn's grasp and walked toward Lady Maclean.

Jesslyn looked toward Branwenn and the other dancing youth, trying to see the danger that Callum was so sure was there. She shook her head. It seemed perfectly innocent to her. Mayhap, 'twas more that

Callum was bent on vexing the poor lass. The two of them did seem to always be at sixes and sevens whenever they met. Sighing, she decided to leave it in the hands of Lady Maclean.

* * *

After his second cupful of the ardent spirits, Bao finally felt able to deal with Callum's wife.

Rising to his feet, he swayed and grabbed the edge of the table for support. Mayhap he'd had more than he should. The room tilted, but after a moment his head cleared and he tripped off the dais and staggered from the hall to the stables. He intended on taking her to one of the caves in the wood. He'd not betray his wife inside her own home.

The stables were deserted, as even the stablemen were enjoying the festivities. Bao patted his stallion's neck. "That's a good lad," he said. He grabbed the saddle and tried to slide it on the beast's back, but the walls of the stall started to collapse and expand and he swayed.

The stallion snorted and stepped to the side. Bao followed and fell to his knees. He'd better sober up a bit more by the time Lara arrived. With effort, he got to his feet again and gave his face a few slaps. Then he took a ladle full of water from a bucket and drank it down. That seemed to help and he managed to get the stallion saddled and ready for travel over the next minutes.

He was just leaning against the stall facing the entry of the stables when she came through it. Her eyes sparked with excitement and her lips turned up in a smug smile as she approached him.

"I've never done it in a stable. How…rustic," she said, looking around. "Is there an empty stall, or…"— she turned her gaze on him—"do you prefer where we stand?"

"I've saddled my stallion. I'm taking you to a cave I know of in the wood. 'Twill be privy and away from the festivities."

She nodded. "Ahh." She sauntered over to where he stood. "I think I'd prefer you here, on the stable floor. Lie down."

"Where is the deed?"

"I'll give it to you while we couple. Will that do?"

He nodded and lay down. She knelt and loosened the ties of his tunic and lifted it over his abdomen. Then, she loosened his braies and brought the cloth away from his pelvis. The old familiar anxiety made his insides tighten. *Can I allow it?* His member lay to the side, resting in the junction of his thigh and pelvis. With a shaking hand she touched him and Bao gritted his teeth as a wave of revulsion swept through him. *Nay!* He thrust her hand away. "Nay, let me." It took everything he had to moderate his voice to a more seductive timbre when he said, "Just watch." He closed his eyes and brought forth a memory of being inside Jesslyn at the waterfall and his cock sprang to life. As he manipulated it a few more moments, he heard Lara's breath grow harsh with arousal and he transferred that sound to his dream lover. *Jesslyn.*

He groaned.

"Lord, you are massive. I've always liked that about

you." His eyes flew open and he watched and waited, tamping down the dread and disgust at what he was about to do, as she quickly undid her gown and chemise, straddled him and trailed the peak of her nipple over his bottom lip. The pungent smell of clove and cinnamon wafted over him and he almost lost his erection. But knowing what she wanted, he closed his eyes again, and with one hand still vigorously massaging his cock, opened his mouth wide, pulling the peak of her breast into it and suckled deeply. He kept his focus on his memories of Jesslyn, which he knew now were all he'd ever have of her and, once his erection was at full mast again, lifted his hands to Lara's breasts and molded one in the palm of his hand as he stroked and massaged the other, feeding on her.

* * *

Lara pressed down a fraction, feeling the large head of Bao's arousal stretching her open in that oh-so-familiar way. It would hurt at first, but she liked it better when there was a bit of pain. That had been the best part of her experiences with her stepbrother. But he always finished too quickly. That wouldn't be the case with Bao. He could go for hours. And, mayhap, if she was rough enough, she could lose this whelp of her stepbrother's making as well. She'd tried often these past moons, but the thing was stubborn. It stayed in her belly with the ferociousness of a priest on a sinner. Placing her hands on Bao's chest, she pressed down, forcing him inside her a bit further. The slight sting was now searing. She trembled and sucked in her breath.

"Fuck me, fuck me now!"

"First give me Branwenn's deed!"

* * *

Callum walked toward the keep. He'd made his rounds, spoken with all his relatives and Maclean clansmen, and now he was ready for bed. The ringing of the bells was another hour away, but he wasn't in the mood for more merry-making. He was troubled over his wife. She was never satisfied no matter what he did to appease her. And he worried for their babe. He'd followed her one day and seen her take a pouch from the old woman that dwelled in the MacGregor wood lining the craggy shore of the ocean. 'Twas well known that she had herbal concoctions that could make a woman lose her babe, if she so desired.

Fearing that she'd try to end her childing condition, he'd stolen the pouch from her casket before she'd had a chance to use the herbs and replaced them with a bit of clove and cinnamon.

Callum was just passing the stables when he heard his wife's exclamation and the reply in a much-too-familiar male voice. Darting inside, he skidded to a halt at the feet of the entwined pair.

His cousin pushed Lara off him and sat up. The look in his eye was one of a trapped animal. Wild and dark.

His wife's bosom and legs were bare, a red bruise and teeth marks marred her right breast. He growled low and unsheathed his dirk. With venom in his voice and his blade in his hand, he said to Bao, "Do you die now, or do I allow you to cover yourself first?"

His cousin staggered to his feet, pushing down the

hem of his tunic over his bare manhood and legs.

"Nay!" Lara cried. "He tricked me into coming here with him and then he tried to force me to couple with him!" Modestly covering her bosom with her hands, she continued, "He's a shameful man. He's been a whore at the king's court for years, you know!"

Callum looked at her searchingly. "How know you this?"

Her eyes widened and darted to Bao as if she were trying to come up with a good answer, and Callum grew more suspicious. "My sister, Edina," she finally said. Then she looked down at her hands as she jerkily closed her gaping bodice and retied the strings. "She told me he's the most celebrated male whore in the court." She lifted her gaze to him once more and moved toward him. With a hand on his arm, she said, "But you saved me before it went too far!"

Callum gave his cousin a long look. There was something very wrong. There was no trace of desire in his cousin's eyes, only dread. In fact, he'd never seen such fear in the man's eyes before. Not even when they were met by a horde of Gordon's that outflanked their own number by three to one. Bao had been steady and sure of the outcome then.

Callum sheathed his dirk. "What did you mean by Branwenn's deed? Does my wife have something that belongs to the lass?"

His cousin remained stonily silent.

Callum glanced at Lara, who had settled a much too innocent mien on her face. This entire encounter between her and his cousin was strange in nature. And how do you force a woman when she's riding astride? In any case, he'd clearly stopped them before it had gone very far.

He looked at Bao. "We'll speak more of this in the morn," he said at last. "Come, you and I shall leave together." He sent his wife a penetrating look. "I'll expect you in our chamber in no more than a quarter hour's time."

* * *

Lara seethed as she watched the two cousins walk away. Though they said naught to each other, there was not the jealous animosity she'd come to expect with male rivals for her favor. Hatred filled her breast. Her husband hadn't even fought for her honor. She had not felt this humiliated since Graeme's letter. After all, she was beautiful. Men adored her. They always had. And she'd gloried in it. Dangled the forbidden fruit of her consent in front of them long enough to get their passions raised and their vows of servitude to her loveliness in her possession. And hadn't she reveled in the number of clashes she'd inspired for her honor? She adored that she could make a man so mad for her that he'd draw another's blood. But it hadn't been until the first time her stepbrother had become so inflamed that he'd forced himself on her that she'd seen the true power she held over men. And the pain he'd given her was proof that they couldn't restrain themselves, that she was capable of overpowering their reason to the point that they became animals. She shuddered. God, how she loved that. But she hadn't known until her sister had told her of it, that a woman could find release the same way a man did. And so had begun her sessions with Bao.

However, 'twas evident that her plans for Bao and Jesslyn had been thoroughly ruined by her fool of a husband. Now, 'twas too dangerous to continue along that track because Callum would be watching the two of them too closely the next days until their departure.

But she could get revenge on her husband. She'd simply begin taking more lovers once they returned home. And this time, if one could not satisfy her, she'd take yet another...and another, until she finally found a man as good as Bao.

At least she'd not given him the deed. She tucked her hand inside her pouch and curled it around the small scroll. Nay, her revenge on her brother was still well in her grasp.

* * *

CHAPTER 10

"Have you seen Bao?" Jesslyn asked Laird Donald. The tower church bells were about to begin chiming and she wanted to stand with her husband, as tradition decreed. Daniel had gone up to his bedchamber a moment before to spend these moments with his wife.

"Not after he went to meet you in the store tower, my dear. That was nigh on two hours past. Actually," he continued sheepishly, "I thought the two of you may have retired for the evening."

"The store tower?" Jesslyn shook her head in confusion. "He didn't meet me in the store tower, sir."

"Aye, he did. He raced with good speed directly to that place upon learning you'd summoned him. Mayhap he still awaits you, lass."

"And who gave my husband this message, sir?"

"'Twas Callum's wife, Lara. Did she not relay it right?"

Lara! Alarmed, but unwilling to burden the older man with her worries, Jesslyn said only, "I must fly, then, for I fear Bao will be quite displeased with me by now." Waving a brief farewell, Jesslyn scurried off toward the tower.

The store tower didn't hold good memories for Jesslyn. It had been the site of her deepest humiliation. Where, in some mad moment of desperation, she'd almost ruined Daniel and Maryn's union by throwing herself at him just before his wife had come through the door. Thankfully, after almost a sennight of separation, Daniel had been able to overcome Maryn's suspicions and they'd reconciled. And, somehow, Maryn had had the generosity of spirit to not only forgive Jesslyn, but befriend her as well.

With leaden feet, she climbed the stairs, the light from the taper creating eerie shadows on the steps and wall, sending a chill down her spine. When the bells began to chime, she nearly jumped out of her skin. "Bao?" she called out. No answer. Mayhap he—*they?*—couldn't hear her over the sounding of the bells. She hurried up the last few steps, rushed to the door of the upper chamber and opened it wide.

Empty, praise be. For she had little trust of Lara, and what Bao had managed to salvage these past sennights with her was fragile.

Except. The chamber looked to be made into a lover's bower. The niggling suspicion was fast becoming a full-blown certitude. Lara had prepared this place to seduce Bao. But, the question remained, had she and Bao met here by some secret design? Had his seeming dislike of the lady been an act to hide his true intent?

Her heart fluttered and her breath caught as she walked toward the blankets and searched for signs that they'd lain together. The makeshift bedding wasn't rumpled. *Thank heavens.*

Her gaze settled on the table as she walked toward it. She picked up the silver chalice and looked into its wide bowl, then gave it a sniff. Clean. The cup had not been used.

Aye, 'twas no doubt Lara's doing, but clearly her husband had remained faithful to his vows. Feeling a little better now, even though she dreaded dealing politely with that strumpet Lara o'er the next days, she left the chamber, closing the door behind her.

As she exited the building, she wondered where next she should look for Bao. Had he gone to their chamber? Aye, mayhap, once he'd spurned Lara's favors, he'd decided to await Jesslyn there. With a lighter heart, she skipped towards the entrance to the keep. Tonight, he would become her husband in truth.

* * *

"What an *ass* he is, Grandmother! He takes great delight in destroying every bit of pleasure I endeavor to have! Why can he not just let me *be*?" Branwenn said as they listened to the bells.

Lady Maclean knew well what was going on between the two, but with Callum and his wife leaving in the next few days, she decided not to broach the subject. After all, neither Callum nor Branwenn seemed in the least aware of what these overt acts of animosity signified. And Branwenn would no doubt be wed the next time they met. "He's only trying to protect your virtue, my dear. He, being a man, is well aware of the trouble a lass can find herself in on a night such as this. Most of these young men are deep into their cups, after all, and their wits have flown to the hills."

"But I was only dancing, and there was a crowd surrounding us. What harm could have come to me?"

Sighing, Lady Maclean shook her head. "None, I wager. But I feared he'd drag you away if I didn't do as he demanded and have you come stand with me."

"He's such an *ass!*" Branwenn repeated. "*I hate him!*" She turned and placed her hand on Lady Maclean's arm. "I'm sorry, Grandmother, I know you love him, but he's the most rude, dreadful, arrogant, mean, suspicious man I've ever met!"

"I know, lass. But, he'll be leaving soon enough, and then you will not see him again for quite a long time, I'm sure."

It did not escape Lady Maclean's notice that a fleeting look of sadness played over the lass's countenance before it was quickly replaced with irritation. "Good. That pleases me greatly."

* * *

When his wife entered their bedchamber not long after the chiming of the bells, Bao pretended sleep. He knew from the disaster of the evening that he'd be taking his sister to the nunnery on the morrow or the day after at the latest, and leaving for Perth from there, but for now he wanted to be near Jesslyn. He feared speaking to her, however, feared breaking the spell he'd conjured in his mind that all was well, would be well with them.

Bao watched her through slitted eyes as she snuffed all the candles before disrobing in the glow of the hearthfire light. His heart nearly pounded out of his chest when she didn't even leave the thin covering of her chemise on this time. When she climbed in beside him and draped herself over him with her head resting on his shoulder, he finally opened his eyes and stared at the shadows above. He wanted her more than he wanted his next breath, but he couldn't bring himself to make a move in that direction. Not after his near betrayal of their vows and not when his thoughts were still ensnared by worry over his sister.

If Callum hadn't interrupted his arrangement with Lara when he had, Bao would now have that deed in his possession. He'd have ruined his chances with Jesslyn for evermore, but at least he'd have protected his sister from that devil, Giric MacBean.

Now, all his plans for his sister, for himself, were crushed into dust.

* * *

Bao had almost drifted to sleep long moments later, but came instantly awake when he felt the glide of Jesslyn's knee over his groin as she tucked her calf and foot between his closed thighs. His manhood, which had been at half-mast since she'd settled into him, now grew turgid and long with the new rush of blood. An involuntary groan burst past his lips.

She lifted her head from his shoulder. "Did I wake you?" she asked softly.

"Nay." His voice sounded gruff, even to his own ears.

"Are you ill from ardent spirits, then?" She struggled to sit up.

Bao sucked air through clenched teeth. "Nay!" He clamped his hand over her naked thigh. "Do not move." He lifted his head, pulling aside the fur-topped blanket at the same time, and slowly ran his eyes up her curved form until they rested on her face. With a shaking hand, he stroked her cheek. "Be you flesh or phantasm?

He felt her relax. Then she defied his order and lifted her hand to his cheek. "I assure you, I be of this world," she replied softly. "I'll draw some water for you, if it please you?"

Mayhap a bit of distance was needed. "My thanks." He slid his hands from her body and dropped his head back onto the pillow. With eyes closed, he listened, imagining each of her movements as she performed her task: The shuffle of her feet across the rush mat; the clatter of the silver cup as the ewer hit its rim; the gentle *swoosh* as the water exited its container; the *glub, glub, glub* as it filled the empty cup; the heavy *bu-bump* as the ewer was placed back on the wooden washstand. And, finally, the soft pad of her feet as she made her way back over to him.

With one knee on the bed, she leaned over him. "Here, lift your head and drink this down." She placed one hand behind his head and the cup up to his lips, then tipped it enough to force him to drink.

Bao's eyes lighted on the coin that dangled between

her breasts as he quaffed the cool liquid. 'Twas the coin she'd refused to take back all those sennights past. Branwenn must have put it back in her possession. He loved his sister. He hadn't noticed it earlier when Jesslyn had undressed. Joy expanded inside him and without further thought, he lifted his hands, molding them to her breasts.

She jerked at the contact, causing a bit of the water to dribble down Bao's neck, but relaxed, and gave him a smile. Without looking, she placed the empty cup on the table next to the bed as she kissed the liquid from his neck. The cup teetered and rolled onto the floor with a *thunk*.

Growling, Bao dipped his head and took Jesslyn's breast into his mouth, warming his cold tongue on the rosy peak as he brought her other knee up onto the bed. His earlier dire thoughts forgotten in the fog of his returned desire, he lifted her hands to rest on his shoulders, then stroked his own down her back and across the rounded planes of her derriére.

She shivered and threw her head back with a moan. She tried to straddle him, but he wouldn't allow it. He kept her where she was, feasting on first one peak and then the other as he lightly traced her supple figure with his calloused hands.

Bao released her nipple and gazed at the results of his loving. "Your breasts are so beautiful," he said, bringing both of his palms up under them to lift and weigh them. "The babe's made them just a bit fuller." He looked up, into her passion-glazed eyes. "You'll tell me if what I do hurts, will you not, my love?"

Highland Grace

She nodded. "Aye," she said, rubbing her nipple across his lower lip.

He tickled the peak with the tip of his tongue, wetting it once more. Then he lightly blew on it, causing the already puckered tip to tighten even further. Bringing it deep into his mouth, he suckled and quickly tongued it, in a replication of what he planned to do to another, even more responsive nub later.

She grasped the back of his head and pressed him against her breast. Her head flew back and a guttural moan erupted from her throat.

Bao gorged on her as he stroked her flesh. He made a slow inventory of her body using his palms and fingertips. He first traced the length of her slim arms up to her rounded shoulders and neck. Then he took a trip down the sides of her breasts to her babe-filled belly and plush hips. He blazed a trail down and over her bent-kneed long limbs and then moved back up to cup the cheeks of her buttocks in his palms, stroking the fine hairs of the feminine outer lips of her labia lightly with the tip of his little finger.

Her moans grew louder. She jerked and trembled and finally climaxed. "Oh, God!" she sobbed. Bao didn't stop. He continued suckling her breast and teasing the sensitive lips of her sex, knowing it would intensify and lengthen her release.

But his seed nearly burst from his loins when he felt the rush of Jesslyn's juices drench his fingers. Groaning, he moved his hands from her buttocks to the curve of her back as she collapsed against him after her orgasm, her arms around his neck and her cheek resting on his shoulder. He pulled the long, flaxen, damp locks away from her shoulders and placed a kiss on one of their curves.

* * *

Jesslyn was still a bit light-headed from the intensity of the release Bao had given her. But she wouldn't be fully satisfied until they'd truly mated. She opened her eyes and saw the blue-veined thick, hard, *ready*, member of her husband. Graeme had begged her to touch him, taste him, but then he'd made her feel awkward, telling her she wasn't doing it right, so it had turned into more of a chore than a pleasure for her. Now she wondered if he'd been comparing her expertise to that of Lara's all those years. Mayhap she really wasn't good at it. She gazed again at her new husband's manhood and she wanted to touch him, love him the way he'd just done with her. Before she could talk herself out of it, she reached down, lifted it in her palm and squeezed.

He jerked and thrust her hand away. "Nay!"

Oh God. She *was* terrible at this after all. "Al-all right."

He put his arms around her and held her tight, his face in the curve of her neck. "I'm sorry, my love. I won't explain why, but I can never bear that touch."

She nodded. At first, she just felt relieved, but then his words sank in and her heart cracked. 'Twas clearly something terrible from his past. Mayhap, at least for now, 'twas best not to know.

"Now, where were we?" he said after a moment, placing his hands on either side of her jaw and bringing her lips up to meet his own.

Jesslyn lay across Bao's chest now, resting on her hip against his thigh with her legs still slightly bent at the knees, but no longer holding her weight. Some primal part of her understood that this man needed to stay in control of their lovemaking; that she should simply relax and give him complete access to her senses in order for both of them to find their pleasure.

He rolled to his side, delving deep into Jesslyn's mouth with his tongue, exploring the recesses, caressing the inside of her lower lip. He suckled her bottom lip a moment before moving down her jaw and teasing the dimple in her chin with the tip of his tongue and then kissing it. His hands positioned her, gently pushing her to her back and lifting her arms above her head. "Don't move these until I say you may," he murmured, meeting her eyes a moment.

Her heart leapt, but she agreed with a quick nod of her head.

Then he caressed her with his mouth and his hands. Everywhere. Over every bare inch of skin. But one. He kissed, licked, touched, pinched, nibbled, stroked, until she was sobbing with the need for release. "Please, take me!" she begged. He'd rolled her onto her side and was tickling the back of her knees with his tongue, following that with open-mouthed suction kisses and nips with his teeth. The action made her womb heavy with the need to be filled.

He raised his head from his ministrations. "How? How would you like me to take you, Jesslyn?"

"However it please you!"

"Then I shall take you first with my fingers. And

then, mayhap, with my mouth—would you like that, love?"

"Aye!"

"And then, while you are still in the throes of release, I shall push myself deep inside of you and mate with you the way I've dreamed of doing again so many times since our day at the waterfall." He pressed her onto her back once more and lifted her knees, spreading her thighs wide as he held them down against the bed. First, he looked at her for long minutes, which made her cringe with embarrassment. Then he bent his head and breathed in her scent before taking a long stroke from bottom to top with the tip of his tongue.

She cried out, her hips coming up off the bed. She dropped her hands to the top of Bao's head.

"Nay, lie still or I can't pleasure you the way I know you crave. And I've not given you permission to lower your arms, either." When she settled back with them flung above her head once more, he lifted his hand from her thigh and slowly entered her pulsing canal with his middle finger.

She twitched and trembled, gave out a soft moan of pleasure, but forced herself to lie as still as she'd been ordered to do.

With his other hand, he opened her labia wide and began his oral onslaught as he stroked in and out of her. He licked and nibbled. He teased her inner lips with the turgid tip of his tongue. When she felt a new flow of love juices rush from her passage, he glutted himself on it, groaning in delight, increasing Jesslyn's need by thrice.

She tossed her head from side to side, a strangled cry pushing past her clenched teeth. "Oh, God," she ground out, a feeling of hot and cold voluptuous pleasure running down her limbs as Bao stroked some inner pleasure center inside her womb. She opened her thighs wider still.

She was already close to climax when Bao began to flick her clitoris with the tip of his tongue as he massaged the sensitive spot in her vagina. She spasmed. "Ahhhh!" she screamed, feeling her orgasm in every nerve ending of her body. Her hips tensed and lifted high off the bed as she splintered into a million specks of starlight. And just as she felt the last wave crashing over her, Bao did something to give her another one. Three times more he sent her reeling into heaven. And, just as he'd said he would, as the last one was ebbing, he lifted her knees over his arms and pushed himself inside of her, riding the wild tide of her release.

* * *

Bao's gaze settled on the junction of their bodies. Black hair mingling with flaxen. Male encircled by female. Hard mating with soft. He closed his eyes tight and clenched his teeth as he struggled to keep himself from coming. She was just as tight as she'd been the first time. So narrow, in fact, that he'd thought he might hurt her again when he entered her. Thankfully, however, she'd been more than ready for him this time. But the feel of her inner muscles contracting around him was almost more than he could withstand without allowing his own release.

He felt her relax back on the mattress and opened

his eyes. "You are so lovely," he said fervidly. His gaze dropped to her slightly rounded belly. Lovely, and carrying his bairn, he reminded himself. "We must finish this with you astraddle me, for I fear I'll be too rough with you otherwise." Placing his arms under her back and shoulders, he rolled to his side and then his back, remaining inside her. Now she lay on top of him, limp, hot and drenched from the dew of her recent exertion.

"Can you stand one more, my love?" Bao asked as he rotated his hips under her, teasing the hooded nub of her pleasure center with his pubic bone. He pressed her hips down further, forcing her to take more of him inside of her. Her sheath tightened around him and Bao gasped.

"Mmm. That feels good," she mumbled. She raised up from her prone position on his chest and, using his shoulders as leverage, allowed him to manipulate her movements in the way he enjoyed.

Bao lifted his head and suckled her right breast into his mouth. He was close, so close. But he wanted to feel her climax around him, feel her milk him of his seed with those strong inner muscles. He nipped the turgid peak with his teeth.

She gasped and her sheath clenched.

Bao threw his head back. "Ahhh!" His hips jerked up just as she pressed down on him. His seed burst forth in the most intense pleasure-pain he'd ever experienced as he held her hips down and ground into the convulsing channel that so snugly clamped around him.

She cried out and collapsed onto his chest.

Bao kissed her temple.

After a moment, she lifted herself from him and he hissed in a breath, his cock still ultra sensitive to the tug of her feminine channel, but he didn't try to halt her retreat.

She rolled off of him and onto her back.

They spent some time catching their breaths and then he rolled over and kissed her, holding her head still with his palms on either cheek. After a long moment, he broke the kiss. "That was better than all the times I've imagined having you again," he murmured against her lips.

She smiled. "Aye."

He took possession of her mouth once more, lifting her limp arms and placing them around his neck, deepening the kiss before stroking his hand over her breast and down her side. He rested his hand over her swollen belly where their babe dwelled and felt the *tap, tap* of his bairn on his palm. He grinned against her mouth. "I believe we awakened the babe."

The babe tapped harder then.

She giggled. "Aye," she said and placed her hand on his arm. "I'm glad you gave me your babe that day at the fall," she murmured. "I've wanted it from the moment I realized its existence. Thank you."

"You *thank* me for getting you with child and then leaving you to defend your condition, take care of yourself and your bairns, without benefit of husband?"

Jesslyn shrugged. "Well, mayhap not that part of the tale."

"Aye, I should hope not."

* * *

"You've truly been traveling around the Highlands for so long? 'Tis so exciting!" Branwenn said to their first footer as he sat with her at the table and devoured his meal. He must not have eaten for a long while, she thought sadly. She glanced once again at her grandmother, who sat a few feet away by the hearth with Laird Donald enjoying a glass of spiced wine. She still held the pouch of salt in her lap that the stranger had given them when he'd requested entry. Branwenn hoped he could afford to give away his meager supply. Tho' he'd told them upon entry that he was of a good family, that his name was Reys ap Gryffyd, and that his father had been lord over a large estate to the south, his clothes were quite worn. But, they were of the finest scarlet and his leather boots, the work of a superior craftsman, giving credence to his assertion of gentle birth. Mayhap, he'd simply fallen on hard times during his journeys.

Reys shrugged. "Aye. It pleases me to meet new people, but the land this time of year is difficult to travel o'er," he replied after swallowing the portion of swan he'd jammed into his mouth.

Branwenn ran her eyes over their guest. He was such a handsome man. With eyes as blue as midnight and hair as black as pitch that fell just over his ears. Shorter than the Highland men liked to wear their own, but still very attractive. And he was tall of stature, too. A good augury for the new year. He was a big man as well. Not as big as Bao or Daniel, of course, but at least as big as that devil Callum. And she'd been eyeing that strange stringed instrument he'd placed next to him on the bench as well. Would he be willing to play it for her later? She hoped so. She loved music. Always had. In fact, Bao used to tease her mercilessly when she was a bairn because she was always trying to make sounds with anything that she found lying about. He especially hated it when she put dried peas in one of the silver wine flagons and shook it vigorously. For hours. The memory made her grin. "By what name do you call that instrument?" she asked, tipping her head in its direction.

Reys glanced down at it. "'Tis a *crwth*; 'tis akin to a stringed lyre." Placing his hand on its rounded base, he stroked the polished wood. "This be an instrument well known in the land of my kin."

"And where be that?"

"*Cymru*, some know it as Cambria."

"'Twas the land of my mother!" Branwenn turned on her seat and called out, "Grandmother! Reys is from Cambria, just as my mother was!"

Her grandmother's nod held indulgence. "We must hear all about you, lad, and what's brought you so far from your homeland," she said.

"Aye," Laird Donald agreed, "Mayhap, after you've finished your meal, you'll come sit by the hearth and give us a song or two and tell us your tale."

"Aye, I've a yearning to do just that," the man replied. Turning back to Branwenn, he asked, "Where be your mother, lass? I've a longing to see a fellow countryman after all this time."

"Alas, she died giving birth to me." His look grew more intent and she felt herself blush. "I was raised by my brother, Bao, who's the mightiest warrior in all this world."

"Bao? An odd name for a Highlander," he said.

"'Tis the name given him by *his* mother; she was from Cathay," Branwenn replied.

Reys's spine straightened and his look sharpened. "Was your mother's name Gwenllian wreic Gryffyd of Penrhos?"

A cold chill ran down Branwenn's spine. "Aye," she said slowly. "How know you this?"

"I didn't, not with any certainty, until now," he replied softly. "She was *my* mother as well."

Branwenn leapt from her seat, as a high-pitched ringing resounded in her ears. "I don't believe you," she said, her voice barely above a whisper. She swayed a moment before collapsing in a heap on the floor.

After a stunned moment, Reys leapt to his feet and pushed the bench aside, then knelt down beside her.

"Branwenn!" Laird Donald shouted. He rushed over to the prostrate figure, lying half on and half off the dais, and placed his hand on her cheek.

"What happened? Is she hurt, Lachlan?" Lady Maclean asked, struggling to rise.

"She swooned, I believe," Reys said.

"Aye, it looks that way," Laird Donald said. "Let's get her into a more comfortable position. Help me lift her onto the dais, lad," he said to Reys.

Lady Maclean came up to stand near Branwenn's prone form, worry in her eyes. Motioning to the young servant that stood next to them all, she said, "Here, lad, get us a bit of water and a cloth."

Grasping Branwenn's limp hand, Laird Donald murmured, "Branwenn? Can you hear me, lass?"

Reys took the dampened cloth from the servant and gave it to Laird Donald to place on Branwenn's brow.

Branwenn's eyes fluttered open. The face of Laird Donald swam before her a moment before she finally focused. Confused, she struggled to sit up.

Laird Donald put his arm around her shoulders and helped her adjust her position.

"What happened?" she asked dazedly, taking the damp cloth away from her face and tucking it in her other hand, which lay limp in her lap.

"You swooned, my dear," her grandmother said.

Branwenn's eyes made a slow scan of the faces of those huddled around her. When they settled on Reys, her head jerked back and she let out a short gasp. In a rush, the memory of their conversation flooded back. Without realizing she was doing it, she held out her hand and grasped her grandmother's wrist.

Her grandmother's sharp gaze settled first on Branwenn and then on Reys as she soothed Branwenn's tensed fingers with a stroke of her own. "Has this young man done something to offend you, Branwenn?" she asked stiffly. "He shall certainly be made to leave forthwith, if such is the case; doubt it not, my dear."

Reys remained silent, but his eyes held alarm and question as they fastened on Branwenn's countenance.

Branwenn shook her head. "Nay, Grandmother, Reys has done naught wrong. I must have risen too quickly and become a bit dizzy. Releasing her grandmother's wrist, she held her hand out to Reys and asked, "Will you help me to rise, sir? I believe my spell is well past now."

With a quick nod, Reys did as she requested.

"Will you play for us now?" Branwenn asked. She could not take her eyes from the man's visage. The longer she gazed upon it, the more she was convinced of their relationship. In fact, there was such a strong resemblance, she was amazed now that neither she nor the others had seen it immediately upon his arrival. But she was not yet ready to make known this twist in her life's tale. First, she wanted to know his reasons for looking for her. Did he plan some mischief, or was his search simply in answer to a need he felt to find a long-lost sibling?

"Aye, with pleasure, m'lady," Reys replied, his mien kind, less tense than the moment before. He turned, retrieved his instrument and descended the dais. Settling by the warmth of the hearth's fire, he began to play. With a voice clear and true he sang in his native tongue:

Hearken, sweet skylark...

When the last note was sounded, Branwenn clapped her hands with glee. "That was lovely. Will you play another?"

"I don't think that a good idea, lass," her grandmother said. "Not after the tumble you just took. I think it better that we find our beds instead and get our rest. The day has been long, and the night, longer still." Looking toward Reys a brief moment before turning back to Branwenn, she continued, "And I'm sure this young man would be pleased to get some sleep as well."

Disappointed, Branwenn replied, "Aye, Grandmother."

Her grandmother turned back to their guest and said, "I've had a chamber prepared for you in the north tower. I shall send a servant along with you to light your way. Mayhap, you'll play for us again on the morrow?"

"Aye, m'lady, if it please you. My thanks for the warm lodgings this bitter eve. 'Tis been awhile since last I rested in such luxury."

"You must stay here as long as you wish, lad. You've a wan look about you that bodes ill for your health. Traveling further in the ice and snow will only worsen your condition, I trow."

"My thanks, m'lady, for your hospitality," he replied before departing with the servant that had been summoned to lead him to his bedchamber.

"What a courteous young man our first footer is," her grandmother said to Laird Donald as he escorted her and Branwenn up the stairs to their chambers. "And, as the legend decrees, the new year is ripe with promise since he stepped o'er our portal."

"Aye," Laird Donald agreed. "And he's a talent with that stringed instrument as well. I've a want to hear much more of his playing o'er the next days until I depart. His voice is one of the best I've heard."

Branwenn was deep in thought. She had to tell Bao

of this discovery as soon as possible. She'd love to wake him now, but she dared not. Not with Jesslyn in the same room. Tho' she loved her sister-in-law dearly, this was not something that she wanted to share with her right away. She needed Bao, needed his strength and his insight. But, most of all, right this very moment, she needed her brother's strong arms around her, comforting her and telling her everything would be all right. Because, tho' she knew instinctively it was true, Reys was not the brother of her heart, the brother who'd raised her from a babe, who'd saved her life, who'd protected her, who'd cared for her, who'd sacrificed his freedom for her. Nay, he was kin by blood, but not by love. Not yet, at least. And mayhap, he never would be, if his motives for finding her were for some foul purpose.

They halted outside the door to Branwenn's chamber. "Good night to you, lass, and happy *Hogmanay*," Laird Donald said before bending down and giving her a kiss on her cheek.

"Branwenn, you look as worn as an old woolen rag. Get some sleep, my dear. There's much to do on the morrow to clean the keep of the remnants of our celebration," Lady Maclean said. And then she, too, gave Branwenn a kiss, adding a quick hug as well. "You're a good lass. I hope you enjoyed your first *Hogmanay* feast with us."

Branwenn nodded and swallowed a yawn. "Aye, Grandmother. I had a fine time. I especially enjoyed the dancing earlier—until Callum decided to meddle and destroyed my good humor."

"Fret not. You'll dance again when we celebrate *Bealltainn* in a few moons time."

Branwenn nodded. "Good night, then." She entered her chamber and closed the door behind her. She was torn. Part of her wanted to wait until her grandmother was abed and then find the chamber where Reys had been settled and question him more fully about his proclamation. But the other, more weary, part of her simply wanted to rest. Her grandmother was right; they had had a very long day. And she was exhausted. Her weariness won the battle and she prepared for bed. Surely, they'd find a way to have a privy discussion some time on the morrow. And besides, that would give her time to speak with Bao first as well. Mayhap, 'twould be better if he accompanied her when she questioned this new-found brother of hers. Aye, that seemed the best solution.

Her worries put aside for the moment, Branwenn went to bed. And dreamed she was a water nymph living in a sea cave, an auburn-haired, green-eyed warrior, her mate.

* * *

CHAPTER 11

Early the next morn, long before the bells of matins rang, Lara stormed across her bedchamber, her arms crossed over her chest and her lips curled in derision. She had no desire to aid the ladies of the keep with whatever duties needed doing after the feast of the night before. And she would be obliged to do it, she was sure, should she leave her chamber for any length of time once the household had awakened. She would much prefer to wander the outer perimeter of the keep in search of a likely candidate for her new pursuit. Most of the men had been released from their duties this day and 'twas the perfect opportunity for her to find a suitable lover.

She'd slept little after Callum and she had exchanged words last eve. He'd left their chamber a couple of hours ago and never returned, so she assumed he'd found a bed in another part of the keep. Which suited her needs perfectly.

Highland Grace

She chewed on her thumbnail. Mayhap, with a bit of wile, she might sneak out. She could go to the stables and have her horse saddled, and then take a ride on the glen. Aye, 'twas still black as pitch, but many of her best trysts had started in just this way.

Tho' the snow was a bit deep, she should be able to cross the landscape, if she was careful. The thought of staying in her chamber all day made her skin crawl. She simply could not be cooped up in this tiny room for hours on end without losing her mind. And, if she were cunning enough, she might just enjoy a tryst with a strong young warrior to help her while away the day.

Her plan firmly set, she rushed to the chest that held her fur-lined gown and cloak and quickly changed into them. With any luck at all, she'd be riding a young buck within the hour.

* * *

A knock came on the door just as the first bell of matins rang out and Bao jerked awake. After a quick glance at Jesslyn to see that she still slumbered, he rose and opened it with care. "Callum," he whispered, "What need you?"

"Have you seen my wife? She's not in our chamber, but no one knows where she went," Callum replied in like tones.

Bao shook his head. "Nay, I've not seen her. She wasn't in the great hall?"

"Nay. Nor the solar, nor the kitchens, nor any other corner of the keep." He looked down the darkened passage toward the stairs. "Where could she have gone?"

"Did you check the stables? Mayhap she went for a ride," Bao said.

Callum's eyes widened. "I pray not. 'Tis barely light out and there is much snow on the ground." He whipped around, saying, "I must find her. She may be endangering our babe," and rushed toward the stair.

"Wait! I'll go with you," Bao said loud enough for Callum to hear.

His cousin halted and gave him a nod.

"We should first go to the stables. If her mare is missing, then we'll know she's gone for a ride," Bao said.

"Aye. But we must make haste."

"I'll be dressed and ready before the taper burns half of a quarter down," Bao replied.

* * *

Bao and Callum moved carefully between the deep snowdrifts that covered the uneven land. The gatekeeper had told them that Callum's wife had left on horseback near an hour and a half past, alone, and that she'd headed toward the glen that bordered the loch. But when he and Callum had searched the glen, they'd found tracks made by two sets of horses' hooves. Bao looked at his cousin's tensed jaw and wondered with whom Callum would find his wife this time. 'Twas likely a man, for she seemed more than determined to cuckold her husband.

They were not far from the ruin where Maryn's attacker had taken her the day he'd tried to murder her. A niggling suspicion entered his head and he turned his horse in the direction of the ruin.

Highland Grace

"Where go you?" his cousin called out, turning his horse to follow.

"Remember you the old roman ruin?" Bao said over his shoulder. "She might be there."

"To the ruin, then."

* * *

Lara lay on top of her fur-lined mantle, on her back in the remnants of an ancient stone building where her newfound lover had brought her earlier. The three walls that weren't tumbled into rubble gave them enough privacy, but the floor was snow-covered earth and there was no roof to the place. Her eyes stared up at the cloudless sky as the young warrior pushed himself inside of her, rocking against her as he panted and moaned.

Naught. She felt naught. Would he never finish? She was ready to ride back to the keep, thoroughly disgusted with the outcome of this tryst.

She'd picked him because of his bulk. After the thrill she'd received with Bao's manhood, she'd always striven to find others of comparable size. And she had found one today—but 'twas not the same. Oh, she'd trembled at that first sensation of pain when he'd taken her the first time, but it hadn't been enough to give her the intense pleasure she craved. So she'd made him take her twice more, but it wasn't working. And now, the initial excitement had completely palled, leaving only a vague feeling of revulsion in its wake. How ugly men were when they rutted. But she had encouraged him this last time to be rough with her, and he was taking great pleasure in that, it seemed. And, with any luck, it might cause her to lose this whelp of her stepbrother's making that she had no desire to carry any longer. That possibility was worth her current disappointment. "Are you almost done? I've grown weary of your fucking."

"Bitch! You know you like this," he rasped, grinding even more deeply into her as punishment.

Lara winced and then laughed bitterly. "Nay, I do not. Make haste, I need to get back to the keep."

"So you like it fast, do you?" he said, and then he slammed against her mons in rapid, harsh strokes, thrusting deep, until, finally, his movements became jerky and, on a long groan, he erupted inside of her again. His breath coming hard now, he rolled to his side, his arm flung over his eyes and said naught further.

Lara rose and straightened her skirts. When a shadow fell over her, she looked toward the door. "He raped me, Callum! Kill him!" she cried, flinging herself into her husband's embrace.

"You lying cunt! You begged me for it!" the young warrior shouted as he shoved his manhood back into his braies and struggled to rise to his feet.

Her husband thrust her behind him and Bao took hold of her upper arm, then dragged her away from the scene, forcing her to stand with him near the place their horses were tethered.

* * *

A battle cry erupted from Callum's lips as he rushed the other man, pushing him against the back wall with a "*whoof*" and a sharp right hook to the jaw. He

Highland Grace

pummeled into the man's abdomen with his fist and pressed his forearm into the man's neck, nearly strangling him with it. "Whoreson! You'll die this day by my bare hands!"

The other warrior struggled to break free, first pounding his fists into Callum's side and then shoving his hand over Callum's face to push his head back. "I did not rape her! I swear it!" he said, his voice choked, compressed.

Callum looked into the reddened face and arrogant gray eyes of his opponent and lowered his fist. He kept his arm against the warrior's neck, however. He forced breath into his lungs as he settled his hand over the pommel of his sword. "Tell me why I shouldn't cut that thing off that dangles 'tween your thighs, Robert MacVie."

"Because I didn't do the like to you when you took the same pleasure of my sister eight years past," the man croaked as he tried to pull free of Callum's hold. "And, God knows, I wanted to kill you then. But I dared not touch the prized grandson of the chieftain of clan Maclean, else my neck be noosed."

Callum stepped back a pace and dropped his arm. "Your sister shared her favors with others before me, and well you know it. Besides, what man says nay to a gift freely offered?"

MacVie rubbed his throat and coughed. "'Tis my defense as well, old friend," he rasped. He gave Callum an angry glare. "And 'twas of further enticement that I had the chance to avenge my sister's disgrace."

Callum growled low in his throat. "She was not

disgraced. At least not by me. And, is she not now wed to the man she strove to make jealous with her antics? She is lady of a great estate, just as your family wanted for her. I know of no lasting disgrace on her for her youthful indiscretions." Callum curled his hands into fists at his sides. "But this...this I can't abide. You've lain with my *wife*. While she carries a *babe* in her belly."

MacVie's nostrils flared. "Mayhap you should keep closer watch on that cold-as-stone whore of a wife of yours then, because *she* came to the soldiers' quarters looking for a lover; I did not seek her out." He flung his arm in the direction of the keep. "I've nearly the whole of the lodge as witness to my claim, should you only inquire there."

Callum's shoulders sagged. He hadn't believed his wife's tale of innocence the night before, but with this new evidence of her treachery, his hope that there was still some way to make the marriage work for both of them was destroyed. "Nay, no need. I believe you." He turned away and closed his eyes tight against the humiliation and anger that seethed within him. "Get you out of here before I change my mind and cut you, as you deserve," Callum said hoarsely.

MacVie moved around Callum and walked outside.

* * *

Bao strode over to the young warrior as he approached his mount. "You are on night watch for the next two moons. Starting now. Go soldier."

Bao noted MacVie's clenched jaw and knew he was struggling to hold back a retort to his lieutenant. With a sharp nod, the man mounted his horse and turned it in the direction of the fortress, kicking it into a canter in his hurry to be away.

* * *

When Callum was at last alone in the ruin, he turned and gave the chamber a quick inspection. His eye snagged on a crumpled scroll where his wife's mantle had been. His brows slammed together. *What is this then?* Some further proof of betrayal on his wife's part, no doubt.

He moved toward it and picked it up. After unfurling it, he scanned the words and his heart dipped into his belly before lodging like a clod of mud in his throat. *Branwenn? A slave?*

And he recognized both signers of the document. He bit back a growl and flung himself out the door, pounding in the direction of his wife and Bao.

"I believe this is the *deed* you demanded from my wife last eve." Callum thrust the scroll in Bao's hand.

Lara rushed him, making a grab for the document. "Nay! 'Tis mine!"

Callum turned a stony glare on her. "Stand back. I'll speak to you later in privy." He took hold of Bao's arm and cocked his head in the direction of the loch, in a petition for them to move a distance away from his wife's prying ears.

His cousin nodded and once they were several paces away, he opened the deed and looked at it. "My thanks. I am in your debt for a lifetime for this."

"Nay, you are not. My wife bribed you with the promise of this document?"

"Aye."

"I've met the stepbrother. He held this from you?"

Bao nodded. "For years, he only held it because I continued to pay his price, but last year he got a glimpse of Branwenn, and now he will not rest until he has her. No amount of coin will appease him."

Callum ground his teeth and looked in his wife's direction. She stood with her hand resting on her palfrey's neck looking back at them. "I tried to get the truth from Lara last night, but she refused to say more than the lie she told when I came upon the two of you. I finally left our chamber, as I was too angry to deal with her any longer. I'd hoped to speak to you this morn, after tempers had cooled, but when I discovered her missing…," he sighed, "well, it turned out a boon for you in the end."

His cousin gripped his shoulder. "Mayhap all will be well between you once she has her babe. It may soften her."

Callum shrugged. "I'm going to take her from here, take her back to our holding, before she can cause more mischief."

"Aye, that is a wise course."

"I shall confine her to a portion of our keep, for at least the remainder of her childing. She is a danger to our babe, a danger to others, and, ultimately, a danger to herself."

His cousin only nodded. Callum studied him a moment. "Last eve Lara said that you were selling yourself at the king's palace. I didn't believe her, but now…with this…. Is it true?"

Bao didn't look at him. He kept his gaze on

something in the distance. "Aye."

Callum stared, wide-eyed at his profile. His throat constricted. "Was Branwenn in the trade as well, then?"

Bao's spine straightened and he did look at him then. His eyes were ablaze. "Nay! She is an innocent and knows naught of that other life I led."

Callum's lungs opened and he was able to take a breath. "Were you that desperate for coin?"

"Not in the way you think." Bao sighed and ran his hand through his hair. "I made enough as a contracted soldier to support us but I was determined to make my fortune so that I could pay Giric's price for not taking Branwenn, but also so that no man could ever again call me slave. I desired a worthy match for my sister as well, and that could not be if I had no dowry for her."

"Does anyone else in the family know of your other profession?"

"Only Jesslyn." Bao looked at the scroll in his hand. "This means more to me than anything else I own."

"Does Branwenn know about it?"

"Nay. And I don't intend to tell her." Bao's eyes drilled into Callum's and Callum understood. "Aye, I'll not say a word."

"Good."

"Keep it safe—or better yet, *burn it*." Callum jogged over to his steed and took the flint and striker from his satchel. When he was back at his cousin's side, he handed them to him. "Let us see an end to this now." From the corner of his eye, he saw his wife turn with her horse's lead and walk away. "Stay where you are!" he yelled at her. When she halted and turned a virulent glare on him, he smiled. "I'm having much the same thoughts about you, *dear*."

His cousin made quick work of setting the scroll aflame and as they watched its edges turn brown, then black with cinder, smelled the smoky flesh-smell of burning vellum, Lara screeched her discontent behind them.

After they'd stomped out the last remaining ember and Callum had helped his wife to mount, the three turned back toward the keep.

* * *

Bao's insides churned, in spite of the rekindled hope for his future with Jesslyn now that the deed was destroyed. Should he tell her about it? About Lara's bargain? About the fact that he'd agreed to it, and would have gone through with it? She'd made love to him last night, freely and passionately, and he knew that had been a huge step for her to make, proof of her restored trust in him. To tell her now that he'd nearly broken their vows—destroyed their marriage again—might be the last death knell for them. Especially with the other indiscretion that hung, like so much dried offal, between them, tho' they'd both managed to ignore it and move forward without speaking of it.

He looked at Lara from the corner of his eye. But Callum was determined to get his wife gone from here quickly. And no doubt he'd keep her under lock and key until their departure in the morn. Mayhap, 'twas not *so* necessary to tell Jesslyn just now. Later, mayhap even sometime after their babe was born, he would tell her.

Aye. That seemed a good plan.

* * *

Lara fumed as she plodded along beside her husband. The two men were utterly silent. They hadn't said more than a handful of words since they left the ruin. Her husband was angry and she couldn't help dreading what he planned for her, but she refused to mewl and beg for his forgiveness. Let him do as he would with her, she thought with false bravery, for 'twould only make her that much more cunning in her devices.

She turned her gaze to Bao. She hadn't finished with him—or Jesslyn—yet. But how to lay waste to them before she departed this place? She'd seen how he'd treated the young warrior and the reverence the man had given him. Mayhap, the best way to ruin him would be to let his warriors learn of his shameful past. They'd not be so eager to obey him then, she was sure.

"We leave at first light on the morrow, wife," Callum told her curtly, finally breaking the silence.

Lara nodded once, but kept her gaze focused straight ahead, not yet daring to meet his eyes.

"I shall see that provisions are prepared for your journey, cousin," she heard Bao tell her husband. "Do you require anything else?"

"Aye. I wish for my mother to stay on here a sennight more, as originally planned. I would rather my mother not have any part in the preparations I intend upon our arrival home."

"'Twill be done. We'll send her home with an escort of Maclean warriors when her visit is done."

"My thanks," Callum replied.

* * *

Bao stepped into his bedchamber an hour later to find his wife up and dressed.

"Where were you?" she asked as she walked toward him.

He'd tell her. Later. For now, he just wanted to be with her, knowing that he would not have to leave her, knowing that he would not have to take his sister to a nunnery. "I was with Callum. He needed me to help him with something."

"Mmm."

"Are you ready to break your fast?"

She smiled. "Aye."

* * *

Jesslyn and Bao had barely finished their meal when they heard Daniel shout, "*Tis time! Grandmother! Jesslyn! Aunt Maggie! 'Tis time!*" as he pounded down the stairs from the upper floor.

Leaping to their feet, they rushed across the great hall, through the arched doorway, and into the antechamber leading to the stairs and the door of the keep.

Bao strode over to Daniel and took him by the arm. "What are you raving about, brother? What mean you, 'Tis time'?"

Daniel ran his hand through his hair. "Maryn. The babe. Her water broke. 'Tis time," he answered.

"That's wonderful! Oh! But, I need to prepare the linens!" Jesslyn said. Turning to Bao, she said urgently, "Have a servant bring up several buckets of water; we'll need to heat it on the hearth. And make sure they bring more peat and kindling as well." She darted up the stairs then with n'er a backward glance.

Bao turned back to Daniel. "I must deal with the water and peat; you need to find our grandmother. Try the kitchen garden."

Daniel nodded and headed through the door of the great hall, evidently intending to take the back way to the kitchen.

* * *

Jesslyn flew through the open doorway of the laird's bedchamber and came to a halt. Maryn was busily poking at the embers in the hearth, humming a merry tune and acting as if naught of import was about to take place. An image of her friend standing at the window upstairs in the solar the day she discovered her childing state, fussing and gnawing at her nails over the fact that she had no idea how to be a mother, flashed through Jesslyn's mind just then. Was this an act or was she truly this calm? Jesslyn decided she'd best tread lightly until she was sure of Maryn's state of mind. "Would you like some help with that?" she asked, coming up beside her friend.

Maryn glanced up from her task, a look of surprise on her countenance. "I didn't hear you come in," she said, and then turned her gaze once again to the hearthfire. Shaking her head, she answered, "Nay, 'tis almost done." She tipped her head to the side and gave it a quick toss, indicating a stool nearby. "Have a seat. Would you like a bit of wine? Daniel was so kind to bring me a flagon-full earlier."

"Nay, I've just had some in the great hall," Jesslyn replied, settling on the stool. Leaning forward, she placed her elbows on her knees and twined her fingers together, saying with care, "Daniel came down to tell us you were in your childbed time. Are you, Maryn?"

She shrugged. "Aye," she said in a barely audible whisper.

Jesslyn's heart tripped and then began beating wildly. She was not prepared for this! She looked toward the doorway and then back at Maryn. Where was Grandmother Maclean? Or Aunt Maggie? Why weren't they here yet? She had no idea what came next or what she should do to help her friend. "Mayhap, you should be abed?"

Dread filled Maryn's voice when she replied, "Nay, not yet. Please?"

Jesslyn jerkily nodded her head. "Al...All right," she replied.

Thankfully, Lady Maclean bustled through the doorway at that moment. "Maryn, my dear, whatever are you doing? You shouldn't be troubling yourself with that hearthfire right now!" She strode over to stand near Maryn. "Here," she said, placing her arm around Maryn's thickened waist, her other hand on Maryn's upper arm, "let me help you over to the bed; you should lie down now."

"Nay, Grandmother Maclean. I'm not ready to lie down just yet," she replied, digging her heels in so that Lady Maclean couldn't move her.

Lady Maclean's arm loosened. "Then let us walk around the chamber together awhile."

Highland Grace

"The water is being brought up now," Maggie said brightly as she walked through the opened doorway. "My son came down just a moment ago and I told him to take Daniel and Bao to the training fields to help Daniel work off his worry. Laird Donald went as well; I believe he's just as distressed as Daniel." She pressed her lips together. "My daughter-in-law is still abed, it seems," she said, disgust in her voice.

Jesslyn rose and took the clean tunics that Maggie held folded in her arms from the older woman and placed them on top of the chest at the end of the bed. They would wear the garments over their own gowns once the childbed began.

Jesslyn was growing more anxious as the moments passed. The only other birth she'd been involved in had ended in death. And there had been so much blood. And screaming. A shudder ran down her spine, taking her by surprise. She cleared her throat. "Mayhap I should find my son and take him to Niall's house for the remainder of the day. He's sure to worry if he isn't allowed to see me otherwise."

"Aye, that's a fine idea, my dear," Lady Maclean said as she strolled with her lumbering granddaughter-in-law away from the hearth. "You mustn't rush back," she said gently, a light of understanding in her eye. "Maggie and I can handle the childbed just fine on our own, if need be."

Maryn held out her hand toward Jesslyn. "Nay! You must be here when my babe comes! Promise me you'll not be gone long!"

Jesslyn's heart twisted. No matter how fearful she

was feeling, it could not compare to the fear her friend must be feeling at this moment. After all, Maryn's own mother had died giving birth to her. She must wonder if she will survive the strain of birth this day. Jesslyn nodded. "Aye. I shall be back in a short while, worry not. I only want to see to my son first."

She stepped over the portal and to the side, as the three servants that had carried the buckets of water and a tub up the stairs and down the passage prepared to enter the laird's bedchamber. A fourth and fifth filed behind the others, carrying peat and kindling. Moving past them, she hurried down the stairs and out of the keep. Her son was most likely at his and Niall's fortress. The two lads spent most of their days there now that it had been completed. *With* mangonel. But they were only allowed to propel balls made of wound-up woolen hose in the weapon, much to their dismay, and her and Lady Maclean's bliss. After both Bao and Daniel had explained the importance of such a tool to a lad's deeper happiness, and had promised to make sure it was made in a way that it couldn't hold anything too heavy, nor hurl very far, both Jesslyn and Lady Maclean had given their permission.

* * *

Bao, Daniel, Callum, and Laird Donald had decided to work on cleaning up the remains of the bonfire instead of going to the training fields. This endeavor required just as much strength and would keep them busy for the remainder of the day. They'd already removed three cartloads of wood and ash from the site, but had at least thirty more to fill before they'd see the bottom of the pile. Where embers still burned, water was used to douse the flames. Most of the warriors were given the day to rest and were either in their quarters or with their ladies, enjoying the holiday from routine. The men assigned to the gate and lookout positions on top of the curtain wall were working in four-hour shifts throughout the day, allowing all of them a bit of extra rest after the late night they'd all had enjoying the *Hogmanay* feast. It was still early, not yet mid-morn, and the first shift would not be relieved for another hour.

Branwenn crossed the courtyard, intent on speaking with her brother about their newly arrived guest—and her evident kin. She'd awakened later than usual and had just come downstairs a few moments before, only to be informed that Maryn was nearing her childbed time. When Branwenn had then rushed upstairs and pounded on Maryn's chamber door, Grandmother Maclean had forbidden her from entering the room, saying unwed lasses were not allowed to see such. The lady had then entreated her to find Daniel and Bao and stay with them.

She was pleased to do her grandmother's bidding, as this tangle she found herself in seemed even more urgent than Maryn and Daniel's forthcoming parenthood. The sun cast a bright ray of light on the fresh-fallen snow that blanketed the earth, blinding her a moment. Halting her pace, she blinked several times. When her vision cleared, she saw Bao lifting a half-burned pine log into a cart. He was bare-chested! She shivered with cold. How could he stand to be so naked in this bitter weather? The man wasn't human. And then she caught sight of Daniel and Callum. Neither one of them were wearing anything on top either! A shiver of a different kind passed through her at the sight of her too-handsome, broad-shouldered, very muscular, nearly-naked nemesis. Tipping her nose in the air, she pressed on, telling herself it had been a shiver of pure revulsion. And he did *not* look like the warrior in her dream last night, not one wee bit.

* * *

"How long have we been doing this now, do you suppose?" Daniel asked.

Callum looked at the position of the sun. "Mayhap a half hour."

"Not so long, then," Daniel said.

Bao clapped his brother on the shoulder. "Worry not. She's under the care of well-skilled hands. Naught bad will happen, only good. And in a short time, you'll be holding your new bairn in your arms."

"That's right, lad," Laird Donald said, his voice robust, as if he were trying to convince himself as well, "and Maryn will be there with you. She's a strong lass, always has been. And she's young, as well. Not in her middle years, as her mother was when she gave birth to Maryn. That makes a difference, mark me well."

Daniel nodded and turned back to the remnants of the bonfire. He lifted another log from the pile and tossed it onto the cart. "I'll not stay down here much longer. I must know how my wife fares."

* * *

"Bao," Branwenn said, motioning with a wave of her

hand to get his attention. When he turned toward her, she said, "May I speak with you a moment? Privily?"

Her brother dropped the end of the log he'd just lifted and strode toward her. "Aye? What need you?"

With a glance past him to the others, she decided she needed a bit further distance from them, in case they could hear their voices. "Put your shirt and tunic back on and let us take a walk."

His eyebrows slammed together with a look of concern, but he said naught further, only turned and pulled on his clothing. Then, clasping her upper arm, he scuttled her out of the upper bailey, across the courtyard, and through the gate of the keep.

* * *

"I wonder what that was all about?" Callum said, staring after the retreating pair.

"Mayhap she's angered because our grandmother will not allow her in the room with Maryn while she gives birth to our babe," Daniel said with a shrug.

"Aye, the lass does like to be in the middle of things," Laird Donald said.

A flash image of her naked, in the middle of his bed, with him straining above her tripped through Callum's mind before he slammed a steel bulwark in place to block it. Feeling guilty and disgusted with himself, he pretended indifference with a shrug, then turned back to his task.

* * *

Branwenn swallowed her complaints as she hustled to keep step with Bao.

They were halfway across the glen, going toward the

wood they'd dwelled in so many moons past, before Branwenn finally spoke. Out of breath, she wheezed, but managed to say, "Bao! We can slow down now. I vow, no one pursues us."

He glanced over at her and slowed his pace. "Too well do I know you. There is something very amiss; I can tell by the panic in those purple eyes of yours. When we're safe in our cave, you'll tell me all, agreed?"

"'Tis much too cold to meet in that barren cave! Why can we not speak out here, where at least the sun's warmth can reach us?"

"Because, I want to be in a more privy place when you give me your tale. We'll build a fire, worry not."

It took a while, but they managed to find enough peat turves and kindling in the cave to build a fire. They'd used the shorter route to their cave, climbing the pine tree and traversing the limestone outcropping that led to the fissure, which led to the opening of the cavern.

The fire was barely built before Bao began his interrogation. "What has you so distraught? And don't give me half-truths. I want it plain and brief."

"I met my brother last night. The one with whom I share blood—"

"*What?*" he barked.

"—is that plain enough?"

Bao's eyes drilled into her and he gave her a grim nod to continue.

"His name is Reys ap Gryffyd; his mother was Gwenllian wreic Gryffyd."

Her brother's brows lowered. "How?" he asked, his

voice grave.

Branwenn shrugged, enjoying herself now. Bao would take care of everything, she had no worry of that. And after the mad dash he had put her through and the rude way he had demanded she give him her tale, he deserved a bit of a blow to his arrogance. "He was our first footer. And Grandmother asked him to stay on as long as he wishes."

He studied her for a long moment. She couldn't read the expression in his gaze. It was dark, guarded. When he spoke at last, he asked, "Are you glad that he's found you?" He looked into the fire. "Pleased to find out you have real kin?"

Branwenn dropped her chin to her knees and shrugged. "I suppose I am." She picked up a chunk of bark that had fallen off one of the logs and tossed it into the fire. "I've not spoken more than a few words to him since I found out our relationship." Shaking her head in self-disgust, she continued, "I actually swooned when he told me! Do you believe it?"

Her brother grinned and returned his gaze to hers. His eyes were sad. "I would have loved to see that."

Branwenn slapped his thigh. "I'm sure you would have, you beast! I know not how Jesslyn stands you!"

"Do not change the subject, for 'tis not that easy to distract me," he said gruffly. "Now, tell me why you were so panicked if you're glad he found you."

Settling back in her earlier position, Branwenn said, "I don't know why, exactly. I suppose I fear that he'll take me from you. That I shall be forced to go with him and live in that other land that I know naught about."

"I will not let that happen. You're mine. *My* sister. I raised you, I provided for you. And Daniel will not let that happen, either. You are his sister as well."

Branwenn nodded. "Grandmother Maclean would no doubt have something to say about it as well. After all, she's set on training me in the ways of a lady. And I trow she's already found a few prospects for husband for me that she will not be happy to give up, either."

Bao rose. "We should get back to the keep, then. I shall meet with this man and learn what his intentions are regarding your newfound relationship," he said as he tossed dirt on the fire to put out the flames. Turning back to Branwenn, he grasped her hand, which she held out for him, and tugged, pulling her to her feet as well.

"Aye, but I want to be there with you when you speak to him," she said as she dusted off the back of her gown with her hands. "After all, it is *my* life you're talking about."

Her brother sighed, but nodded his head in agreement. "But I shall send you from the room if you become peevish. Understood?"

"Aye," she answered gaily, thoroughly unconcerned with Bao's threat.

* * *

CHAPTER 12

Branwenn led Bao to the north tower where Reys ap Gryffyd was lodged. After climbing the spiral of narrow stone stairs that led to the top-most chamber, she knocked on the thick wood door that filled the arched limestone doorway to Reys's chamber.

Reys turned at the sound. He'd risen only a few moments past and had still to put on his shirt. One side of his face was shaved, while the other still held soap. "Aye?" he called out. As he scrubbed the remainder of the herbal lubricant from his cheek, he strode to the door and opened it, believing one of the servants was on the other side. "Oh, beg pardon," he said to his guests, swinging the door shut once more and grabbing his shirt from the chest to put it on. When he was sufficiently covered, he opened the door again. Looking from Branwenn to the massive black-haired, slant-eyed warrior just behind her shoulder, he moved to the side and said, "Come in."

***

Branwenn scanned the chamber. The man was certainly tidy, she thought. He'd neatly folded and stacked his clothing in the chest at the end of the bed and his shaving implements were meticulously aligned on the top of the washstand. One of the linen cloths he must have used to bathe himself earlier had been folded lengthwise and hung on its wooden rod on the back of the stand, and his *crwth* leaned against the corner of the recessed seat of the window. Still gazing around the place, she said lightly, "This is my brother, Bao."

Reys acknowledged him with a slight nod.

Bao's nod was curt, she noticed, and he stood with his arms crossed over his chest with his feet spread. "So you believe my sister shares your blood? What proof have you of this rather odd notion?"

She gave Bao a questioning look, but remained silent. She'd already told him who the man's mother had been, and the resemblance they shared to one another was quite distinct, she thought.

"My home is Penrhos, on *Ynys Môn*, part of the kingdom of Gwynedd, in the land of the *Cymru* kings. My mother was the daughter of a *pencerdd*, the chief poet to Prince Owain Gwynedd. Her name was Gwenllian wreic Gryffyd." His gaze settled on her. "Just as was this lass's mother...and our father was Gryffyd Duy ap Kenneric, the *penteulu*, head of Prince Llywelyn ap Iorwerth's *uchelwyr teulu*, his noble warriors," he said the last with a bit of hesitation. His gaze returned to Bao. "My pardon, but speaking of my father is not an easy endeavor, as I lived with the broken spirit of the man for nigh on thirteen years until he took his final breath on the blood-soaked ridge overlooking the castle at Mold." He turned to Branwenn and said, "He took a Norman arrow through his eye in their campaign to wrest the fortress from the Norman invaders' grasp. The castle was captured, but our father paid the ultimate price."

Branwenn stared. "My father was the head of a Cambrian prince's noble fighting force?"

"Aye. And I, as well, served in the *uchelwyr teulu*. At least I had done, until I set out on my quest to find you."

She cocked her head. "How did you find me?"

"My father learned that our mother's body had been left at a small kirk near Duglyn. When he arrived there, the priest told him that a foreign looking lad of around ten summers had given instructions for burial and had given him our mother's full name, along with her betrothal ring, should her family ever come searching for her. Even with that, it has taken years, and the backing of my liege, to find you."

"And now that you've found Branwenn, what is your aim? To take her back to Cambria with you?" Bao said, his words clipped.

Reys nodded, "Yes—"

"Nay!" Branwenn said loudly and moved behind Bao, clinging to the back of his tunic.

* * *

Bao's heart stopped momentarily and then thrummed to life once more, beating a rapid tattoo in his chest. "Never," he said darkly.

"The lass is promised to one of the march lord's nephews. She must return with me and wed the man. Prince Llywelyn has decreed it. He's got the backing of King John of England and he needs the alliance to extend his influence further south."

"You had no idea the sibling you searched for was a lass—how could this prince have made a decree for her to wed?" Bao said.

"According to the dictate, if my sibling proved to be female, she is to wed the nephew. If my sibling proved to be male, then he is to wed the niece," Reys replied. "In either event, Prince Llywelyn intends to provide either the dowry or the bride price. That is how intent he is in this pursuit."

Branwenn peeked from behind Bao's arm. "And why can you not wed this niece, then?" she asked.

"Because I'm wed to someone else."

"You're wed? Where is your wife?" she asked.

"At home in Penrhos, taking care of my little ones."

She edged to the side a bit, but remained standing behind Bao. "You've bairns?"

"Yes, twin girls."

"Twins! How many summers are they?"

"They just past their second year not one moon ago. I've yet to see them, tho' I've tidings they fare well," Reys said. Bao heard sadness in his voice and that softened his anger toward the man, but there was still more to be confirmed. "How is it that my sister is sufficient to fulfill this requirement?"

Reys regarded him a moment before speaking. "We

are cousins, twice removed, to Prince Llywelyn. 'Tis a close enough relation to make an alliance."

* * *

Jesslyn was thrilled when Lady Maclean finally got Maryn to rest on the bed awhile, tho' her friend still chafed to rise every few moments. It had been seven hours since her water broke and her pains were coming in earnest now. They'd placed the childbed chair near the hearth, tho' Lady Maclean thought Maryn might be more comfortable if she had the babe on the bed. The tightening pains in her belly were more frequent and lasting a bit longer than they had been and Lady Maclean told them it wouldn't be long until the babe began to crown.

Daniel had surprised and horrified them all by checking on his wife's progress every hour for the last six, but he was so worried and determined, his grandmother had allowed the lapse.

"I need to stand again, Grandmother Maclean," Maryn said. "I feel another pain coming on." She lifted her arm in a silent bid for assistance.

Jesslyn side-stepped the older woman, saying, "Let me help you this time."

Unfortunately, another contraction began the moment she stood up and she gasped and leaned against Jesslyn for support.

Daniel opened the door just then and came inside. "How are you fee"—he looked at Lady Maclean, his eyebrows slamming together—"Why the hell is she out of bed again?!" He crossed the room to Maryn's side in four strides and took Jesslyn's place. Putting his arms around her, he held her to him to support her weight. "You need to rest," he said more gently.

She raised her dewy, heated face to Daniel and replied, "Nay, 'tis easier to bear the pains when I'm upright."

"Aye, 'twas the same for me when I had Callum—remember, Mama?" Maggie said.

Lady Maclean nodded. "Aye, you said it relieved some of the strain on your back."

"May I have some more of that water?" Maryn said to Jesslyn.

Jesslyn walked over to the washstand and poured some of the icy liquid out of the ewer into a silver cup. A servant had chipped some of the ice from the well and brought it up to them just before Daniel arrived. "Here, Maryn, drink this down and then I shall get you another cupful."

Her friend nodded and drank down the cold liquid.

"I've been going out of my mind with worry these last hours. I'm staying here with you through the birth of our babe," Daniel stated as she rested once more against his chest.

"Daniel!" Lady Maclean interjected, "That simply cannot happen. This is an untidy business and your wife deserves her privacy."

"If Daniel wishes to stay with me, I'm glad of it. After all, he got me into this state, he can certainly help to get me back out of it," Maryn said.

Daniel grinned at her. "You must not be in too much pain if your sharp tongue is still in such good form."

Maryn's eyes narrowed as she glared at him. "Ha!" But she turned back to Lady Maclean and added, "Besides, you know he's knowledge of the healing arts. It might be useful."

Lady Maclean shook her head. "Nay, lass—"

"And his presence comforts me," Maryn said with more force.

With a sigh of resignation, Lady Maclean nodded curtly. "Aye, all right then."

Maryn hunched over and cried out.

"Take a deep breath, lass, and then let it out on a sigh," Maggie instructed.

She pressed her cheek against Daniel's chest, allowing him to take most of her weight while she did as Maggie told her to do. When the contraction passed, she said, "My back aches!"

Daniel rubbed the muscles on either side of her spine, concentrating on the lower area where she seemed to have the worst pain. "Does that feel better?"

"Aye. Keep doing that, it helps."

Jesslyn was having a hard time swallowing down her panic. In only a few moons' time she would be in this very position. She could see that her friend was weary to her bones and, with each new pain, grew weaker still. How was she ever to find the strength to push the babe from her when the time came? Involuntarily, her hands fluttered up and covered her belly. Just then, the babe tapped against her womb and a warm glow filled her. She smiled. For the chance to hold her babe in her arms at last, she would—and could—do whatever she must.

Another moan erupted from her friend and she held

tight to Daniel. He placed a kiss on the crown of her damp head and continued to massage her back.

"As soon as this one passes, we need to get her back to the bed, Daniel," Lady Maclean said, coming up beside the two and placing her hand on Maryn's cheek. "Are you ready to have your babe, now, lass?"

Tears fell from the corner of Maryn's closed eyes. "Aye," she said on the sigh of her released breath. "But I must inspect the guardrobe once more before I do."

A tender smile crossed Daniel's countenance.

There must be some privy memory attached to her words, Jesslyn thought as he placed a kiss on the tip of Maryn's nose. "Need you my help, or do you prefer Jesslyn?"

"Jesslyn, please."

"I shall have more water prepared for the childbed," Lady Maclean said.

When Jesslyn emerged from the guardrobe with Maryn a few moments later, Daniel wrapped his arm around his wife's back once more and assisted her in her trek across the chamber.

"If you're staying, then you can get up on the bed behind your wife and help her push, when the time is right," Lady Maclean said to Daniel as they walked toward the bed. "Do you want to put on one of these tunics?"

Daniel shook his head, his eyes never leaving his wife's face. "Nay. 'Tis too hot in here as it is."

Jesslyn looked over at Lady Maclean, her brows raised in disbelief.

Maggie had her back turned away from the others as

she gathered more linens from the chest. "Nay, 'tis still a wee bit cold, I trow," she replied absently.

* * *

Nora Mairy MacLaurin made her entrance an hour later. She had a shock of red, curly hair and the biggest, bluest eyes her parents had ever seen. She was perfect, or so Daniel stated to Bao when he knocked at the door not long after learning the news of the birth. "Grandmother and Aunt Maggie said the same when I met them downstairs. I know there was still a bit of worry that the babe had been injured in some way by the blows Maryn received from that murderous horse marshal, Clyde Ramsey."

Daniel's jaw clenched. "Aye," he said grimly, "but God be praised, the babe was unharmed."

"How is your wife?"

Daniel gave his brother a tired grin. "She's well. Pert and fiery, just as I like her."

Bao returned his brother's grin and gave him a clap on the shoulder. "That pleases me, brother. Can Jesslyn be released from her duties yet, or does Maryn still have need of her?"

Jesslyn heard her husband's voice and a thrill of excitement passed through her. She rushed to place the last of the soiled linens in a basket for one of the servants to take down to be washed and, nervously running her hand over her veil and skirts, scurried to the door. Maneuvering herself around Daniel, she said softly to Bao, "Maryn has just fallen asleep. The babe is resting next to her as well." Turning her gaze to the new father, she said, "The babe will need to be placed in her cradle, do you want me to do it before I leave, or would you like to take care of the task?"

"I shall do it. You must find your rest as well; 'tis been a difficult, yet marvelous, day for all of us."

Jesslyn nodded and slid through the narrow opening in the doorway, straight into her husband's embrace.

Daniel quietly shut the door, leaving them their privacy.

"'Tis good to see you. I've missed you," Jesslyn said against her husband's chest.

"I've missed you, as well. Let us retire to our chamber, you're clearly weary and in need of rest."

Jesslyn nodded and allowed Bao to lead her to their chamber on the level above.

"What is *this?*" she exclaimed happily when she saw the steaming tub of water sitting by the hearth as they came inside.

"I thought you might enjoy a hot soak in a bath after the ordeal you've been through," Bao replied. "How *is* our babe, anyway? Is she well? I worried you might be putting yourself under more strain than is wise in your condition."

"Worry not. The babe has more strength than do I. In fact, she's moving about right now."

"Here," Bao said, lifting the filet and veil from her head, "let me help you undress. While you bathe, I shall find a servant to bring us our meal. We'll eat in our chamber this eve. I've much to tell you and I want to hear about my new niece, as well."

Jesslyn was so weary, she simply nodded and allowed her husband to do most of the work of getting her out of her garments.

"How went the childbed?" he said as he untied the laces holding her gown together on the side. "Was it hard for Maryn?"

Jesslyn pressed her lips together and gnawed on the bottom one, nodding. "Aye, 'twas hard for her. Tho' I trow the hardest part for her was the waiting. She was so weary by the time the babe's head crowned, I worried she'd not have the vigor she needed to push the babe from her. But once Nora was finally ready to be born, she slipped from Maryn with no difficulty, it seemed. And having Daniel there actually seemed to ease her."

He looked up from his task and met her gaze. "Would you like for me to be in the chamber with you as well, when the time comes for our babe to be born?"

Her drooping lids widened in surprise. "Would you"—she began to yawn—"want to be?" she finished behind her hand.

He nodded. "Aye, I would. I've a bit of experience, since I aided Branwenn's mother when she was in her childbed." He went still, his gaze intent. "Are you sure you can stay awake long enough to bathe and eat your supper?"

"Aye. The hot bath will ease my aching body, and tho' I'm weary, I'm even more famished."

He chuckled. "All right, then. Let's get you in the tub. Would you like a bit of the lavender oil added to the water?"

Jesslyn nodded, "Mmm, that would be nice, and the lavender soap, as well, if it please you. My thanks."

* * *

After settling his wife in the steaming bath and retrieving the herbal enhancements she required, Bao left the room in pursuit of a long-overdue discussion with his grandmother as well as a meal for him and Jesslyn.

He found his grandmother in her bedchamber readying for slumber. After bringing her a cup of wine to ease her thirst, he settled next to her by the hearth. "I've something of some import to tell you, Grandmother, which has to do with Branwenn and, mayhap, a coming war.

She sat bolt upright in her chair. "Tell me!" she demanded, the weariness instantly clearing from her eyes.

"Remember you the first footer, Reys ap Gryffyd?"

She gave him a short nod. "Aye."

"He has proved to be Branwenn's brother by blood."

She looked into the hearthfire a moment. "That explains Branwenn's odd behavior here in the great hall last eve." She glanced at him, saying, "She swooned—did she tell you?" before turning her gaze once more to the hearthfire.

Bao nodded. "Aye."

She pierced him with a purposeful look. "Give me the entirety of it, then," she said brusquely.

Bao told her all he knew of the man and his mission, explaining to her the reason that the fortress might come under siege since he did not release Branwenn to return with her brother-germane to his homeland.

Highland Grace

"Does Daniel know of this?" she asked when Bao paused to take a sip of his wine.

"Aye. I spoke with him about it just after I met Reys earlier today."

"And he's in full agreement that we should fight her kin to keep her from them?"

Bao nodded once. "Aye," he replied shortly.

"We all think of Branwenn as one of our own but, I must say, I cannot agree that we should keep her from her blood kin, whether we agree with their plans for her or not."

"You think it fine to send the lass off with strangers, blood kin or nay, when she is quite set against it?" Bao asked, disbelievingly.

His grandmother seemed just as astonished by his attitude. "The lass must wed, and if her blood kin can wed her to a nobleman, I see no real difference in what they planned for her from what our own plans for her have been."

Bao leapt to his feet. "The *difference* is that her kin are strangers to her—and to *us*—and so too will be this unknown nobleman to whom they are set on binding her for life! What if he's cruel, or depraved, or diseased? You know well that it is not beyond the realm of the possible that a royal prince might wed her to the worst sort simply for his own gain." Bao's lungs were blowing hard by the time he finished his diatribe.

She took a deep breath into her lungs and, slapping her hands on her knees, said, "Well, it seems we must prepare for war, then."

"Aye," Bao ground out. "We must." He forced

himself to calm down and settled back onto his stool. "I want to make plain that Reys will do all he can to urge his cousin withdraw his decision to use Branwenn as a pawn in his devices to gain influence in the march regions, so war may not be the final outcome." Sighing, he shrugged, adding, "Of course, there is no surety of success."

"When will we know if an army's been raised, do you suppose?"

"It should take Reys another few sennights to reach his homeland, and then, mayhap, a sennight more to gain an audience with the prince. If all goes well, the prince will either completely withdraw his edict or, mayhap, at least agree to certain conditions we insist upon for Branwenn's protection. If Reys cannot convince their royal cousin of these terms, then we will go to war." Bao shrugged. "Once negotiations are concluded, 'twill take at least a fortnight for his army to be raised and about a moon for them to arrive on our doorstep, I trow. I do not expect the siege before the spring."

* * *

When Bao returned to his bedchamber an hour later he was pleased to find that Jesslyn slumbered peacefully on their bed.

As he stood gazing upon her, she slowly opened her eyes, turned onto her back and stretched her arms over her head, flexing her feet and toes at the same time. He smiled down at her and caressed her thigh.

"Mmm. What hour is it? Have I slumbered long?" she asked.

"'Tis an hour past the vesper bell, you must only have slept for a short time after your bath. Our meal is being brought up now; you should dress. He retrieved her chemise and robe from atop the chest at the end of the bed and held them out to her. "Do you need me to assist you?"

She scurried to sit up, grabbing the garments. "Nay, just don't allow them entrance until I've put these on!"

Bao chuckled and moved toward the door to the chamber. "Worry not. I've no desire for any other than myself to behold the ripened treasures of your womanly form."

"And I have no desire for any other to see me in my nakedness evermore," she replied as she shimmied into her clothing.

A knock came at the door and Bao called out, "Hold a moment," and then, "Enter," when Jesslyn was covered once again. The servants trailed in carrying a small table, a trencher of food, a flagon of ale and some fresh water for the wash stand. Once the table and supper were placed by the window, where Bao indicated they should go, he turned back to his wife and assisted her to her seat.

As the tub and water was cleared out of the chamber, Bao and Jesslyn ate their meal, saying little.

When he saw that Jesslyn had finished eating, he said, "Mayhap, we should settle by the hearth."

She nodded, "All right." Bao assisted her to her feet and they walked hand-in-hand to the chair by the fire. Bao settled her on his lap and she wrapped her arms around his neck, then rested her head on his shoulder with a sigh. "This is nice."

Bao kissed her forehead. "Does Alleck stay at Niall's this night?" he asked, suddenly remembering the lad. The day had been so long, so eventful, that he had forgotten, until now, that Jesslyn had sent Alleck there while Maryn was in her childbed.

She nodded lazily. "Aye. You must speak with him on the morrow, tho'. It seems he and Niall got themselves into some mischief early this morn. They lobbed wet hose they'd rolled into missiles at Niall's sister and her wee friend."

Bao guffawed before he thought better of it.

She slapped his chest. "This is exactly the reason Grandmother Maclean and I didn't want them having that mangonel in the first place."

"Now, Jesslyn, lads need their sport. And I'm sure the lasses weren't harmed by such play," he said with a grin.

She lifted her head and looked at him. "They were still wailing and as mad as wet hens when I took the lads over to Niall's house to beg forgiveness."

His grin evaporated. "You made them beg forgiveness? That seems a bit harsh. After all, a lad must have his pride."

His wife sat up, her back straight as a board. "And what of a lass's pride? Does she not have that right as well?"

"Aye, certainly," Bao replied. "But she should keep her distance from a lad's fortress, else she find herself the target of his defense machine."

With a sigh, she relaxed back into her previous

position. "Aye, you are right. The lasses *did* seek to break through the lads' fortress wall."

"And were the lasses made to beg forgiveness as well, then?"

"Aye, but not before much persuasion. They were, after all, the defeated party."

Kissing her brow again, he placed a hand on her thigh and the other at her waist, bringing her more snugly against him. "Good."

"The lads also took one of the blacksmith's buckets of water that he uses to cool his tools."

It was his turn to sigh. "All right. I shall have a talk with him about it in the morn."

They were silent, both lost in their own thoughts and enjoying the physical closeness their positions on the chair allowed.

"Of what are you thinking?" she said after a while. "You've been pensive since your return to our chamber. Is all well?"

Bao took a deep breath and released it before answering. "Our guest, the first footer of last eve, is my sister Branwenn's brother by blood."

She bolted upright and would have toppled from her perch had Bao not tightened his hold on her. She stared at him, her eyes wide with shock. "How know you this?"

"He's been searching for her for two years, tracing first the trail his father, Gryffyd Duy ap Kenneric, had taken directly after my father abducted Branwenn's mother and then looking for all dark-haired lads or lasses of Branwenn's age throughout the towns and boroughs of the Kingdom of Alba."

"Her father was able to track his wife? How did he not find her before her death?"

"It took several days for him to learn of her seizure as she had not been taken from her home, but had been taken on the way to her sister's holding when my father attacked her traveling party. When she didn't arrive as planned, her sister's husband sent out a search party and found the slain bodies of her bodyguard, but there was no sign of her. He sent a missive to Branwenn's father telling him of the snatching and in which direction he should follow. He then immediately set out to track the fiends who'd stolen her away, but my father was able to divert their search in another direction long enough for him to lose them completely. 'Twas only after many moons of continued searching that Branwenn's father finally came upon the kirk where his wife lay buried."

"Were you with them when they stole her?" There was quiet horror in her voice.

Bao didn't answer immediately. When he finally spoke, his voice was gruff with impotent rage. "Aye. I was with them, but not among them when they committed the crime. Nay, I was left in a wooded copse to guard another captive, a merchant my father was using as cover to his schemes. He and his band of mercenaries pretended to be the man's bodyguards as they traveled across Cambria reaving and wasting."

She lifted her palm to his chest and soothed it with a gentle caress. "You were but a bairn; there was naught more you could have done to protect the lady from your father's villainy."

"Aye, there was more. I could have skewered him through the heart as he slept."

"You were but a lad. Hardly yet capable of finding your way through this world on your own, nor of breaking the bonds of slavery to your father."

Bao laughed in self-derision. "Nay, 'twas over two years more before I was released from my bondage by his death. Unfortunately, 'twas not before his heinous crimes against Daniel's mother and her father."

"Nor, I trow, before he made you a whore."

His gaze sharpened on her, his muscles tensed. 'Twas an apt and true guess on her part. "Nay, not before that either," he said, keeping all emotion from his voice.

His wife's eyes pooled with tears and he watched, in detached fascination, her throat work before she said, "How old were you? The first time?"

He didn't want to say. *He didn't want to say!* But her eyes, her gentle caress brought the answer forth in spite of the cool iron taste of fear on his tongue. "Ten summers." He managed to keep his tone matter-of-fact.

"So young!" He saw how hard she swallowed, saw her hand fly to her stomach, and he knew she was fighting to keep the bile down.

"Aye. But I was mature for my age," Bao replied, giving her the rationale he'd been giving himself all these years. "'Twas not many hours after Branwenn's birth, in fact. 'Twas the bargain I made with the bastard in exchange for his allowing Branwenn's mother to be buried properly...and in exchange for Branwenn's life as well. In order for me to keep Branwenn safe, I swore to do the thing he'd been trying to get me to do for several moons prior."

"But you were his slave, did you not do whatever he demanded anyway?"

Bao shook his head. "Nay. Not this. And tho' he tried beating me into obeying his command, I wouldn't yield—and he wouldn't slay me for my refusal, tho' I know he hated me, hated my foreign blood." Scrubbing his fingers across his brow, he continued, "I still understand it not, for he had many chances to do the deed, if he'd so desired."

"I'm glad he didn't," she said, pressing her damp cheek into his chest.

"Ssh, you mustn't cry so. Not for me. 'Twas a long time ago and I wasn't under his power, nor that of the procuress to whom he sold me, for very many moons afterward. And Branwenn is worth every horrid moment, I assure you."

She lifted her head and looked at him. "However did you manage to free yourself from the procuress? And where was Branwenn?"

"Branwenn was with me. I was the only male in the whorehouse, the rest were women. The other whores and the maids that worked in the house helped me take care of my sister during the time I was there." Restless now, Bao said, "I have need of a bit of ale."

He rose to his feet and settled Jesslyn on the chair he'd just vacated before walking over to the table and pouring out a bit of the substance into a flagon. Lifting it to his lips, he drank deeply and then set the container back in its place. The conversation had veered into darker territory than he'd intended. He took several deep breaths and released them before turning and walking back to the hearth. Once there, he remained standing, crossing his arms over his chest and gazing into the flames. "Suffice it to say that I soon met someone who sponsored me as squire. He took both me and Branwenn into his home." He didn't know why he didn't tell her then that it was Giric who'd taken them in, Giric to whom he'd given his service, both in battle and the bedchamber.

He turned and looked at her. "Understand you this: Tho' I eventually was able to win tourneys, become a knight in the King's guard, and earn a good amount of coin for my service as a warrior, I was determined that I would never be a slave to anyone again. So, by my own choice, I sold myself to the ladies of the court, set Branwenn up with a nurse in a modest cottage not far from the royal castle near Perth and gave her the best life I could make for her."

"Does Branwenn know of your sacrifice?" she asked softly.

Bao looked away a moment, then looked back, tightening his crossed arms over his chest and giving his wife a piercing look. "Nay, and I don't want her to learn of it; at least not until she's older. I want to keep her innocent of that part of my past as long as possible."

She gave him a slow nod. "Aye, that seems best. She's such a sensitive lass, I worry how she would respond."

More comfortable with this turn in the conversation, though it still weighed heavily on him, he said, "Aye, tho' our worry may be needless." He settled on a stool across from Jesslyn. Leaning forward and resting his elbows on his knees, he continued, "She may be traveling to Cambria with Reys ap Gryffyd soon, her brother-germane."

A look of horror came over her countenance and she stood up. "What mean you? Why would she leave with this stranger, brother or nay?"

Bao rubbed his tired eyes and sighed loudly. "Because, she is a member of the royal family of Gwynedd. The prince persuaded Reys that 'twas of imminent import that, should he find his sibling, the lad or lass be wed to one of the Norman march lords' kin to expand the prince's influence in that region."

"Does Branwenn desire such a fate?" Clearly shaken, she reached behind her and found the arms to the chair, using them to lever herself back into the seat.

"Nay, she does not."

"Yet you intend to allow him to take her?" There was a note of accusation and sheer shock in her tone.

"Nay, I do not. She will not be forced to leave, not while Daniel and I still breathe. I've already begun to strengthen our battlements and prepare for the siege."

Her jaw dropped open. "S-Siege?" Her voice cracked on the word.

"Aye. Tho' we don't believe 'twill come to that. At least, Reys believes not. He vowed he'd speak to his cousin, the prince, and dissuade him from such action. In any case, 'twill be many moons before we see a legion arrive, we have plenty of time to prepare."

"But what of your grandmother and Maryn? Branwenn? Alleck and me?" She leapt to her feet. "Oh, my God! What of Maryn's babe?" Worrying her bottom lip, she began to pace.

Bao rose as well and took hold of her shoulders, halting her nervous stride. "Worry not. Our scouts will give us plenty of warning, should a legion approach. The women and bairns will be lodged at the Donald holding and will never be in danger, I swear it."

She gazed into his eyes a moment. "Aye, but our *men* may be, it seems," she said at last.

Bao wrapped his arms around her and ran his fingers through her hair, cradling her face in his hands. He kissed her then. Gently, reverently at first. But with ever increasing desire as the moments passed.

She leaned into him, returning his passion with an ardor of her own. "Make love to me, Bao. Now."

Bao lifted her in his arms. He reached the bed in four strides and sat her down on the edge. Placing his hands on her shoulders, he pressed her to her back before gathering her calves over his forearms and bringing her buttocks to the edge of the bed. He knelt between them and stroked his hands up her thighs, raising the hem of her garments at the same time. When her lower half was free of encumbrances, he arranged her limbs over his shoulders, opened her labia and settled into them for a long, humid kiss. Almost immediately, her thighs began to quake. Soon, she began to strain, to struggle, to cry out her pleasure, until finally, at last, her inner muscles convulsed around his tongue. When she settled, he stood. "I hope you're ready for me because I can't wait to be inside of you another moment." He unlaced his braies, settled his hands on the back of her calves and opened her wide, bringing her knees down to rest on the bed. He entered her with a hard push, not stopping until he was fully sheathed.

Jesslyn caught her breath and bit her lip to keep from crying out. It burned, but it felt so good to be filled by him that she cared not.

Bao pumped into her, moaning her name as he felt the strong muscles of her canal take him in their tight grasp. He rubbed the nubbin of her sex as he moved, feeling the gush of her juices around him, smoothing the way even further for his swift invasion.

He came hard, groaning loudly as he held Jesslyn's hips and rammed into her. With a final deep thrust, he was finished. She cried out and his eyes flew open, worried he'd hurt her.

"Don't stop!" she said, tossing her head as she churned against him.

Realizing she was on the verge of another release, he continued to stroke into her, teasing the sensitive nub at the apex of her sex with his thumb at the same time. He leaned down and clamped his mouth over the nipple that pebbled under her robe and sucked hard.

"Oh, God!" she cried out. And then she climaxed powerfully. After a moment, she settled back with a sigh.

Bao lifted his head and gazed at her. Her eyes were closed and her face was flushed and dewy from their recent exertion. She ran her tongue over her parched lips and Bao took advantage. Bending down, he captured her tongue, suckling it a moment before nipping at her bottom lip with his teeth. "Let's get you settled more comfortably on the bed," he said against her mouth.

She nodded drowsily and brought her legs down over the edge of the bed as Bao moved away from her.

With gentle hands, he lifted her to her feet and made quick work of getting her out of her robe and her chemise. After he had her settled on the bed, he bent and placed a tender kiss on her damp brow and brought the blanket up over her shoulder. She opened her eyes and looked into his as he leaned over her. "Come to bed," she said.

Bao nodded and tossed off his own clothes. When he was settled beside her, she rolled over and put her head on his shoulder. She lifted her hand and caressed the scar that made a raised pattern on his chest, just below his collarbone. "Will you tell me how you received this now?"

Bao sighed and shook his head. "Nay, love. 'Tis a long and very unhappy tale and I fear 'twould ruin our current feelings of bliss."

"All right," she said. She raised up and kissed him.

Renewed ardor pulsed through him, making his cock hard again. He groaned, sending his tongue between her teeth. Without conscious thought, he ran his palm over her thighs and derriere. When his hand skimmed over her rounded stomach, reason at last overrode lust and he forced himself to break the kiss. With lungs blowing, he rested his brow against hers and said, "'Tis much too soon for more of that, I trow. You and our babe need your rest."

Wrapping her arms more snugly around him, she settled her head back on his chest. "Mmm-hmm. Mayhap a bit."

Bao took in a deep breath. Mayhap…mayhap he *should* tell her now about what Lara had attempted, what had almost happened between them last night. The burden of keeping it from her had been weighing on his conscience all day. And her reaction to what he'd done as a youth had quieted his demons more than he'd ever thought possible.

He decided to ease into the telling. "Callum and Lara leave at first light on the morrow," Bao said into the silence. He quickly explained the scene he and his cousin had come upon earlier and Callum's reaction.

"Poor Callum!" she said. "Has he told his mother or Grandmother Maclean yet?"

Bao shrugged. "I know not. Nora's birth has been on everyone's lips this day, and I've not seen Callum since this morn."

"How wicked Lara is. How will he bear being wed to such a lady—and what sort of mother will she be to her bairn?"

"I know not, but I tell you this: If ever a man deserved to be released from his vows, 'tis he."

Jesslyn nodded. "Aye, but he would never attempt it, because of the babe."

"Aye," Bao agreed. "I fear you are right." He cleared his throat. "There *is* something I—"

She sat up. "I found the bower she arranged for the two of you last night and thought at first you had betrayed our vows with her. But when I saw that naught had been used, I knew you'd kept your faith with me."

Bao's ears started to ring. "Aye, about th—"

"If you hadn't, well, 'twould be the end of us. Faithfulness to one's marriage vows is sacrosanct, and must not be trifled with for any reason. Ever."

Bao squeezed his eyes shut. *Oh, God.* He could never tell her. She'd never forgive him. Ever.

***

CHAPTER 13

A rapid knock came on the door of Bao and Jesslyn's bedchamber early the next morn, waking them both.

"Get you dressed," Daniel said urgently to Bao when he opened the door. "The clan elders are gathered in the great hall and demand your presence forthwith."

Yawning, Bao scrubbed his hand through his tousled hair and looked at his brother through squinting, sleep-filled eyes. "Know you of what they wish to speak?"

Daniel's jaw clinched. "Aye. I shall explain once you've dressed."

Bao nodded and shut the door, leaving his brother to stand in the passage until he and Jesslyn were fully attired.

Jesslyn, having risen while he and Daniel were speaking, was busily completing her morning ablutions at the basin as Bao walked toward her.

Highland Grace

"The elders wish to meet with me," he explained as he watched her dry her face before taking a nearly-sheer yellow cotton thing from the chest that held her clothing. He turned toward the basin then and began lathering the soap to wash and shave his face, saying, "They await my arrival in the great hall."

She tossed the saffron chemise over her head and quickly shimmied into the garment. "Think you it has to do with Daniel's bid to make you chieftain?" she asked as she did the same with her gold velvet gown embroidered with red roses along the neck and sleeves.

"Nay," he replied as he began to scrape the stubble from his cheek. "There's something amiss, but I know not what. Daniel will explain as soon as we've readied ourselves." They said naught more as Bao hurriedly dried his face with the linen cloth and then grabbed a shirt and hose from his chest and put them on. Once his black-woolen tunic, leather belt and boots were in place as well, and his wife's hair was adorned, he opened the door and beckoned with a wave of his hand for Daniel to enter.

His brother moved through the doorway, not stopping until he stood in the middle of the chamber. He crossed his arms over his chest and stared at Bao for a moment without saying a word. When he finally spoke, his voice was filled with anger. "Robert MacVie came to speak with me before dawn. It seems he was given a bit of information last night which could, if handled poorly, cause you to be banished from this place, this clan, for evermore. Unfortunately, the other guard overheard and gave the tale to one of the clan elders before I could speak with you first. I sent him to my MacLaurin holding to deliver a missive before he had a chance to spread the tale throughout the entire fortress." Walking a step closer to Bao, he asked grimly, "Is there something you wish to tell me, brother, about the work you did at the king's palace? I mean, other than soldiering?"

Bao felt the blood leave his face as lightheadedness set in. *Blood of Christ!* Lara, the vicious bitch, had somehow managed to tell all before he'd mustered the courage to speak with his family. He'd not fully appreciated the depth of the woman's spite and now he would pay the price, it seemed. A sense of doom settled in his chest and, with a dull voice, he began his explanation. "Aye, there is...."

His wife walked over and stood next to him, taking his hand as she listened to his halting reply and it gave Bao courage.

* * *

"Jesslyn has been in there for two hours now. How much longer will the meeting continue, do you suppose?" Maryn asked Branwenn and Maggie softly as she held her sleeping babe to her breast.

The three ladies were seated in the solar, awaiting the end of the meeting so that they could learn what the elders had determined to do about Bao.

Maggie looked up from her embroidery and shrugged, silently shaking her head.

"I know not, but I pray 'twill be soon," Branwenn replied. Bao had evidently cautioned the others not to tell her the reason he had been summoned, nor why his wife had been so determined to speak on his behalf, but Branwenn knew there was something amiss. Else, why would everyone insist upon keeping the information from her? And, she wondered, what could it possibly have to do with Callum? He'd been called upon to speak with the elders as well. Aye, there was something very, very wrong, Branwenn could feel it in her bones, and she was hurt and angered that her brother refused to allow her knowledge of it.

Reys ap Gryffyd had left at dawn to return to the Gwynedd realm in Cambria and speak with his cousin, Prince Llywelyn. Branwenn still could not think of Reys as her brother, nor fathom having a relation as noble as a prince. Her mind churned. What if Reys was not successful in his bid? What if Bao and Daniel were forced to battle for her right to remain here? And, *whatever was the purpose of this secret meeting regarding Bao?* Might he be banished? *Oh, Lord.* Feeling panicked now, Branwenn forced herself to focus instead on the tapestry on which she was working. When she realized she'd dropped a stitch several loops back, she sighed and let her hands fall into her lap.

A knock came on the door just then and Branwenn started. "Enter!" she called out a bit too loudly.

In the next second, Jesslyn moved across the threshold into the chamber. "The meeting has ended," she said, giving both Maryn and Maggie a steady look, "and all went well. Tho' whether he will be chieftain has still to be decided."

"I'm pleased that Robert MacVie came first to Daniel with his tale instead of spreading it through the ranks, as it likely had been intended," Maggie said.

"Aye," Maryn said. "And thanks be to heaven that Daniel learned that another soldier had overheard the tale as well before he could cause trouble for Bao."

Branwenn sighed loudly and dramatically flung her arms wide in frustration. "What was the warrior *told?*" she prodded.

"That is for your brother to reveal, and he is not yet ready for you to know of this," Jesslyn told her. "Just know that it is something about his past and be glad that all has turned out well."

Branwenn groaned behind clenched teeth and shook her head in disgust. She rolled her eyes, but prodded no further. 'Twas evident she'd get no information from this quarter. Nay, if she was to learn anything, she'd have to wait and speak with Bao. Her heart ached that he was keeping a secret from her. Especially when the rest of the family had been made fully aware of it.

"Do you know who gave Robert the tale?" Maryn asked.

"Nay, I do not," Jesslyn said. "They spoke not of it while I was in the great hall. However, I believe the men know who it was but are not speaking of it, yet."

"Aye. I'm sure all will be revealed in time," Maggie said.

* * *

Jesslyn was just passing Callum's chamber on her way to the stairs leading to her own when the door swung open. "Lara! Are you well? Callum said you were in need of a bit more rest this morn."

"Aye. In fact, I was just coming out to find you.

Have you a moment to speak with me?"

Alarm bells sounded in Jesslyn's head, but no polite excuses for refusal came immediately to mind, so she nodded and said, "Aye."

"Come inside, then. The hearthfire is warm and quite pleasing on such a cold day as this."

Once the two were comfortably seated near the hearth, Lara said, "You must be in utter delight over the attentions you receive from your husband. I know I certainly was."

Her stomach trembled. "What mean you?"

Lara laughed. "Lord, that mouth of his, those fingers! He knows just how to combine their strumming to send a woman into her utmost bliss. Several times." She sat forward, as if a kindred conspirator. "And don't you adore that enticing brand he has on his chest? 'Twas given him by a jealous lover, you know," she said. "Of course, the long scar on his hip is from a blade, 'tis clear. What a warrior! Oh, Lord! And doesn't he have the *mightiest* cock?" She giggled. "However do you take it? All at once, or a bit at a time?"

Jesslyn hadn't been able to drag in more than the smallest of breaths since Lara's first volley. "When?" she managed to say, though it was barely audible, even to her own ears.

"Ah," Lara said, giving her a knowing nod. "Several times, actually. I paid my price for him each time I visited my sister in Perth these five years past. But most recently, the night of the *Hogmanay* feast, first in one of the tower chambers and again in the stables."

A warm damp began under Jesslyn's arms. "The tower room was untouched."

"Aye, we didn't even make it to the pillows, so wild was he to mate with me." She sat forward a bit more. "He took me where we stood—we never even shed our clothing!" she trilled.

Her look turned conspiratorial again. "Tell me, does it burn a bit for you as well when he first enters you? I shall wager it does. No matter how prepared he makes a lady, it still hurts at first."

Jesslyn was torn between rage and heartbreak. Disillusion and disgust at herself for being gulled again so easily with a soft word, a sensual touch made her physically ill. Rising from her seat, she said jerkily, "I must leave." Then she stormed across the room, threw open the door and fled down the corridor, the stairs, across the antechamber, through the door of the keep and across the courtyard. Anger and horror put wings to her feet and on she sped, through the arched gateway of the fortress and down the pebbled path toward the village. She didn't stop until she had her back pressed flat against the inside of the door to the cottage.

Bao and Lara had evidently enjoyed each other many times. The hypocrisy of his words the night before, of his pretense of disgust at the lady's shameless betrayal of Callum, hit her all at once and a strangled cry burst from her throat. She bit down hard on her lower lip to keep from splitting the air with a second, more deafening one. What a fool she'd been! Why, oh why, had she not paid more attention to the qualms she'd felt upon finding the lovers' nest that night? Instead, she'd proceeded with her plan and given him her body again. Revulsion filled her as she recalled how openly eager she'd been for his attentions—and that, mere hours after his adulterous tryst with Callum's wife! The lecher! When would she ever learn?

She groaned. Thoroughly humiliated, her chest tightened and her breath hung suspended like a noose in her throat. She was bound for a lifetime with a man who broke, and likely would continue to break, his vows of faithfulness willfully and without regret. When she thought of how fiercely she'd defended him, waxed on about his good character, his strength, his courage, she wanted to retch. Pressing the heels of her palms over her eyes, she whispered aloud, "And I was the one to *initiate* the loving!"

Lord, how she dreaded telling the others of her disgrace. But she must. Pushing herself away from her position against the door, she stood with her spine straight and her shoulders back. Because she wouldn't live with the man a moment longer. *Not one moment longer.* Wiping the tears from heated cheeks with the back of her hand, she gazed around at the front chamber where she'd cooked so many meals for herself and her son and began to scheme. It wouldn't take long to have a few things brought down from the keep. Just enough to make the place habitable once again. Walking over to stand in the doorway of one of the bedchambers, she scanned the empty bedframe. First, she would need two freshly filled mattresses brought down. Her and her son's personal belongings were meager and wouldn't take long to gather. A few cooking and eating utensils, linens for the beds, kindling and wood for the cookfire, peat for the hearth, and mayhap a bit of food as well, just to get them started. Aye, it shouldn't be more than an hour, mayhap two, before she and her son were settled once more in this tidy cottage.

* * *

Bao stood in the courtyard watching as Callum, Lara, and their retinue slowly made their way through the gate of the fortress. Bao absently took the familiar pouch from his belt and held it in his palm for a moment, feeling the weight of the treasure that was hidden in its folds. Callum had given it to him only moments ago. He slowly loosened the string that held it closed and peered inside. It held two smaller pouches, and he knew what they contained: More of his mother's dowry and trousseau that his father had stolen from her and then, ultimately, given to Callum when they'd journeyed here not long after Branwenn's birth. He'd been angered, yet powerless at the time to retrieve his mother's possessions his father had so callously given away.

Callum had apologized for not returning them sooner, but Bao saw no reason for such, as he'd not been back to the Maclean holding for any length of time since Bao's first arrival this summer past. Besides, Bao had known where the coins were: he'd found them during the time he and Branwenn lived in the wood. He'd almost taken them back then, but had decided against it. They were not his to take, they were his mother's, and she was dead.

Highland Grace

Bao scooped out a handful of the Cathayan coins and allowed them to slide off his palm and back into the pouch. Then he unfurled one of the black scarves with its red woven symbols and imagined it covering his mother's thick, silky black hair. With a sigh, he tucked the scarf back in it's pouch and set his mind to current matters.

'Twas time to find his wife. Believing her most likely to be with the other ladies in the solar, he headed there first, but was quickly informed that she had quit their company close to an hour past with the intention of resting in her bedchamber. He headed there then, glad that they'd have this time to themselves, but again was thwarted in his pursuit of Jesslyn when he found the chamber empty.

Stepping back into the passage, he closed the door behind him and stood for a moment in thoughtful debate as to where else to look for his wayward wife. Mayhap she's visiting Niall's mother, he thought. Or mayhap, she decided to inspect Alleck's fortress once more after the lads' unwise use of the mangonel this morn past.

A half hour later Bao was out of ideas. He'd looked in every place he could think of to look for Jesslyn and had yet to find her. He was coming back through the village when he glanced up and saw her with a bucket in her hand stepping through the doorway of the cottage. Highly curious at her reasons for being there, as 'twas not her usual ale-making day, Bao rushed to meet her before she'd had time to shut the door behind her. With his forearm resting against the door, he asked,

"What do you here, my love?" He took the bucket from her and placed it on the table by the hearth.

She didn't answer right away, and her face looked grim, which immediately brought an answering tension in the tendons of his neck and shoulders. Folding her arms across her chest, she said, "I'm preparing the place for habitation. Mine and Alleck's."

"What? Why?" Moving around her, he closed the door and leaned against it with his arms crossed as well. "Were your words to the elders all lies, then?" Dread, like an iron fist, gripped his insides. "Are you sickened by what I revealed to you last night—have you realized you can only despise a man such as me?"

"Aye, I *am* sickened." Bao's knees went weak. "And aye, I *do* despise you!"

All the air went out of his lungs and it was all he could do to remain standing. Every part of him started to tremble, his legs, his arms, his stomach, his cheeks, his lips.

"But I am not sickened in the way that you mean. I'm sickened by the fact that a lad so young was forced to sell himself and go against his nature to perform the works of Eros in order to survive."

He'd not told her that, and yet, like so much else, she'd somehow figured it out. The vise grip around his lungs released and he was finally able to take in air. It made his head spin. "All right then, why have you left me?"

She turned away from him and, with jerky movements, took one of the folded cloths from the table and dropped it into the bucket.

Highland Grace

He wanted to rush over and shake her, force her to give him her answer. *Tell me!* But he didn't. He was treading kraken-infested water here. 'Twas best to let her say what she would in her own way, her own time.

So he watched her in silence. After she wrang the cloth of most of its moisture, she rolled a cake of lye soap in it to lather it up before using the worn piece of material to scrub the table. "Because I've had enough of your fickle nature," she finally said.

Bao dropped his arms and pushed himself away from the door. "My fickle nature?" His heartbeat tripled. "What mean you 'my fickle nature'?"

"Lara."

Christ's Bones! "Whatever she told you, it isn't true," he ground out. He walked a step closer to where she stood, bent at the waist and furiously scrubbing the non-existent soil from the tabletop. "Will you tell me what lies the woman gave you so that I may defend myself?" he asked with less heat in an effort to soothe her anger.

Her movements came to an abrupt halt. Rising from her position, she looked him straight in the eye. "Not only did she tell me, very precisely, a certain way you have of making love, but she described your body as well. And in a way that only one who'd had intimate knowledge of both would be able to do."

His hands balled into fists at his side, his heart started its pounding again, and Bao stood motionless. He forced in a deep breath and released it before he answered. "Jesslyn..." He wanted to tell her the whole sordid tale, starting with his discovery of Lara's identity and ending with her attempt at revenge for his destroying the deed. "Jesslyn, I...I..." But he was unable to turn his jumbled thoughts into coherent words.

Her eyes moved away from his, down to the cloth, lying in a wet mound on the table. She picked it up and threw it with a *plop!* into the bucket of water. "She had the *gall* to ask me if I could take your manhood inside me all at once—or if I had to take you a bit at a time! I was mortified."

Oh, God. "The woman was a client of mine," he began carefully, "but I-I only learned it when she arrived here and revealed such to me. She...always wore a mask, you see." Jesslyn's eyes lifted to his again, but there was skepticism in their depths. "I should have told you of this sooner," he rushed to say, "but I feared it would ruin the fragile accord we'd managed to build o'er these past sennights, so I remained silent. I see now, I should have told you of this as soon as I found out who she was."

"Aye, you should have. How many more former lovers will I be obliged to meet, do you suppose? The number must be legion, I suspect, after so many years spent in such amorous pursuits." She threw the rag on the table again and started scrubbing. "One probably cannot travel more than a mile in any direction without meeting up with one or more of them."

He put his hand over hers to halt it's movement, but she jerked it away. "They were *clients*, not *lovers*," he said. "At least not in the way that you mean, and I was very particular. I kept only a few at a time, Jesslyn, and they are most all securely settled in the king's court, fear not. The likelihood of you ever meeting another of them is almost naught," Bao said.

She looked up once more into his eyes and shook her head, then she turned and walked away from him, her arms crossed over her chest once more. Turning back to face him, she continued, "I saw the tower chamber with its wine, its pillows, its candles. A veritable lover's bower. And she had you again, it seems, in the stables just afterward. *Twice* she had you before...before you and I—*argh!*" She swung around, turning her back on him.

"We didn't couple in the tower chamber, I swear it," Bao said. "The woman tricked me into believing you'd requested my presence there and then she followed me." Sighing, he scrubbed his fingers across his brow and squeezed his eyes shut. "She wanted me, that much is true," he finally said. "But I rebuked her, rejected her advances. Then—then she made an offer that could not be refused." He walked over to Jesslyn and turned her around to face him. "She held a deed of ownership, Jesslyn. With Branwenn as the property transferred. Signed by Jamison Maclean and Lara's stepbrother Giric when Branwenn was only sennights old. But Callum came upon us before—"

Jesslyn whirled around, turning her back on him. "Aye, Lara always has *something* which will entice my husbands from their vows."

"What mean you, your *husbands*?"

"Tell me, is she as adventurous in bed as Graeme once said she was?"

"*Graeme* broke faith with you?" he asked unbelievingly. Graeme, the standard upon which all others were compared? The ideal of all that was manly and perfect in husbandly conduct? The man Bao had secretly feared he'd never match up to in Jesslyn's regard? All his hopes evaporated. Just like that. And he could swear the hammering in his head was the sound of the last nail in his crucifix.

"Where is this deed?"

"Burned."

"Convenient."

"Callum can vouch for its existence."

"Mmm. Still, we've not yet been wed two moons and in that time you have broken your vows of marriage to me with as many women."

"Jesslyn…about that time in the wood—"

She whirled around to face him. "Nay, I'll not hear more lies and excuses. I no longer want to be wed to you."

"It wasn't as it s—"—She spun around and hurried toward her bedchamber—"Jesslyn, please!"

In the doorway, she turned. There was naught in her eye, neither anger, nor sadness, only resignation. "Just go."

Bao's shoulders slumped in defeat, but he nodded and turned away. With swift strides, he departed the cottage, quietly closing the door.

* * *

Jesslyn wandered into her chamber and lay down on her bed. Twining her fingers together over her belly, she looked at the rafters above as threads of the words she and Bao had exchanged went through her mind. Mayhap she was being stubborn in her unwillingness to forgive Bao his caresses of another for the sake of his sister's freedom, but no matter how she tried, she simply could not feel comfortable with him again. Not when she also knew that he and Lara had lain together—lord knew how many times—prior. And not after having dealt before with a husband who found that same woman's caresses far superior to her own.

Thankfully, none of her other family knew of Lara and Graeme's affair—not even Daniel—until today, when she'd told Bao. 'Twas something that had happened not long into her and Graeme's union, when he'd left their cottage after an argument. He'd accused her of being too timid with him, of being too rigid in her understanding of when and where a man and his wife should make love and she'd accused him of being a deviant for wanting to mate with her on the same table from which they ate. He'd accused her of being cold, unwomanly—even said he'd wed her only for the sake of his bairn. She rolled on her side and bit down hard on her lower lip. How long would it be before Bao complained of just the same with her? A moon? Two moons?

Would he storm out as Graeme had? Not return until early the next morn, leaving her to wonder and worry, as Graeme had? Would he lay down beside her, smelling of another woman, of venery, of stale ale, as Graeme had?

A dry chuckle escaped her throat. Oh, how relieved that younger Jesslyn had been when her husband had returned that morn. She'd even begun to apologize until she'd gotten a whiff of him. Then she wouldn't let him sleep until he told her where he'd been. He'd finally relented and told her about Lara, the letter he'd written breaking their affair, and the woman's subsequent arrival back on her uncle's holding in order to keep their relationship going with the promise of a lieutenancy.

He'd sworn it had been a singular event—something that would never occur again. That the cruel words he'd said to her earlier had been said in anger and that he was happy to be wed to her. That he loved her.

Jesslyn let out a whimper and covered her eyes, tormented as she recalled the vicious words they'd exchanged then. Their earlier quarrel had been naught to what had taken place afterward. What had begun as a dispute between two people trying to learn to live together had, with her discovery of his faithless actions, turned into a fight that had had the ability to break the bonds of their union for evermore.

She'd almost left him, even gotten as far as packing a satchel and wrapping the babe in a warmer blanket for traveling. But, he'd stopped her and she'd let him. Nay, she'd been too young, too unsure of her ability to care for herself and a bairn, and too unwilling to leave Alleck without a mother to care for him.

So she'd kept the peace. And, after a time, when she'd believed he'd truly broken the affair and devoted himself only to winning her love back, she'd forced herself to forgive the transgression.

Except, he hadn't broken the affair. And how her

insides cringed now, how she squirmed to remember how he'd gulled her into believing she was enough for him. How devotedly she'd served him, cared for him. Loved him.

But now, with Bao, she wasn't about to do the same. This time, she was older, wiser, a lady who'd been forced by circumstances to fend for herself—and done well at it. Aye, she'd not forgive this time; she didn't have to.

* * *

When Bao arrived back at the keep, he made a direct dash up the stairs to his bedchamber and locked himself in. Fate—everything—was against him. He paced over to the hearth and poked at the fire, then fell into the chair nearby and gazed, unseeing, at the gray-blue sky outside the window.

He was ill-prepared for this. What did he have to offer her that might persuade her to stay with him? He was naught but a soldier and a whore. Aye, he had coin. And, because of her, he had this keep as well. But what were they against her disgust of him?

To push, or not to push? 'Twas a thin line he walked, with snapping, raving monsters on either side. He bolted from his chair and grabbed the few items of his that hung on their hooks, then tossed them in his chest. He was just gathering the items off the washstand when a knock came on the door.

"Enter!"

"What's this? Are you leaving? Why? What happened?" his grandmother said as she shut the door behind her.

"'Tis a long tale, and one I won't burden you with, but aye, I'm traveling back to Perth forthwith."

Her gaze grew keen as she regarded him in silence for a moment. "Where is your wife?"

He turned back to his packing. "She's living back at her cottage. She'll be up here soon to gather Alleck as well, I'm sure."

"I believe I shall go have a little visit with her."

"Don't, please. She will not appreciate the company just now."

"Oh, I shan't stay long." She turned him around to face her with a hand on his arm. "And you cannot leave, you know. Have you forgot our dread of siege by Branwenn's royal kin?"

Bao's hands, full of sundries, stopped midair. "Blood of Christ!"

She went up on tiptoes and kissed him on his cheek. "G'day. I'll see you in an hour or two."

* * *

CHAPTER 14

Bao remained in his chamber, awaiting his grandmother's return. It was foolish, mayhap even insane, but still a last remaining ember of hope in his chest refused to die out. His grandmother was a persuasive woman. She might be able to turn around Jesslyn's decision to leave him. And that was all he needed. Just a crumb of her willingness. He could build upon that, he was sure of it.

When the knock came on the door, he jogged over and opened it. "Did she tell you why she left? Does she still insist on staying in the cottage?"

His grandmother sighed and nodded as she handed him her mantle. "Aye, lad. She refused to stir from that place, no matter what good reasons I gave her to do so."

Bao stood quiet and still. Folding his arms over his chest, he bowed his head in resignation. After a moment of silent contemplation, he said, "Does she have all that she requires?"

She walked over to the chair by the hearth and sat down creakily. "Aye, as far as I could see," she said. "Tho' 'twould be best to make sure she's a large enough peat stack available to her right away. The nights are even more bitter with cold than are the days."

"Aye, 'twill be done." He moved to the door and flagged down one of the servants, then gave him the order to get the deed accomplished. Afterward, he strode to the stool opposite his relative and lowered himself onto the seat. Leaning forward with his forearms on his thighs, he said, "What am I to do? How can I allow her to stay there on her own in this weather while she carries my babe in her belly?" Pointing to the window, he continued, "Even now the snow drifts pile high against the curtain wall, and once the sun has set, the cold will pierce like a dirk, straight to the bone. The cottage will not hold heat well and that cannot be healthy for either her or our babe."

"Aye, but the lass is adamant. She'll not live here with you another moment longer. Those were her precise words, as I remember."

"I swear to you I did not break my vows to her, Grandmother." He jumped to his feet and began to pace. "But, I would have. For Branwenn, I would have." He lowered his head into his hands.

"Callum was right when he called his wife an adder," Lady Maclean said coldly, her heart aching as she watched her grandson anguish over his predicament.

Lowering his hands to settle on his hips, he looked over at her. "I shouldn't have told you of that afterward," he said sheepishly.

She shrugged, ignoring his unease. "She's the devil's own, I trow. And my poor, dear Callum is yoked, like some miserable ox, to her for life."

She stood and walked over to him. After giving him a long look, she said, "You asked me before what you should do, and now I will answer: You must not let one night pass with the two of you housed in separate places. And, since she is set on staying in the cottage, there too, shall you reside as well." She turned then and walked back to her chair. Sitting down, she continued, "I think it best you know that I put her to bed before I left. Her back was aching, I could tell, and that is not a good sign at this stage in her childing. Not a good sign at all."

It felt as if strong hands crushed his throat. He swiveled around and jogged to the door. "I'll retrieve Alleck once I check on her."

"No need. She sleeps peacefully."

Bao halted and turned to look at his grandmother.

"Get the lad first and be gone to your new dwelling," she said.

When her grandson was gone, Lady Maclean leaned back and smiled. That last took a bit of nimbleness of mind. Aye, she'd put Jesslyn to bed, and aye 'twas for an ache, but not one that was a danger to her babe.

If all went as she planned, the two of them would be back at the keep, back in each other's embrace in no time.

* * *

Branwenn watched Alleck as he sat on the back of

his calves, clearly fascinated with the wee babe, Nora. "Her grip's so strong! And her legs and arms are so fat!" he exclaimed. "But her skin is very soft." He giggled with glee. "An' see how merry she looks with that red hair standin' straight up and no teeth!" He looked up with wide eyes at Lady MacGregor. "She's grinnin' at me!" he said. Looking back down at Nora once again, he said, "But she needs to learn not to slobber so much."

"Nay, lad," Lady MacGregor said, "the babe only needs to belch the wind from its belly."

The lad's shoulders sagged in disappointment. "Are you sure?"

Branwenn, too, looked to the other lady for confirmation, since this was all so new and wonderful to her as well.

Lady MacGregor nodded sagely, lifting Nora from her cradle and holding the babe up to her shoulder before beginning to lightly rub and tap the babe's back. "Aye. She's a bit young yet to be smiling. Tho' I'm sure, in only a wee time she'll give you one in earnest."

Nora burped loudly and a bit of her earlier meal settled on the cloth Lady MacGregor had placed over her shoulder.

"Eewww!" Alleck said, scrunching up his face at the sight.

Branwenn agreed, but prudently held her tongue and her visage still.

Just then, her brother, Bao, opened the door of the solar and briskly walked inside. "Alleck, your mother wishes for you to remove to the cottage where we'll be dwelling for the next while."

Alleck's lower lip extended in a pout and his brows slammed together. "Why must we live at the cottage again? I like it here!"

It didn't escape Branwenn's notice that her brother looked uncomfortable with the subject as he answered, "Your mother has decided that she prefers it there, and we men must make sure that she is as comfortable as can be. Especially while she's still got your wee brother or sister in her belly."

"I don't want to," Alleck said sulkily.

"Aye, but you must. Your mother wants you with her."

"But I want to stay up here with Nora!" Alleck balked, pressing himself against Branwenn's skirts.

Branwenn grinned and settled her hand on Alleck's shoulder, thoroughly enjoying watching her brother try to deal with this stubborn lad. Especially after Bao's own willful insistence that she remain ignorant of some vital piece of information about his past. She was still quite determined to speak with him regarding that slight, but with all the discord happening around her, she'd thought it best to defer that conversation to a later day.

Bao's eyes narrowed as they rested on her briefly before returning to his stepson. "You'll be able to come visit her again on the morrow, but for now, you must say your farewells and come down to the cottage with me."

Alleck picked at a scab on his knee through a hole in his hose. "When's my brother goin' to be finished bein' made?"

Bao sighed, and Branwenn thought 'twas no doubt because he knew the lad was stalling for time. "Around *Bealltainn*, in May."

Alleck cocked his head to the side and peered at Bao through narrowed eyes. "How long away is that?"

"'Twill be a few more moons 'til then, Alleck," Bao said, his tone holding a bit less patience than before.

Alleck crossed his arms over his chest and gave him a mutinous look. "That's too long!"

"Mayhap 'twould be best for Alleck to stay here," Lady MacGregor interjected, "at least for this first night."

Her brother studied the obstinate set of Alleck's countenance a moment before reluctantly agreeing. "Aye, all right," he said with a brief nod, "*if* Jesslyn agrees to the arrangement as well—all right, Alleck?"

Branwenn thought that a good plan, as she suspected Alleck's behavior was in reaction to the strained dealings between the adults around him.

"All right," Alleck agreed dejectedly.

* * *

Jesslyn had remained on her bed with a sick head since before Lady Maclean departed a bit over an hour past, but she jumped up off it and rushed to her doorway when she heard the front door of the cottage open, followed by the clomp of heavy footsteps across the threshold. *Bao!* Her palpitating heart sank into her stomach. "What do you here?"

His eyes narrowed on her, studying her. "You are supposed to remain in bed. Grandmother said you'll risk losing the babe if you don't. Go to bed Jesslyn. We can speak of this later, after you've rested awhile longer," he said, then he continued directly to Alleck's bedchamber with the wad of clothes that filled his arms. She heard the *shwish-plop!* of male garments landing on the mattress in the next instant and it made her grit her teeth.

"I only had a headache, 'twas naught to harm the babe. Why would she say such?" Her own eyes narrowed then and she stormed over to stand in the doorway of her son's room and crossed her arms over her chest. "*Get out!* I told you before that I didn't want to see you again!"

He turned and faced her, miming her stance. "That's certainly a pity. But, as I intend to live where you live, at least until my babe is born and I know it's well, my visage is a thing which you will need to grow accustomed to seeing quite often."

"Nay!"

"We are wed," he said matter-of-factly, "and we will live as husband and wife, whether it be here, at the keep, or up a tree. I assure you, I care not where you choose."

Jesslyn sputtered, too stunned by the man's audacity to retort.

In the meantime, he turned back around and proceeded to re-fold the few articles of clothing he'd brought with him.

Jesslyn ground her teeth together and swallowed back a scream of frustration. A mental image floated across her mind of manfully tossing the vexing man out on his ear. *If only she had the strength!*

Forcing a calm into her voice that she didn't feel, she said, "You cannot stay in this chamber. Alleck will be here soon."

"Nay, he will not. He was not keen on the idea of moving back here—quite adamant against it in fact—and begged that he be allowed to remain at the keep with the others. When it became clear the only way to get the lad here would have been to carry him out, Maggie thought it best we allow him to remain there for this one night and, because of the tension between you and me, I agreed with her and left him behind."

A sense of utter defeat filled her. "Why will you not just let me be?"

Bao stopped what he was doing, but didn't turn, simply stared down at the pile of folded clothes on the mattress. "I think you know why, if you'll only believe it."

Jesslyn's heart did a giddy flutter before she forced reason to pound it into pulp. She straightened. "I will not allow myself to be gulled again. Not by you, or any other man." She walked with as much dignity as she could muster to her bedchamber and shut the door behind her. Leaning against it, she gulped air into her lungs and dabbed the tear from her cheek with the back of her hand. She hadn't realized until this moment that she'd even shed it.

* * *

Bao stood with his arms akimbo, staring blankly at the closed door to his wife's bedchamber. 'Twas clear by the color in Jesslyn's cheeks and her vigor that she was not as ill as his grandmother had led him to believe. Still, she'd done him a favor. For he was now well-entrenched in this cottage with his wife, and he intended to take heed of his grandmother's sage advice to remain so.

The rest of the day and night passed with no further words exchanged between them.

Once Bao realized Jesslyn didn't intend to leave her chamber if he was in the front room, he returned to his own bedchamber and closed the door. He was glad when he heard her preparing a meal for herself about an hour later; he'd begun to worry that she would forego eating while he was in the cottage.

After having his own meal of stale bread and a bit of cheese, he lay on his back on the bed and pondered what tactic he might use to soften her hatred of him.

The only thing he was good at was sex and soldiering. He'd just have to cull from both pursuits in his efforts to wear her down.

* * *

The next morn, Jesslyn sat on the edge of her bed and listened for any sounds of movement in the front room of the cottage. She was desperately hungry, but her pride wouldn't allow her to exit her bedchamber until Bao had left to go to the training field for the morn.

She hadn't slept well. Every sound that had come from the direction of the other chamber had awakened her. And the babe had been restless as well, kicking and jabbing her rib cage all night long. Tho' it angered her to admit it, she'd also missed having Bao next to her, as she'd grown used to having him there these past sennights.

She let out a despondent sigh. Why, oh why, must she keep falling in love with faithless men? What was it in her makeup that attracted her to such vile creatures? Just look at how her heart refused to melt for Daniel. Nay, it seemed clear to her now, he was simply too trustworthy for her twisted heart to love. If a man did not charm her to her marrow and proceed to treat her as if she were naught, then she simply could not want him.

A scratching noise on the door jarred her from her musings and she looked up.

"Are you well?" Bao said.

Why did the sound of his voice always produce a heart flutter? She gripped the side of the mattress. "Aye, I'm fine! Go away!"

* * *

Bao sighed and walked back into his bedchamber to finish dressing. After tying his hair back in a thong, he strode out into the front chamber, checked to make sure there was fresh peat on the hearthfire as well as plenty of water and food for Jesslyn, and then left the cottage. If he was ever to try and seduce her into mellowing her feelings toward him, he must find a way for them to be in the same place at the same time. An idea struck him, and he started to jog. He must speak with Maryn right away if they were to put this new plan into action by this eve.

He grinned. Jesslyn wouldn't say nay to her good friend. Of that, he was certain.

Highland Grace

* * *

A clamor sounded from the front room with the distinct sound of a door banging open. Jesslyn jumped up from her prone position on the bed and stared at the closed door to her chamber, afraid to open it, in case it was Bao. Tho' she felt guilty for her idleness, she was still so weary from lack of sleep and worry that she'd lain back down after her meal earlier in the morn.

"Mama! Mama! Guess what?"

All the muscles in Jesslyn's body relaxed at the sound of her son's voice. "Aye," she said cheerfully, pulling the door open, "what have you to tell me, my wee lad—and don't I get a hug first?"

"Aye!" Alleck shouted, and jumped like a rabbit over to her, then threw his arms around her and rested his cheek on her rounded belly.

Laughing, she said, "You're getting really good at that!" Jesslyn stroked her fingers through her son's tousled hair. "So, what has you in such good spirits this morn?"

Alleck craned his neck to look up at her. "We're having a feast this day! With lots and lots of sweet things!"

Her brows lifted. "And why are we having a feast?"

"For Nora! 'Cuz she's just borned and Aunt Maryn wants us to have a merry time," he answered, bouncing up and down in excitement, which forced Jesslyn to reposition her feet in order to keep her balance.

"Ah!" she said, nodding her head in understanding. "When are we to go to the keep for this glorious feast?"

"After the chimes at sext."

"That leaves us just enough time to wash and dress, then."

"Why do I hafta wash? I'm not dirty—I haven't even been over to me and Niall's fortress yet!" he complained.

Jesslyn bent back one of her son's ears and looked behind it. "Alleck! You're filthy! Didn't you bathe before you went to bed last eve?"

Her son dropped his chin to his chest and, clasping his hands behind his back, shuffled his feet. "Nay," he mumbled, "Branwenn said I didn't hafta."

"Aye? Well, you're having one now—and one again before you go to bed!" she said, moving him toward the hearth. "First, I must heat some water."

"I hate baths! They're for lasses! Lads are s'posed to get dirty—Bao said so!"

Alleck had no idea that he'd said the one name that would bring Jesslyn's temper to a boil. "Well, *Bao* can remain as *filthy* as he *pleases*, but *no* son of *mine* will walk around like a *ragamuffin!*"

Alleck plopped down on the stool by the hearth, crossing his arms over his chest and sticking out his lower lip, but wisely held his tongue.

Jesslyn worked silently for a time, preparing the water for her and her son's bath and slowly allowing her temper to decompress a bit before speaking again.

Alleck broke the silence. "I don't wanna live back in this ol' cottage. I don't hafta, do I?" he asked, agitatedly kicking the air with one foot while he rested on the stool.

Jesslyn looked up from her task. Sighing, she said,

Highland Grace

"You can *sleep* at the keep, if it pleases you, but I want you here each morn to break your fast." It seemed the best solution until she could oust the belligerent man who'd taken up residence in Alleck's chamber. Alleck didn't need to be privy to the problems she and Bao were having, in any case. Not, at least, until they'd come to a decision regarding the future of their marriage.

"Good!" Alleck exclaimed, clapping his hands and bouncing on his seat.

"And!" Jesslyn had to yell to be heard over the ruckus her son was making. "You must have your bath *here* each eve."

That deflated his glee a bit. Sighing loudly, he said, "Aaall riiight."

* * *

Bao's sister cornered him in the courtyard, outside the chapel. "I understand there's actually something I don't know about you," she said bitingly, "that *everyone else* does!"

"Well, not *everyone* else," he replied half in jest.

Branwenn slapped him on his bicep. "You know what I mean."

Pressing his lips together, he scrubbed his fingers across his brow. "Aye," he said at last.

She crossed her arms over her chest. "Pray, enlighten me."

Bao looked away, scanning the top of the curtain wall. When he turned back to her, all earlier humor was gone. Lifting his hand to her cheek, he held it a moment in his palm, stroking the rise with his calloused thumb. "You're so *young*," he said, "so innocent. I can't bear to ruin that with my tale of shame."

She lifted her hand to cover his. "Not *so* young, not *so* innocent. Remember you that I'm old enough to wed...and that I understand things that other unwed lasses my age may not," she said, pinkening with the gentle reminder of her eavesdropping adventure at the waterfall.

Bao shook his head.

She nodded hers.

He relented. "I...," he started, "I was a...whore," he said the last rapidly. His sister's violet eyes became as wide as saucers, taking up, it seemed to Bao, the whole of her face. Her throat flexed as she swallowed.

"When?" she whispered hoarsely.

Bao shrugged. Shaking his head, he said, "Since just after your birth and up until I came back here to wed Jesslyn."

"Oh, my God!" Branwenn turned and walked a few paces away from him. Turning back around, she said, "Why? Why did you do such a thing, Bao? You worked so hard as a soldier—I know you made enough for us just from that!" She didn't give him a chance to answer before she said, "So that's where you were all those nights when you were home from one of the King's campaigns." She turned and chewed her thumbnail. "I resented that you left me by myself with that nurse until the wee hours of the morn. I believed you were out carousing with your friends, or mayhap romancing one of the beauteous ladies at court." She whirled back around. "But 'twas not *romance* that you were up to. Not at all."

Bao strode up to her and opened his arms. She huffed, but walked into them. "Nay, 'twas not. 'Twas a business arrangement so that I might give you the future you deserved. Build a dowry for you. Make sure neither one of us would be pressed under the thumb of another again." He stroked her silky black hair and took in a deep breath. Then he proceeded to give her the whole of it, even the most shameful part of it, baldly, honestly, and without any glossing of words.

His sister listened intently. She squeezed him more tightly as he spoke, rubbing her cheek against the rough, woolen fabric of the tunic, and he knew her heart had not been swayed from her love of him, for which he gave silent thanks.

"And did you tell Jesslyn all this before you wed her?" she asked when he'd finished speaking.

Bao shook his head, "Nay, not all," he shrugged, "but, aye, the most recent part she was given before our union. The rest she guessed later."

"She must truly love you, Bao, to have wed you knowing that you'd been involved in the venereal trade," Branwenn said quietly.

He frowned. "Nay, 'twas not love that brought us together, 'twas honor and duty. But I had hoped that one day she might feel such for me." He stepped back a pace and threw his hands into the air. "But now—now—she's cloistered herself away in her bedchamber and refuses to come out when I'm in the front room of the cottage, refuses to even speak to me other than to say 'Go away!'"

* * *

Branwenn stood silent, gazing at her brother with new eyes, her mind a jumbled mass of thoughts and memories. She'd always thought of him as infallible, mayhap even a bit immortal, able to fend off all comers. After all, she'd yet to see him lose a joust, or any other test of strength or reason, and the knowledge that there had been a time in his life when he'd been forced to go against his own nature, to do things he surely couldn't have even fully understood at that age, sickened her physically and broke her heart. And he'd done it all for her! *For her!* *God!* When she thought of her own selfishness, how often she'd begged him for new clothes or other ornaments, complained of her situation, complained of his absence, and finally, how she'd fought with him when he'd insisted upon leaving her here to be trained as a lady so that she might wed well, she wanted to crawl into a hole and die of shame. And, even worse, was the fact that she'd been prepared to allow him to—even had *expected* him to—defend the fortress and keep her safe from this cousin-germane, this prince, who had decreed that she be wed to a nobleman from a Norman house.

She determined at that moment, that should an army be raised and brought to their doorstep, she'd not allow one single drop of blood to be spilled. Nay, she'd meekly go to this other land and wed whomever she must. 'Twas only right to sacrifice her life for Bao's since 'twas clear he'd done even more for her.

Vaguely, she noticed her brother turning and beginning to pace back and forth with his hands clasped behind his back and his head lowered. He was telling her something about why Jesslyn was vexed and not speaking to him, about Maryn and a feast, but her mind refused to turn from her own thoughts about the feared siege and wedding a foreigner. *Would he be old? Cruel?*

"Branwenn? Branwenn? *Branwenn!*"

She blinked at her brother and gave herself a mental shake.

"Aye?"

"Have you not been listening?"

"Oh. Aye. Ummm, worry not. Jesslyn will give you her heart—although I still believe she already has—I doubt it not, but it may take some time. Be patient, Bao."

"'Tis not in me to be patient! I cannot wait and watch as she slowly slips further away from me!" he said in a near shout. "Action is what is needed, I'm sure of it."

"And, pray, what action would that be?" Branwenn asked.

"I-don't-know!" he yelled in frustration.

A giggle slipped out before she could stop it and she slapped her hand over her mouth.

Her brother looked at her in disbelief. "You laugh at me?"

Sobering, she said, "I'm sorry. 'Tis just that I've rarely seen you get so vexed. 'Tis usually I who have the bursts of ill temper, not you."

"Well, get used to it, for I've a feeling I'll not be calm again for some time to come."

* * *

The door to the cottage opened with a *snick* and Bao silently stepped over the portal into the front chamber late that night. Tho' the feast had put him side-by-side with Jesslyn, he'd had little luck melting her cool demeanor. Every warm word he gave her was rebuffed with short, cold replies—or not at all—and the one time he'd attempted a small touch, just his fingertips to the top of her hand, she jerked it out of reach as if his hand were a pit viper.

He looked around the quiet room. The hearthfire was still ablaze, but there was no sign of Jesslyn. Quietly, he closed the door behind him and pulled the mantle from his shoulders. He hung it on a peg next to the door and then moved toward the hearth. A flagon of ale sat on the table along with a cup. Bao poured a bit out and took a long swallow before sitting down on one of the stools. Gazing around, he marveled once more at Jesslyn's ability to make even the most humble lodging warm and pleasing.

She'd managed, in only this short time, to fill the cottage with bits and pieces of her own personality. She'd hung two large tapestries on the north and west walls, he noticed. Tho' they added decoration to the otherwise stark surroundings, they also served a useful purpose by blocking the bitter cold from seeping through the cracks into the cottage. A gentle smile of affection formed on his countenance as he studied her handiwork. She was no seamstress, as she'd vehemently attested so often since they'd begun living together. There were places where the threads were a bit too slack, causing gaps to be formed where the loosely formed loops lay on their sides, and others where the cloth was puckered by the threads having been drawn too tightly. But Bao thought the work beautiful. Worth more, in his estimation, than ten others of finer construction made by the hands of other, more talented, ladies.

Bao's spine straightened in shock, his mind finally grasping the full of what he gazed upon. The two tapestries were both depicting warriors, in full battle gear, sitting upon their destriers facing slightly sideways. They were almost identical, but mirror images. Each held his helmet under his arm and looked straight ahead. There was one very glaring difference, however: The color of the warriors' hair. In the tapestry on the left, the man had hair the color of midday sunshine; the man on the right had hair as black as the midnight sky.

When had these tapestries been formed? And why had she chosen to hang them where she would be reminded each day of, what she believed were, her *two* faithless husbands? Was this meant to rankle? Or was it an indication of some softening in her hatred? Bao knew not.

It did rankle, he admitted to himself. Being forced to look upon the visage of the man she'd loved enough to remain with, even after the man's admitted infidelity, was not going to be an easy task. Especially while he, himself, stewed in his own jealous juices and flailed about trying to win back the heart of his one true love.

In fact, he wouldn't do it. Bao bolted to his feet and strode over to the offensive needlework and yanked it from its perch before heading toward the door. He grabbed his mantle and rushed out of the cottage once more. He'd find another tapestry at the keep and bring it back with him to hang in the place of the other. He'd keep his own likeness there, however. It seemed fitting that she should gaze upon it each day; after all, he was her husband now, and if he had anything to say about it, he'd also be her lover again in not so many more days.

* * *

Jesslyn woke the next morn with a bit of a sick head. She still felt groggy, but was determined to get more done this day than she had the day past. Alleck would be here any moment to break his fast, and she wanted to be fully dressed and ready to spend some time with him when he arrived, so she quickly rose and began her ablutions for the morn.

The feast had been more enjoyable than she'd expected, even with Bao in attendance. Fortunately, she'd managed to avoid him most of the evening and he hadn't been able to speak with her for any length of time, as she could see he had been hoping to do. She wasn't ready for another confrontation with him just yet. She felt her resolve slipping and she needed the time to bolster her reserve, for she wasn't about to give in to her body's desire to lay with him once more. Even if she did have the most erotic dream about him last night—and it had involved those damned berry tarts!

God's teeth! Why had she ever made them for him in the first place? She remembered that day, right here in her front chamber, when he'd avidly devoured—how many? Two? Three? Lord, she didn't know for sure. But watching him eat them had for evermore emblazoned in her mind the thought of those berry juices being licked just as fervidly from her own skin. By him.

Her pulse thrummed, but she quickly turned her mind to more mundane pursuits: Getting water for their meal, cleaning the hearth out, washing their clothes, going to the forest to pick some wild winter berries. Damn! She *must* let go of that fantasy—and in all haste. For Bao was sure to be sitting with them this morn, breaking his fast as well. And she certainly had no desire to reveal, in any small way, that she was having such carnal thoughts about him.

The door slammed in the front chamber and she heard the distinct sound of her son's steps. "Mama, I'm here!" she heard him shout.

Jesslyn quickly opened the door to her bedchamber and stepped into the front room. "Good morn, my brave, fine, laddie—what on earth are you wearing?" It looked as if he'd clasped together a mishmash of various metal rings of quite varied original use. She immediately recognized several worn and bent-up brooches, what looked to be stud rings from a horse's bridle, and—were those the hooped handles of a clothing chest? There were other metal loops attached as well, that were of an origin outside of Jesslyn's understanding.

Alleck looked down at his clothes and said, "'Tis my mail armor. Maryn helped me make it to wear in me an' Niall's fortr'ss." He looked back up at his mother then and patiently explained, "'Tis what warriors wear in battle." He shrugged. "I'm sure to need it when the prince comes to get my Aunt Branwenn."

Bao came out of his chamber just as her son said the last. "How know you of this?" he asked sharply.

Alleck looked sheepish. "Ummm. I think I might've heard...ummm...." he stalled.

"Aye?" Jesslyn prompted.

"Uncle Daniel told me!" Alleck finally said.

"*Daniel* told you?" Bao repeated in disbelief.

"Weeelll," Alleck shuffled his feet and twisted his ear, "he didn't tell *me*, but I...ummm...heard him sayin' it to Aunt Branwenn this morn."

"And where were you when you heard this?" Jesslyn asked with no little bit of suspicion.

Alleck dropped his chin to his chest. "In the buttery," he mumbled.

"Pardon?" she said, thinking she'd surely not heard correctly.

"In the buttery," Alleck repeated a bit louder, still with his chin on his chest.

"And why, pray, were you in the buttery?"

"'Cuz I wanted to bring you some of the wine you liked from this day past."

That softened Jesslyn's ire immediately and she went to her son and hugged him tight. "That was awfully kind of you to think of me. But you mustn't listen to others' conversations without their knowledge."

"You'll not be here if the prince does send an army, Alleck," Bao told him. You and your mother will travel to Laird Donald's holding with Grandmother Maclean and your Aunts Maryn and Branwenn, should our fortress come under siege."

Jesslyn, who'd been resting her cheek on the top of her son's head, lifted her own and began to look behind her at Bao. Her eyes halted on the north wall.

"Why can't I stay—" Alleck began.

"Where is my tapestry?" she said sharply. The tapestry of Graeme had been replaced with one she recognized from Alleck's bedchamber at the keep, depicting a *Bealltainn* scene.

"I thought Alleck might like to have the tapestry hang in his own chamber," Bao answered, his tone all-innocence. "It *is* of his father, is it not?"

Narrowing her eyes at him, she shook her head in disgust, but decided against arguing with him about his presumptuous action in front of her son. "Aye, it is. And, for the time being at least, I shall allow the tapestry to remain there."

"I want to help you fight the prince's army!" Alleck said belligerently.

Bao broke eye contact with Jesslyn, allowing her to win the glaring contest, and looked back at her son. "Ah! But who, then, will protect the ladies? It is the highest honor and the gravest duty I bestow on you, Alleck, the protection of our most cherished family members."

Alleck's shoulders straightened and his chest swelled with self-importance and pride. "Aye, I'll keep them safe!" he vowed.

"Good, I shall be trusting that you will," Bao said.

* * *

Bao met Daniel on the training field later that morn to discuss building a second mangonel to be placed on the newly constructed south tower of the curtain wall. The north tower had been equipped with its own war engine just after the completion of the towers' construction a few moons past.

"Nay, let us begin by having archers man it; they will halt the onslaught of Llywelyn's men, should they get past our defenses and make it to the wall. We can place a mangonel there later, if the need arises," Daniel said.

"The gardener, even now, is searching the periphery of the curtain wall for any vines or other such that might be used by our foes to climb to the top."

"Make sure he pours boiling water on the roots so that they do not return. And he must look for new growth each sennight and kill that as well."

"Aye, I shall speak to him directly," Bao replied. "Have we enough murder holes above the gate—should we make more?"

"We have enough."

"And we'll fill the moat with water," Bao stated.

"Aye," Daniel agreed solemnly.

"Additional barns and stables will need to be built as we'll need more livestock. About seventy-five cows and, mayhap, twice that in sheep should be brought into the bailey," Bao said. "Do we have plenty of grain, or will we need more?"

"Laird Donald said he would send more from his own stores, so we should be well stocked."

"I've spoken with the marshal. He'll oversee his

staff and make sure that we have more hauberks, cables, cords, and other such supplies completed in no more than a fortnight."

"That pleases me," Daniel said. "We'll need thousands of arrows. Have you spoken to the bowyer?"

"Nay, not as yet. I shall meet with him later this morn," Bao replied. "Have we time to finish the barbican?"

Daniel nodded and sighed. "Aye, but 'twill be difficult. I'll need to entice the master mason and his workmen with additional coin to do the work during such bitter weather." Daniel rubbed the tense muscles in the back of his neck. "This siege will be costly."

"Aye, but Branwenn is worth the sacrifice," Bao reminded his brother. "And I've gold and silver enough to furnish this keep with twelve such barbicans, if need be," Bao added.

Daniel gave Bao a curious look. "Aye?"

Bao nodded once and said shortly, "Aye."

Daniel shrugged when Bao said naught further. "I've received missives from my clan, the MacLaurins, as well as the MacGregors. They are both ready to send backup forces as soon as we give them the word. Between the improvements we continue to make to the defenses of this fortress and our ally clans, we should rout the aggressors before our provisions run dry."

"Good," Bao replied.

* * *

CHAPTER 15

The day after the *Uphalieday* feast, Lady MacGregor and Laird Donald departed for their own holdings, leaving the Maclean keep much quieter than it had been in over a fortnight, when the first of the festivities, the Yule, had occurred.

Tho' Jesslyn was not as hostile toward Bao as she had been in the beginning, he was still no closer to a full reconciliation with his wife than he had been the day she first moved back to the cottage.

Bao walked slowly across the snow covered glen toward the forest. His head down, he swung the stick he held in his hand in violent arcs, in unconscious imitation of the broad strokes he used with his battle ax in war. What tack should he take with her now? He'd done as he'd set out to do, when possible. He'd tried to entice her, remind her of her desire for him, by means he was a bit abashed to remember. At every opportunity, he had found an excuse to disrobe in front of her, at least from the waist up. Just this morn, he'd pretended to become overheated while he chopped wood for her. He'd taken off first his tunic and then his shirt in an effort to gain her attention. And nearly frozen himself in the process. But it was for naught. He had ended up chopping enough wood for the entire keep's cookfires for the next twelve annals and she'd never turned her eye to him. Not once. She'd blithely continued speaking with Niall's mother by the well while he'd performed for her like some smitten youth.

This was no right conduct for a warrior, a man of means, one who'd battled his fiercest challengers—and won. He must do as Maryn and Lady Maclean had advised he should do. He must woo her, win not only her heart, but her mind as well. He'd won many less evenly matched competitions, after all. Why then could he not win this fight to regain her good opinion?

Before he realized his destination, he'd trudged through the snow and stumbled along the well-known path that led him to the waterfall. He hadn't been back here since his return to the holding and now he gazed in amazement at the difference the snow and ice made in the aspect of the place. Where there once was rushing water tumbling loudly over the cliff, there was now a silent, thick sheet of ice and snow. And the pool was completely frozen over. In fact, a light blanket of snow had covered it so completely that he couldn't at first discern where the land ended and the pool began.

* * *

Jesslyn made her way through the dense blanket of snow that covered the floor of the wood, determinedly heading in the direction of the waterfall. She'd decided to take the longer route this morn, the one that led her to the opposite side of the pool from the path that she'd been taking these past few morns. The sun was brightly shining and the air was crisp, smelling of fresh-fallen snow, and she felt the need for a bit more exercise. She had made the trip to the fall several times in the past days, her mind plagued by thoughts and memories of both her husbands. She'd hoped that, by coming back to this enchanted place, she'd gain some clarity in her muddled mind and heart and she'd finally decide what she should do about her marriage to Bao.

She found the place just as beautiful, just as soothing, as she had during the summer when the lush green foliage and the white frothy fall had settled her restlessness. Now the trees were like well-ornamented ladies of winter, bare of their summer clothing, they stood draped in their diamond-like crystalline baubles, their arms and shoulders cradling their white-powder mantles. And serenity was there for her, in the hush, as well. Which she desperately needed after the display of muscle she'd been a witness to this morn. She was dangerously near to losing the battle between her body and her mind and that scared the hell out of her. Between Bao's seduction and the rest of the family's constant harrying to trust her husband, she was closer than she wanted to admit to giving in to her body's and her heart's desire and reconciling with Bao. But her mind was just not ready to give him her trust. No matter how hard she tried, she couldn't seem to get past the images of Bao, half-naked, in the wood with the village lass, nor of him completely bared by, and being pleasured by, Lara. They fed on her deepest fear. The one she'd had from the beginning. One that had aided the delay in consummating her marriage to him. He would grow bored with her, bored with their marriage bed, as Graeme evidently had done. How could he not, when his prowess and experience far outstripped that of Graeme's and even Graeme had complained of her lack of adventure? Nay, 'twas much better that they end it now before more damage was done. Or *was* it? Ahhh! She just didn't *know!* She'd been bombarded by each member of Bao's family at every turn to give him another chance, to believe him when he swore his loyalty, swore he'd never betray her trust again. She worried her lip with her teeth. She'd already made peace with the incident in the wood sennights ago and seeing how deeply loyal he was to his sister, even to the point of breaking his marriage vows, she couldn't help but begin to believe his heart's ability to remain true.

She shook her head and sighed as she walked between two large trees towards the edge of the pool, then stopped short. There, on the other side of the pool, stood Bao. As if it were being drawn by some unknown force, his gaze met hers.

He would know now that she had been thinking of him. What should she do? Her mind raced. Should she turn and run? (Well, at least walk quickly—after all she was a bit too round now to *run*.) Or, mayhap, she should behave as if she cared not that he'd found her here, at their lovers' bower. Nay, that would require being near him, speaking to him in this place filled with so many erotic memories. Alone. Too dangerous.

She whirled around and quickly began following her tracks back in the direction from which she'd just come.

"Wait!" Bao shouted, bolting forward without thinking, across the frozen snow-covered pool. He'd almost made it to the other side when the ice and snow gave way and his right leg fell through the break into painfully frigid water. "Aaargh!" He grabbed hold of the icy ground, but still slid further in before finally finding purchase on a tree root that protruded from the ground just under a shallow layer of snow.

Jesslyn turned when she heard Bao yell out in distress and immediately rushed back to the pool. "Ohmygod!" she cried. She looked around and grabbed a dead branch from the ground and thrust one end toward him. "Hold on to this, I'll help to pull you out!"

Bao grabbed hold of the branch with his right hand and, using his left elbow for traction as well, was able to get out of the water with Jesslyn's aid. He rolled onto his back at the side of the pool, breathing hard, his eyes closed and his hands resting on his abdomen. His clothing was now almost completely drenched from the icy cold water of the pool. His limbs and torso, at first so numb they had no feeling, were now tingling so painfully, it felt as if large needles were puncturing his skin, with barely a space between. After a moment, he began to shiver uncontrollably.

"Bao, you must rise. We need to get you home at once where we can get you out of these wet clothes," Jesslyn said, grasping his shoulders and giving him a little shake.

"Just give me another moment," Bao replied. He didn't think his limbs would hold him yet.

"Nay! You must come with me now or you'll surely perish from the cold." Jesslyn grabbed his hands and labored to pull him upright. "Bao! Help me! Rise to your feet!" she demanded.

Feeling lethargic and a bit dazed Bao strained to comply. Tho' it was difficult, he managed to lumber to his feet.

* * *

Jesslyn put her arm around his waist and pressed him to move forward. Why, oh why had she taken this route? It would take them at least a half of an hour to get to the cottage. What would she do if he became ill...or worse? Her mind balked at that, refusing to go further down that path. Nay, she assured herself, he would be all right. She would see it so.

They had gone about a hundred paces when she saw the entrance to the cave she'd discovered this morn as she made her way to the waterfall. With so many trees and vines stripped of their leaves, the entrance and its clearing in front were now in plain sight. She said a quick prayer of thanks and struggled toward the cave. Once she had gotten Bao out of his wet garments and wrapped him in her fur-lined mantle, she would leave him here, sheltered from the wind and frost, while she hurried back to the village to get help.

"This be where Callum's coins were," Bao said groggily, looking around.

Jesslyn gave him a curious look. Why would Callum

leave his coin in a cave? Bao's eyes were half-closed. Mayhap he was confused. Oh God. What if he was already catching a fever?

She was pleased to find that there were remnants of a fire a few paces inside the opening. Mayhap she'd find the means to build one as well. Thank heaven the sun was brightly shining this day, for it allowed enough light inside the first several feet of the cave for her to help Bao sit down. By the time she had him settled on the ground, she was winded and her back was aching from the strain of taking so much of his weight as they traveled.

"There are peat turves and kindling stacked further back along this wall," Bao said, limply pointing in the direction she would find them. "And the tools to start it are in a crevice above it," he said weakly.

"Thanks be to God," she breathed aloud, her suspicion confirmed. Ignoring her own discomfort, Jesslyn immediately gathered up a few of the cut turves and placed them in the center of the fire ring. She then searched the crevice for the striker, flint and tinder box with which to start the blaze. Her heart sang when she also found a pan. She would be able to heat some snow and make him drink the warm water. That should warm him, shouldn't it? She prayed so.

* * *

Bao began to shiver once again. It had been happening in spurts up until now, but the coldness of the ground, added to the fact that he was still wearing frigidly cold, wet clothing, sent his body into fits of tortured jerking and quaking. He lay down and rolled to his side, curling up in a fetal position, his teeth chattering loudly.

* * *

Jesslyn took off her mantle and placed it next to the fire she'd just built. With the added light the fire provided, she was able to clearly see Bao's worsening state and rushed to his side. "Bao, you must help me. I will not be able to get your tunic and shirt off by myself." She pressed him to his back and then struggled to lift him to a sitting position.

His head lolled to the side. "Dnnn...mmfff," he said irritably through clacking teeth, his eyes a bit glassy.

"I *must* move you, at least while we get these wet things off of you," Jesslyn said firmly. Thankfully, Bao gave her no more trouble and, though his movements were jerky, he aided her in the removal of his garments. Afterward, she retrieved her mantle and, tho' it was difficult, managed to get the garment, first around him, and then stretched out beneath him. The fur lining would help to warm him, as well as shield him from the coldness of the cave's floor.

She was relieved when, after only a few moments, his teeth stopped chattering. Quickly, she gathered up her pan and went outside once more. After filling the container with snow, she returned and held it near enough to the flames to melt it and warm the liquid.

* * *

Bao watched Jesslyn work. Her movements were so sure, yet there was grace in them as well. Grace. Wasn't that what he'd been seeking from her—mayhap, even from the day he first met her? Her good will and her pardon—her love?

His wife sat the pan down and took her head covering off. She absently brushed the back of her hand over her brow before placing the wimple on the ground next to her. Distress and the heat of the flames were causing her skin to become damp. She loosened the tie holding her chemise closed and stroked away the dew that had formed on the heated skin between her breasts with the tips of her fingers.

Bao's pulse raced and his manhood shot to full attention. Aye, he'd sought all of those things—and her body as well. Christ's Bones! Did she have no idea of how her movements were affecting him? When she touched herself in that way, it reminded him of when his own hands had done the same.

As even more blood rushed from his head to his male member, so too, did his better judgement speed from his mind. In a flash, all of his good intentions of wooing her, winning her trust, flew away, like so much faery dust, as he was struck with an idea. A way, tho' not so honest, of touching her once more, holding her, making love to her. Surely, 'twould melt her anger, her reserve with him, as well. He grinned but then quickly sobered and closed his eyes when she looked up suddenly.

"I've warmed some water for you and I want you to drink the whole of it, all right?" Jesslyn said.

Bao lifted his eyelids only slightly. Seeing the concern in her countenance, he experienced a momentary pang of conscience. But he was using the only means he knew how—the only means that had ever worked for him—so he squelched the feeling and instead used her concern to his advantage by shivering dramatically once again. With a jerky nod of his head, he answered, "Aye."

Her brows came together in worry. She quickly brought the liquid over and kneeled down next to him. Then she helped him to raise himself up to a sitting position so that he could more easily swallow it.

Bao bent his knee, concealing the evidence of his desire before she could see it, and then drank down all of the fluid. The warm water did feel good going down and, amazingly, was the final thing he needed to give him his full recovery. But he wouldn't let Jesslyn know that. Nay, he had other things in mind which would not only warm his blood, but warm hers as well. And mayhap, if he were very fortunate, it would warm her heart also, enough to make her finally accept him back into her life.

Lying back with a sigh, Bao placed his arm over his eyes and groaned. Loudly. "I'm so cold! I can't seem to get warm." It was difficult, but he managed to clack his teeth together fast enough to make it seem genuine, at least to Jesslyn. "I need more heat! Hold me, I beg you!"

* * *

Jesslyn's heart pounded with dread. Without thinking how absurd the exercise would be, she looked around for anything else she might use to cover him. Of course, there was naught. What else could she do to warm him other than to do as he asked and use her own body's heat? Jesslyn stood up.

Bao opened the mantle and his arm quaked as he did so. "I'll better feel your heat this way," he explained when she hesitated. "But hurry, I grow ever colder and I need your warmth."

Jesslyn shrugged and nodded jerkily. Lifting her skirts, she settled herself on top of him, laying her head down on his chest. She could feel his chill through her garments. Even his manhood was cold—and very hard, she noticed—where it pressed against her belly. Was that a reaction to the freezing water to which he'd just been exposed? Lord! What if it was *frozen?* Was that possible? She knew not. She knew dangerously little about the symptoms of overexposure to the cold, nor how to hasten recovery from it. She only knew that, in spite of that worry, her body responded to the contact, softening and readying for his masculine invasion. She ignored the reaction, concentrating instead on her patient. It worried her that, even after quite a few moments, he continued to tremble beneath her, and his skin remained like ice. She feared leaving him to get help, but what if she wasn't able to warm him enough? Mayhap it would be better for her to get Daniel here. He would know exactly what to do to hasten his brother's recovery.

A severe quaking took over his previous trembling and Jesslyn held him tighter. "I should find Daniel, he'll know what to do," she said anxiously.

"Nay!"

Jesslyn lifted her head and looked at Bao.

"Nay," he said less forcefully. "I'm sure I shall be warmed enough in no time by your own ministrations."

Jesslyn stared at him, mentally struggling with the quandary of what would be best for her to do, but finally, she nodded. She placed her cheek back on Bao's chest. Unable to think of any other way to warm him, she began to furiously rub his arms with the palms of her hands. "Is this helping?" she asked after a moment.

"A bit, but I can't feel your heat through all these layers you wear," he complained. "Mayhap if you took them off and we were skin to skin?"

"I don't think that a good idea."

Bao shuddered and groaned.

Jesslyn sat up and quickly untied the strings holding her gown together before lifting it over her head, with Bao's rather eager help. Then came her chemise. She tensed, fighting back a shudder of delight, when Bao's fingertips accidentally grazed the sides of her breasts as he lifted the thing up and over them before bringing it over her head as well. She felt his hot, moist breath against the sensitive peak of the left one in that split second when the material covered her eyes, making her nipples pucker and her passage throb in reaction. In moments they were lying entwined beneath her gown, with the mantle wrapped around both of them. This time, she lay on her side, halfway on top of Bao, with one arm and one leg draped over him—a much more comfortable position for her and her babe. She was overcome with guilt. While Bao was fighting for his life, her body betrayed her own good intentions with its piercing response to his nearness. With extreme effort, she cleared her mind of all the carnal thoughts his unintentional touch had incited. After a bit his quaking stopped, but he was still trembling, and his breathing was too rapid for her liking. Without lifting her head from his shoulder, she placed her hand to his brow. It was warm, but not hot enough to indicate fever. "Are you warming up?"

Bao, who had his chin resting on the top of Jesslyn's head, grinned broadly. Aye, he was warm—mayhap a bit *too* warm. "Aye, I'm not so cold now, but I think 'twould help if you rubbed my skin, as you were doing before."

Jesslyn nodded and tried to rise up in order to use both hands on him, but Bao wouldn't allow it. Shrugging, she began her massage using just the one hand. She vigorously rubbed his arm, his chest, his abdomen, and the top of his thighs, careful to stay clear of the area she desired most to touch the longer she stroked his body. Lord, he was magnificent. All sinew and smooth, golden skin. And the battle scars only added to his masculine beauty. They were proof of his might, proof of his prowess as a warrior. She pressed her lips together to keep from caressing the dark brown nipple directly in her view with the tip of her tongue. How she craved to cover his massive chest with moist open-mouthed kisses.

* * *

Bao fought to keep his breathing at an even meter, but was rapidly losing the battle. With every new sweep of her hand, he grew more aroused. He moaned. A shudder of intense pleasure traveled through him.

"Are you growing chilled again—is your manhood

frozen?"

Bao snorted and started to laugh but quickly turned it into a brief cough followed by a clearing of his throat. "Beg pardon," he said in a strained voice. "Aye. I think it must be. Will you warm it?"

She rose up, resting her arm on his chest and gave him a questioning look. "But I thought it bothered you to be touched there."

He sighed. "Aye, it does," he said, feigning sufferance. "But I cannot allow it to remain frozen for much longer. It serves a duel purpose, if you recall?"

Her eyes widened in understanding and she nodded.

God, he loved this woman. "I have an idea," he said with false humility. "Mayhap, I could put it inside you and thaw it in that way?" he asked innocently. It was a struggle, but he managed to keep a serious mien when he rushed to add, "You wouldn't have to move, or anything—we wouldn't really be *doing* the deed."

There was a very long pause and then: "Al...All right," she replied. But he could see in her eyes that she struggled with her doubt at the intelligence of her decision.

Bao trailed his hand down her waist toward the junction of her thighs, with the intention of beginning his assault on her senses to prepare her for his entry, but when she straddled him, he positioned the head of his erection against her opening, and she gently pressed down. With only a bit of resistance, he slid right up inside of her tight, wet sheath. Sucking in a breath through his teeth, he bit back a groan, his heart pounding so hard in his chest he thought it would surely burst. She had been more than ready for him, it seemed. An acutely pleasurable surprise.

She shuddered. "It's cold...hard and cold." Placing her hands on his shoulders, she wiggled in an effort to get him as far inside her as she could. He felt her passage tighten in reaction, before she forced it to relax. "How does that feel?"

"Hot. Good," Bao croaked. His hungry gaze wandered to Jesslyn's full, white breasts. The rosy peaks were so turgid, partially from the chill air of the cave, he assumed, that they were little more than tight, pink balls. He craved to caress them, to put his mouth on them, but he dared not. At least, not for just a few more moments. He had to maintain the facade just a bit longer, else she'd surely bolt.

She threw her head back and closed her eyes, tossing her long, golden hair off her shoulders. The movement caused a bit of a glide up his shaft and he sucked in a breath. She settled back and pressed down, clearly intent on keeping still, but then her canal pulsed and he felt the hot dew of more of her juices warming him. It was evident that she bit her lip to keep from crying out. He watched her breasts rise and fall with her rapid breath, felt her feminine channel tighten around him.

Bao bit back a groan of agonizing desire, but managed to remain silent as he continued gazing at his wife. Whatever she was thinking of, he wanted to be part of it, for it was evident that it was extremely arousing to her.

She squirmed and a throaty moan burst from her throat.

Bao's heart slammed against his ribs and he ground his teeth together in an effort to stay still. He wanted to move so badly now, to stroke inside her until they both found completion, that hot and cold chills ran rampant along his nerve endings.

She opened her eyes and he captured her gaze. When he saw that her pupils were so dilated with desire that her eyes appeared to be as black as midnight, his blood flamed higher still. Past reason now, he sat up, brought his arms around her and feasted. First on her left breast, and then on her right.

* * *

Jesslyn moaned in delight, too far gone with desire to think clearly any longer. She straightened her legs and wrapped them around his waist, just as she'd imagined doing a moment before, and then she twined her arms around his shoulders and curved her back, giving him better access to her aching breasts.

Bao eagerly obliged, bringing his hands around and molding them in his palms. He laved the tight peak he'd just kissed and then rolled it between his teeth, tugging it slightly at the same time.

Jesslyn jerked at the sharply pleasurable sensation and then groaned when he took it into his mouth and suckled, softly tickling it with the tip of his tongue as he did so. She started to pant and mewl, every muscle atremble, the longer he worked on her until, finally, unable to control her own body's compulsion another moment, she began to move. When he grasped the cheeks of her buttocks in his hands and rotated her hips several times, pressing the head of his cock against her womb, she shattered. "Bao!" she cried out, her head thrown back as thousands of tingling shocks traveled from her convulsing center out to her limbs and even to the tips of her fingers and toes, her skin pebbling in their wake.

* * *

Bao arched, tugging Jesslyn's hips up and down rapidly as he shot to the stars, finding his own release in her hot, moist, pulsating channel.

Collapsing back on the ground, he brought Jesslyn with him as he limply helped her position her knees at his side once more. They were both winded, their breath coming in jagged gasps and their hot skins damp with the dew of their exertion.

Bao's mind was in a state of blissful peace, blank of all thought, his body and heart in that same condition as well. They were mates, truly husband and wife once more. He rested in a dazed stupor with his eyes closed as his breathing slowly returned to a normal meter.

* * *

Jesslyn's mind, however, was anything *but* restful. Thoughts were flying at lightning speed, zipping from one event to the next, connecting each thing that had happened, and 'twas not long before she'd worked everything out, come to a somewhat slanted form of the truth. With a jolt of pure fury, she sat up and scrambled off of Bao and onto her feet. "You tricked me!" she said, grabbing up her chemise and throwing it over her head—backwards. Dammit!" she shouted in frustration and then quickly readjusted the garment, ripping seems in the process.

Bao opened his eyes and sat up, crossing his forearms over his bent knees. His eyes were glazed with slumber. He'd evidently dozed while she'd boiled. "What?" he asked.

Jesslyn tossed her gown over her head and battled to pull it down over her body. "I said: *You tricked me*, you spawn of Satan!" Her voice, tho' muffled inside the gown, was strident enough, she was sure, for Bao to hear and understand it.

Luckily, she had her shoes on—*she'd never taken them off!* Nay, she'd been much too concerned with Bao's welfare, and he'd evidently been much too concerned with tricking her into coupling with him! But it worked out beautifully for her now, for she was fully dressed—except for her mantle—and would leave him here with at least a crumb of her dignity still intact. "Get up, you black-haired deceiver!" She grabbed the edge of the garment and tugged hard, shouting, "Give me *my* mantle!"

Bao tried to rise, but with her yanking on the material he was resting upon at the same time, he lost his balance and stubbed his toe on the ground in the process, breaking the skin covering the joint. *Good.* He deserved it, she thought. Finally, he managed to stand. Hopping on one foot and rubbing his abused digit, he said, "Jesslyn, I beg you, do not leave without allowing me to explain! I was desperate, can you not see that?"

Pressing her forefinger into her chest, she retorted, "Aye, I see! I do *indeed* see! You hadn't had a woman in—how many days? Six? Not even a sennight! But that must have seemed a century to one such as you.

You're clearly not used to celibacy," she continued sarcastically. "Which is why, I'm sure, you enjoyed servicing all those women in court. One of your lovers liked you so well, she even put a brand on you!"

"That is not—"

"Aye, do not deny it—Lara told me all about it. And now you've used my concern for your health as a means to satisfy your own lecherous lusts!" How he must have reveled in her foolish and lack-witted conclusion regarding his manhood! Mortified and furious, unable to face the proof of her mental blunder that was bared, and clearly healthy, before her, she whirled and rushed toward the entrance of the cave.

* * *

"'Twas not like that—I swear it!" Bao scrambled to find his clothes and put them on. They were still damp, wet through in some places, but he cared not. He had to follow her, make her understand that he had been desperate to find a way to reconcile with her. That he hadn't tricked her only as a means to mate. His boots were wet and stiff, but he managed to get them on his feet with only a bit of added effort, ignoring the pain it caused his sore toe. He quickly doused the fire using snow from just outside the entrance and, after gathering up Jesslyn's wimple, ran to catch up to her.

* * *

Jesslyn stumbled blindly ahead, her only clear thought, to reach her cottage and bar the door from Bao before he could intercept her.

Bao raced as fast as he was able with stiff boots, a sore toe, clammy clothes, and deep snow drifts, but he did finally reach her. He slowed his gate and walked silently beside her, gazing at her fury-filled countenance. He handed her the wimple.

Jesslyn growled low in her throat, but took it. Fortune was not shining on her this day. She looked straight ahead, refusing to acknowledge his presence any further.

Bao was at a loss as to how to soothe Jesslyn's temper enough so that she would listen to him, for he could see that her intent was to ignore his presence. "The brand is from no lover, Jesslyn. 'Tis one my father gave me to show the world that I was his slave."

It took everything in her not to bend, not to look in his direction, not to forgive him just a little, but she must remember: he'd use her for his own pleasure until the inevitable discontent set in and then his eye would begin to wander. Just as Graeme's had done.

"I love you," Bao said into the silence.

She snorted. "There is more to love than coupling."

Bao turned toward her and, walking in a sideways fashion, continued to stay beside her. With hands palm-side up, he said, "I know that. I do! I love you, Jesslyn, and all I want is for you to love me, to trust me."

Jesslyn ground to a halt and turned to Bao, her hands clenched into fists. "Trust! You want trust from me after the foul way in which you tricked me into warming your"—she glanced down and vaguely pointed in the direction of his groin—"*you know what!*" she replied coldly, her cheeks heating with chagrin. "You use sex as a weapon. You use it to manipulate, not as a means of showing your deeper feelings. You've used my desire for you against me for the last time." She turned and stormed ahead once more, angry that she'd broken her vow to herself to *not* speak to him *ever again*.

Bao rushed to catch up. He sneezed, and then sneezed again. And then, he sneezed again. He sniffled and coughed. Blood of Christ, but it was cold out here! It felt as if he were wearing sheets of ice from neck to foot. He shuddered and cleared his throat. It felt a bit raw of a sudden.

Jesslyn ignored him, convinced this was yet another ploy to gull her into attending him.

Bao realized his attempts to explain, to gain her understanding, had actually deepened her anger toward him, so he decided to say no more until her temper had cooled. He continued to walk beside her however, unwilling to abandon his nearness to her, no matter how bitter was her manner toward him.

They'd nearly made it to the door of the cottage when another sneezing fit caught him by surprise.

Jesslyn took the opportunity to hastily step over the portal and slam the door behind her, barring it to keep him from entering.

"Jesslyn!" Bao croaked, pounding his fist against the wood.

Crossing her arms over her chest, she leaned against the door, her heart racing.

"Jesslyn, open this door or I'll break it down!" Bao rasped, his throat feeling thicker and achier with each passing moment. But at least he wasn't cold anymore. Nay, in fact, he was burning up. He pressed his forehead into the door as he leaned against it for a moment, placing his forearm above his head and resting it on the portal for additional support. Sweat beaded on his brow and he absently wiped it on his sleeve. The cloth was nice and cold, so he decided to cool his cheek on it for a moment as he awaited her reply. His head had started pounding a few moments past, but he reasoned that it was because he hadn't had a meal in more than half a day. The notion that he might be truly ill had yet to sink into his muddled brain.

Jesslyn finally noticed the change in Bao's voice and her concern for his welfare once again overrode her better judgement. She turned and slid the bar from its rest and then opened the door a crack.

Bao stumbled and fell forward.

Jesslyn shrieked and moved out of the way of the door before it hit her as it swung wide with the force of his massive weight.

Bao landed with a thud face down, half in and half out of the doorway to the cottage. He groaned in pain.

"Bao!" Jesslyn exclaimed, squatting down and placing her hand on his brow. "You're burning up with fever!" Guilt assailed her. She should never have allowed him to walk all the way back home in these wet clothes.

"Nay, I just got a bit hot from the walk home," Bao said, rolling over with a grunt and then rising to his feet.

Jesslyn allowed Bao to assist her to rise and then rushed over to grab her bucket from its position by the hearth. "You must change into dry clothing without delay."

* * *

Bao was feeling a bit lethargic now, but he was more than ready to get out of his clammy garments and into fresh, dry ones so he moved slowly toward his bedchamber. Once there, he took a dry shirt out of the chest at the end of his bed and, with a bit of strain to his aching muscles, was finally able to get himself out of his boots, tunic, shirt and braies.

He felt a bit odd, a bit light-headed. The mattress was so soft and inviting to him that he decided to rest there a moment before putting his shirt on and returning to the front chamber. The cool air of his bedchamber was like heaven against his hot skin. He flopped onto his back and sprawled out, rejoicing in the crisp air that cooled his armpits and groin. After a moment, he turned onto his stomach, allowing his backside to receive the cooling treatment.

* * *

When Bao didn't return to the front chamber, Jesslyn went to his doorway and peeked in. Her heart did a little flip in her chest. He was bare from head to foot and so gorgeous, that in spite of her hurt, her anger, and her disgust at herself, her mouth watered.

He was sound asleep. Mayhap that was for the best, because she must bathe him down with cool water to try and break the fever. She'd already been dreading doing the deed since she had, not one hour past, just proven to herself that she had no self-restraint where a wickedly naked and awake Bao was concerned. But, she'd treated fever often enough to know that the bathing must be done.

Turning, she hastened out of the cottage and drew water from the well. Afterward, she would consult with Daniel and get some herbs for Bao's throat and cough. So far, his cough was dry, and she was determined to keep it that way. If the phlegmatic humor moved into his lungs, his fever could rise.

Thankfully, Bao never fully awakened during her ministration to him and the bath was completed with no added embarrassment to her. Upon speaking with Daniel, she was cautioned to remain at the keep and not go near Bao again until he was recovered. This, as a precaution against the fever being transferred to her and possibly harming their babe. Which, of course, was fine with her, as she had no intention of ever speaking to the man again. However, that did not mean she wouldn't worry over his recovery. He was, after all, the father of her unborn bairn, even if he was a no-good, rotten manipulator.

It was decided that she would use her chamber at the keep and that Bao would remain at the cottage, nursed by Daniel, Branwenn, and a few servants.

* * *

Bao's recovery took several days, which gave him plenty of time to think about his dilemma. He had blundered, badly.

Jesslyn was right. Using his body as a means of persuasion was a habit he needed to break. There was more to their relationship than mere lust and 'twas time that he convinced her of that fact. No matter how long it took, he would prove his devotion to her and not touch her, or attempt to seduce her again. And in time, when he didn't stray from her, she would finally believe him, trust him, and then they could finally settle into their union.

He was dressed in his shirt and braies, standing at the washstand shaving, when he heard the knock on the door. Turning, he called out, "Enter," and then turned back to gaze into the silver mirror as he scraped the last of the bristle from his chin.

"Good morn, Bao," Jesslyn said.

A thrill of shock and pleasure rushed over him and he looked over his shoulder. "Good morn," he answered softly.

"Daniel told me that you were recovered enough for me to see you."

"Aye. I'm feeling fit, actually."

"That pleases me. I was worried."

"I'm sorry for that."

She shrugged and looked away. She was tense with nerves, he could tell, so he turned his attention back to his morning rituals. He laid the knife down on top of the washstand and gazed in the mirror as he wiped the soap from his face, but his heart was racing and his palms were sweaty. "I'm moving back up to the keep, so you shall not have me in your way much longer."

"My thanks." There was both surprise and relief in her voice.

They were silent for a time and Bao strove for calm as he continued his ablutions. Her nearness made his heart pine, made his body ache for her touch.

"I am sorry that I made you ill," she said at last.

"Please, will you forgive me?"

Bao looked at her. "You didn't make me ill. I made myself ill with my own foolish behavior." He walked a step toward her. "And it is I who begs your forgiveness for my dim-witted attempt to trick you into giving me your good opinion again. I should have known not to treat you in such a manner. 'Twill not happen again, I swear it."

Jesslyn gave him a grim nod and then cleared her throat. "I've spoken to Daniel and he has agreed that, if you agree to it as well, Alleck, the babe, and I will move back to the MacLaurin keep to live once he and Maryn return there this summer."

A one-ton weight decended on his chest—it must have—for his lungs locked up and his chest cavity wrenched. He staggered back and leaned heavily against the washstand. "Nay, I do *not* agree to it."

"You'll keep me prisoner to you in a bad marriage, then? A slave to your will?"

He whirled around and gripped the edge of the washstand, his gaze blindly settling on its contents.

"If 'tis a son I have," she said, "then he'll train with you instead of one of our allies, if it please you to do so."

She was killing him and she didn't even know it.

"All right?" she prompted.

He squeezed his eyes shut. "All right."

"My thanks." She turned and left the chamber, left him. Left him standing there with his mind numb, his heart in tatters.

* * *

CHAPTER 16

Several sennights later, on the feast of Saint Brigid, Jesslyn cradled Nora in her arms in the great hall, cooing and speaking to the fiery-headed babe in low, dulcet tones. What a wee imp she was going to be. She was sure to give her father fits, and Jesslyn couldn't say that that thought gave her one moment of unease. Not after spending the past hours being chastised by the man for "tormenting" his brother.

"Has she finally fallen asleep?" Maryn asked softly as she settled on a stool next to Jesslyn and peeked around the blanket resting against the babe's cheek.

"Not yet, but soon, I trow," she replied in a whisper. "Her eyes have been drooping more frequently in just the past few moments." She slowly rose from her seat. "I should take her up to her nurse now so she may take a nap."

"I shall come with you," Maryn said. She tipped her head in Bao's direction. "Our lady guests certainly are enamored of your husband."

Jesslyn glanced in his direction and shrugged slightly, taking care not to jostle the babe and wake her. "What care I who occupies his attention?" But she did. She'd been gnawing on her jealousy all during the festivities. And now, when his eyes met hers briefly, when they warmed, when his mouth quirked in a quick smile before he looked away again, her heart melted a little.

"You shouldn't," Maryn replied. "He's a vile creature. When I think of what he was!" She shuddered. "He should have been banished; he has no place here with honorable folk such as us." Jesslyn felt her cheeks heat with her sudden anger as Maryn continued her tirade. "I tried to explain as much to Daniel, but he'd hear naught of it" she said, her voice filled with disgust. "It seems he's determined to defend his brother to the end."

Jesslyn forced in several long calming breaths, but said naught else. They arrived at Maryn's bedchamber door and quietly entered. She gently placed the babe in her cradle and quickly left the room, leaving Maryn whispering instructions to the nurse.

Jesslyn strode toward the stairs, intent on getting as far away from her ex-friend as possible. She couldn't believe the vicious words the woman had given her! Poor Bao! He had no idea that his own sister-in-law held such contempt for him. And after all he'd done to run her would-be murderer to ground! What a faithless friend she'd turned out to be!

She heard the soft pad of rushing footsteps behind her and sped up. "I'm sorry!" Maryn said breathlessly when she caught up to her, but Jesslyn didn't acknowledge her, simply continued to look straight ahead as she walked.

"I didn't mean those things I said, I swear it! I was only trying to see if you still cared for Bao enough to defend him."

Jesslyn stopped short and turned to face her. "What a foul thing to do! I shouldn't ever speak to you again!"

"I know!" she cried. "Say you forgive me, I beg you," she said coaxingly.

Jesslyn sighed loudly and rolled her eyes. "I forgive you."

Maryn grinned happily and clapped her hands.

"But don't ever try that again!"

"Nay, I shall not," she promised. "There's no need," she added cheekily, "now that I've seen your reaction." She paused only the length of a heartbeat before adding, "You love him. Desperately, in fact."

Jesslyn took in a deep breath and released it slowly. "Aye," she finally replied. "But love alone cannot save this union."

"Why not? Love is the strongest, best bond there is between a man and a woman! Why shouldn't it be enough to heal your hurt, to bring you back together—and keep you together?"

"Nay, it is *trust* that is needed to bind two people; love merely brings them together in the beginning, and sweetens the relationship as time goes on."

Maryn opened her mouth to argue, but was cut off by Jesslyn's next remark.

"Oh, I'm not saying 'tis not important, or even

highly desired in a union. I'm simply saying that one can have a happy, contented union without love where there is trust, but happiness and contentment cannot exist where love abides without trust."

"And you cannot trust Bao?"

"Nay, I cannot."

"Will you do something for me?" Maryn asked softly.

"Aye," Jesslyn responded, a question in her look.

"Will you have your evening meal here at the keep, as you used to do?"

"Aayyye," she drawled, suspicion in her voice.

Maryn gave her a slight smile. "Even if Bao is invited as well?"

Jesslyn narrowed her eyes at Maryn and shook her head at her friend's shameless meddling. "All right," she finally answered on a sigh.

* * *

A fortnight later, Jesslyn was on her way back to her cottage after spending the morn sewing with the ladies in the solar. She'd just turned off the path and was heading to her front door when she caught a glimpse of Bao and her son walking hand-in-hand toward the lad's mangonel. She stopped short and watched them.

Alleck's bright countenance turned up to the tall warrior and he said something to him. In the next instant, Bao had him hoisted into his arms and Alleck hugged him so tightly, she thought he'd choke the poor man. *"My thanks, Papa!"* she heard him yell. It caused a sharp spasm in her heart and before she realized it, a tear leaked from her eye. *If only....*

She threw her shoulders back and continued her march toward her cottage. No use wishing for things that would never be. She hadn't told Alleck that they were leaving with Daniel and Maryn. After discussing it with Daniel, they both decided that 'twould be best to tell him closer to the day of their departure. In any case, her son would begin his training with Daniel come September, as had been promised by Daniel to her husband Graeme before he died. And Daniel had been much like a father to Alleck these past years since Graeme's death. Alleck would soon recall their closeness when they were home once again at the MacLaurin holding.

* * *

A troupe of traveling players passed through on their way to a faire in the next county near the time of the *Alban Eiler*, the feast of the vernal equinox, and Lady Maclean thought it a fine time for a celebration. Jesslyn's childbed time was nearing and her gate was a bit lumbering, but she looked forward to the entertainment.

That evening, after the feast, the great hall was filled with soldiers and tinkers, alewives and midwives, ladies and maids, lads and their lasses. For the hundredth time, Jesslyn's eye scanned the crowd and landed briefly on Bao and his bevy of lady friends before moving back to the players.

"They vie for his attention like hounds on a bone," Maryn whispered to her.

Jesslyn quirked an eyebrow at her. "Of whom do you speak?"

"Bao, of course! The young women of good family and marriageable age are all abuzz with the prospect that the new laird and chieftain of clan Maclean will soon be free to wed again, now that you plan to petition for annulment on the grounds of consanguinity within the fourth degree."

"Mmm. As long as they do not let my son hear of it, I care not."

Maryn's hand settled on top of hers. "And yet, his eyes are only for you."

She couldn't help it, she looked. "Nay, they are not. He's listening avidly to—" with a jolt she realized *exactly* to whom he was speaking. 'Twas his lover, the one from the wood. A jealous fist twisted her insides and broke her heart. Again. Which angered her. Again.

"To whom? Oh, I see. 'Tis the MacGilvie lass. She's not a worry." Maryn leaned closer and whispered, "She's carrying a babe in her belly and is to wed soon. Oh! I see Daniel waving me over. I'll return in a moment."

Jesslyn felt weak, dizzy. Bao got the lass with child and now she was being bartered off to whatever young lad would have her. This time, when Jesslyn looked in Bao's direction, she allowed her gaze to remain. The MacGilvie lass stretched up on her tiptoes and whispered something in Bao's ear. He nodded and, in the next instant, she settled her hand on his arm and he led her out of the great hall.

Another tryst? Jesslyn didn't allow herself time to think. She rose from her stool and followed the two. This—this would be the final proof she needed to show

Daniel and Maryn that she was right to end this marriage and give him the freedom he clearly craved.

* * *

Bao led the lass across the antechamber and out through the door of the keep. At the bottom of the steps, he stopped and looked around. "Over there. No one is about, they're all inside the hall. We should have the privacy we need."

When they were ensconced in the darkness afforded by the night and the shadow of the chapel, he said, "Of what did you need to speak to me in privy?"

"I did a favor for you once and—"

"Of which I paid you handsomely."

"Aye. But I wondered if you might do a favor for me now?"

"What do you need?"

"I need you to promote Jamie in your ranks."

"My men get promoted when they deserve it, not before, and not for any other reason."

"But my mother found the coins a few moons ago that you gave me that day in the wood and when I explained where and why I got them,—I had to, else I'd have been banished—well, now she believes that you are the father of my bairn, not Jamie. She's heard the rumors that you are granting your wife an annulment and she will not be still until I agree to wait for you—to wed you instead."

"I understand not. How could she believe such—'tis clear you are not far enough along, even if I had bedded you, for this babe to have been conceived then."

"She believes 'twas you I was with on Hogmanay,

not Jamie."

"And why does she believe that?"

"Because I told her as much that night when she questioned me. The lie just flew from my lips. She hates Jamie. She cornered me outside the soldier's quarters, where Jamie and I had...and I thought if she believed 'twas you, then she wouldn't punish me as harshly."

"And what good will my promoting Jamie bring you?"

"Do you not see? My mother's opinion of Jamie will rise and she will see that 'tis best to wed sooner rather than later. And, once the babe's born, 'twill be clear that 'tis not yours."

"Lass, you are being naïve. If the lady truly believes that I fathered your bairn, she'll not rest until you are the lady of the holding."

She let out a long sigh and she wrang her hands. "What am I to do? I love him. He loves me. We want to wed."

"I could speak to her, explain..."

"Explain? Your wife saw us together. She doesn't know that you arranged it so that she would find us there, so that she would believe that we coupled. My mother has already told me that she believes your bedding me is the reason that your wife is leaving. All 'twould take is for her to speak to your wife, for your wife to confirm what she saw, and... well...."

Jesslyn stepped from the shadows. "*I* shall tell her there is no way—"

"—Jesslyn!" Bao said.

"—'tis Bao's babe when she speaks to me." She

came toward them. "And his family will concur, for all of them know where and with whom Bao was with the entire evening."

* * *

"And then the two of you made love in the cave?" Maryn asked the next day as she and Jesslyn sat in the solar enjoying some mulled wine.

"Aye. Nay. Oh, I don't know!" Jesslyn jumped to her feet and walked over to stand at the window, looking out at the courtyard and training fields. "We...coupled, aye. But I cannot say that *love* had anything to do with it."

"Can you not?" Maryn asked disbelievingly.

Crossing her arms and rubbing them, Jesslyn shrugged, "'Twas a demon trick on his part."

"*Jesslyn*," Maryn pressed, her voice chiding. "You lie to more than me with that response. You lie to yourself." Maryn placed her cup on the table before rising from her stool and walking over to stand next to her. Wrapping her hand around Jesslyn's upper arm, she gently squeezed and coaxed, "You *love* Bao—and he *loves* you."

Jesslyn shrugged once more, unable to speak past the constriction in her throat.

"Avow it this instant or I shan't do any more of your sewing for you!"

Jesslyn whirled to face her. "All right! I love him! He loves me!"

Maryn's gaze gentled.

Jesslyn's shoulders shook with grief as she struggled to stem the tears that flowed from her eyes. "I fear there is something lacking in me. Something that will lead him away. Else, why would Graeme have betrayed me?"

Maryn pressed her lips together in an effort to keep back the sharp retort that came to mind. She took in a deep breath and released it slowly. "I do not like speaking ill of the dead," she started carefully, "but...did you not ever consider that his faithlessness was a weakness—a *lack*—in his own character?"

"Even if it were, how do I know that Bao has not the same weakness? Just look at the way he gulled me into mating with him! His abstinence didn't even last a full sennight! What will he do when the babe is born and I am unable to couple with him for two moons?"

"Ah! Now it is clear to me. This groundless fear is the cause of your continued stubborn refusal to reconcile with Bao," Maryn said, with a nod of her head. "Well, let me assure you...there are other means of pleasuring your husband."

Jesslyn warred with herself over whether to tell Maryn the truth. "That is not possible," she finally said. "I can tell you naught more on the matter, so please do not press me to confide it."

Maryn's eyes narrowed on her a split moment before she gave a nod. "All right," she said. "But think on this awhile: Bao abstained for quite some time after you wed and his eye did not stray once from you. You are his prize, the one he craves. And, tho' he did use some trickery to gain his ends, 'twas with you that he mated, not any other. And he hasn't had another since you and he first made love."

"How know you this?" Jesslyn asked.

"He said as much to me two nights ago when he asked my advice on what he might do to win your trust." Maryn strolled toward her stool and sat back down. "Oh, there was one occasion in Perth, that evidently ended quite embarrassingly for him, in which he couldn't, shall we say, hoist his manly sword? But after that, there was no one."

"Why did he not tell me of this himself?"

"Mayhap, because he didn't think you would believe him? You have, after all, accused him of lying at every turn," Maryn replied. "In any case, his telling me was an accident, I believe. At first, he only said how absurd your fears were, considering the fact that he'd been with no one but you since last summer. I prodded, and he rather unwillingly gave me the full of it." Maryn sat forward, resting her elbows on her knees and loosely twining her fingers together. "I only break that confidence, for confidence it was, because I think that by telling you, 'twill finally give you the assurance you need to trust in Bao's love, in his allegiance to you."

Stunned, Jesslyn plopped down onto her stool with her hands clasped in her lap.

"He loves you, Jesslyn," Maryn stated again. "And what is more, he is devoted to you. All it will take for you to have your heart's desire is to let go of all these groundless worries and run into your husband's waiting arms."

Jesslyn rose to her feet, saying "I've an errand I just remembered. I shall see you at the noontime meal." And with that, she rushed from the room.

Maryn followed her a few steps behind. *"I hope he is sufficiently thawed first!"* she called down the stairwell to Jesslyn's fleeing backside.

Jesslyn cringed. Why had she told her of that? She should have known Maryn, with her wicked sense of humor, would not be able to restrain herself from teasing her about it. The sound of womanly laughter echoed in the stairwell. Jesslyn's shoulders scrunched. Aye, Maryn was certainly enjoying that bit of humiliating information. And then, before she realized, she was laughing as well. Suddenly, she felt cheerful, as light as air. She recalled Bao's reaction when she'd asked him the question and laughed even harder. The lecher had been hiding his own amusement!

* * *

Jesslyn found Bao overseeing the work on the new tower. "Will you walk with me to your bedchamber? I've left something there for you that I wish to give you."

The spark of hope in his eyes as he nodded and motioned to one of the men to take over made her smile.

"So, now that you know I never broke my vows to you, will you consider staying with me?" he asked as they walked toward the keep.

"Aye."

* * *

Bao's heart raced and his palms sweated as he shut the door behind him and leaned against it, watching her. What should he say to her? His mind was a blank.

"I made you some berry tarts," Jesslyn said into the

silence, lifting the basket slightly that resided on the tabletop near the hearth in indication of what it held.

Bao cleared his throat and crossed his arms over his chest. "My thanks," he finally said. He knew better than to press her to stay. He must tread very carefully with her, let it be her decision to be with him—if, as he hoped, 'twas what this errand was truly about.

She shocked the hell out of him when she lifted her hands to the tie of her chemise and loosened it, then pulled it open and ran her fingers over the rise of her breasts. "'Tis a bit warm in here, is it not?" she asked in a sultry voice. Untying the strings that held her gown together on the side, she loosened it as well.

Bao swallowed a couple of times.

She smiled. "Is it not?" she repeated when he didn't reply, skimming the gown and chemise off her shoulders a bit, just enough to bare another few inches of her bosom.

Bao blinked and cleared his throat. "Aye, it is." He would not walk one step toward her, he swore silently, else he might ruin his chances with her for evermore. He would not use his sexual prowess on her again unless she begged him to do so.

She took a step toward him, not covering herself when her bodice gaped open even further, allowing him a clear view of her excited nipples. Her eyes traveled from his face, down his torso, and halted briefly on the area where his tunic tented over his arousal, before she lifted her gaze once more to his own. "Bao," she said throatily, "I believe part of you"—she tipped her head toward the evidence of his desire and openly gazed at it, making him grow even more turgid—"is suffering a chill and needs a bit of thawing." She looked into his eyes once more. "I'd be pleased to hold it inside of me again to warm it—for as long as it takes," she offered suggestively.

His mind and sight were so fixed on the wanton display before him, that it took a moment for her words to register. When they did, his heart lifted and he grinned. She had turned his own method of trickery back on him. In two strides, he was before her. Without breaking eye contact, he lifted her in his arms and strode toward the bed. "You look a bit piqued, you should take a nap."

She brought her hand up to his face and stroked her thumb over his lips before leaning up and giving them a gentle kiss. It thrilled him beyond reason when she melted into him. It had been so long since he'd been allowed to hold her, kiss her. Without prompting, she opened her mouth to receive his tongue and gave him hers in return.

After a time, Bao lifted his head and gazed into her bemused eyes, out of breath, but eager to follow this through to its most pleasurable conclusion. "I want to touch you, taste you, all over, if you'll allow it."

Her smile was warm and her eyes held longing when she shook her head. "I shall touch *you* instead."

Her words hit like rapid, hard blows to the abdomen, forcing all the air from Bao's lungs, for he knew what she meant to do. It felt as if they had collapsed, so tight was his chest now. But, he knew also that he must attempt this thing in order for their union to fare well. With effort, he took a deep breath. Nodding slowly, he said, "I do not know for how long I shall be able to bear being touched there. Even by you."

"All right." Her eyes met his and did not waver. "Take off your clothes," she commanded softly.

Bao settled her back on her feet and took his time disrobing, not only for the added reprieve he received in doing so, but also in an attempt to heighten the sense of anticipation in himself.

When he finally dropped the last garment to the floor and stood bared to her gaze, she tipped her head in the direction of the hearth and said, "Sit in that chair over there."

Bao did as she wanted, but his heart raced and his muscles tensed. He placed his sweaty palms on the arms of the chair and grasped the edge in his hands. He'd never before felt this odd combination of trepidation and desire. Even the first time he'd bedded a woman he'd been filled with lust, not fear.

Bao watched as she took two of the large pillows from the bed and walked over to stand in front of him. "Lean back and open your legs wide so I can kneel between them."

"Is that wise? The babe…"

"I can manage it, I assure you."

He nodded. Tho' his hands clenched and unclenched the wood, he did her bidding and she placed the pillows on the floor and went down on her knees, resting her hands on the taut muscles of his thighs. She gazed up at him as she ran her hand over them. "I like the feel of the course black hair on your limbs. It tickles my palms and fingers."

His lungs wouldn't cooperate and he was getting lightheaded. He held tighter still to the ends of the wood armrests and his knuckles turned white. A crush of panic gripped him and he squeezed his eyes shut. His heart pounded in his ears and he swallowed hard.

Her sensual touch halted mid-thigh. "Whatever you're thinking of, stop," she commanded softly. "Open your eyes and look at me. Think only of me and what I'm doing. Naught else. At least for as long as you can do so."

Forcing himself to do as she instructed, Bao slowly lifted his lids and watched her.

"I see I must start in a different place." She took her hands from his thighs and placed them on her breasts, lifting them and caressing them the way he craved to do. His breath, what there was of it, caught in his throat and his rapid heartbeat tripped in his chest with both lust and shock.

"I was asked to do this once before, by Graeme, but I was much too shy to try it then. However, if this will help you to concentrate only on me, only on what is taking place between us in this chamber, then I am more than willing to overcome my own abashedness to gain that end."

Gripping the arm of the chair even tighter, his mind spun. "My thanks."

She twirled the rigid nipples between the thumb and forefinger of each hand and gave him a sultry smile when his arousal twitched against his stomach in reaction.

"Let me touch you, love. You're driving me mad," he ground out.

She shook her head. "Nay, not yet. But if you could, where would you touch me next?"

Bao's lungs worked just fine now, his breath coming faster and harsher. "I'd touch the heat of you, stretch you open with my fingers and take the honeydew it offered, up to its hidden pearl."

She nodded and placed one of the pillows behind her, then gingerly laid back. Lifting her legs over his knees, she did exactly as he'd described.

Bao moaned. The sight of her long, feminine fingers manipulating her lovely sex brought him dangerously close to climax. He craved to touch her, taste her. Now his hands grasped the armrests only as a means of keeping them from their purpose. He found her childing body intensely erotic; she was his very own golden fertility goddess. Whatever panic he had been feeling in the moments prior was gone in the wake of his overriding passion for her. "God, you're so lovely down there. Make yourself come," he begged. "I want to see you fly apart."

He could tell she was fighting her embarrassment, but she did as he asked. In no time, her eyelids drifted shut and the rosy hue of her cheeks and chest turned carmine and damp. A long, low moan escaped her lips.

Bao's breathing turned harsher still. She was close, he could tell by the gathering of her muscles, the trembling of her thighs. "Slide your finger into your sheath, feel how it quivers."

He could almost feel those inner muscles around his own digit as she did his bidding. In the next instant, her head flew back and she cried out, "Ahhh! Ahhh!" Her body remained taut, suspended in its pleasure for a moment and then she settled back on the cushions, her breath coming hard and fast. Her eyes opened and they stared hazily up at him a long moment.

"God, you are so beautiful," he said, stunned. She'd managed, with her openly erotic display, to send his panic flying. Now, all he wanted was her, in whatever manner she would allow.

Slowly rising back up onto her knees, she stroked his inner thighs once more. "I want you," she said throatily, easing her hands ever upward toward his aching cock.

"I want you, too," he said hotly, keeping his eyes, his thoughts only on her.

She managed to shock him again when she said, "I want to suck you, curl my tongue around this glorious manhood of yours." Then she coiled her fingers around him and stroked up, teasing the head before stroking back down. She did the same several more times and a drop of seed emerged.

He groaned, his abdomen tightening and trembling in pleasure. "All right. You may try putting your mouth on me," he said gruffly.

She rose up, balancing on his thighs and opened her lips, taking him between them and licking off the cum at the same time.

Intense pleasure rushed through Bao's veins. His eyes shut of their own volition and instantly a memory of Giric taking him this way, his grinning eyes as he molested his much-younger quarry, flashed through Bao's mind. "Stop!" Bao yelled, thrusting her from him.

She sat back with a stunned look on her face.

Bao leaned forward and covered his eyes with the base of his palms, forcing the foul images of his youth from his mind. "I'm sorry. I suppose 'tis just too soon for that." Lifting his gaze to her face, he said, "Forgive me?"

"Aye," she replied. "Make love to me, Bao. Now."

Bao rose from the chair and lifted his wife in his arms. He reached the bed in four strides and lay her down on her side. He settled behind her and lifted her leg over his arm. "I need to be inside of you now. All right?"

"Aye."

He entered her with a hard push, not stopping until he was fully sheathed. "Oh, God, Jesslyn. You, Alleck, our babe—you are everything to me. Everything."

* * *

CHAPTER 17

As the white and gray frost of winter slowly melted into the lush green and vibrant color spectrum of spring, Jesslyn and the ladies prepared for the birth of her babe while Bao, Daniel, and their soldiers continued preparing for the possible invasion. With a bit of difficulty, due to a late snowstorm, the barbican was completed and the final defense requirements were met. Tho' there had been hope that the babe would be born prior to the arrival of the army, it was not to be so.

On a bright April morn, only three sennights before the babe was expected, the Maclean scouts arrived with Reys ap Gryffyd bearing news that Llywelyn and his army were only days behind and would make camp on the other side of the wood while the required truce conditions were being considered.

* * *

"So this is my answer, then?" Bao said harshly to

Reys as the man was finally allowed to enter the great hall. Bao and Daniel had left him to cool his heels in the antechamber while they consulted with their scouts.

Reys held his hood in his hands, twisting it slightly. "Yes. I've spent these past moons seeking to turn my cousin from his purpose, as you and I agreed, but the effort was in vain." Reys looked from Bao to Daniel before saying, "He's quite adamant that Branwenn must return with us to Gwynedd."

"—Nay!" Daniel said.

"—That will not be," Bao said at the same time.

"The betrothal contracts have already been signed," Reys continued doggedly. "She is to wed Gaiallard de Montfort, nephew thrice removed to Guillaume le Maréchal, Earl of Pembroke as soon as possible." He slapped the woolen hood against one palm before grasping it once again in a tight fist. "My cousin wouldn't even allow more than a few days lead time for me to meet with you prior to his arrival here." Reys looked from one huge, fierce warrior brother to the other and waited. They stood silently glowering at him like one massive wall of human flesh and bone, their legs spread and their arms crossed over their heaving chests.

Without moving his eyes from Reys, Bao called out, "Steward Ranald!"

When the steward appeared in the doorway, Bao said, "Have the ladies' things packed immediately for a long visit to the Donald holding."

The portly steward nodded once and quickly departed.

"Branwenn cannot leave here," Reys said anxiously, "else there will be no negotiations. Llywelyn will strike forthwith and he will show no mercy."

"So be it," Daniel replied solemnly.

With a curt nod, Bao reiterated, "Aye, so be it."

"Be assured, he will attack the Donald fortress as well," Reys warned.

"Then he will not find out," Bao said forcefully. He was behind Reys in two strides and, before the man could know what Bao intended, he had looped his arms through Reys's and pressed his forearms against the back of the man's head, forcing it forward in an unnatural position.

Reys's arms flailed out to the side. "Wha—!" he wheezed.

Bao had locked the man inside a human vise. "You will be our prisoner, it seems, until this is finished," he growled through clenched teeth.

* * *

Intent on finding out what her fate would be, Branwenn rushed into the chamber and came to an abrupt halt. "Bao! What do you?" she shouted.

Bao tightened his hold.

"Aaargh," Reys cried out.

"I only seek to make our *guest* comfortable, as he will be staying here for quite some time it seems," Bao replied.

Reys lifted his foot and slammed his heel down hard on Bao's toe, grinding it in for good measure.

"Yeeowww! You spawn of a cur dog! You'll think twice before trying that again!" Bao swore, then he tossed Reys to the floor and sat down on him, hard, knocking the wind from the other man's lungs with a loud *whoosh*.

Spurred into action by the struggle, Branwenn flew over to the two men and yanked on Bao's upper arm. "Release him this instant! Are you addled?" she asked hoarsely, winded now from her own exertion.

Daniel let out a loud whistle that nearly broke all of their eardrums.

The tussle came to an immediate end.

"Get up Bao," Daniel said shortly.

Bao looked over at Daniel, his hands still clenched around Reys's skull. "What be the problem, brother? Surely, you do not expect me to allow this whoreson to leave here now?"

"Nay, I do not. However, we are not going to abuse our guest while he is here, either," he replied.

Bao reluctantly rose to his feet and aided Reys to his as well before turning to Daniel. "He's not to be a part of the negotiations, either. I do not want this prince to learn Branwenn is no longer here."

"Agreed." Daniel replied with a nod.

Branwenn looked at Reys. "Why are you being treated like this?" she asked in confusion. She turned then to her other two brothers without waiting for a reply. "Why are you treating him in this manner?"

"Because," Bao snapped, "I do not trust him to keep our confidence. He has informed us that Llywelyn will not negotiate, will begin the siege immediately, in fact, should he find out that you have been allowed to flee."

Branwenn's heart pounded in her chest. She turned

back to Reys then. "So he is still insisting that I wed this relation to one of the Norman march lords?"

Reys pressed his lips together and nodded once. "Yes. He will not be thwarted, it seems."

"And would you? Would you tell Prince Llywelyn that I've fled?" Branwenn asked. Now that the time had come to surrender herself to this stranger, she found she couldn't do it. As it was, she didn't want to be wed, but the thought of doing so with none of her family around petrified her. Was it *so* terrible to allow her mighty warrior brothers to fight to keep her with them? After all, Maryn had told her that Daniel never lost any battle—and she, herself, knew that Bao was the bravest, smartest, most unbeatable force of any of the king's soldiers. And the two of them *were* quite determined that they could win this thing.

Reys nodded his head grimly and she was sure she saw regret in his eyes when he said, "Yes, I would. I must. For he is my sovereign lord and it is my duty."

Words flew from her mouth with a force of their own before she'd fully realized she'd made her decision. "Then there is naught for it but that I flee and allow my brothers to use their skills and their might to push the man back from whence he came. For, be assured, I *will not* return with him!"

"I think it be time that we show our *guest* to his new lodgings," Bao said snidely and then he called out to the two scouts he had told to remain outside the doorway earlier. "Take him to the upper chamber of the donjon and lock him in. Make sure there is no means of escape and keep a guard outside his door at all times," Bao instructed.

After the scouts had departed the hall with Reys in tow, Daniel said, "Once our family is safely at the Donald keep—and now, I wonder if they shouldn't be sent even further, to the MacLaurins at least—and the villagers who do not travel there as well are safely behind these walls, we'll send a missive to Llywelyn informing him that we keep Reys with us as our guest. Any negotiations will be done in the glen, with only the two of us meeting with him. Reys will not be allowed an audience with his cousin again until after the siege is done."

Bao nodded. "We must send the women and Alleck from here. Now. Before another minute has passed. I shan't be able to think clearly while their lives are in danger." He turned to Branwenn. "Make haste to the Donald holding. Go!" He said, turning her and slapping her on the behind as he had so many times when she was a wee lass.

"Ouch!" Branwenn yelled dramatically as she scurried toward the door.

"That didn't hurt and well you know it!" Bao called out to her retreating form, finding his first smile since Reys's arrival. His heart ached at the thought that she might be lost to him for evermore if Llywelyn discovered their deception. Sobering he looked at Daniel. "I fear Jesslyn and the babe are in no condition to travel as far as the MacLaurin holding now. If we can hold our secret, and hold our fortress, until after the babe's birth, then they should be able to travel there soon after, as long as the weather permits."

Highland Grace

"Aye, I had not thought of that. You are right, Jesslyn cannot travel such a distance just now." Daniel sighed and scrubbed his hand through his hair. "We'll hold our own, fear not. Not only until our wives and family can get to my MacLaurin clan, but until the other clans have arrived to set upon our adversaries' hind shanks."

"Aye, but before that can happen, we must *inform* them of such," Bao reminded him. "And I think it best that we send six messengers in just as many directions. The prince will be expecting us to gather our allies, and I fully expect him to attempt to stop the missives from getting through. However, he'll not expect he'll need to hinder more than two, I'd wager."

"Aye, that be a sound plan. We must not tarry another moment." Daniel called for the steward to gather six of the fleetest messengers and then quickly wrote out the missives and stamped them with his seal.

"It is done," Bao said finally when the last messenger scurried from the chamber a quarter-hour later.

"Aye, it is done. And now we wait."

Hearing his wife's voice just outside the doorway, Bao replied, "Nay, and now we say our farewells to our women," as he rushed from the chamber.

* * *

CHAPTER 18

Jesslyn lay curled on her side on the bed late that night in the chamber she'd been given at the Donald holding recalling the scene in the courtyard earlier that day. Bao had made her vow that she would be careful these next days until the babe was born. She'd grown quite round and her movements had become ever more lumbering with the added weight. He worried that she would not be able to climb and descend the stairs without falling, but she'd assured him that his worries were for naught, that tho' her movements were a bit slower than before, she was still quite strong and capable of carrying herself up and down stairs as needed. When she'd arrived and attempted just that, however, she'd been shocked to find that one of Laird Donald's men had been instructed to *carry* her to her chamber! She chuckled and shook her head. She'd relieved him of *that* notion soon enough.

She smiled. Bao had been in such a state, worrying that she would be afraid to deliver her babe without him by her side as he'd promised he would be. And no matter how much assurance she'd given him that she no longer felt so fearful of the childbed time, that she looked forward to it now, that she was *past* ready to be done with her childing state and hold her babe in her arms, he would not be settled.

Jesslyn sighed and sat up with a bit of difficulty, dangling her feet over the edge of the bed and resting her palms on the mattress at her side. Her breathing was somewhat labored from the effort, but she was growing used to that effect now that her childbed time was drawing near. She arched her back in an effort to ease the ache in it.

A knock came on the door and she called out, "Enter!"

Maryn opened the door a crack and peeked inside. "How feel you? Need you a cup of warmed wine?"

Jesslyn motioned for her to come inside and rose from her place on the bed. "My thanks, but nay, I need no wine," she said, answering the last question first. "My back aches, but in all other respects, I feel quite fit." She toddled over to the chair by the hearth and slowly levered herself into the seat. "You cannot sleep either, I see."

"Nay!" Maryn said anxiously, settling in the seat opposite. "I cannot stop worrying about my husband's safety—and Bao's as well, of course."

Jesslyn had been fighting back the panic each time it threatened to rise in her breast, but with Maryn's words, she lost the battle. Clasping her hands together, she began her old habit of twisting her fingers together. "Aye, and there is much to fear. Of which I have personal experience, as you recall." Her eyes pooled with tears. "Oh, Maryn! What if Bao is killed? I cannot bear to lose another husband! And this time, I shall have *two* bairns to raise on my own!"

Maryn took Jesslyn's hands in her own. "I shouldn't have voiced my foolish worries to you. For foolish they are," she said soothingly. "You must remember that Daniel and Bao are seasoned warriors who have fine, tactical minds. They've thought of every ploy this Prince Llywelyn may try and will overcome each of them. You will see. And you must not forget that, even now I wager, Callum and his clan of MacGregors as well as the MacLaurins are preparing to counter the prince's strike with one of their own." She sat back and smiled, though it didn't quite reach her eyes. "Why, 'twouldn't surprise me in the least if this whole mess was over and done with before *Bealltainn*."

Please, let it be so, Jesslyn prayed silently. An image of Graeme unfurled once more in her mind's eye. Dead, battered, one arm gone, he had been soaked in blood from the sword wound that had sliced through the links of his mail armor into his neck, nearly severing his head from his body. They'd laid him out on a stretcher and carried his body home to her. She shuddered. "You are much too innocent in the ways of war if you believe such," she replied sadly. "Nay, we shan't see our husbands again for many moons, if at all."

Maryn jumped to her feet. "Nay! I will not listen to

such talk! 'Tis bad luck, I know it is." Now *she* twisted her fingers together. Turning, she walked a few paces away. After a moment, she straightened her spine and threw her shoulders back. "Nay, we must believe that all will be well, that is the only way we will make it through this without losing our wits, I'm sure of it."

Jesslyn nodded and forced her panic back down deep once more. "Aye, you are right. For our own soundness of mind, we must not think on the worst."

* * *

A moon passed without word from the Maclean holding, so Laird Donald sent one of his men to scout out the situation, in stealth, and report back to him.

The man arrived back in the late afternoon, winded and distressed. With horror in his voice, he gasped out the news. "The enemy army is legion, Laird. More men than I've seen assembled in my lifetime. And they are well equipped. They've war machines positioned on the north and south side of the barbican and bombard it mercilessly. "There were many lying dead along the battlements."

Laird Donald rose to his feet and began to pace with his head bent and his hands clasped behind his back. "And the Macleans? Do they hold steady?"

"Aye, so far. But I know not for how much longer they can do so. For the numbers against them are vast, as I said."

"Have the MacGregors or the MacLaurins arrived?"

The man shook his head. "Nay, Laird. I saw no other warriors outside the fortress other than the enemy's."

"I wonder what is taking them so long to arrive?" Laird Donald mumbled to himself before looking up at his man and saying, "I need you to gather three others and journey to the MacGregors' land. Hopefully, you will meet up with them along the way, but if not, you must carry the message to Laird MacGregor that he and his men are needed forthwith to aid in this war against their allies, the Macleans. Mayhap, the missive did not make it to them. If that is the case, you will travel to the MacLaurins as well. Understood?"

"Aye, Laird."

* * *

Branwenn scurried into the shadows of the stairwell when the scout walked out of the great hall into the antechamber. She'd heard everything. The Maclean allies had not arrived yet. And Bao and Daniel were outnumbered by thousands of men. Men with war machines capable of tumbling the Maclean fortress! She should not have left her fate in the hands of her loving brothers. For her, they may be killed. For her, they may leave two widows and their bairns. For her, they may watch their clansmen, and those of their allies, perish. It had finally become clear to her that she was being selfish, that she had willingly fallen back into her youthful habit of allowing Bao to solve her problems for her. Of *relying* on him to solve her problems for her. But she was a woman grown now. She must stand on her own and do what she must, do what was best, do what would engender the least amount of grief and destruction to those for whom she cared most. Do what she had sworn to herself she *would* do if the prince laid siege to her family's holding. She straightened her spine and threw back her shoulders, a new purpose in her stance. She must surrender herself to the prince and wed with whomever he had contracted for her hand. It wouldn't be so horrid to do so, she was sure of it. After all, Reys had never mentioned her future husband in any disparaging manner. He must be as fine a man as any her grandmother had in mind, surely. 'Twas settled then. She nodded once for good measure. She would give herself over to the prince. She plucked her thumbnail against her front tooth. But first, she must plan a way out of here and figure out how she would get to this prince before anyone found out what she was about.

* * *

"I cannot understand why none of our allies have shown up yet. Do you think it possible all of our missives were intercepted?" Daniel shouted to Bao over the din of battle. They stood in the curve of the south tower stair, watching the battle progress through the arrow slit. This was one of several of the quieter regions of the fortress where they could meet to make battle plans and give each other news of what was happening in their area of the fortress where they each battled to keep the enemy from breaking through.

"Aye, 'tis the only explanation," Bao shouted back. He shrugged and winced from the sting it caused the injury he'd received this morn from a stray arrow. It had gone into his chest, just below the collarbone. He'd yet to get the arrowhead out, instead simply breaking off the wooden shaft and occasionally dousing the wound with *uisge beatha*, as Daniel had recommended. "The man has more wit than I suspected. That was a grave mistake on my part. 'Twill not happen again, I assure you."

"It is not time to worry yet, brother. Remember you we made provisions for such an outcome in our planning, that Laird Donald will send a scout here when he receives no word from us. I've no doubt he'll quickly get word to the MacGregors and the MacLaurins once he learns of our situation. Our task is to keep the enemy from overtaking us until that time."

"Aye. But I think it best that we build the second mangonel. If we can destroy more of their towers and ballistae, 'twill delay their advance."

"Get the men on it at once," Daniel replied. "Where is Derek?" The man had been the lieutenant before Bao's arrival, and would be again once Bao took over his duties as Laird of the Macleans. Derek was now serving as second lieutenant and was an integral part of the tactical decisions regarding the siege.

"He's overseeing the defense of the barbican. Since he is the most skilled with the mangonel, he's set himself the task of destroying the tower containing the battering ram that approaches before it reaches the gate," Bao replied, absently rubbing the area around his wound.

"Good," Daniel replied. Then, noticing Bao's movements, asked, "Will you make it until the bombardment ceases for the night for me to tend that wound?"

Bao nodded. "Aye. I am not losing much blood

from it."

Daniel gave him a curt nod and moved past him down the stairs. "I'll see you in two hours in the north tower. And make sure Derek is there as well."

"Aye," Bao replied as he followed behind his brother.

* * *

One of Laird Donald's scouts returned a fortnight later. Their mission had been a success and forces were on their way from both the MacGregor's and the MacLaurin's to meet the enemy army on the field.

"I have tidings of the Macleans, as well, Laird," the scout said.

"Aye, speak up, man," Laird Donald said anxiously.

"One of the brothers has been wounded," the man replied.

"Wha—which one?"

"I know not," he said. "The wound itself was not mortal, but it must have festered before it was tended properly and now they fear he'll perish from the fever, Laird."

Laird Donald turned and walked toward a bench and then numbly collapsed upon it. "How am I to give this dreadful report to my daughter...my guests?" he said hollowly, his eyes fixed on some point far in the distance. He looked into the eyes of the scout and said, "Jesslyn, Lady Maclean, only three sennights past, brought her son into this world. What will be my words to her if it be her husband that may perish?"

* * *

Branwenn hastened up the stairs to her chamber and

sat down hard on the bed, chewing her thumbnail. She'd heard all, of course. She'd just begun descending the stairs, intending to ask the cook for a chamomile tincture for her menstrual cramping, when she saw the man go through the portal of the great hall and immediately set about listening to the exchange. She'd discovered that her only means of learning news of the siege was to do thus, for Laird Donald held much from them. He was a kind and good man, but he strove to protect them too much, revealing as little detail as possible when he spoke of the siege.

The first sennight after hearing news of her brothers' fight against the Prince, she tried twice to get past the guards, but had twice been turned back. Afterward, it had taken a fortnight of close observation to the routines of the keep to devise her new plan. And now, 'twas clear, she must tarry no longer. She would fly, and fly quickly. She would not even wait until night fell to do so. She would wear the drab, brown tunic and tan hose of a villein that she'd worn last summer while she and Bao lived in the wood. The hood would cover her hair and she'd wear it low enough to shadow her face as well. With a bit of soiling to her cheeks and her hands, she should pass through the gate easily enough.

But the trip would be a brutal one on foot. If only she could acquire a cart and ox. The wheels in her mind spun with possibilities. Aye, a cart would make the entire process easier. And hadn't she seen just such a conveyance filled with horse dung sitting outside the stables this morn past? She'd borrow the thing and make sure that it was returned to its owner within a day of her arrival at the prince's camp.

Rising to her feet, she then hastened to the chest that held her clothing and rummaged through the contents, flinging out each piece of her villein costume as she came upon it. With a cart, she should be able to reach the prince before dusk. And by morn, the siege on the Maclean holding would be over. But she would insist upon seeing her brothers before she departed. She must. Worry for their welfare was tearing at her insides. Which one labored for his life? If it be Bao, she'd die of a broken heart before she ever left this land. But what if it be Daniel? Oh, God. Her heart could not stand the pain that worry gave her either.

Within moments she had gathered her villein attire into a basket and covered it with a cloth. To any who might see her, 'twould look as if she carried bread or some other foodstuff. There would be no suspicion raised, which meant it would be several hours before the alarm would be sounded that she was missing.

She'd leave a note, of course. Here, in her chamber. She looked around for a prominent spot where the missive would be seen immediately upon entering. The top of her chest. Aye, that would do nicely.

She quickly scribbled out her tale; where she was headed, and with what purpose. Surely, by the morrow they would all be reunited in peace once more. And then they could spend all their energies on making her brother well again. Before she left them all to meet her destiny.

* * *

"My son is so big, I cannot believe he sprang so easily from my loins!" Jesslyn whispered, awestruck and happy as she held the sleeping babe in her arms and gazed upon him. It was well past noon now and she'd just awakened from her nap. She looked up, into the eyes of Lady Maclean. "But, thanks be to heaven, he did. For I believed I would labor to give him birth at least until the curfew bells that day."

"I as well," Lady Maclean replied. She leaned forward and placed her hand on the back of the babe's head. "He's a handsome lad, this Bao Li," she murmured. "He's the look of his father, with that black hair and the slight slant to the eyes. But I can see you in him as well. He has your chin and brow, it looks to me."

Jesslyn glanced down once more at her new son and said, "Aye, he's lovely. Bao will be so amazed! He was sure he'd have a wee *daughter* come *Bealltainn*."

"Aye, that he will be," Lady Maclean agreed softly. Settling back on her perch on the mattress next to Jesslyn, she said, "I should go and check on Branwenn and see how she fares. 'Tis not like her to lay abed this long, even while she flowers."

Jesslyn nodded. "Where is Maryn?"

"She's in her chamber, I suppose," Lady Maclean replied, not ready to speak with Jesslyn about the possibility that Bao may have been injured, that he may now lie fevered inside the battle-torn Maclean fortress. Earlier in the day, while Jesslyn still rested, Laird Donald had given the news to both her and his daughter that one of her grandsons had been wounded.

Highland Grace

Even now, the memory of the tortured cry that Maryn had emitted before collapsing to the floor sent chills down her spine. She feared that Jesslyn would have a similar reaction and thought it best to allow the new mother a bit more rest before revealing the dreadful message to her that they had received.

"Give her my thanks when you see her. I don't know how I would have gotten through these past sennights without her strength, her courage, and her friendship."

"Aye, she's a brave lass." Lady Maclean rose from the bed and leaned down, kissing her granddaughter-in-law on the cheek.

Jesslyn grasped the older woman's hand in her own. "And I thank you as well. You've now brought *two* lovely, healthy, great-grandbairns into this world."

Lady Maclean squeezed Jesslyn's hand before releasing it. "Would you like me to put the babe in his cradle before I leave?"

Jesslyn shook her head and gazed once more at her slumbering son. "Nay. I shall place him there a bit later. I want to enjoy the feel of him in my arms a while longer."

Lady Maclean nodded and quietly departed, leaving the mother and son to enjoy their peaceful and innocent time together. For it would be so no longer once Jesslyn learned of the possibly fatal wounding.

* * *

It was late afternoon by the time Branwenn abandoned the ox-drawn cart along the southern banks of the loch. All had gone as planned and she'd managed to depart the Donald holding soon after she'd devised her escape.

With some apprehension, now that she was so close to her goal, she steadily walked in the direction of the wood, knowing only that the prince camped somewhere on its outskirts. The camp would be mostly deserted at this time of day while the battle raged, but there would be guards manning the outer perimeter, and her greatest fear was that they might strike her down before she had proffered her surrender. Even with that dread chance, she pushed herself onward. For the prospect of ending the siege and preventing any further bloodshed was worth the risk.

* * *

Lady Maclean sat down on the edge of Jesslyn's bed and handed the note to her. She anxiously watched the emotions race across the younger woman's face as she read it.

Jesslyn's eyes were riveted on the final words of the note. *"Fare you well,"* Branwenn had written, *"You will be for evermore in my heart and in my thoughts."* There was such finality in the words and in the tone, as if Branwenn expected that they'd not be seeing each other ever again. Dropping her arm onto her lap, Jesslyn limply held the letter in her hand. "But why?" she asked at last. "Why would she surrender herself into this man's control when our allies are on their way to aid our cause?"

Maryn, who had been standing a bit away while Jesslyn read Branwenn's note, came over to settle on the other side of her, placing a comforting hand on her shoulder.

Lady Maclean took the missive from Jesslyn's limp fingers and placed it on the bed beside them. She glanced at Maryn and then turned her gaze once more to Jesslyn, her mouth forming into a grim line. "I had hoped to tell you of this on the morrow," she finally said, "after you'd had a bit more rest."

Jesslyn sat up straight, alarm filling her countenance. "Wha—"

"One of Laird Donald's scouts arrived earlier this day with word from the Maclean fortress."

Jesslyn's heart leapt into her throat. Swallowing past the pounding swell of fear that lodged there, she grasped the older woman's arm and rasped, "Aye?"

Lady Maclean placed her hand over that of her granddaughter-in-law's and soothed it with a soft caress. "One of my grandsons was injured and is now battling a deadly fever."

Jesslyn released her hold on the other woman's arm and blindly reached up, taking hold of Maryn's hand instead. "The scout knew not which of our husbands is ill?"

"Nay," Lady Maclean replied sadly. "I believe Branwenn went to the prince's camp in order to end the siege and get inside the fortress to see her brothers."

"Then we must go home as well," Maryn said anxiously.

"We cannot. We must first hear that the siege is done or we risk all our lives," Lady Maclean cautioned.

"When will we learn if he has withdrawn his army?"

Jesslyn asked.

"Laird Donald sent a scout back to the battleground the moment he read Branwenn's missive. If all goes well, we should know by the morrow. But 'twill be late in the day, I fear, for the negotiations will take several hours and he must wait to find out their terms in order to relay them to Laird Donald," Lady Maclean replied.

"So we may be able to leave day after next?" Jesslyn asked.

Lady Maclean nodded and patted her granddaughter-in-law's hand. "Aye. That is as I surmise, but do not be surprised if they will not allow us to return for several more days. They may want to bury the fallen soldiers and clear the war debris before we arrive."

* * *

Prince Llywelyn sat inside his tent that eve going over tactical maneuvers with his marshal. He regarded the drawing of the Maclean fortress, endeavoring to find any weakness he might have missed the many past times he'd studied the illustration. "We must break through that wall!" he said harshly, slamming his fist on the table in frustration. "The demons have thus far managed to tumble two of my siege towers with their mangonel." He looked up, his eyes drilling into those of the other man. "Destroy that mangonel! 'Tis the only way we'll get close enough to the wall to use the battering ram on it."

"Aye, Your Highness," the marshal replied gravely. "We've attempted such already, but as yet to no avail. We'll be successful this next attempt, I assure you, now that the perrier is built. The engine is easily set again and is quick to fire, Your Highness."

"Pound the thing with it, then. And protect the men who man the sling with a hundred bowmen."

"Aye, Your Highness."

A shrill screech came from just outside the tent followed by the sound of an angered girl's voice. "I have already surrendered, you idiot! Cease twisting my arm from its socket!"

The prince and his marshal looked toward the entry to the tent just as a girl in humble dress was thrust inside, followed by one of the men assigned to guard the camp. "On your knees before the Prince!" he stormed.

Branwenn fell forward, taking all her weight onto her knees and hands, her wrists bent and her fingers snapped back almost to their breaking point. "Owww!" she yelped, and then, unable to hold her weight with her injured wrists, collapsed face down in the dirt.

"Pardon, Your Highness," the guard rushed to say, "but this youth claims to be your cousin, the Lady Branwenn, but I think it the newest plot by the devil Macleans to spy upon us."

Branwenn gingerly lifted herself up, first onto her elbows and then up into a sitting position resting back on her calves and the undersides of her feet. "I *am* Branwenn Maclean," she said forcefully, rubbing the bitter sting from her sprained appendages. "This is no sinister device to steal your war secrets, I swear it." Branwenn gazed at her cousin, this prince who held her life, her fate, in his hands and was amazed to see that he was not the demon she'd expected him to be. He was quite handsome, in fact. And not at all the aged man with the graying hair and beard that her mind had envisaged all these moons. His hair was dark, like hers, and he did not shave the bristles from above his upper lip, instead allowing them to grow in long strips from just under his nose to either side of his jawline, making an arrow effect. His eyebrows vee'd, much like her own, above dark, penetrating eyes. He wore a tunic of the finest scarlet, trimmed in saffron, over mail armor, the hood of which rested on his shoulders and back. A crown of gold perched atop the short-cropped mass of hair on his head, intimidating her more than she was willing to admit, even to herself.

The prince sat back in his chair and lazily stretched one leg out straight in front of him under the trestle table he sat behind. There was a long scroll of parchment with a drawing on it which he held open in front of him using his forearms as braces against the curling edges. Unfortunately, it was too far away for Branwenn to see clearly, but she suspected it might be an image of her family's castle.

"I've come to surrender myself into your hands, so you may end the siege of my home."

Prince Llywelyn looked first to the guard and then to his marshal and cocked his head in the direction of the entrance. "Leave me with this youth." As the two men made their departures, he studied her. "Why dress you so meanly, lady?" he said at last. And then, looking past her out through the opening of the tent, he queried her further, "And where be your Highland protectors? Had they not courage enough to meet me face-to-face when they surrendered their prize?" He glared down at the map in front of him. "There must be some secret passage that allowed exit," he mumbled, evidently to himself.

"My brothers know not of my purpose, Your...Highness," she said, struggling past the appellation.

Prince Llywelyn looked up from his musings and gave Branwenn a piercing look.

"With some bit of stealth and cunning did I leave from my safe haven at the Donald keep. It required that I clothe myself in the guise of a villein," she explained.

Prince Llywelyn sat forward. "Your Highland *brothers*"—he sneered when he said the word—"defied the codes of chivalry and hid my prize from me?" he growled.

"Nay! You mustn't believe them unchivalrous, Your Highness. They only sought to protect me, and their ladies, until the victor of the siege was named. Surely, you can see that a besieged fortress is not a place for lady wives and their bairns, nor a dearly loved sister and her aged grandmother."

Prince Llywelyn relaxed back once more. "Aye, I can see the wisdom in that decision. *If* it was, as you say, only for the duration of the siege, and not a ploy to keep me from my prize."

Branwenn bristled. "I beg you, *Your Highness*, cease labeling me your *prize!* Else, I swear, I shall not remain the calm lady you see before you now."

Amused, by the girl's show of spine, one side of

Prince Llywelyn's mouth quirked in a smile. "This, then, is how you behave when you are calm? My bones quake at what may be your behavior when you are truly roused, then, *my prize*," he provoked. She was a beauty, he was pleased to discover. Not tall, and very slight. Seemingly too delicate to have made it here on her own. The fine bones of her face set into stark contrast her large violet, tip-turned eyes and fleshy red mouth. Her hair was still covered by a hood, but her brows and lashes were as dark as pitch in color. Just as her mother's had been. Aye, Gaiallard de Montfort would be pleased with his bride. And the more pleased this relation to the Earl of Pembroke was in his match, the greater the bond between the two families, which could only translate into more power for the Prince of Gwynedd.

Branwenn's cheeks flamed with ire. She stood up, even though he'd not given her leave to do so as yet. "Is this how it is to be then?" she asked, her fingers curling into fists inside her chafed palms. "I am chattel and will be treated as such?"

"Nay, lady, not mere chattel, but something of much greater worth. For, with your union to the Earl of Pembroke's nephew, I will gain the means by which to extend my realm."

"And so I am to play the pawn in your plot," she stated stiffly. "This...this nephew to whom I am to pledge my troth...is he to be so ill-used as well? Or does he also gain from this match born of avarice?"

"It is not only greed that drives me in this contract I draw with the march lord, lady. The Cambrian people have suffered greatly at the hands of the Norman invaders. I seek to put our land, our people, back under the control of the natives. That is my first, and most desired, purpose," the prince explained. "The man I seek to wed you to is Gaiallard de Montfort. And he gains what you gain as well: A vast demesne, its fortress, and jurisdiction over its tenants."

Branwenn's heart nearly leapt from her chest. She'd believed her new husband would be a member of the march lord's household. She hadn't expected to be responsible for her own house. Not in Cambria. She had no knowledge of that land's customs, nor what would be expected of the lady of the holding. "I..." she started hoarsely. She cleared her throat. "I am expected to be lady of a keep in a strange land? Does this man know I was not raised a lady? Have, in fact, only just this past year begun my training? Surely, he will be greatly disappointed in me, Your Highness."

A twinkle came into Prince Llywelyn's eye as he regarded her. "Gaiallard is full aware of your upbringing, lady, fear you not. And I am more than certain that he will be quite pleased with you, lady skills or nay."

Branwenn's shoulders drooped. She sighed and nodded, saying, "Then the siege is done? You'll send a messenger at first light to convey that I have surrendered?"

Prince Llywelyn nodded. "Aye, lady. And pleased I am that we will for home so soon since my arrival here."

"But I will be allowed to say my farewells to my

family before we depart?" she hastened to ask.

"Aye. And forget you not, your brother, Reys, is prisoned in that fortress you call home. I shan't leave this land without his company."

"Worry not, Your Highness. My brothers have not harmed your cousin, you shall see."

"*You* are my cousin as well, fair lady, forget you not," Prince Llywelyn admonished gently. He hadn't expected to like the girl quite so much, but she was such a charming mix of beauty and fire, so full of spirit and wit, he found himself completely enchanted by her. Aye, she'd bring him what he desired, and in not so distant a time.

* * *

"Christ's Bones!" Daniel shouted as he released his grip on his brother's wounded thigh. He and Derek had been attempting to hold Bao still while Daniel tried to inspect the gaping gash left from the arrowhead his brother had yanked from his groin area where his thigh met his pelvis. "Even in his slumber, Bao will not allow me to tend this wound!" He looked up, into the worried face of his second lieutenant. "And that is the one, I fear, that is causing his fevered stupor."

Derek nodded grimly. "There is a stench of putrefaction in that region."

"Aye, it festers, that is certain." Speaking through clenched teeth, he ground out, "I should not have waited so long to tend it."

"It could not be helped," Derek consoled. "The whoreson prince sends his first volley earlier and earlier each day, and the battle was already raging by the time we discovered your brother had not come from his chamber this morn. We could not bear losing another commander."

Knowing Derek spoke the truth, Daniel nodded, sighing. But it still did not sooth the raging guilt he felt. "He must have received this arrow the same day he got the other one in his chest, but he never told me of it," he said finally. Agitated, he ran his fingers through his hair. "I should have realized when he became dizzy last eve that he was ill, but he'd had *uisge beatha* with our meal and I thought him only a bit sotted." He glanced at Derek, smiling slightly in spite of his worry, as he explained, "'Tis truth that he does not hold his spirits well," before turning his gaze back on his brother and somberly continuing, "I discovered the wound when I helped him to his chamber and then out of his chain and hose."

"Did he not allow you to tend it then?"

Daniel shook his head. "Nay. He had it bound in a bloody rag, but said 'twas only a scratch, that 'twould heal on its own without my tending it."

"He fought hard all these days past, and he limped not," Derek said, surprised.

"Aye, which is why I thought he'd spoken the truth about the nature of the wound."

Derek nodded. "But when he failed to meet us in the south tower...."

"Aye, I did begin to worry then. Tho' when I hurried up here afterward, I never believed I'd find him laid so low," Daniel confessed. "All I had time to do was to bathe him down with cool water, pour *uisge beatha* on the wound, and force a ptisan down his gullet before I returned to the fray."

"And now he grows worse;" Derek said, "he awakens not from his fevered slumber."

Daniel's worried gaze traveled from his brother's damp brow to the blood-soaked binding around his upper thigh. He took in a deep breath and released it slowly as he rubbed the back of his neck and pondered his dilemma. When he finally spoke, he did so with a new determination, saying, "I must tend this, I *must*. There is no choice."

Derek nodded. "Aye," he agreed. "But we will need to bind his arms and legs beforehand. And even then, it may be necessary to bring another soldier in to help me hold him while you clean the wound."

"Aye," Daniel said and moved swiftly toward the door. He opened it and told the guard to gather rope and bring it back to the chamber with due haste. He turned and walked back to stand at his brother's bedside once more. "Why does he fight me so?"

Derek shook his head as he gazed down at his friend and commander. "I know not."

"My brother endured a different kind of torment from our scurrilous sire than the man gave to me. Mayhap this odd reaction is due to some evil on that man's part."

Derek nodded.

The guard came through the open doorway with the rope and handed it to his laird. Daniel and Derek quickly tied down Bao's appendages. Afterward, the guard and Derek took their positions beside their lieutenant as Daniel cut the binding away and doused the festering wound with *uisge beatha*. Looking up at Derek and the other man, Daniel said, "Get a good grip on him, for I must cut out the dying flesh. But be you careful that the stitches of his other injury are not opened."

The two men nodded grimly as they pressed Bao even further down into the mattress.

* * *

Bao was deep in a vivid nightmare. He was a lad of ten summers once more and under his father's control. Thrashing his head from side to side, he began to yell as he strained to free himself from his father's black-hearted soldiers who held him down while his father came ever closer with the dirk he would use to cut the horrid emblem into his flesh.

* * *

Daniel made the first cut, slicing out part of the rotting tissue.

"You have already put your mark on me! Why mark you me again?" Bao cried.

Daniel looked up anxiously when he heard his brother mumbling incoherently.

"He still slumbers," Derek assured him.

"Aye, but I hope not for long after the wound is cleansed," Daniel replied. He turned his attention back to the surgery he performed. "The edges of the flesh are too ragged for me to stitch; I'll need to burn them closed instead."

Derek and the other man nodded.

He doused the wound once more with the *uisge*

beatha.

"*Nay!*" Bao yelled and fought even more furiously against their hold.

Daniel waited for Derek and the other soldier to gain control of Bao's appendages once more. When his brother finally settled, he asked, "Have you a grip on him?"

Derek nodded curtly.

Daniel went back to his task, dressing the injury with a poultice of cobwebs to stop the bleeding. He then took the cautery iron from his healer's box and held it over the flame of the small brazier. It didn't take long for the iron tip to become red-hot. "Bao will undoubtedly fight this with even more strength," he warned Derek and the guard.

"Worry not, we'll keep him still," Derek replied determinedly as he braced himself to take the brunt of Bao's resistance.

Daniel lifted the poultice from the wound and pressed the ragged edges of the gash together as much as he could before setting the red-hot tip to his brother's tender flesh, searing it closed.

* * *

Bao screamed in agony. "*Why father? Why?*" he asked as his father pressed a hot firebrand to his groin.

"*Because you would not go with my soldier and do as he asked,*" Jamison Maclean said evilly, "*you have earned my wrath!*"

"*Nay! Nay!*" Bao pleaded once more, tossing his head from side to side.

"*Do you forget you are my slave? You will do anything I tell you to do!"* Jamison roared.

"I will not submit to him, no matter what you do to me!" Bao screamed back.

* * *

Daniel lifted his eyes once again to his brother's tormented countenance. He'd understood his words this time, but not their context. It was evident that Bao was in the midst of a terrible dream. Daniel quickly finished cauterizing the wound and placed a poultice on it to soothe the ache before binding it in clean linen. He sat back and took a deep breath. "It is done," he said. "Now, let us untie his bonds and allow him his rest."

A few minutes later Daniel closed the door to Bao's chamber behind him, resting his back against it and closing his eyes. His brother's fever was still raging, but at least he'd been able to tend the injury that had caused the illness. Bao was strong. Surely, he would fight this fever and recover. He must. For 'twould be cruel indeed for fate to have brought his brother back into his life only to take him away before he'd had the chance to know him well.

* * *

Branwenn and Prince Llywelyn rode their mounts through the gateway of the keep the next morn, picking their way over fallen and charred debris. It was as quiet as a tomb inside the courtyard, as all who resided there stood silently gaping at the procession before them. A stench of death and scorched wood permeated the air. So this is what war looks like, Branwenn thought sadly. This is what her brothers trained themselves to do, trained their soldiers to do. This is what Bao had been a part of most of his life. Branwenn's eyes fell upon a cart that was loaded six-deep with the bodies of fallen soldiers. She quickly dropped her gaze to her hands, fearing she would recognize some of their youthful faces, fearing that she may have even danced with one or two of them the night of the *Hogmanay* feast, and unable to bear the thought that it had been their last.

Prince Llywelyn halted his destrier and Branwenn followed suit. Lifting her gaze, her eyes immediately locked with her brother, Daniel's. He stood just outside the door of the keep, at the bottom of the steps.

Branwenn leapt from her mount and flew into Daniel's embrace, her eyes streaming with tears of joy and sadness. "So 'twas Bao, then, that was wounded? Please, tell me he still lives!"

Daniel kissed her damp cheek and hugged her tight. "Aye, he lives. But he's quite ill, Branwenn. I thought cleaning his wound would revive him, but he has yet to awaken and his fever still rages."

"I must see him!" she said, struggling out of her brother's arms.

Daniel looked up into the visage of the man who was now her guardian. "Aye," he said. "And while you are there, your cousin and I will share some ale in the great hall."

Prince Llywelyn nodded curtly and dismounted, handing his reins to the stableman who rushed up to attend him.

No one spoke as they ascended the steps and

entered the keep.

"We will not stay long, only a day or two while we replenish our supplies, and then we will depart for my kingdom," Prince Llywelyn said as he stood beside the two in the antechamber of the great hall a few moments later.

"I cannot leave here without knowing my brother will recover!" Branwenn cried.

"Then we must hope that your brother becomes well before we leave this place two days hence," Prince Llywelyn replied staunchly.

Branwenn fell to her knees before the prince. "I beg you, Your Highness, please do not force me from my brother's side while he is in peril of dying!"

Prince Llywelyn's eyes softened as he gazed at her. He lifted his hand to her face and held her chin in his palm. "How can I say 'nay' to a request so sweetly given?" He nodded curtly. "We shall stay until the man is well out of danger." After only a brief pause, he continued, "Whether he be fully recovered or nay. Will that suffice, my dear?"

Branwenn took her cousin's hand in both of her own and kissed the top of it in gratitude. "My thanks."

Daniel's worst fears fled as he watched the exchange between the two. 'Twas plain that the prince held affection for his young charge, that he would not treat her ill once she was officially given into his care. "We have much to discuss, Your Highness."

"Yes," Prince Llywelyn replied as he helped Branwenn to her feet. "And this lady is anxious to leave my presence to attend her brother."

Branwenn bowed her head and performed a quick courtesy before scurrying toward the stairway and quickly ascending them.

The two men watched her leave.

"She's a high-spirited youngling, but quite beautiful," Prince Llywelyn stated.

"Aye. And that is why she will need a strong, but patient, man for her mate," Daniel replied. He turned his eye to his guest and studied his profile. "Is her intended such a man, Your Highness?"

"He is strong, for certain. He's a highly skilled knight in the Earl of Pembroke's legion. In fact, until only recently, he's been undefeated at tournaments." Prince Llywelyn turned and followed Daniel into the great hall. "As you surely know, it takes great patience to become so skilled."

Daniel waited for his guest to settle himself into one of the chairs by the hearth before asking, "Aye, but will he be so patient with my sister?"

Prince Llywelyn sighed. "I will gain a promise from him that he will treat her thus before I allow the marriage contract to be signed."

"That eases me greatly," Daniel said. "Because Branwenn surrendered herself into your hands, you have no obligation to negotiate further terms regarding her welfare. But as a brother who loves her dearly, I must know the details of the contract."

Prince Llywelyn nodded. "You already know the pith of the thing, but ask me what you will and I will answer you honestly."

Over the next two hours, Daniel did just that. By

the end of that time, his worries had been lessened and he was assured that the man to whom Branwenn would be wed was as worthy of her as any he or his grandmother might have found for her.

"And now," Daniel said, "we must sign our truce so that I can bring my other family members home."

The two men rose from their seats and settled at the high table.

Prince Llywelyn indicated that his man should bring the rolled document up to them and he and Daniel quickly did the deed.

"It is finished," Prince Llywelyn said afterward.

Daniel gave his steward the signal to have a missive sent to the Donald holding. If all went well, he should have his wife and babe in his arms by sennight's end. "Aye, it is finished," Daniel agreed. "And now, instead of enemies, we are allies."

"That is good. I've a need for more allies," Prince Llywelyn said.

* * *

CHAPTER 19

’Twas nearing the hour of midnight four days later and Jesslyn sat at Bao's bedside anxiously bathing him with a cool, damp cloth. Daniel told her that Bao had awakened briefly several times o'er the past days and his fever had lessened, but not completely fled. His recovery had looked good, in fact, until sometime early this morning when another infection set in and he'd had to open the wound near his groin, clean and drain it, and then close it up again. The infection had put Bao into another fevered stupor.

Maryn and Lady Maclean were tending to Bao Li and Nora at Jesslyn's cottage. Until Bao's fever broke, they must keep the babes as far from the illness as they were able. The two ladies had agreed to sequester themselves in that cottage until the danger had passed.

Bao moaned in his sleep and his hand trembled and jerked. Jesslyn lifted the cloth from his brow and gazed worriedly down at him. The images his fevered mind conjured must be of the evil sort, for he did not rest easily. "Bao?" she said for what seemed the thousandth time that eve. "Bao, can you hear me? 'Tis Jesslyn, your wife." She took his trembling hand into both of her own and placed a kiss on the abraded knuckles. "We've a son, my love. A strong and handsome *son*." She started to laugh but it turned into a choked sob. "You were so certain 'twas a lass we made that day that you had me believing it as well. We never even spoke of a name for a lad! I hope it pleases you—I named our son Bao Li. Branwenn told me that 'twas the name of your mother's father."

Bao opened his eyes. "He...was a great...warrior," he rasped.

Jesslyn smiled through her tears and grasped Bao's hand even more tightly in her own. "Aye, love, just as *you* are. Just as our *sons* will be someday." She placed the palm of her hand on his brow. "You're still quite warm. Does your head ache? I can make a ptisan of betony for you."

"Nay, lovely enchantress, I need naught more than to hear your sweet voice and feel the touch of your gentle hand on my brow."

For the first time seeing the glassy look in her husband's gaze, Jesslyn's own brows came together in consternation. "Know you not who I am?" she asked anxiously.

Bao's mouth quirked in a lopsided smile. "Nay, goddess, but if you would give me a bit more time, I vow that I shall *know* you better, and more deeply, than you've ever been *known* by any other."

The carnal promise in his words made her blood rush in spite of her worry. "I am your wife. Jesslyn."

Bao chuckled. "A goddess would wed a mere mortal? Nay. I know you are naught more than a dream—a wish—that my slumbering mind has conjured." His eyes drifted closed and it looked as if he were falling back into a stupor once more. She shook him and tried one more time to tell him of his son, but he didn't answer, so she settled back into her ministrations.

Jesslyn remained at Bao's bedside the remainder of the night. Just before dawn, his fever finally broke and he at last fell into a restful slumber. Relieved and tired to her very core, Jesslyn disrobed and settled next to him. After only a few moments, she fell into a deep, dreamless sleep as well.

* * *

A sharp ray of sunshine pierced Bao's eyelids and he threw his arm over them as a shield. It was then that he became fully aware of the familiar soft curve of silken, heavy breasts against his side, of lavender-scented hair under his chin, of a long limb settled over his calf. He pressed her to her back and, biting back the shot of searing pain to his injured thigh, rolled onto his side and opened his mouth over her nipple.

She moved beneath him. "Mmm."

He lifted his head and looked into her sleepy eyes. "G'morn, love."

Her eyes flew open and her head shot up off the pillow. "You are awake! How fare you?" Her hands grew busy then, feeling first his brow, then his cheeks, then running over his chest to the wound in his shoulder. "How are your wounds, do they pain you?" she asked. When her hand started toward his groin injury, he took hold of it and brought it to his lips instead.

"I fare well—better still, having awakened with you in my arms once again, where you belong."

"I've missed you." She raised up and gave him a kiss.

Bao stroked his fingers through her tousled hair and held the back of her head in his hand as he brought it down to rest once again on the pillow. He deepened the kiss, devouring her lips, delving deeply into the recesses of her mouth with his tongue. After a time he lifted his head and gazed down into her bemused blue eyes. "I've missed you, too. So very much." Gazing down at her flattened stomach, he said, "Where is my daughter?"

She burst out laughing.

Bao gave her a stunned look. "What?"

Her cheeks billowed as she tried to stop laughing, which then made her snort, which then made her laugh even louder.

Bao grinned, let out a chuckle, too. He had no idea what had his wife so tickled, but he loved her laughter. 'Twas surely the sweetest music he'd ever hear.

After another moment, she gained control of her mirth and wiped the tears from her eyes, saying, "I hope you do not object to a son, for 'tis a *son* that we have."

Bao gaped at her. "A-a...*son?*" He sat up and stared straight ahead. "I know not how to care for a son—

I've raised only a lass!"

Jesslyn sat up then as well and placed her arms around his neck, resting her cheek on his shoulder. "Aye, you do. Just look how well you've done with Alleck!"

"Aye, but he's not a *babe!*"

Jesslyn giggled and stroked the worry from his countenance, giving his cheek an affectionate peck. "And what, pray, do you believe will be so different in caring for a male babe rather than a female babe?" she asked. "They both cry when they need changing, or are hungry, or don't feel well, or just because. We do the same for both genders: We change their swaddling clothes, we feed them, and we hold them and comfort them. We love them."

"You named him Bao Li," Bao stated after a moment.

"Remember you now?" Jesslyn asked. "You were quite feverish last eve when I told you."

Bao nodded his head slowly and looked off in the distance. "Aye," he replied. "I thought it a dream. A lovely goddess, made of pure gold light, sat at my bedside telling me the story of my grandfather, the great warrior prince." He looked down into his wife's eyes once more. "Just as my mother would do each eve when she put me to bed."

Jesslyn narrowed her eyes and dropped her arms to her sides. "Aye. And you tried to charm your way into the *lovely* goddess's bed!"

"Nay, into *your* bed," he stressed, vaguely recalling now what he'd said.

"But you did not *know* it was me!"

"I was raving, my love," he reminded her. Then, with care to his wounds, he twisted around to fully face her and cupped her face in his hands. As he gazed intently into the limpid pools of her angry sky-blue eyes, he told her softly, "But last eve was *not* one of those casual dalliances—nay, it held much more meaning. For when my eyes beheld the golden enchantress, I felt exactly as I did the first time I saw *you*."

For a long moment, she looked into his eyes. "I want to make love to you, Bao."

His heart tripped. "Aye. But we cannot yet, can we?"

She shook her head. "Not for a few more days."

He trailed his eyes down her torso and gazed at the golden hair covering her mons. "Open your legs," he demanded darkly.

"We can't...you know," she reminded him again, but she followed his command.

Bao grinned. "Aye. But we can do this...." He stroked her between her thighs. "And this...." he blazed a trail with his tongue down between her breasts, over her quivering abdomen, to the apex of her womanhood and laved it once, twice, three times in quick succession with his tongue.

Jesslyn moaned in ecstasy, her abdomen tightening, quivering in anticipation.

Bao lifted his head and continued his question, saying, "Right?"

Her nod was exuberant.

"Good." And then he proceeded to do just as he'd

promised. After her first climax, he moved back up her body, needing to love all of her. He kissed her lips and delved deep inside her mouth with his tongue, allowed his hands to stray over the recovered curve of her waist, up to the ripe, rose-tipped mounds of her breasts. She squirmed beneath him and he captured one of those peaks between his lips and suckled gently as he caressed her slick, swollen labia with his fingertips. He wanted desperately to push a finger in, but fought the urge, instead using that finger to taunt another orgasm from her. It wasn't long before she peaked, and at it's pinnacle, she reached down and stroked his manhood in the same rhythm with which he plied her.

Bao jerked, ready to pull away, but then forced himself to allow the touch. He *had* to get over this aversion. He just had to. Closing his eyes, he concentrated only on the moist, hot feel of her, on the fact that 'twas her hand on him and in the next second, his head flew back and a moan flew from his dry throat. His hips jerked involuntarily in time with her hand. "God that feels so good." Without realizing he did it, his fingers quickened their motion and as she crested a third time, she tightened her fist around him and squeezed hard.

He gasped. "You make my head swim."

Slowly, she settled back onto the mattress and opened her eyes. Her gaze settled on him as she caught her breath. "My thanks for letting me touch you."

He let out a strained chuckle. "'Tis my pleasure, I assure you."

She surprised him when she raised up and gently

pressed Bao to his back, careful of his injuries. "I think I can do this right, if you'll let me."

His heart started pounding, and not from desire. "What are you about, love?"

She shook her head and then, before he could stop her, she took him into her mouth. Using her hands as well, she employed the ancient rhythm that would bring his seed up. Bao gritted back the immediate shadow of revulsion that threatened and forced his eyes, his mind, only on her and how much he loved her. He fisted his hands in her hair and watched her lips take him, felt her tongue against the underside of his erection. In no time, there was only pleasure as he bucked and moaned, tossing his head from side to side as his wife teased him and stroked him, sucked him and pleasured him.

His orgasm was a raging fire in his veins. A bellow of delight burst from his throat as his seed spewed from his sex into the loving cavern of her warm mouth. He collapsed back and peeked at her through one eye. She seemed to be savoring the victory, for her smile was smug as she rose from her position on the bed and washed her face at the washstand.

"You are much too good at that for *my* own good, my love."

She swung her head around and gave him a wide-eyed look. "Truly?"

"How can you even question such after the force of the eruption I just had?"

She shrugged and turned back to her ablutions. "Graeme said I didn't do it right, that—"

"Graeme! 'Tis always Graeme! Clearly he was an

idiot." He sat up and rested his arms on his bent knees. "I am truly sorry if I offend, but I am tired unto death of being compared to a dead man."

She turned and faced him. "You are right. I shan't do so again. You've proved yourself more my mate than Graeme ever was."

He grinned. "'Tis glad I am to finally hear you admit it."

Her eyes softened and her lips turned up, but she said naught further. With a shrug, she turned back around and dropped a cloth into the basin of water.

He lay back and watched her as she warmed the dampened cloth in her hand before turning and walking back toward the bed. Lifting the cloth to his belly and groin, she cleansed him of the remnants of their loving. The grace of her movements, the unconscious femininity of her, fascinated him. Her golden hair lay in soft strands over her breasts, tickling and snagging on the rosy peaks. He lifted his hands and rested them on her upper arms, drawing her down on top of him. Then he rolled her onto her back and gently moved the hair away from her right breast. "You are so very lovely. Perfect, in fact." He stroked his tongue around the circumference of the peak a few times.

Her voice was gentle when she said, "So are you."

He lifted his head and looked at her, shocked to hear her say such. "Nay, not by miles. I've seen too much, done too much." He moved a lock of her hair off of her cheek with his finger, enjoying the silky feel of her cheek as he did so. "But you make me feel that I *could* be a better man. Someday."

Highland Grace

"Come here. I want to hug you."

For some reason, that made his heart feel like a starburst exploding in his chest. He grinned and did as she requested.

It was long minutes before they rose from their bed and dressed. Bao, who was feeling much recovered, even after the morning's pleasurable exertions, would not even consider staying in his sick bed until Daniel looked at his wounds again. Jesslyn had reminded him of Branwenn's surrender, that there was a truce made, that his sister would be leaving for Cambria now that he was well enough for her to say her farewells to him, so he insisted upon meeting with the prince and then seeing his sister.

* * *

"Bao! I've been so worried!" Branwenn said as she pressed her cheek even further into her brother's chest. It was late, well past sunset, and they were standing in the center of the solar. They'd been given this time alone by the others to say their farewells in private, for she would leave at first light on the morrow. Never, she supposed, to cross the threshold of this keep again. She held Bao with all her might and he, in turn, was almost squeezing the breath from her lungs, but she cared not. She stood in a state of melancholy bliss, memorizing the wonderful, comfortable feeling she had when he held her thus, knowing this would be the last time she'd ever be held by her brother, her protector, her hero, again.

"I am well, little one, do not fret," Bao said as he lifted his hand to the back of her head and stroked her hair.

"But what if you hadn't recovered? I would never have forgiven myself for being the cause of your death!"

"Branwenn," Bao chided, "you must not think of what might have been—you must only think of what *is*, else you'll surely make yourself daft."

Branwenn nodded her head and squeezed him a bit tighter.

He tightened his hold as well and dropped his cheek to the top of her head. "I am quite well now, I assure you."

Branwenn swallowed past the lump in her throat and nodded again, but said naught further.

"Do you desire that I travel to Cambria with you and Prince Llywelyn?" Bao asked softly. "I could stay until you are well wed."

Branwenn shook her head. "Nay. You must stay here with your family," she said thickly. Her throat was clogged with unshed tears, tears she was trying valiantly not to release in Bao's presence. It would only make this parting more difficult, and it was time for her to meet her destiny with the courage of a woman grown, not the fear of a wee lass.

"Do you like your cousin, the prince?"

Branwenn sighed, shrugging. She nodded. "Aye, well enough, I suppose. He's younger, and more handsome, than I'd expected. And kinder, as well."

"Aye, he seems to hold affection for you, which eases my mind. He will take good care of you while you are under his protection. And Reys cares for you as well. He's sworn on his life to watch over you in my stead."

"Aye," Branwenn agreed, "and this man for whom I am intended is a bold warrior—unbeaten at the tournaments, at least until recently, I've been told. He will be a good protector, I'm sure," she said, managing to keep most of the fear from her voice.

"It tortures me that a man I've never met will soon have control over your life. I wish you hadn't given yourself over to the prince," Bao chastened. "Daniel and I had sent for our allies and we would have won the day. You would not have had to go so far away from us then."

Branwenn pulled back a bit and gazed up into her brother's worried countenance. "But how could I have had even a small kernel of happiness for the rest of my life if you or Daniel had been killed in the process? In the end, 'twas much more important to me that I leave with you well and happy than that I stay with one of you cold in your grave because of me."

"But *our* happiness will be tempered by sadness at your parting, for I know not if we will ever see each other again."

"Mayhap my new husband will be kind and allow us to visit in a few years," Branwenn said.

Bao nodded, but his eyes held little conviction. "Aye, mayhap he will."

"What think you of your son?" Branwenn asked, needing to change the subject. Her heart was overflowing with sadness and she couldn't bear another moment of the pain—'twas time to think on things more joyous.

Bao grinned. "He's almost as handsome as his father."

"*Almost!* He's at least twice your looks, brother mine!" Branwenn teased, but her face crumpled and her eyes filled with tears before she could stem their flow.

"Branwenn!" Bao said. He rocked her in his arms, rubbing her quaking shoulders while she cried out her sorrow. "He's beautiful!" she wailed. "*All* your bairns will be lovely!"

He cleared his throat and she heard him swallow before saying, "And so, my comely sister, will be all of yours."

* * *

Bao had remained with Branwenn until it was time for her to depart, reminiscing on their lives together. By the time Branwenn left the solar just before dawn, Bao had felt slightly more ready to give her over to her brother-germane's keeping. And now that he'd seen her off, said his final fairwell, even lied to her that he'd seen his new bairn to ease her heartache, 'twas time to meet his son. At last.

As he came down the hall toward the stair, he was intercepted by Maryn.

"Good morn to you Bao. I thought you would surely be with Alleck and Giric hunting in the wood."

Alarm shot through him. *"Giric?"* Without realizing it, he gripped her arm. "Mean you Giric *MacBean*?"

"Bao! You're looking wild-eyed. Calm yourself. And, aye, 'tis Giric MacBean—our *ally* we summoned during the siege—with whom the lad's gone hunting." She lifted her hand to his brow. "Are you still fever— Where are you going?"

Bao didn't answer, didn't halt, didn't turn, he plowed forward and leapt down the stairs three at a time.

"What is wrong?" Maryn called down to him. He heard the pad of her footsteps behind him. "Stay here!" he shouted back.

* * *

"He was too fast for me to catch up to, Jesslyn," Maryn said between gulps of air. "Something is amiss. Something dire. Oh, God. My heart won't stop pounding."

"I'm going after him. If there's danger to my son, I won't stand here doing naught."

"I'm coming with you. We must have someone find Daniel and tell him to follow as well."

"Aye—Did Bao have his sword?"

"Nay—only his dirk."

"We must take him is sword, then."

* * *

Bao followed the trail Giric and Alleck left—'twas easy enough, as Giric clearly believed there would be no suspicion of his purpose from any quarter. Did he even know Bao was here at the Maclean holding? Even if he did, he no doubt knew of his injury and the fevered stupor he'd been battling, thought himself safe to do as he would with the lad.

He'd torn open his groin injury when he'd flown down the stairs earlier and the searing pain helped to keep his thoughts focused and the dizziness that threatened a swoon at bay.

* * *

"There he is!" Maryn pointed to the copse of trees up ahead. "I can see movement just there, where the sun lights the break in the trees."

"Aye...*yes!* Yes, 'tis him!" Jesslyn kicked her mount into a gallop and her friend did the same.

* * *

Bao dismounted and tied his horse's reins to a tree outside the same cave where he'd tricked Jesslyn into coupling with him long sennights past. His heartbeat's rapid meter increased as a near-dibilitating dread took hold of him. Weak-kneed and lungs blowing, he moved with silent tread to the mouth of the cave. A drop of salty sweat pierced his eye and he pressed his palm to it, then swept an arm over his face to mop the moisture.

The acrid smell of a peatfire hung heavy in the air as he took his first step through the mouth of the cave and saw the reflection of the blaze's licking flames bathing the cavern wall in a sheen of rust and ochre. They were further into the recesses than Jesslyn and he had gone, and that increased his dread further. The cave held it's cold and when it sliced through his sweat-soaked shirt, it sent a shiver through Bao. Just then, an arced form severed the wall's glow with a dark eclipse and, as if reliving his own nightmare, he heard Giric say, "See how much better we can judge your strength now that you are bare?"

Bao bolted forward.

"Just look at how the sinews in Gowan's arms and chest flex as he hefts the sword. A warrior must—"

"Get your filthy hands off my son!"

"Papa!"

Bao wrenched Giric's arms behind his back and slammed him against the wall. The man's cheek made a satisfying *thwak* as it met the stone.

"Ahhh!" Giric struggled to free himself, nearly losing his footing on the slick moss that populated the edges of the floor nearest the walls of the cave, but Bao yanked him back up, nearly jerking the man's arm from its socket. Giric let out another cry of pain then said in a strangled tone, "I was only showing the lad how to heft a sword!"

Bao slammed him into the wall again and turned his head to look at the other lad—older than Alleck by a few years, but also stripped down to his braes.

"You are Gowan?"

The lad's eyes were wide with fear. His lip trembled. "Aye."

"How do you know this man?"

"Papa, why are you vexed? Did I do something wrong?"

Bao turned his gaze on Alleck and did his best to temper his tone when he said, "Nay, lad. Will you do me a favor?" When Alleck nodded, he continued, "Take your clothes and go out to where I've tethered my horse. I'm worried that the beast is getting lonely out there all by itself." He knew Alleck loved horses and was relieved when the lad's eyes sparked with joy and he scurried to do Bao's bidding.

Bao turned his gaze back on Gowan and the lad finally answered his question. "I-I am his squire."

Bao growled through gritted teeth. "Get thee from

here as well. Now."

As the lad rushed to obey, Giric tried to struggle free again and Bao leaned into him. The air went out of the man's lungs with a *whoosh* and only when his face turned a deep purple-red did Bao lessen the hold again and allow him to breathe. "You are vile."

The man snorted just as Jesslyn skidded to a halt three feet from where they stood. "Get out of here," Bao told her.

"I brought your sword."

"Leave it and go."

"Is this one of the men who—who touched you when you were a lad?"

"Aye."

"You can't kill him. You'll be tried and hanged—or worse."

"Aye, Bao. Listen to the lady, for she speaks the truth."

Bao rammed his knee into Giric's ass, just where he knew it would cause the most pain. Giric grunted. "Did you touch my son?"

"Oh, God, Bao—did he? Did you?" In the next instant, Jesslyn was there beside them.

"Nay. 'Twas only a lesson in sword—*ah!*—play."

"Bao, his eyes are growing glassy. Let him go." Jesslyn's hands dragged at Bao's arms. It surprised him how her touch sent a wave of calm through him, enough so that he was able to release his quarry and step back.

Giric fell to his knees, then rolled onto his side, struggling for air, and Bao let him.

"How did you know?" Bao asked her. "Maryn?"

"Aye."

"You shouldn't have followed me. This is no right business for a gentle lady."

"My son—and you—are, and will always be, my business."

Giric raised up into a sitting position. "This act you put on for your lady is sweet, actually, but we both know how much pleasure you received with me. A hard cock and moans of pleasure are not signs of disgust. Are they, Bao?"

* * *

Jesslyn's eyes flew to her husband's face. His cheeks were ruddy and his eyes—his eyes held shame. Shame and revulsion. For himself, or for Giric? No doubt, both. Hot anger ripped through her chest and she turned her sights on Bao's molester. "He was a bairn. He had no choice but to submit to you—you—you defiler of innocents!"

The man had the gall to smirk at her! "Aye, but did he have to *enjoy* it so much?"

Would a gentle lady—a mother—be subjected to as high a penalty for murder as a knight? Her fists clenched at her side and she took a step toward him, but Bao swung his arm out in front of her, successfully halting her stride. "Nay," he said.

She spit on Giric instead. "His body responded in spite of his will, but his mind is forever tormented by it!" She swung her gaze to Bao. "I've changed my mind, he must die." She slid his dirk from the sheath before her husband could stop her and lifted it in preparation for the kill.

A clamor came from the entry to the cave and in the next instant Daniel was there with them, his arms akimbo as he looked on with fevered eyes at the scene before him. "What goes on here?"

Bao remained stonily silent.

Just like him, Jesslyn thought. She shot around him and rushed over to Daniel, pointing back at Giric. "This—this is—"

"NAY!" Bao bellowed. "Do not say it."

"Bu—"

Giric struggled to his feet and dusted off his tunic. "G'day, Daniel. Your brother seems to think I was up to no good with the lad Alleck. I assure you, my squire and I were only teaching the lad a bit of rudimentary swordplay. How to heft it, being the first lesson."

Jesslyn saw a light of understanding in Daniel's eyes as he narrowed them on Bao. "I see."

It surprised all of them when Daniel tore over to Giric and pummeled his fist into the man's groin. Giric screamed. Doubled over, he staggered out of Daniel's reach. He stumbled, and before anyone could catch him, he fell, hands-first, into the fire. This time, Jesslyn's screams echoed his. Daniel and Bao sprung into action. Daniel reached him first and rolled with the man in an attempt to put out the flames.

It wasn't until long minutes later, after the flames were extinguished, and after Daniel had tried unsuccessfully to revive him, that Jesslyn got a good look at the man's injuries. His face, hands, and lower arms were burned. But it was his countenance that captured her gaze. One side of his face was charred and bloody and he no longer looked like the comely, brown-haired man he'd been just moments earlier.

"The burns have put him in a stupor. He may not live until morn," Daniel said. "We must get him back to the keep, though it makes my stomach churn to give him shelter."

"Even if he lives, he'll not be the man he was," Jesslyn said.

Bao shocked her by speaking for the first time since he stymied her words earlier. "What am I to do with this vermin? Allow him a decent burial? He may not have gotten to Alleck, but he's certainly done something to his squire"—he drilled his gaze into hers—"where are they? Still outside?"

"Maryn took them back to the keep."

"Good."

* * *

Two hours after returning to the keep, and after leaving Alleck and her babe in the care of the nurse, Jesslyn returned to her bedchamber, intent on finding her husband. He'd disappeared after helping Daniel get Giric into bed and getting his own wounds reclosed and redressed. Thus far, she'd had little luck finding him. But after she was told by Steward Ranald that he'd seen Bao going upstairs not a quarter-hour past, she felt confident she'd finally located him.

With care, she opened the door and looked inside. Aye, there he was. Seated by the fire, brooding.

She placed the basket of berry tarts she'd brought him on the floor, then walked over and settled in his lap before he could give her protest. Happily, he allowed it, even wrapped his arms around her as she rested her head on his shoulder. "Does this hurt your wounds?"

He shook his head, but said naught. Just continued looking into the hearthfire's flames.

After another moment, she lifted her head, turned his with her hand on his cheek and kissed him on the mouth.

It crushed her a little when he didn't return it. She stroked her tongue over his bottom lip in a bid for him to open, but instead, he stood up, dropped her into his place on the chair and strode toward the washstand. "I'm not clean," he said, and she knew he meant more with those words than simply the literal.

He splashed water on his face several times, then grabbed a towel and buried his face in it.

"You're beautiful. I love you."

He wouldn't face her. Instead, when he took the towel away, he turned and leaned his palms on the washstand. "How can you? After what Giric told you about me."

She rose from the chair and took a step toward him, then stopped. "Did you think my words to him were lies? You were a bairn, Bao! Just as Gowan is—would you blame him for what Giric did to him? Condemn him as vile if his body's natural responses betray his will to do otherwise?"

He shrugged. After a stretch of time that seemed endless to Jesslyn, he finally spoke. "I hate myself. I'm sick—disgusting."

How it was possible for him to both break her heart

and fire her wrath at the same time, she could not say. Her hands shot to her hips and she stormed over to him and yanked him around. "You go see your son, see what you created, then you come back to me and tell me you still hate yourself. You'll find him in the solar with Alleck and the nurse."

* * *

Bao didn't go directly to the nursery. Instead, he went to find Gowan. Jesslyn's words had struck deep. She was right. He'd never blame Gowan for any response he might have had to Giric's forced touch. Why then, was he so quick to blame himself?

He found Gowan on the training field, squiring for Derek. After taking the lad aside, he said, "I want you to stay here and squire for me, if you would like. I've just sent a missive to your family and we should hear from them in a sennight, mayhap a fortnight at the latest."

Gowan's gaze dropped to the ground. "What did you tell them?"

"Naught about what Giric was up to with you. I told them that, due to Giric's hand injuries, he'd no longer be able to do battle, so would have no further need of a squire."

Bao put his hand on Gowan's shoulder. "What he did to you…he did to me as well, when I was near your age."

Gowan's head shot up, his eyes wide as saucers. "He *did?*"

"Aye. 'Tis why I think you and I were destined to meet. I know how you feel, the shame you feel, but you are not to blame. He is. And today, he paid for his villainy. We must be content with that and not hate ourselves any longer. All right?"

The look of relief on Gowan's face was a treasure in itself to Bao, but when the lad told him that Bao would be his liege from this day forward, he knew he'd made a friend for life.

* * *

A few of the Gordon allies were still camped outside the keep. They'd arrived soon after the truce had been signed, and some had stayed on to rest themselves and their mounts before taking the journey back home. When Giric surprised them all and recovered enough to demand he be allowed to return to his stepfather's—the Gordons—holding near the MacGregor's, Bao agreed to Daniel's request that he be allowed to do so. It was not until later that evening that he was able to finally visit his newborn son, Bao Li.

As he approached the opened door of the solar, he heard Alleck say, "And there's a loch with really, really big fishes in it." The babe was squeezing Alleck's finger in his small fist and grinning up at him and that drew a smile to Bao's lips as well.

"See! You are grinning! 'Tis not just wind, like Callum's mama said."

Bao quietly leaned against the wooden doorjam with his arms crossed over his chest, content to just continue listening and watching the interplay between the two. The nurse looked up from her sewing and started to speak, but Bao motioned with his fingers over his mouth for her to remain silent. When she nodded and resumed her stitching, Bao turned his attention back to his two sons.

"When you're just a bit bigger, I'll take you to the loch and we can catch some fish—you'll like that, will you not?"

Bao Li kicked his feet and bobbed his arms up and down in response. "Guuuu."

"Aye, *'twill* be good," Alleck agreed, nodding and smiling. "Me and Niall have a fortr'ss, too. 'Tis only for us lads—no lasses can come inside. *You* can help us defend it from 'em."

Bao's heart expanded in his chest with love and contented delight. He hated to interrupt the private conversation, but he couldn't wait one more moment to hold his new son. "And what mischief are you planning to get your new brother into, my son?" he asked, straightening and taking a step into the chamber.

Alleck started and twisted around, nearly toppling over in the process. "*Papa!*" he said at the top of his lungs. "You're here!" He jumped to his feet and flew at Bao's knees, flinging his arms around them in glee.

Bao winced at the jarring his newly reclosed groin wound was being subjected to before lifting Alleck up and hugging him tight, scrubbing his son's mussed flaxen hair at the same time. It made the wound in his shoulder burn as well, but he ignored the added discomfort. "Aye, I am quite fit. And how fare you?"

"I'm good." He dropped his gaze to Bao's chest. "I'm sorry I was playin' with Giric's sword—are you still vexed at me?"

Bao lifted Alleck's chin and made him meet his eyes.

"I was never vexed at you. I was vexed at Giric—'tis an old, dull story that I'll not bore you with now. So"—he tucked a lick of Alleck's hair down—"what else have you been doing since your return from Laird Donald's holding?"

Alleck's eyes grew animated. "We found some more stuff for our fortr'ss in the glen!—I'm glad it didn't get blowed up during the siege—There was a bunch of broken up stuff out there. Uncle Daniel said it was from the prince's army, but that we could have as much of it as we could carry. We even found some arrows!" Alleck's shoulders sagged, his lower lip protruding a bit. "But Mama wouldn't let me keep 'em. She said I'd be too *tempid* to use 'em on the lasses."

"If you give me your vow that you will not point them at a living thing, I will have some made for you and teach you how to use them. You can only shoot them on the training field and they can only be aimed at the targets that are set up for their use there. Agreed?"

Alleck bounced up and down in Bao's arms, nodding exuberantly. "Aye!" he shouted and squeezed his arms around Bao's neck, making Bao bite back a groan.

"I love you!"

He closed his eyes and pressed the lad closer still. For at least the millionth time since finding Alleck in the cave earlier that day, a wash of relief flooded his spirit. "I love you, too." He had to swallow and clear his throat before he could get his next words out. "Now, introduce me to my new son."

Alleck scrambled out of Bao's arms and skipped

over to the cradle where Bao Li lay gazing around wide-eyed and drooling. "He looks like you, Papa! See? 'Cept he's got blue eyes, like me an' Mama."

His injuries caused Bao's movements to be a bit stiff as he made his way over to the side of the infant's bedding. Gazing down at his cheerfully innocent, driveling bairn, he was filled with wonder. He did not know now what he had been expecting to see; mayhap a babe with the aspect of Alleck—flaxen-haired and with the look of the Highlander in him. Instead, here was a clear link to his own Cathayan heritage, to his mother. A sense of complete contentment settled over him in that instant. *"I did it, Mama,"* Bao thought. *"I did what you wanted and made a family—became a part of a family. And I'm no longer a slave, no longer bound to another as chattel and no longer bound in mental bondage, either, by my past."* Now, all that remained was the present and the future and it held a sea of possibilities. "He's beautiful," Bao said softly. "Perfect."

Alleck rolled his eyes. "That's what Mama keeps sayin'!" Shrugging, he studied his brother closely once again. "He jes' looks like a fat wee babe to me."

Bao smiled and tousled Alleck's hair. "You'll understand one day when you have a bairn of your own."

Alleck shrugged once more, rolling his eyes. "Growed people are always tellin' me stuff like that."

Bao laughed and tousled Alleck's hair even more this time. "You will, I promise."

Alleck sighed and scraped his hair flat. "Aye," he said, tho' his voice held no conviction. He bowed his head and rubbed his finger across a groove made by a scratch in the side of the cradle, his brow furrowed in thought.

"What ails you, son?" Bao asked.

Alleck shrugged.

"Worry you that your mother will not allow me to make you those arrows?" Bao guessed.

Alleck shook his head.

"You believe me that I'm not vexed with you, do you not?"

"Aye."

Bending down even further in order to see Alleck's face more clearly, Bao said, "I truly am well, I'll not perish."

Alleck nodded. "Good," he said softly.

"Alleck," Bao said in some frustration, "tell me what ails you, else I will not be able to help."

Rubbing his cheek on his shoulder, Alleck began, "Bao Li is your *true* son—is *Mama's* true son. If you love him more than me..." With a loud sigh, he shrugged again. "I shall not be mad."

Stunned and quite honestly appalled, Bao did the only thing he knew to do in that moment: He came down onto his knees and wrapped his arms around the lad. He hugged him tight, holding the back of Alleck's head in his palm and pressing the lad's cheek against his shoulder. The action wrenched his wound, but he paid no heed. "You are as much my *true* son as is this babe—and I know your mother feels just as I do, for she has told me so." Taking hold of Alleck's shoulders, Bao drew the lad away from him a moment so that he could look into his countenance as he continued, "Remember you the first day we met? By the loch?"

Alleck nodded. "I thought you was a magic giant 'cuz you wored no tunic—only that blanket around your waist. And you left the magic coin in my shoe."

It was Bao's turn to nod. "Aye. But did you know *why* I left the coin for you—why I spoke to you that day?"

Looking down at his toes, Alleck shrugged.

"Because I saw myself in you; saw the lonely lad I had been when I was just your age and felt a connection to you even then." Bao stroked the hair away from Alleck's brow and lifted the lad's chin, forcing Alleck to look him in the eye. "And when I wed your mother and became your papa, I felt twice blessed. For I could not have loved you more or been more proud to be your father had I beget you myself."

Alleck shrugged and bit his lip, breaking eye contact with Bao and looking to his right.

"Know you that your Aunt Branwenn and I are not related by blood?" Bao waited for Alleck to nod before he continued, "And yet, even now, she would stay here with us and not go with her brother-germane, had she the choice. *Blood* is not what makes us love you; 'tis *you*, Alleck, the brave, strong, clever and merry lad that you are, that makes us love you."

Alleck couldn't bring himself to meet Bao's eyes, but he nodded slowly and again rubbed his cheek against his shoulder as he settled into Bao's arms once again.

"You believe me, don't you son?"

"Aye," Alleck said softly.

Bao could tell that the lad wasn't thoroughly convinced, but he reasoned that time would surely show Alleck that he was, and always would be, his and Jesslyn's first-born son. Looking back now, he could almost convince himself that it had been kismet, fate, that had brought the two of them together, for his life had been mightily altered after meeting this bairn.

"Don'cha wanna hold Bao Li?" Alleck asked after a moment.

Smiling, Bao said, "Aye."

Alleck moved out of Bao's embrace and watched as Bao lifted the babe into his arms.

"He weighs much more than Branwenn did!" Bao said with some surprise.

Alleck giggled. "It's cuz he's a lad, Papa! He's a warrior, not some puny lass!"

Bao grinned as he looked from the gurgling babe in his arms into Alleck's shining countenance. "Aye. How witless of me to forget."

"You're really silly, Papa." Alleck slowly worked his way to Bao's side and leaned into him a bit.

Bao absently reached down and rested his hand over Alleck's flaxen pate as he spoke to Bao Li. "How would you like to take a walk to the training field, my wee warrior?"

The nurse jumped up from her position in the corner and hurriedly took the babe into her arms. "It be much too bitter outside as yet for the young one," she admonished.

* * *

'Twas just past sunset when Bao returned to his

bedchamber, returned to his wife, with one purpose in mind.

As he shut the door behind him and leaned against it, he allowed his eyes to settle on her. She'd clearly believed he'd return hours prior—and that her ploy would be successful—for she was already in bed, naked. Unfortunately, she slept.

With a sigh, he began to undress. Tomorrow would be soon enough. The day had been long and eventful.

As he approached the bed, she opened her eyes and looked at him. "Finally," she said and sat up. Her silken hair swayed over her shoulder and pooled on her thigh.

"Aye, finally." In two strides, he was at the bedside. Without breaking eye contact, he brought his hands up to her face and stroked his thumbs over her lips before dipping his head and giving them a gentle kiss. After a time, he lifted his head and gazed into his wife's bemused eyes. "I want you to touch me again, as you did this morn past."

Her eyes grew round and then she grinned. "'Twill be my pleasure." She turned and plumped up his pillow. "Lie down and let me love you."

Afterward, Bao marveled. "Christ's Bones! Do I still live?" he gasped as he lay dazed, dizzy, elated, and spread-eagled on the bed. He was so much in love at that moment, he thought his heart would surely burst from it. From the vicinity of the washstand, he heard his wife giggle and it brought a smile to his lips.

She'd done it. Done what he'd begun to believe was the impossible. With her love and her generosity, she'd broken down the last barrier. Not once had his mind strayed to his past. Not once. It had been as it always should have been with her. Perfect. Wonderful. Untainted.

While she was still at her ablutions, he looked over at the table next to the bed and grasped the treasure he found there, bringing it down to his side, hidden from view.

After she'd settled once again beside him, bathed him off, and rolled her body into his, he said, "I've a craving for something sweet."

She lifted her head. "Sw—?" she began in confusion, but giggled when she saw the berry tart in his hand.

He took a bite of the tart and chewed. "Mmm. You know how much I love these comfits." Then he dribbled some of its juice onto the tip of her breast and licked it off.

She moaned and turned onto her back, arching.

"You liked that, did you?" he purred. This time, he allowed even more of the juice to dribble onto her breast. It ran down the sides and onto the mattress. "My pardon," he said, "you may sleep on my side of the bed tonight." Her only answer was to press against him. Taking the hint, he positioned his palm under her breast and lifted it before opening his mouth wide and drawing it deeply into its recesses. He suckled her then, massaging the breast until he got what he craved. A blissful moan rumbled up from deep inside him. This—This, he thought, must be the ambrosia of which the ancients had spoken.

Jesslyn gasped in shock and desire as she felt him draw nourishment from her.

After a moment, Bao raised his head and gazed into her passion-filled eyes. "I hope you don't mind, I wanted a bit of milk with my tart."

Thankfully more amused than shocked by the bawdy jest, she chuckled and shook her head before lifting it from its resting place on the pillow and kissing him, sucking and nibbling the remnants of the tart and milk from his bottom lip.

"I want you inside me, Bao."

He groaned and tucked his head into the curve of her neck. "Believe me, my love, I want that too. But we cannot."

She shoved at his shoulder and he lifted up and caught her eye.

"Aye, we can. 'Tis been long enough. I spoke to your Grandmother about it and she says that I have all the signs of being fully healed. Please. Please let us just try."

Bao wanted to say no, he really did, but somehow what came out of his mouth was, "Aye, all right. But I'll have to prepare you first."

She grinned. "I was hoping you would say that."

"Spread your legs, vixen."

She did and he settled his head between them. After dribbling berry juice over the hood of her clitoris, he lapped and nibbled, then started a gentle suction. When he'd brought her to peak twice, when he could easily slide his finger into her, when he could feel the soft swell of her inner flesh, touch her turgid bud with his tongue, he knew she was ready to receive him.

He slid up her limp form, leaving hot kisses along

the way until at last he was cradled by her womanhood. "Open your eyes, Jesslyn."

Her lids drifted open and he stroked the hair off her damp brow with the palm of his hand. "Wrap your legs around me."

She did more than that, she wrapped her arms around him as well. And then she lifted up, just as he began to press down. In the next second, he was home. "Oh, God. I love you so much," he said and scorched her mouth with a long, deep, ravenous kiss. He started to move then, slow, gentle, and she matched his rhythm.

He felt her turn her head to his cheek, felt her lips caress the shell of his ear and then she whispered. "I love you, too. Give me another babe—not now, but soon. Next year. All right?"

"Aye." A surge of pleasure took him by the shorthairs and his movements grew more rapid. He grasped her hips, held them up so he could plow more deeply.

She winced.

He paused. "Am I hurting you?"

"A little, but...mmm. It feels good, too. Don't stop."

He began to move again. For the next few moments, their cries of passion melded in the room. Both ground out the other's name as they climaxed, first Jesslyn, then Bao.

Afterward, when they were both near to unconsciousness, he managed to say, "You are serious? You truly want another babe so quickly?"

"Aye, I do." She raised up and propped her head on her hand. "Don't you?"

He grinned. "Oh, aye, I surely do."

* * *

EPILOGUE

It was a bright, warm morn in July when Daniel, Maryn and Nora departed the Maclean keep, heading back to the holding that held Daniel's heart, back to his mother's clan, *his* clan, the MacLaurins. Bao had been officially named laird and chieftain over the Macleans the sennight after Branwenn's departure, but Daniel had wanted to wait until Nora was older to make the long journey home.

"I'm going to miss you desperately," Jesslyn said to Maryn. They stood beside the cart that held her friends' chests and other belongings. She quickly scanned it to make sure it was well bound with rope.

Maryn followed the line of Jesslyn's sight. "Can you believe how much more we're taking back with us than that with which we arrived?"

"I know. A babe, for one thing," she gently teased, giving her friend a quick glance before turning her eyes back to the cargo loaded on the cart. "It seems so long ago now," she continued wistfully, "so much has changed between us since that time." She looked back at her friend and grasped her hand in both of her own. "Back then you were a stranger, a rival to the life I'd mapped out for myself and Alleck. But now you are not only my dearest friend, but my sister as well."

"Aye," Maryn replied. "Which means we *will* see each other again. *Often*. Daniel promised."

Jesslyn laughed. "I made Bao promise the same thing to me! Although, 'twas not very difficult; he adores his brother, after all. And since Branwenn has been lost to him, he feels an even greater need to keep close ties with his other family members."

"Daniel feels the same way," Maryn said.

"I wish Grandmother Maclean could have been here," Jesslyn lamented, squeezing Maryn's hand.

"Aye, but with Lara's death, Aunt Maggie needs help taking care of Callum's wee daughter." Callum's wife had run off with the outcast and permanently marred Giric in the moon after *Bealltainn* and was found a sennight later. Both were hiding in a cotter's hut on the Gordon land, with her near death from a fall she'd taken on one of her wild rides across the glen. Callum had been summoned immediately and he had stayed by his wife's side until she'd finally succumbed to her injuries and passed away.

"Aye, and Callum needs her comfort as well, I'm sure," Jesslyn replied.

Maryn nodded. "He's always been close to Grandmother Maclean." She sighed, saying, "Poor Callum, he's had quite a bad time of it this past year or so."

"Aye, he has. But he's strong and he's matured over the past moons since I first met him—he'll be fine."

"You are right, I know you are, but I cannot help but worry for him. We've been friends for many years and I hate to know he's suffering so."

"He'll be fine," Jesslyn repeated, feeling the need to assure herself as well as her friend. She took in a deep breath and slowly released it as she gazed around the courtyard. "This place will seem like a tomb with you and Daniel gone." She turned her gaze back onto her friend. "And who will I get to do my sewing?" she jested.

"I know Bao will do it for you, if you ask." Maryn answered cheekily.

"Ha! Ha! What a wit you are," Jesslyn replied with a grin.

Daniel and Bao walked up beside them then. Daniel put his arm around his wife's waist, drawing her up against his side. "What has you grinning?" he asked Jesslyn. "Never say you are *glad* to see us leave, dear friend of mine."

Jesslyn's eyes misted as she gazed at her handsome auburn-haired friend. She ignored his jest and said instead, "Thank you. Thank you for bringing me and Alleck here. Because of you I have another love and a new babe. I have the life I craved, but never thought I'd find again."

Daniel placed his hand on Bao's shoulder and squeezed, giving it a little shake at the same time. "You're a fine chieftain, Bao. Our grandfather would have been proud to pass on his legacy to you." Daniel gazed around him, taking in the scenery for the last time. "We must leave now, Laird Donald will be waiting." Maryn's father was to meet them along the road and travel with them back to the MacLaurin holding. He had agreed to a long visit while Maryn settled in as mistress of the MacLaurin keep.

After a few more moments of final farewells, Daniel, his family, and his entourage departed.

Jesslyn and Bao stood in the courtyard for quite some time after the dust had finally settled, sad but filled with hope for their future.

"I meant what I said, you know," Jesslyn murmured. "I *do* have the life I craved, the love I craved."

Bao turned and wrapped her in his arms, hugging her close. "'Twas my brother that I thanked, but in truth, 'tis you who have my deepest gratitude. You saved me, lightened my soul, brought depth and meaning to my life."

"As did you for me."

"Will you meet me later? At our special place?" Bao murmured against her ear.

"Our special place?" Jesslyn asked in confusion.

"The waterfall, my love."

Jesslyn smiled and sighed, snuggling even further into her husband's comforting and loving embrace. "Aye, that sounds wonderful. The weather is just right for a swim."

"I'm sure Alleck will not mind spending a bit of time with his wee brother and the nurse while we are gone."

"Nay, he will not. As a matter of fact, I believe he's

up in the solar with them right now. He's very sad that Maryn and Daniel had to leave, even tho' he'll see them again a few moons hence when he begins his training. I tried, but I couldn't get him to come down to say farewell to them this morn."

"Daniel and Maryn spent some time with him last eve while you were with Bao Li. They said their farewells to each other then," Bao reassured her.

Jesslyn nodded, rubbing her cheek against her husband's chest.

Bao kissed her forehead.

They stood that way—content, joyous, and silent—until the terce bell chimed. Then, in unspoken accord, they at last turned and, arm-in-arm, slowly made their way back toward the steps of their home.

The End

Thank you for reading
Highland Grace : Book Two : Highlands Trilogy

If you enjoyed Highland Grace, I would appreciate it if you would help others enjoy this book, too.

Lend it. Please share it with a friend.

Recommend it. Please help other readers find this book by recommending it to friends, readers' groups and discussion boards.

Review it. Please tell other readers why you liked this book by reviewing it.

Author updates can be found at
http://www.kesaxon.com

Connect with K.E. at:
http://www.facebook.com/kesaxonauthorpage

ABOUT THE AUTHOR

K.E. Saxon is a third-generation Texan and has been a lover of romance fiction since her first (sneaked) read of her older sister's copy of *The Flame and the Flower* by Kathleen E. Woodiwiss. She has two cats, a 26-year-old cockatiel, and a funny, supportive husband. When she isn't in her writer's cave writing, you can find her puttering in her organic vegetable garden or in her kitchen trying out a new recipe. An animal (and bug) lover since before she could speak, she made pets of all kinds of critters when she was a kid growing up. Her mother even swears that she made a pet of a cockroach one time (but K.E. doesn't believe her). She likes to write humorous, sexy romances.

* * * *

OTHER BOOKS IN THE MEDIEVAL HIGHLANDERS SERIES:

THE HIGHLANDS TRILOGY: The Macleans

Highland Vengeance
Book One

A Family Saga / Adventure Romance

DANIEL AND MARYN'S STORY

* * *

Highland Magic
Book Three

A Family Saga / Adventure Romance

CALLUM AND BRANWENN'S STORY

* * *

The Cambels

Song of the Highlands
Book Four

A Family Saga / Adventure Romance

ROBERT AND MORGANA'S STORY

Now the rascal Highlands warrior knight from Highland Grace and Highland Magic has his own romance adventure!

HIGHLAND MAGIC
Book Three
The Macleans – The Highlands Trilogy
(The Medieval Highlanders)

The third in the Highlands Trilogy, HIGHLAND MAGIC begins where HIGHLAND GRACE ended, giving you Branwenn and Callum's story.

Set in the turn of the 13th century Scottish Highlands. After fleeing her wedding to her Norman betrothed and being swept into the Irish Sea during a storm, Branwenn Maclean finds herself once more in the land of the Highland Scots. Little does she know, however, that the maimed man who drops through the ceiling of her hiding place is none other than Callum MacGregor, the man who both vexes and beguiles her.

Callum awakens in a darkened sea cave believing he's being nursed by a sea nymph. Little does *he* know, however, that the fey creature is in actuality none other than his massive warrior Maclean cousins' foster sister, Branwenn, the lass that has taunted and haunted him since his first encounter with her one year past.

Read an excerpt on the following pages.

Excerpt from Highland Magic

PROLOGUE
Cilgerran Castle, Southern March Region, Cambria
The Betrothal Feast, July 1205

Gaiallard de Montfort settled back in his chair and studied the chaos all around him. This betrothal would bring him the demesne he'd been craving, but at a price for which he was growing more resentful as each day passed. He was expected to wed an awkward rustic, a mere girl! He, whom the ladies of the court had given the title 'golden wolf', both in and out of the bedchamber. Oh, she was pleasing to look upon. Her dark hair framed her face in a becoming enough manner and accented her most attractive asset: her large eyes bore the color of kings in their amethyst depths. But even his young sister had more curves than this boyish girl. And she was as green as his page—and just as unschooled in the ways of the court, mayhap even more so. How many times now had he been humiliated in front of his comrades by her graceless overtures and simple dress? If he had not given her, as a betrothal gift, the lovely purple velvet dress she now wore with the gold embroidery edging the square neck and sleeves, or the gold silk chemise beneath it, he had no doubt she'd now be wearing that godawful saffron woolen thing she'd worn to at least five of the seven previous evening meals this past sennight. Had she no understanding of the place she would be taking, had already been expected to take by his side? She was no good representative of his position in the hierarchy. In fact, she had made him a laughing-stock at court. And

Excerpt from Highland Magic

last eve, when she'd stumbled upon him with his sister—well, she would simply have to grow accustomed to such encounters as they were a well-established part of life amongst those of noble birth. He clenched his jaw to keep from groaning aloud in frustration. Why, oh, why had fate not been kinder to him? If all had gone as he'd planned, he'd even now be presiding over the demesne of *Castell Crychydd* with his chosen mate, Caroline de Montrochet. Now, there was a beauty, a perfect example of nobility, virtue, and womanliness. Gaiallard's eyes were drawn once more to the trestle table below where the lady in question now sat nibbling a portion of sea fowl.

* * *

Branwenn watched her betrothed from the corner of her eye. He'd made it plain these past days that he was not as pleased with this match, with her, as he'd first pretended. And last eve—*last eve*! She'd stumbled upon him in his sister's chamber. The poor lass had been in a distressing state, her gown torn and hanging from her shoulder, exposing red marks on her tender arm and chest where the drunken knave had abused and beaten her. Would he have gone further still—done the thing Branwenn feared had been his true purpose, if she had not interrupted his savage attack? And 'twas clearly not the first time the lass had been the outlet for his violent lust either, for there had been older bruises in plain view as well. She turned her sight on the lass, Alyson, who even now sat much too quietly with her silver-blond head bowed and her hands demurely folded in her lap. The poor dear had barely touched the food on her trencher, nor the wine in her goblet. She was far too young to have been exposed to such lechery, for she surely was not more than twelve summers. Aye, 'twas truth that according to tradition, she was a woman full-grown, capable of becoming a wife, should her father contract such an arrangement, but in Branwenn's view, 'twas much too young an age to be expected to perform such duties.

Reys ap Gryffyd dipped his head and whispered in her ear, "Have you second thoughts so late in the game, then, Branwenn? If so, you've dallied too long, my little dove, for your vows will be heard before the bishop and all this fine assembly in but a few hours' time at the morrow's morning mass."

Branwenn bit her lip and turned her troubled gaze to the dark-haired, blue-eyed man she'd only discovered to be her kin a mere seven moons past when he'd been the first to cross the threshold of her heart-family's keep, the Macleans, after the feast of *Hogmanay*. He'd come there to find her and bring her back to Cambria to wed this flaxen-haired Norman nephew thrice removed to the Earl of Pembroke that sat at her other side. For the marriage would make a blood alliance between her Cambrian cousin, twice removed, Prince Llywelyn, and the Norman usurper, Guillaume le Maréchal, the Earl of Pembroke. And tho' she liked Reys well, even from their first meeting, she still did not feel the same strong bond with him that she felt for Bao Xiong Maclean, the man who'd raised her, the man who, in her heart, was her brother in truth. Should she tell Reys of her discovery? She'd been debating that very question these past hours since finding her betrothed with his sister. And tho' the hour was late, she needed some guidance, some words to soothe her worry. "Brother, I have something I must speak with you about in all haste, but it must be in privy, for I have no wish for any here to learn of what I must tell you."

Reys had been jesting with her, believing that she was merely uneasy, as any new bride would be, at the prospect of her wedding. He sat forward and truly studied her worried countenance for the first time that eve. With a brief nod, he said, "Meet me in the chapel after supper. 'Twill be empty, as all here will be enjoying the pipers and players afterward. Say that you wish a few moments alone to pray and light some candles. No one will say you nay, even this eve before you wed, for your desire to pray will be seen as an act of true piety, a great virtue for a new bride."

Branwenn's shoulders relaxed for the first time that eve. With a sigh and a nod, she said, "My thanks."

* * *

An hour later, Branwenn, on her knees in the chapel with her head bowed and her eyes closed, felt someone settle beside her.

"We are alone now—all are in the great hall enjoying the players. Tell me what troubles you, Branwenn," Reys whispered.

Branwenn slowly opened her eyes and, settling back to rest upon her calves, she dropped her clenched hands to her lap and turned her gaze upon this almost-stranger who just might give her the heart's-ease she so desperately craved. "I know not how to begin...."

Excerpt from Highland Magic

Reys placed his hand over hers. "Begin by telling me the thing that is giving you the most dread."

Branwenn dropped her gaze to her lap and nodded. She took in a deep breath and released it on a sigh. "Aye, 'twould seem to be the best place, I trow." She cleared her throat. "Last eve..."

When she didn't immediately continue, Reys dipped his head in an effort to see her countenance. "Aye, last eve—what happened?" he prompted.

"I came upon my betrothed in his sister's bedchamber,"—she lifted her gaze to her brother's once more and said in a rush—"he had *beaten* her, Reys! There were purple and red marks on her chest, her shoulders—even her arms! And her gown was torn, it looked as if he'd ripped it away to expose her breasts. And what is more, I could see other, older bruises on her flesh as well. Godamercy, Reys, I do believe he intended to...to...bed her!" There, she'd said it.

Reys's eyes widened even further in shock and disgust. *Why, the lass was barely out of swaddling clothes!* He'd known Gaiallard to be a man who enjoyed the sexual privileges bestowed upon him due to his noble birth, but he'd had no true understanding of how dissolute, how morally corrupt, the man had become until just now.

Branwenn's eyes misted with unshed tears. "I knew not what to do—I fled the chamber and have said naught about it to anyone, not even Gaiallard."

"You cannot wed him, then. You must away this very night." Reys pressed the base of his palm into his eye.

Excerpt from Highland Magic

Branwenn grabbed hold of his wrist and held tight. "But how can I not? 'Twould mean war—war with not only the Earl of Pembroke, but with the King of England himself, for he has decreed that this match must take place!"

Reys nodded and turned his gaze upon his sister once more. "Aye, and forget not that our cousin will surely skin me alive before hanging me on a gibbet to rot—and he'll lock you in the tower gaol for all eternity, I doubt it not." He turned and faced Branwenn fully. Taking both her hands in his own, he said, "But we must at least try to release you from this contract. I will speak with our cousin forthwith. There must be a way to delay this wedding, at least until I can procure our cousin's agreement to free you from this bad bargain."

Branwenn dipped her head and gazed down at their clasped hands. 'Twas no use. Her fate was set, and there would be naught to stop it. For, she knew her cousin would never agree to such a thing; his empire was much more important than she in the scheme of things. "My thanks, brother, tho' I know not how you shall manage such a feat." All at once struck with an idea, she lifted her head once more and gazed, wide-eyed with hope, into the midnight-blue depths of Reys's eyes. "I beg you, do not be angered—or hurt—by the proposal I am about to make, for I mean you no injury—"

"Aye?" Reys said anxiously, "have you a plan then? Tell me quickly, I swear I shall listen without prejudice."

Branwenn tightened her grasp on her brother's

Excerpt from Highland Magic

hands and leaned forward a bit as she said, "Would it not fulfill the spirit, if not the letter, of the contract were *you* to wed *Alyson* instead?"

"Wha—?"

"Nay, hear me out before you balk. Do you not see? This is the best solution for all. The lass clearly needs a protector and you—well, I know you do not like speaking of the recent tragedy that befell your poor wife and bairns,"—Reys looked away, his mouth set in a grim line, and Branwenn brought her hand up to his cheek and gently forced him to look at her once more—"but you know that you are now free to wed. And you told me yourself, when first you found me in the Highlands, that the contract would have been fulfilled whether you'd found a brother *or* a sister, for the brother would have been contracted to wed the niece. You were not free to wed then, and I, for my own reasons, agreed to return to Cambria with you."

Silence reigned for many long seconds as Reys struggled to breathe past the heavy pain of guilt and longing that now gripped his chest.

Branwenn remained still, fearing that any movement on her part would send her brother fleeing from this sanctuary, from her, leaving her honor-bound to fulfill the terms of the contract.

At last, Reys gave his answer. "Gather only the most precious of your belongings, only what you can easily carry, and meet me in the stables in half an hour's time."

"You will arrange this thing, then?"

"Aye." He rose to his feet and brought her up with

Excerpt from Highland Magic

him. "As you said, 'twill fulfill the intent of the contract, if not the actual terms set down in writing."

"How will I get past the gates—to what destination will I travel?"

"Dress in those same lad's clothes you wore as a disguise when you traveled to our cousin's war camp on the edge of the Maclean holding last spring. I know you kept them, so pretend not otherwise. The disguise will aid in your escape."

"But to where?"

"I shall tell you more when we meet later. For now, suffice to say, you shall be safely out of Gaiallard's influence by the time the ceremony is to begin. Now, make haste to your chamber."

Branwenn nodded and, without forethought, flung herself into her brother's embrace and held tight. "I do believe I shall miss you," she said, wonder in her voice.

Reys smiled and gave her a bit of a squeeze. "And I you as well, you little midge."

"However will I repay you for such a sacrifice?" she whispered brokenly. She kissed him on his cheek and fled without waiting for a reply.

* * *

Reys watched her leave before collapsing onto the bench directly behind him and covering his face with his hands. Branwenn was right, this was the best solution. For, he no longer cared who he wed, as his heart had died with his love, his wife, and his sweet little girls, in the fire at the convent where they were staying two moons past. And he must wed—he must have offspring, a son, to inherit his position, his property. 'Twas the way of things, and he was honor-bound to fulfill his duties. At least he liked the young lady. And by wedding her, he would not only free her from her brother's wicked clutches, but give both himself and her a few years' time to heal before embarking on the more amorous aspect of the wedded state. Surely the lass would appreciate a bit of a reprieve from such duties—at least until she was older.

And he would not subject his sister to the same type of evil that their dear mother had been forced to endure the last moons of her life, the same evil even Branwenn in some indirect way had endured as well during that exact time—for his mother's kidnapping and enslavement at the hands of the murderous Highlander, Jamison Maclean, had occurred while she'd carried Branwenn in her womb. 'Twas for the sake of his mother's sweet memory that he had at last settled on the decision to, in effect, embark on this act of treason by securing his sister's safe passage away from her betrothed and her signed contract to wed. He must somehow find the words to convince his cousin and the Earl of Pembroke the propitiousness of this change in plan.

Reys rose to his feet and hurried towards the front entrance of the chapel. But first, he must get his sister as far from Gaiallard's clutches as possible—and to a place no one would ever think to search for her. For 'twas no feat of reason to imagine the tirade that would ensue when Gaiallard realized he would lose his chance at the demesne he so coveted.

* * *

Excerpt from Highland Magic

The bar across the door lifted with less effort than Branwenn had been expecting, but with more sound. Anxiously looking over her shoulder at the still-slumbering maid settled on a pallet only a few feet from where Branwenn now stood, she breathed a sigh of relief and opened the door to her bedchamber. 'Twas just past midnight and the corridors were dark. Tho' it chafed her to do so, she took a valuable moment to stand with her back against the wall as she allowed her eyes to become adjusted to the much darker outer perimeter of her chamber. Oh, how she'd love a candle at this moment, but she dared not risk it. Nay, 'twas much better that she remain quiet and hidden as she descended to the lower level of the keep. The way down to the courtyard of the castle would be manned with servants and, mayhap, even soldiers, but she would not quell her intent to escape this place this very night.

Twenty minutes later, she'd made it to the stables. "Reys?" she whispered into the darkness.

"Aye, over here." he whispered back.

Branwenn moved in the direction of the voice. "Where are you? 'Tis as dark as pitch in here. Will you not light a taper?"

"Nay, 'tis too dangerous. The stableman that was left to guard the horses slumbers in the corner, but we must be careful not to wake him. The sleeping herb I put in his ale will not last long, I fear."

"I see—Oh!" Branwenn stumbled over a rise in the straw-covered earthen floor.

Reys swept his arm around her middle to catch her before she fell. "Watch your step," he cautioned. He

Excerpt from Highland Magic

led her to her mount then and took her hastily-packed satchel from her nerveless hands. "I shall travel with you as far as the coast and then I shall return here, for I must be back by sunrise."

"The *coast?*" Branwenn asked dazedly.

"Aye, the coast. There are trade ships there. One of which will take you to my wife's cousin in Ulster on the northeast coast of Ireland. None will think to look for you there, for no one knows of my friendship with the man."

"But I thought...I believed you'd be sending me back to *Aber Garth Celyn*, to our cousin's estate."

"Nay, 'tis the first place Gaiallard will look for you, youngling."

Branwenn's brows drew together in confusion. "Why would Gaiallard look for me—he shall surely be relieved that he will not be forced to wed a ceorl such as he clearly believes me to be."

"Because he shall lose the demesne he was to gain with this alliance, tho' I do not believe he is aware of such now. I think he is under the belief that he is to be given sovereignty over the demesne, no matter what lady he weds, that he was just to receive it sooner, if he agreed to this alliance."

"I see." Branwenn felt dizzy, her thoughts spinning madly about inside her skull like one of the Persian dervishes her brother, Bao, had told her of. "You will not be traveling with me?" she said weakly after a moment.

"Nay, I cannot, for the meeting with our cousin and the Earl cannot wait. Surely you ken, 'twould not be

Excerpt from Highland Magic

good for them to discover you gone before I explain the new scheme to them. And the bishop has traveled many miles to be here—as have most of the guests." He shook his head and sighed. "Nay, the wedding must take place, and at the time originally planned. The only difference will be that 'twill be I and the Earl's niece who wed for the sake of the alliance instead of you and that devil *Gaiallard de Montfort*." He'd said the name as if it were the bitterest of tinctures upon his tongue. Reys placed his hands on her waist and lifted her onto her mount. "We must away in all haste; there is no more time for discussion, else I'll not be back in time to stand before the bishop and exchange vows with the lady Alyson," he said as he walked the animal out into the courtyard.

Branwenn was surprised to find his mount already saddled and ready to go. How had she missed seeing the animal earlier? She shrugged. No doubt, her mind had been much more occupied with not getting caught at the time.

After Reys mounted his steed, 'twas not as difficult as Branwenn had anticipated for them to depart the holding. The journey to the coast took two hours.

The wharf was dark and dank. More abandoned than Branwenn had been expecting, even at this dim hour of the morn.

"Stay upon your horse," Reys cautioned as he handed her the reigns of his own mount, "and do not move more than a pace or two from this spot until I return, for I shall not be long. I must negotiate your safe passage with the captain of this vessel."

Excerpt from Highland Magic

"Aye," Branwenn replied with a nod of her head. After her brother had been gone a few minutes and she was convinced that she'd not be accosted by any wayward, drunken seamen, she relaxed a bit and took stock of her surroundings. The wharf had the smell of the sea—no surprise. But there was the smell of something else as well. 'Twas as if the sea creatures had crawled to the shore to die, for the smell was caustic, harshly bitter, the air filled with the smell of rot.

In another moment, Reys came into view once more. His expression was somber as he briskly walked up beside her mount. "I've secured passage for you on the Irish ship, the *Maighdean mhara mhear*." He took hold of Branwenn's hand. "I wish there were another way, but there is none."

"I care not—"

"Branwenn, heed me well. These are men of the cloth—monks from Strangford Lough on the coast of Ulster. They are just returning from Cumberland with more stone and iron ore for the abbey they are building. If all goes as planned, you shall arrive there in a matter of days. I have claimed corody for you as a kinsman of Prince Llywelyn, so you may stay with them until all is settled. I will come for you then, so do not stray from that place until that time. 'Twill not be long, I vow it."

Branwenn's heart pounded in her chest. Tho' her hand trembled with fear, she managed to slip it from her brother's embrace. Taking a deep breath, she straightened her spine, and showing more courage than she felt, she said, "Worry not, I shall do as you say. For, where else could I go without fear of discovery? I

Excerpt from Highland Magic

do not dare go back to the Maclean holding, as I wish no harm to come to any there—nor do I wish for them to ever discover that I was almost wed to such a man as Gaiallard de Montfort."

"We must make haste, then, for the barge will sail in but a quarter-hour's time. These mariner monks use naught but the sun's bright beam during the day and the star's light that twinkles in the northern sky at night to guide them. But fear not, they've assured me they've made this same journey many times since their patroness, the wife of John de Courcy of Ulster, founded their abbey but a few years past."

Reys took the reigns of his and Branwenn's mounts and led them to the ship's loading plank. After helping her to dismount, he placed the scroll in her hand and settled his own long-fingered hand over hers. "Use this document as your introduction to the abbot. The letter explains that you are my brother and that you are also the cousin of Prince Llywelyn.

"But—"

Reys lightly covered her mouth with his fingertips. "Nay, my little dove, it cannot be helped. You must continue in your disguise until I come for you, else you will not be allowed to remain at the abbey—corody, or nay. And do not take those clothes from your frame at any time during the voyage, not even to bathe, for 'twould not do for these men of the cloth to discover that a member of the fairer sex is on board their vessel."

With a stiff nod of the head, Branwenn turned and gazed at the huge sailing vessel she was about to

Excerpt from Highland Magic

embark upon. The ship was long, with at least 25 to 30 oars on each side and a long mast that hung suspended over the entire length of the deck.

"There is more I would give you before you are gone," Reys said, turning and rummaging inside the leather satchel he had attached to his saddle. A moment later, he was lifting her hand, palm up, and placing a small leather purse upon it.

Branwenn's brows drew together. "What is this?"

"There are silver coins inside—enough to purchase several more moons of shelter and food for you than what I have arranged already with the monks."

"But, you said you would return for me soon...."

"Be at ease, little one. I shall take not one moment longer than I must, but I cannot allow you to travel so far—and with strangers, tho' men of the cloth they be—without *some* bit of coin, just in case. Do you see?"

With a long, forlorn sigh and a shrug of her shoulders, she sadly nodded her head. "Aye. I do see. My debt to you is growing greater and greater."

"Nay, you owe me naught. I beg you, trouble yourself no more on that score." Reys took hold of the hand she held the purse in. "Look inside," he coaxed, loosening the string that held the neck of the pouch closed. "For you will find something of our mother's which I wish for you to keep. I planned to give this to you on the morrow, as a gift to celebrate your wedding, but, I confess, I am much more pleased to give it to you now as a token of my great affection for you as my sister."

Still holding the scroll, Branwenn managed—rather

Excerpt from Highland Magic

awkwardly—to place two fingers inside to find the object he spoke of. She discovered it immediately and drew the cold, circular band of gold metal and amethyst gemstone out of the pouch.

"'Twas our mother's betrothal ring. The same ring, in fact, that Bao gave the priest at the kirk he had our mother buried in. The ring was left with the priest as a means to prove that 'twas truly her grave, should her family come searching for her there."

Branwenn's hand began to shake with more violence and her eyes filled with tears. "This was my mother's?" she asked brokenly. 'Twas lovely. The small, polished, oval stone was set high on the narrow gold band.

Reys took the ring and settled it on her finger before Branwenn's next thought had time to form. "There now, I knew you were a near twin to her, but now I have proof. See how nicely it fits you?"

"Aye," she replied wonderingly, "I thought it surely too small for my hand." She looked up, into her brother's eyes and said, "I thank you for this memento of my mother."

Reys gave her a brief nod. "We have tarried long enough, I trow," he said abruptly. "Come," he continued in a softer tone, "we must find the captain and get you settled in the space he's allowed you in the hold before the ship sails." And with a bit of gentle pressure to the base of Branwenn's spine, he prodded her to begin ascending the rough, wooden plank of the ship.

* * *

The vessel had been at sea for no more than three

Excerpt from Highland Magic

days and three nights when brigands, pirates of the sea, rammed into the side of their ship sometime around the chimes at midnight, bombarding it with large stones flung from a mangonel, and sending missile upon missile of fire-tipped spears and arrows onto the deck, killing many of the men who were unfortunate enough to be on duty at the time.

"GET YOU DOWN BELOW, LAD!" The grey-robed captain pushed Branwenn toward the stair leading into the hold. "'Tis the safest place for you. Fear not, we will rout these robbers in little time."

Branwenn did as she was told, fearing she'd be more cumbrance than aid were she to stay above and attempt to fight.

Despite the captain's assurance, she was still not free of doubt that all might be lost. And if it were not for the tempest of severe proportions that howled down upon them with a deafening force mere moments after she'd settled in her snug nook below deck, making the pirates' fiery offense upon them moot, Branwenn was certain that she and all who were still alive aboard the vessel would have been doomed to a watery grave at the hands of the greedy robbers.

The sounds of attack now silenced, Branwenn went directly against the captain's orders and, after slinging the long strap of her satchel, which held her dearest possessions, around her neck and over her shoulder, went topside.

The brigands' much smaller vessel slipped away into the darkness on thievish feet and in moments, the monks' galley was once more alone on the sea.

Excerpt from Highland Magic

Unfortunately, it had sustained quite a bit of damage in its hull and the vessel began to take on water. In minutes, it lurched to its side, sending anything that was not nailed down slamming against the railing. Branwenn had barely stepped two paces away from the stair leading below deck when she was sent flying against the railing herself. She only had time to grab hold of a stray plank of wood before she was swept off the ship and into the dark, cold, unforgiving depths of the frigid, briny water.

Tho' the wood acted as a buoy in the violently tossing sea, she was still buried beneath the crashing waves, forced down, down, down, into the unrelenting dark chasm. She held tight to her anchor in the storm, and, after long, terrifying seconds, she was finally thrust back up, like some volcanic spew from an island mound, until she at last broke free of the surface of the abyss and was once more able to draw breath into her burning lungs. When her mind and vision cleared, she realized the tide had propelled her much too far from the vessel to be seen or heard.

Holding tight to her plank of wood, she allowed herself to drift, fearing that if she fought the tide, she'd only end up at the bottom of the sea. For the next few hours, she could do no more than wait. Wait for the light of dawn and keep her mind occupied with any thoughts other than the terrifying ones that niggled at the edge of her mind. Nay, she refused to think upon what sea monsters might even now be skimming under her and around her dangling feet. Nor would she think upon what she would do if she did not find land soon.

Excerpt from Highland Magic

Instead, she filled her mind with happy thoughts, dear remembrances of the merrier times. Like dancing—dancing for the very first time—around the *Hogmanay* fire this past winter. How gleeful she had been then. Until, of course, that pompous man, Callum MacGregor had spoiled it for her. Nay, she would not think of him. Instead, she forced her thoughts back to more pleasant aspects of that night. Aye, had not the hall been lovely, with the mistletoe, holly, and hazel adorning the trestle tables, and rowan branches above every door? And the scents! Of roasted swan and berries, of juniper, of ale. Aye, that was a happy time.

At long last, dawn arrived in a mist-shrouded glimmer of mauves, pinks, and blue-greys. As the sun came up over the horizon and lit the world around her, Branwenn studied her surroundings. Her heart pounded with joy in her chest, for there, in her sights, was land! And she was near enough to the shoreline—of whose sovereign soil, she knew not—to paddle the rest of the way inland.

* * *

Made in the USA
Lexington, KY
22 July 2015